Praise for Catherine Palmer
and her novels

"Catherine Palmer's writing shines with romance and the inner struggles of the heart."
—Francine Rivers, bestselling author of *Redeeming Love*

"Catherine Palmer…understands hurts as well as joys, and portrays them authentically and insightfully."
—Randy Alcorn, bestselling author of *Deadline*

Praise for Gail Gaymer Martin
and her novels

"*The Christmas Kite* is a tender romance, the story of two wounded people learning to live and love again. And I guarantee that little Mac will steal your heart. Settle into your favorite chair and enjoy."
—Robin Lee Hatcher, bestselling author of *Loving Libby*

"Gail Gaymer Martin's best book to date. Real conflict and very likable characters enhance this wonderful romantic story."
—*RT Book Reviews* on *Loving Hearts*

Praise for Lois Richer
and her novels

"Richer creates family dynamics that are realistic and engaging in this story of forgiveness and reconciliation."
—*RT Book Reviews* on *Yuletide Proposal*

"[A] lovely Christmas story."
—*RT Book Reviews* on *The Holiday Nanny*

Catherine Palmer is a bestselling author and winner of the Christy Award for her outstanding Christian romance. She also received the Career Achievement Award for Inspirational Fiction from *RT Book Reviews*. Raised in Kenya, she lives in Atlanta with her husband. They have two grown sons.

Gail Gaymer Martin is a multi-award-winning novelist and writer of contemporary Christian fiction with fifty-five published novels and four million books sold. *CBS News* listed her among the four best writers in the Detroit area. Gail is a cofounder of American Christian Fiction Writers and a keynote speaker at women's events, and she presents workshops at writers' conferences. She lives in Michigan. Visit her at gailgaymermartin.com. Write to her online or at PO Box 760063, Lathrup Village, MI, 48076.

Lois Richer loves traveling, swimming and quilting, but mostly she loves writing stories that show God's boundless love for His precious children. As she says, "His love never changes or gives up. It's always waiting for me. My stories feature imperfect characters learning that love doesn't mean attaining perfection. Love is about keeping on keeping on." You can contact Lois via email, loisricher@gmail.com, or on Facebook (loisricherauthor).

That Christmas Feeling

Catherine Palmer
Gail Gaymer Martin

&

Yuletide Proposal

Lois Richer

HARLEQUIN® LOVE INSPIRED®

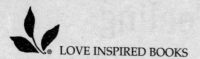 LOVE INSPIRED BOOKS

Recycling programs for this product may not exist in your area.

ISBN-13: 978-1-335-00545-8

That Christmas Feeling and Yuletide Proposal

Copyright © 2018 by Harlequin Books S.A.

The publisher acknowledges the copyright holders of the individual works as follows:

Christmas in My Heart
Copyright © 2004 by Catherine Palmer

Christmas Moon
Copyright © 2004 by Gail Gaymer Martin

Yuletide Proposal
Copyright © 2012 by Lois Richer

www.Harlequin.com

Printed in U.S.A.

CONTENTS

THAT CHRISTMAS FEELING

* * *

CHRISTMAS IN MY HEART
Catherine Palmer

&

CHRISTMAS MOON
Gail Gaymer Martin

CHRISTMAS IN MY HEART

Catherine Palmer

***

"I will honor Christmas in my heart
and try to keep it all the year."
—Ebenezer Scrooge in *A Christmas Carol*
by Charles Dickens

For the other three FABs:
BB Heil, Lucia Kincheloe and Kristie McGonegal.
Thanks for supporting me, praying with me
and loving me these many years.
I love you all!

Chapter One

Never again, Claire Ross fumed as she stepped through the front door onto the porch of her aunt Flossie's house. So much for spreading the Christmas spirit. Lifting the fragrant pine wreath she had brought as a gift, Claire jammed it onto a nail in the door and stomped across the sagging wooden floorboards.

She had never met a more irascible, heartless, crusty old windbag! The woman was impossible. Picking her way down the damp and splintered steps, Claire vowed that this first time she had visited her great-aunt would also be the last. No wonder the entire Ross family had disowned Florence Ross. She deserved it.

"And stay gone!" a voice crowed behind her.

Claire swung around in time to see Aunt Flossie point a double-barreled shotgun into the gray Missouri sky and pull the trigger. At the deafening blast, a pair of doves fluttered screeching out of a nearby oak tree, five yowling cats hightailed it from under the porch and every dog in a three-mile radius of Buffalo, Missouri, began to bark. Stunned, Claire watched as her aunt grabbed the Christmas wreath off the front door and sent it sailing like a Frisbee across the yard.

"Don't need Christmas 'round here!" Aunt Flossie shouted. "Don't need it, don't want it!"

Breathing hard, Claire stared at the tiny, white-haired woman. Flossie wore a faded pink bathrobe with its terry-cloth loops picked into long strings by the horde of cats that lived in and around old Ross Mansion. The robe's hem hung uneven and frayed around her thin ivory calves. Socks—one navy, the other black—were rolled to her ankles. And a pair of men's leather work boots with steel toes and untied laces anchored her feet.

Hair splayed out like dandelion fluff, Flossie stared at her niece. Her sharp blue eyes narrowed as her mouth turned down. "This is my property," she sneered. "You stay off!"

"Believe me, I have no intention of ever—"

A wailing siren drowned out Claire's words as a blue car sped toward them down the narrow paved road. Emblazoned with the word *Police* in bold white letters on the side, the squad car pulled to a stop beside the gray picket fence that surrounded Flossie Ross's yard. The siren died, the driver's door swung open and a man Claire instantly recognized as Robert West, Buffalo's police chief, stepped out.

"Miss Ross," he called as he rounded the fence and strode down the driveway. "How many times have I told you not to go firing guns inside city limits? Now, give me that thing!"

"You can't have it, you ol' turkey buzzard!" Shaking the weapon, Flossie tottered down the steps. "Get outta my yard!"

Claire's fury at her aunt shifted to concern as the

chief stalked toward the old woman. Rob West was not a man to defy. Six feet four inches tall, broad shouldered and narrow hipped, he had been quarterback of Buffalo High School's winning football team and a state-champion wrestler. Though Claire had returned to her hometown the previous summer and had been teaching high school history since the start of the fall semester, she had yet to cross paths with Rob.

Not that she'd been looking for him. In school, Rob had been a popular, handsome athlete and the beloved boyfriend of the prettiest, blondest, curviest girl in their class—the sweetheart he had married the day after his graduation from the police academy. Until a teacher paired the two mismatched freshmen for an ongoing four-year research project, Rob had paid scant attention to Claire Ross with her coarse red hair, ghostly pale skin and rail-thin body. It didn't help that she adored school, loved to read and made it perfectly clear she thought Rob West was as dumb as a Missouri mule.

Still, they had somehow ended up becoming friends—easily teasing each other, sharing ideas and even confiding secrets. He called her Clarence and sneaked her pieces of her favorite brand of bubble gum. She called him a nincompoop and a lamebrain, and she blew bubbles, which he mashed onto her nose.

In the course of the four years, Claire made sure the research project progressed, and eventually she even convinced Rob that Buffalo's role in the Civil War really was an interesting topic. He made sure the other guys didn't malign skinny Claire behind her back, and she actually ended up getting a date to her senior prom.

"What are you shooting at today, Miss Ross?" Rob

asked. "Is a stray dog after your cats? Or are you mad at the garbage truck again?"

"It's her." Flossie pointed a thin finger at Claire. "She's trespassing on my property."

Rob's bright blue eyes focused for the first time on the younger woman. His brow furrowed as he took off his hat. "Claire Ross? Is that you?"

"Of course it's me," she said. "I drove all the way over here to bring my aunt a Christmas gift, and she—"

"She started right off griping about my cats!" Flossie cut in.

"Everybody in town gripes about your cats," Rob retorted. "You're in violation of city ordinances, Miss Ross. Only four cats are allowed per household. A city license is required. You've got to have proof of current rabies vaccinations for each cat. And it's against municipal code to allow your pets to run loose off your property."

"So what? They're not my cats anyhow. People drop 'em here, and I take 'em in." She gave a loud snort and shouted, "I'm a kindhearted animal lover, that's all!"

"How many cats do you have now? It was sixteen the last time I came out here."

"Who cares? Sixteen or twenty, what difference does it make? They're not doing harm to anyone."

"They stink, Miss Ross. Plain and simple, you've got an odor problem. Not only that, but your property is a public eyesore. You've got cats on the roof, cats in the trees, cats in the basement—"

"Not in the basement. I keep that locked."

"The point is, ma'am, you've got to get rid of some of the cats and clean up this place."

"Or what? You ain't out here about the cats anyhow. You're here to get that woman off my land!"

Rob glanced at Claire again. His face registered surprise for a second time, as if he'd failed to remember her from a moment before. She clamped her hands on her hips in frustration. Bad enough that she had been invisible in high school. But now? At twenty-eight, she thought she had improved a tad. She filled out her clothes in the right places, she had earned a master's degree in history, she had been the assistant curator at a museum in Savannah, Georgia, and despite recently having her wedding canceled only a month before it was scheduled, she certainly had plenty of confidence.

"I'd heard you were back in town," Rob said. "Teaching history at the high school, someone told me."

"And trying to be a kind niece." She glanced down at the pine wreath. It lay half in a puddle of icy water and half in the mud. Bright red berries, pretty ribbons and silver bells were forlornly buried in the fragrant branches. "It's real, you know. I bought it at the florist shop and brought it over here for my aunt. I hoped it would cheer her up."

"Cheer Miss Ross? You've got your work cut out for you there." His mouth tilted into a grin. "But as I recall, Clarence, you never objected to hard work."

So he did remember her after all. To her dismay, Claire felt her cheeks grow warm. "Well, I just didn't expect—"

"You planning to arrest that woman, Chief West?" Flossie demanded. "She's the one in violation of city code. She's trespassing!"

Rob turned to the older woman again. "Miss Ross, Claire is your niece. It's almost Christmas, and she's trying to be neighborly."

"Neighborly? I didn't ask her to come over. I never invited her—and I don't want her!" Flossie shook her fist. "Now, you just make her get off my land, because I don't tolerate…"

"Did you actually go inside the house?" Rob asked Claire as her aunt ranted and stomped around on the porch. "I've never been able to get through the front door."

Claire nodded. "The smell is awful. It can't be sanitary."

"I've sent social workers over here to check on her, but she won't let them inside."

"I barely set foot in the foyer before she went after her gun. All I saw was torn wallpaper, piles of newspapers and cats. Lots of cats."

Claire mused for a moment, recalling stories she had heard told around the family dinner table. A clapboard confection of nineteenth-century turrets, gables, balconies and gingerbread, the old house had been built by a wealthy Ross ancestor in anticipation of a promised railroad that never came to town. Generations came and went, and the family fortune dwindled. Now only Florence Ross and her cats remained in the dilapidated, sagging structure.

"When I was a girl," Claire told Rob, "my father used to say that Ross Mansion was a showpiece inside. He believed it was filled with family treasures—artwork, antiques, historical items. But if that's true, everything is probably ruined."

"I'm afraid so." Rob's blue eyes clouded. "Your aunt is an animal hoarder, Claire. It's part of the spectrum of mental illnesses known as obsessive-compulsive disorders. Miss Ross collects cats. Most of them are feral. She can't turn them away, she won't get them neutered or spayed and they've infested the house and grounds.

People call me at all hours of the night to complain. The cats yowl and fight and dig up gardens and tear into trash cans—"

A second shotgun blast shattered the conversation and set the dogs barking all over again. "Hey, both of you trespassers!" Flossie screeched. "Get out!"

"That does it." Rob swung around and marched up onto the porch. "Hand over your weapon. Do it now, Miss Ross, or I'll take you in."

With one hand he grabbed the shotgun. With the other he dipped into the gaping pocket of Flossie's shaggy pink robe and took out a fistful of unspent shells.

"I've got a rifle inside the house!" she squalled at him. "It's a .22, and I've got a pistol, too. I have the right to bear arms!"

"Not in my town you don't. Not anymore." He stepped around her and pushed open the front door. "I'll just go in there and—"

"Don't go in! Don't go in!"

He vanished, the old woman scurrying through the door behind him. Claire let out a breath. But her relief evaporated when Rob reappeared again immediately, his face contorted.

"That house is a public menace," he scolded Flossie, who stood glaring up at him. "I can't even breathe in there without a face mask."

"Good!" she snapped back. "Don't breathe. You can just die, for all I care!"

"Miss Ross, your neighbors have been pestering me about you for years, but I've been patient. Too patient. Today you've pushed me over the edge. I want this place cleaned up by Christmas, or I'll ask the city to condemn it and evict you. The cats have to go. The waste has to be cleaned up—and I don't mean with mop water. You'd better get some disinfectant. And paint. I want you to paint these outside walls and the picket fence, too. You hear me?"

"I don't hear a thing!"

"And no more gunshots!"

As he strode toward his squad car, Claire caught his arm. "Wait, Rob, you can't do this! Aunt Flossie is too old to clean and paint the house. And she's too mean to obey you."

"Then we'll have to evict her."

"How can you even say that? If you turn her out of the house, what's to become of her?"

"She can move in with you," he retorted.

"Are you crazy?" she called after him as he opened his car door.

"Not as crazy as your aunt."

As the blue car made a U-turn and sped off in a cloud of dust, Claire clenched her jaw. That dumb Rob West always had been too big for his britches! What an ego—calling Buffalo *his* town, threatening to evict Aunt Flossie and ordering Claire to take her in. As if Claire would ever consider opening her pristine little bungalow, her precious sanctuary and refuge, to that impossible woman and her umpteen smelly cats!

No way. Absolutely not! She owed Aunt Flossie nothing. The woman had never played any part in Claire's life. A lifelong spinster, Flossie had avoided family gatherings, never invited anyone over and certainly made it clear she wanted to be left alone. So clear, in fact, that the whole Ross family had readily agreed to deed her their stakes in the mansion. Despite its rumored treasures, the house held no claim on anyone's affections. Not if that meant encountering Florence Ross and her bitter, biting tongue.

"He stole my gun!" Flossie fumed, turning her small blue eyes on her great-niece. "Did you see that? The police chief stole my shotgun!"

Claire hesitated. Her urge to rebuke the bedraggled creature was mitigated only by the knowledge that Rob West always meant exactly what he said. If Flossie didn't get rid of the cats and clean up the house, he would have it condemned. Claire's parents were out of town for the winter, and as her great-aunt's nearest living relative, she would then become legally responsible for the elderly woman.

"Aunt Flossie, do you know who I am?" she asked.

"Of course I do. You're Jim's girl. Listen, you better tell your daddy to get his sorry hide over to the police station and bring me back my shotgun!"

Picking up the muddy wreath, Claire shook her head in frustration. She had come here to be kind, not to take abuse. Life had been difficult enough lately. While preparing for her wedding only nine months before, Claire had learned that her fiancé was seeing another woman. After canceling the nuptials, she'd stayed on in her job at the museum as long as she could. But her deep-seated unhappiness had convinced her she needed a new beginning.

At first the idea of coming home to Missouri felt like a step backward. When her mother mentioned that a teaching position had opened up in Buffalo, Claire immediately rejected the idea. She was a museum curator, not a high school history teacher. And she had no interest in returning to the little town she once had so eagerly fled. But the chance to escape the pain of her broken engagement and start life over changed her mind. After talking with her pastor and praying about the situation, she had embraced the opportunity and made the move.

As it turned out, Claire found she enjoyed teaching and appreciated Buffalo far more than she'd expected. Most important, as the darkness in her heart began to fade, a new dream took its place. Why not open a small museum dedicated to the town's unique history? To that end, Claire already had approached several of the city aldermen. If they could find a suitable location, she explained, then she would help gather the necessary historical artifacts and set up displays. Volunteers could staff the museum during visiting hours. Local schoolchildren certainly would benefit, and a small entrance fee might help the museum pay for its upkeep. Though the aldermen were skeptical that such an expense could be justified, they had agreed to look into it.

Feeling a bit lonely as the holidays approached, Claire had been trying to make herself reach out into the community. She joined her church's special Christmas choir, attended a play, even accepted a position on a committee. Bringing the wreath as a gift for her great-aunt had seemed a perfect way to honor the holiness of the season and to express her own newfound hope that her life had truly taken a turn for the better.

Now this.

Claire took a step toward the porch. "My father isn't in town, Aunt Flossie. The day after Thanksgiving my parents drove their RV to Texas to spend the winter. No one else is here, either. Dad's brother, Jake, moved to St. Louis three years ago. And his sister, Johanna, is on a mission trip to Haiti until next summer. I'm the only Ross around. So it's just you and me."

Flossie bent over and picked up a gray-and-white-striped cat. "Well, go on home, then," she said, her voice softening as she rubbed her cheek against the animal's fur. "I don't need you or any of the rest of 'em."

"You're planning to paint the house by yourself?" Claire stepped onto the porch. The odor emanating from the open front door would have made a skunk swoon. "And clean it up? And get rid of all the cats? That's what Chief West said you have to do."

"I don't care what that ol' buzzard said." Flossie set the cat back on its feet. "This is my house."

"Yes, but he has the power to condemn it. And he's only given you two weeks."

"Who cares? I have the deed to this house! It's mine!" She frowned as Claire stepped past her and went into the foyer again. "Hey, what are you doing? Get out! Get out of my house!"

"Oh, no...oh, Aunt Flossie..." Claire gritted her teeth to keep from gagging as she edged around a waist-high stack of newspapers. Swags of cobwebs draped from the chandelier overhead. Was it crystal? Impossible to tell with all the dust. The wallpaper, once a flocked velvet maroon in an Oriental pattern, hung in shreds. Fraying ropes held cockeyed pictures in heavy gilt frames, their art obscured by soot and dirt. The rug had rotted out from under the piles of damp newspapers, and everywhere lay evidence that the cats had ceased to use their litter boxes years ago.

"Aunt Flossie, this is..." Claire tried to think of adequate words. "Well, it's just—"

"Just *get out* is what it is! I didn't invite you in! I don't want you, and I don't need you!"

"And I don't care!" Rounding on the much smaller woman, Claire jabbed a finger at her. "You're stuck with me, Aunt Flossie. You can either clean up this disgusting mess, or that nincompoop Rob West will turn you out of the house and make me take care of you! Do you understand that? Do you see that you have no choice in this, and neither do I?"

Flossie's narrow lips went white. "I heard the man. I'm not deaf."

"Then what do you plan to do about it?"

"Why, I'll clean it, of course."

"You will?" Her aunt's capitulation stunned Claire. "You'll throw out all the newspapers? And you'll wash the floors?"

"With disinfectant."

Claire eyed her. "What about the cats?"

"Fare-thee-well to the cats." Flossie flipped her hand in a jaunty wave. "I'll call the animal shelter to come get 'em."

"All of them?"

"Every one."

Letting out a breath, Claire set the wreath on an old chair with upholstery that had been clawed to shreds. "Fine, then. I won't bother you anymore."

"Good."

Grateful, she stepped back out onto the porch. "Because it's really not healthy for you in there, Aunt Flossie," she said, feeling a little guilty about the relief she felt. "It's not safe for your food, for one thing. I mean…do you have enough to eat? Do you need anything, because I could—"

The door slammed shut in her face. Claire stared at it for a moment, fighting fury, biting back rage.

"And a merry Christmas to you, too!" she called out as she turned and headed for her car.

Rob West took his seat at the far end of the long polished oak table, directly across from Mayor Clement Bloom. The last place he wanted to be on a frosty December night was tucked away in the dank county courthouse basement with the mayor and a bunch of other community-spirited citizens. Not that planning the Christmas parade didn't rank fairly high on his priority list.

Rob enjoyed his role as a public servant, because it meant getting out of the office and mingling with Buffalo's residents. Every able-bodied man, woman and child in the area always turned out for the annual parade—police sirens wailing, fire trucks blasting their horns, floats rolling by, endless thrown candy soaring through the air. Not only did the police force cordon off streets and control traffic, but the chief of police traditionally joined the mayor in leading the procession through town. The Christmas parade created the perfect opportunity to promote goodwill, and Rob welcomed it.

But tonight his focus was elsewhere. Trouble had come to Buffalo. Throughout the fall the local police, the highway patrol and the Dallas County Sheriff's Department had noted an increase in methamphetamine traffic in the region. Somebody was cooking and distributing the illegal drug. But who? And where?

Methamphetamine manufacturing had become one of Missouri law enforcement's biggest headaches. The largely rural state provided meth makers with an ideal setup. From farmers' fertilizer tanks they stole a primary raw ingredient for the drug. And they used the many isolated farms and forests as hideouts in which to cook the highly explosive and pungent mix. As the public's appetite for the drug grew, meth manufacturing had gradually crawled into Missouri's towns and cities. But until this year, Rob had seen very little activity in his territory, and he was grateful.

His force—an assistant chief, a corporal, five patrolmen and a secretary—had more than enough to handle as it was. Domestic altercations were the most common of their calls. Petty stealing cropped up now and then. And traffic accidents sometimes occurred around five in the evening when cars attempted to negotiate the narrow streets of the town that formed the junction of U.S. Highway 65 and Missouri Highway 32.

"Well, I guess this committee probably ought to come to order," Mayor Bloom spoke up. A hefty fellow with a big mustache, Clement Bloom was Buffalo's lone veterinarian. "Who's here? Let's see, we've got Chief West, a'course. Mrs. Hopper, you represent the board of Realtors, right? Jerry, you're speaking for the downtown merchants. By the way, the store windows look real good this year."

"I think so, too, Mayor." The owner of the local drugstore grinned. "The middle school art classes came to the square and painted them."

Rob checked his watch. He had two men out patrolling side streets and alleyways in search of any suspicious activity. As soon as the parade meeting ended, he would join them in his own squad car. The past few weeks, he had worked far into the night in the hope of ferreting out the source of the methamphetamine that was entering his jurisdiction. But so far, few clues had crossed his radar screen.

"We've got silver bells and green holly and gold stars," Jerry was saying. "It's not just your usual Santas and reindeer. There's even a window with a scene from Dickens's *A Christmas Carol*. You know, Tiny Tim and Scrooge and everyone. I thought the kids were real creative with their painting this year."

"Any complaints about the manger scene on the barbershop window, Mayor?" One of the local pastors had come to the meeting to represent the ministerial alliance. Various church choirs would be performing on the parade floats. "Last year someone griped that the schoolchildren shouldn't be allowed to paint Bible scenes—due to the separation of church and state."

"And we all know who made *that* complaint," Mrs. Hopper put in.

Rob nodded along with the others around the table. Jack Granger, the local atheist, liked to voice his opinions in the newspaper and at city council meetings. Every town had its colorful characters, Rob realized. Buffalo enjoyed perhaps more than its fair share. In addition to Granger, they had "The Walker," a fellow who claimed he had been wounded in Vietnam and had a steel plate in his head. They had Mr. Chin, an Asian gentleman who appeared out of nowhere every now and then. Wearing white gloves and a black hat, Mr. Chin strolled around the square, peered into shop windows, got himself a haircut at the barbershop and vanished again. And then there was Florence Ross.

The image of the vituperative old woman had barely entered Rob's head when the meeting room's door swung open and Flossie's niece stepped in.

"Sorry I'm late," Claire Ross said, pulling off a pair of bright blue wool gloves. "The high school secretary gave me a message that we were meeting at the public library, so I went over there. When nobody showed up, I made a few phone calls and found out you were here. Whew!"

She let out a breath and smiled broadly—until her eyes fell on Rob. Instantly serious, she pulled off her hat, releasing a billow of auburn curls, and took the only chair available. Right next to his.

"Good evening, Chief West," she said in a low voice, flashing her green eyes at him. "No one told me you were on this committee."

"I'm on all the committees. It's part of the job."

Hard as he tried not to, Rob couldn't help staring at the woman beside him. What had become of skinny Claire Ross with her too-big mouth, her pasty white face and her straight hair that stuck out in all kinds of strange directions? And who had replaced her with this curvaceous, full-lipped, porcelain-skinned, red-headed beauty?

Ol' Clarence had never sported curls in high school. And those eyes! Hadn't they once been a sort of muddy olive? Tonight they sparkled like emeralds as she glanced across the table.

"What?" she whispered, flipping the word at him. "Have you forgotten who I am again?"

"You didn't used to have curls."

"That's because I ironed my hair." She shrugged. "I gave that up in college. Quit staring, you lamebrain. It's me."

He tore his focus from her and tried to concentrate on the mayor, who was outlining the parade route.

Bloom was famous for his visual aids, and tonight he had brought along a map drawn in black marker on a large sheet of neon-green poster board. He held a laser pen to create a tiny white directional point.

"Now, we'll have the marching bands gather over here in the usual spot," he was saying. "And the floats—"

"Excuse me, Mayor, but you've put the bank on the wrong corner of the square." All eyes turned to the speaker, Mrs. Hopper. "In my work as a real estate agent I see a lot of maps, and this one is incorrect, sir. The bank should be across the street."

The mayor studied his carefully executed drawing. "Well, I'll be. Are you sure?"

Rob leaned toward Claire. "What do you mean, you ironed your hair?"

"With an iron. On an ironing board." She tipped her head to one side and demonstrated. "Straight hair was in style."

He eyed the curls that bounced and bobbled down her shoulders and onto her soft blue sweater. Clarence Ross had curls. How about that?

"So, what do you think, Chief West? Uh… *Rob?*" The mayor leaned over and cleared his throat. "About blocking off the streets around the school? Will that be a problem?"

Collecting himself, Rob stared at the map and tried to make sense of it. "We'll block off the usual streets. Just like every year."

"But we were discussing the idea of moving the marching bands over here." He pointed at the green poster board. "Because what I was saying was that the local cable company has asked to have a float this year.

And several clubs at the high school want to do floats, too. Isn't that right, Miss Ross?"

Claire pulled a sheet of paper from her purse. "That's correct, Mayor Bloom. The Spanish club and the chess club each would like to create a float."

"The chess club?" Mrs. Hopper frowned. "What kind of a float can that be? Kids playing chess? What's interesting about that?"

"The students are planning to make large chess-piece costumes and walk around on the float as though it's a chessboard. It's a way to draw attention to their club, which they feel doesn't get as much community support as athletics."

"No question about *that*," Mayor Bloom said.

Bloom had never played on a school sports team, and Rob had considered him the quintessential nerd. That is, until he'd returned to town with "D.V.M." attached to his name and set up a bustling veterinary clinic. Nothing nerdy about that.

"All right, Miss Ross, we'll let the two clubs build floats," Bloom continued, "if you'll speak to the school superintendent about our parking problems."

"Certainly," she said. "I'm sure we can work something out. And I would think the police force can figure out how to adapt to the changes, even though it might be a little confusing for them at first."

Rob stiffened at the dig. "No problem, Mayor."

"Well, I guess we're about done here, then. Mrs. Hopper has typed up the order of entries in the parade. Like always, she put a float or two between each of the marching bands. She's got the squad car with the chief and me leading the parade, and the fire truck with Santa at the end. Looks like it's all in good shape. You can go ahead and hand out copies of your list, Mrs. Hopper. The police are on board to control the traffic, and Miss Ross will take care of the parking issue. We've got city sanitation set up to clean the streets after the horses. There's always a lot of candy wrappers lying around, too. And finally, we've got the parade route worked out." He eyed his neon map again for a moment. "I'll move the bank to the correct corner for the diagram that'll go in the newspaper. Anything else? All right, then we're adjourned. See you at the parade."

Chairs scraped back across the tile floor as Mrs. Hopper passed around her list of parade entries. Never much good at sitting for long periods, Rob stood and stretched his muscles. Claire was speaking to the preacher as she pulled on her gloves and hat. Rob considered walking away without another word to her, but the woman had clearly baited him with that crack about his police force. Besides, he had a little matter to lob back at her.

"Excuse me, Miss Ross," he said as she made to sashay past him without even a flick of her green eyes. "Do you have a minute?"

She paused, and the pink in her cheeks brightened as she faced him. "If this is about my hair—"

"It's about your aunt, Florence Ross. The cats are still on her property, I'm still getting phone calls in the night and when the wind is right, you can smell her house clear across town. I gave her till Christmas to clean up the place. Time is slipping away fast. But you're smart enough to know all that already, so I just wanted to make sure you'll be available to take her with you when I go over to condemn the place."

The blush drained away as fast as it had come. "Aunt Flossie hasn't done anything?"

"Nope. As I told you before, she has a mental illness. The cats are the focus of her obsessive-compulsive disorder. There's no way she'll give them up without a fight."

"But she told me…" She pursed her lips. The room had cleared out now, and she raised her voice. "Rob West, I always knew you were thick, but I never thought you were mean!"

"For your information, I am not thick." Setting his fists at his waist, he took a step toward her. "And you know good and well I'm not mean. It's my job to uphold the law—"

"By throwing a helpless old lady out onto the streets in the middle of winter?"

"Flossie's not helpless. She has you."

"She doesn't want me. And I don't want her, either."

"Now who's mean?" He shook his head. "Have you forgotten what you used to tell me, Claire? You grew up in that fairy-tale family who went to church every time the doors opened. And you used to preach at me, remember?"

"I did not preach."

"You preached all the time. You'd say, 'Rob West, you've got to do your homework if you ever want to amount to anything… You'd better stop that cussing, because civilized people don't swear… I won't have you taking the Lord's name in vain in front of me, Rob West… If you want to turn into a decent human being, Rob, you ought to go to church and quit messing around with Sherry and drinking with your buddies after the game.'"

As he spoke, Claire's mouth slowly fell open. She folded her hands together, and the hard emerald in her eyes softened to mossy green. "I don't remember any of that," she told him.

"Well, I do. I remember every bit of it. And most of all, I remember that you told me I had to take care of people. You said loving people was a lot more important than winning state football championships and wrestling trophies. Caring about the needy, the hungry, the homeless was what God expected of us, and it was all that really mattered in the long run."

When she didn't speak, he continued. "I thought you were the goofiest, dorkiest girl I'd ever known. But I listened to you, Claire, because everything you ever said to me made sense. Your words took me all the way to the police academy, where I was trained to do exactly what you said—take care of people. Because of your preaching at me, I married Sherry when I got her pregnant and she threatened to have an abortion. I stayed with her even though we lost our baby and the marriage was rocky all the way to the day she died in a car accident two years ago. The words you said to me over and over for four long years of working on that never-ending research project took me to church and led me to give up trying to control my life and to surrender it to Jesus Christ."

She moistened her lips, her eyes fastened to him. "Rob, I—"

"And now you're telling me you don't want to take care of your aunt? You won't look after an elderly mentally ill woman with no family but you? What happened to you, Claire? Where's the girl I knew in high school?"

She pushed her purse strap up onto her shoulder. "This isn't high school, Rob. People do change. And besides, you have no idea what I've been through. You don't know anything about me."

"Yes, I do. I know you're still smart, you're about a hundred times prettier and you're mean."

"I am not mean!"

"Excuse me, but I have to turn out the lights and lock up." He stepped around her.

"I am not mean!" she repeated, following him to the door and up the stairs to the main level. "I've worked very hard to recover from my own issues, I'll have you know."

"Issues." He flipped off a main switch, instantly casting them into darkness.

"Yes, issues. My fiancé left me for another woman, I had to quit the job I'd trained for and loved, and now I'm back in this little podunk town trying to start over. I have a tiny house, but it's mine. It's my home, and I'm not letting some ornery old woman who never cared about me or any of my family move in!"

They stepped out of the courthouse into the night. "Like I said, Clarence. You're mean."

As he walked away, she called after him. "My name is Claire!"

"Rence," he shouted back.

"Claire!"

"Rence!" He got into his squad car and backed out into the street. How about that, he thought as he drove off to look for meth dealers. Claire Ross had had those curls all along.

Chapter Two

Just as Claire pulled her car to a stop in front of Ross Mansion, a cascade of light, fluffy snowflakes began. Like goose down from a torn pillow, the white clumps gathered on the windshield and danced across the car's hood. She paused, soaking in the heater's comforting warmth before finally switching off the engine. For a moment she dropped her forehead onto her gloved hands that still clutched the steering wheel.

"Not what I want to do," she murmured through clenched teeth. "Are you hearing me, God? This is *not* what I want to do today! I don't like Aunt Flossie. I don't want to help her. And I'm furious with Rob West for shaming me into this! But I'm here, Lord, bad attitude and all. You promised to work things out for the good of people who love You and are called according to Your purpose. I do love You, and I know You want me to be kind to my great-aunt. So, please…even though I realize I'm doing this badly…please help me."

Letting out a long sigh, Claire opened the car door and stepped into the snowy morning. Bitter Missouri wind instantly penetrated her heavy winter jacket to the very marrow of her bones. Her cheeks ached. Her fingers went numb. Her eyes watered. Even her teeth hurt.

Shivering, she trotted across the yard, her boots crunching on the frozen crabgrass that no doubt would bloom with a sea of golden dandelions in the spring. Good grief, what was wrong with Florence Ross that she couldn't at least have a decent yard?

After living near the ocean with its difficult climate and soil, Claire had come to appreciate that in Missouri, people tended their perfect postage-stamp lots with the loving care a mother gave a newborn child. They fertilized, weeded and reseeded until thick green grass covered every inch of ground. They sodded, dethatched and aerated. They planted flowers and bushes and trees, and they spread decorative mulch around everything that rose more than an inch above the smooth plane of their lawns. If all that wasn't enough to satisfy, Missourians liked to add trellises, fountains, birdbaths, gazebos and collections of concrete statues—gnomes and cherubs and fairies. Early in the morning elderly ladies could be spotted with their dandelion forks, rooting out the pestilent weed with the passion of zealots. And nothing made a Missouri man prouder than to circle his yard several times a week atop his riding lawn mower.

Florence Ross, on the other hand, seemed determined to cultivate the perfect breeding ground for every dandelion seed, crabgrass root and burr that made its way into her neighbors' yards. Claire knocked on her aunt's door a second time. No doubt those three cats huddled up against the outside of the brick chimney joined their feline companions in spreading fleas, chiggers and ticks everywhere they roamed. Not to mention dragging scraps of garbage from the trash cans into one yard or another.

"Aunt Flossie!" she shouted. "Open up! I'm freezing out here."

No wonder the townspeople reviled the elderly spinster. Claire felt sure that everyone up and down this street would be thrilled if the police chief condemned Ross Mansion and kicked Flossie out. But the very thought of the foul-tempered woman ever setting foot inside Claire's clean, quiet house sent prickles of horror down her spine. It also had motivated her to hurry over this Saturday morning and start rounding up Aunt Flossie's feral felines.

"Hey!" she hollered, hammering with her fist on the solid oak door. "Aunt Flossie, you'd better come down here and—"

"Get offa my property!" The door opened an inch, and the barrel of a .22 rifle slid through the gap. "And I mean business!"

Claire stepped back and swallowed a gulp of surprise. Okay, this was another gun. Yes, indeed. And most certainly it would be loaded.

"Aunt Flossie?" she croaked out. "Uh, it's me. Your niece, Claire Ross."

"I know who y'are. I told you not to come back here!"

"But you also told me—"

"Then get off my porch!" The door opened wider, and Flossie glared as she brandished the rifle. "I don't want you here!"

"And I don't want to be here," Claire snapped back. She grabbed the rifle barrel as she had seen Rob do, and stepped to one side. "You promised to get rid of the cats and clean up this place, Aunt Flossie. You promised!"

"I don't give a bucket of spit what I said! Let go of my gun and—"

"You let go! I'm here to round up cats. I've brought a net and a pet carrier, and every last one of them—"

The gun went off with a deafening boom, jerking out of Claire's hand and blowing a hole through the porch roof. Claire jumped backward as though she herself had been shot. Flossie wobbled for a moment, then toppled to her knees. The .22 clattered onto the icy porch.

"Get out!" Flossie screeched, her fingers gripping the filthy marble threshold. "Get off my land!"

"You nearly hit me, you crazy coot!" Claire smacked open the door with her hand. "You could have killed me! Now, get up off that floor, Aunt Flossie. And don't even think about going for the rifle."

As the woman reached out for the gun, Claire kicked it across the porch. It spun on the slick wood, sliding in circles until it dropped off the steps and into the yard. Vaguely aware of an approaching siren, Claire stepped over her aunt and into the reeking foyer of the aging mansion.

"Get up, Aunt Flossie!" she commanded. "You're not going to shoot me. I am going to round up your cats— and you're going to help me."

Her aunt was still on the floor, crouching on hands and knees. "Get away from me," she huffed. "Go on. Get outta here."

"Aunt Flossie, you have no choice in this." Claire glanced out across the yard at the squad car pulling to a stop. "Now you've brought the police again. Oh, great, it's Rob West. Well, this is just perfect. He'll probably throw you out right this minute, and I'll have to... Aunt Flossie?"

Needles of alarm shot through Claire as she knelt beside the woman still huddled in the doorway. Unmoving, Flossie breathed heavily, her wispy hair drifting in the chill wind that sucked around the corner of the old house. Claire laid her hand on her aunt's back. A knobby ridge defined her spine, and her shoulder blades stood out beneath the ragged pink bathrobe.

"Aunt Flossie, are you all right?" Claire asked softly.

A gnarled hand shot out and clapped her on the shoulder. "Back off before I have to coldcock ya! Look what you did—busted both my knees. Elbows, too, probably."

"I never touched you. You fell when you shot off that—" Claire bit off her retort. "Oh, never mind. Just let me help you up before we both freeze."

As she reached around her aunt's scarecrow frame, a pair of boots thudded toward them across the porch floor. "Good morning, ladies," Rob said. "Would one of you care to explain—"

"She fell," Claire cut in. "What does it look like?"

"She pushed me," Flossie spat out, her breath fogging the marble threshold. "Knocked me down and broke both my knees!"

"I did *not*—"

"Just be quiet, both of you." Muttering in disgust, Rob scooped Flossie into his arms and headed through the front door. "The apple doesn't fall far from the tree is all I can say."

"What is that supposed to mean?" Claire demanded, following him into the foyer and slamming the door shut behind them. Rob made for a room from which came the only evidence of warmth in the mansion. "Because I'll tell you one thing," Claire went on. "I am nothing like—"

"Aw, shut up!" Flossie squawked. "And put me down, you big galoot! Who do you think you are, hauling me around like a sack of potatoes?"

"Sack of feathers, more like it. What have you been eating anyhow, Miss Ross? Cat food?"

Rob tromped into what must have been the parlor at one time. Claire gaped at the appalling sight. An ornate marble fireplace belched gray smoke upward to the soot-blackened ceiling twelve feet overhead. Stacks of newspapers, magazines and advertising circulars lay moldering on the faded carpet. Antique settees and chairs that once might have been lovely leaned like old haystacks, covered with papers, clothing and cats. Everywhere—cats. Skinny and yellow eyed, they stared at Claire from atop ornate valances, an old upright piano, curvy-legged tables and mantel shelves. They peered out from under cushions and from behind Oriental pots whose foliage was long gone.

And the smell! Claire raced for a window as Rob kneed a pile of newspapers from one of the old settees and placed Flossie on it. Throwing back a velvet curtain that turned to dust in her hand, Claire reached for the sash. A cat that had been basking in the pale winter sunshine leaped to its feet, arching and hissing at her. With a gasp of surprise, she swatted the cat off the sill and jerked upward until the old window slid open a crack. Chill air rushed into the room as Claire headed for another window.

"What're you doing, girl? Trying to freeze me out of house and home?" Flossie squirmed as Rob attempted to wrap a moth-eaten afghan around her. "Hey, you're the no-good devil who stole my shotgun! And she knocked my .22 off the porch. Thieves! Robbers! Help! Some-body help me! I'm being attacked!"

"Hush now, Miss Ross," Rob ordered. He spoke over her high-pitched cries into the radio on his shoulder. "Dispatcher, this is Chief West. Send Bill Gaines over here to Ross Mansion, would you? And tell him not to turn on the bells and whistles, please. Ten-four."

"Who's Bill Gaines?" Claire asked, stepping around a heap of unwashed pots and pans on the floor.

"Paramedic. He's with the fire department. We'll let him check Miss Ross over and see if she needs to be transported to a hospital. Meanwhile, you and I can start rounding up these cats."

"No sirree, you don't!" Flossie rolled off the settee and staggered to her feet. "Nobody touches my cats! And I'm not going to a hospital, either. Where's my pistol? I'll show you, Buster Brown. Just you wait and see what I can—"

"Get back on that couch, Miss Ross," Rob com-manded, depositing her on the settee a second time. "Now, stay there, and I mean it."

"What're you planning to do? Handcuff me?"

"If I have to, I sure will." He heaved out a deep breath as he turned to Claire. "What do you suggest we put the cats in?"

"I borrowed a pet carrier from my neighbor."

"*One* pet carrier?"

"Well, I didn't expect to have any help, you know. I thought I'd catch a cat or two and take them over to the shelter. Then I'd come back here and—"

"Did you call the Buffalo shelter to ask how many stray cats they can manage?"

"I didn't…think…"

"Clarence? You didn't think?" He grinned for the first time that day, his blue eyes twinkling despite the smoky pall that darkened the room. "Obviously this is a situation that calls for brainpower. Leave it to me."

With a wink, he headed for the parlor door. As he talked into his radio again, Claire heard the fire engine pull up in front of Ross Mansion. Flossie was already back on her feet and fairly spitting nails. Blocking out the sound of her great-aunt's verbal venom, Claire greeted the paramedic and the two volunteer firemen who stepped into the room. Looking as though they had entered a genuine haunted house, the three men paused, their eyes wide and their Adam's apples working to control the gag reflex.

"Uh, seems like Miss Ross has a blocked chimney over there, Bill," one of the firemen spoke up. "How about we take a look at that?" After a glance for confirmation, the two crossed the room to inspect the smoking fire. Bill picked his way toward the tiny creature who was dancing around like an imp from the bowels of Hades.

"All of you better get gone!" Flossie ranted, shaking her fists. "And leave my fire alone. Why, I'll have you know it takes me a good hour to start it every morning, and I'm not—"

"Aunt Flossie, the paramedic is here to look at your knees," Claire cut in. "You said they were broken."

"Do these knees look broken?" the older woman hissed. "Why, they could carry me to Kathmandu and back! You think I'm about to let some goggle-eyed greenhorn take a gander at my legs? Is that what you think?" Rising to her full height of just under five feet, Flossie stared at Claire. "Well, you're wrong, girl!"

"Sit down, Aunt Flossie!" Claire shouted, taking the woman by the shoulders and forcing her back onto the settee. "Sit down *now!* And if you so much as squeak, I'll tell Rob to handcuff you."

With Flossie bawling like a calf at branding time and Claire doing her level best to restrain her, Bill managed to sneak in a quick examination of the elderly woman's knees. As the paramedic retreated from the hail of verbal abuse, Rob returned to the parlor with Claire's pet carrier, the fishing net she had brought and word that the local shelter could handle ten cats and the nearby town of Bolivar would take the rest. The head of Buffalo's animal rescue was on her way with several humane traps and other equipment.

"I'm afraid you're going to have to cuff Miss Ross, Chief," Bill said, eyeing Flossie. "I got a look at her knees, and I suspect they're all right. But I'm telling you… I think we may have some other problems going on. I'd like to check her over. She may need to see a doctor."

"What's wrong?" Claire asked. Flossie was headed for the door, murmuring that she was going to fetch her pistol. "Is my aunt sick?"

"Hard to say, but I think for sure she's got…well, fleas. Maybe other things, you know."

She grimaced. "Lice?"

"Not sure. She definitely looks anemic to me. There are bruises all over her legs, but everybody knows the only place she ever goes is to the corner grocery to buy cat food and a few supplies. So I'm thinking she bumps into the furniture, maybe. Then there's the matter of her teeth. Vitamin deficiency, low iron, you name it. Her general nutritional condition looks pretty bad…"

His words drifted off at the sight of Rob West hand-cuffing Florence Ross to the arm of her carved mahogany settee. Her free fist pounding his broad shoulders, Flossie wailed and screeched and threatened the police chief with every manner of legal action and vengeance imaginable.

Claire could only stare in dismay. How on earth had things gotten so out of control here? Exactly who was responsible for Florence Ross? Did the state of Missouri owe her help—the Division of Family Services, Meals on Wheels, Social Services or whatever? Were Buffalo's public servants—the police force and the city aldermen—liable for keeping an eye on their elderly and infirm residents? Should the Ross family have been looking in on their recalcitrant relative, a hermit who had unequivocally disowned all of them? Or was Aunt Flossie supposed to be capable of maintaining her own health and habitation?

The sight of the elderly woman cuffed and snarling at everyone in sight sent a curl of flame through Claire's chest. The truth of the matter was, Aunt Flossie had brought this on herself. She had alienated everyone to the point that no one wanted to go near her. For all they knew, she could have dropped dead weeks ago, and no one would have been the wiser.

Angry at her aunt, her family, the police, the state government and even herself, Claire snatched up the fishing net and dropped it over the nearest cat. A gray-striped bag of skin and bones, the animal instantly sprang to life—yowling, hissing, turning circles inside the nylon net, tangling claws and teeth and tail in a mass of freaked-out feline hysteria.

"Look at her! Look at what my niece is doing!" Flossie hollered. "She's killing Oscar!"

Oscar? This cat had a name? Struggling to keep the animal trapped, Claire reached for the pet carrier. As she tugged it toward the netted cat, a claw caught her hand and raked a line of torn flesh.

"Ouch!" she cried, tumbling backward into one of the haystacks of clothing and newspapers. The cat escaped the net in a blur of gray fur. Ears flattened against his head, Oscar made for the open window and vanished with a flick of his long tail.

"Nice try, Clarence," Rob said, reaching out to help Claire to her feet. "But I believe this is a job for two."

"Fine, then." She handed him the net. "See if you can do it."

But the cats were on to their game now. Warily eyeing the enemy, they crouched with skinny muscles coiled and sharp claws dug in, ready to bolt. The two firemen had managed to put out the fire, and Claire was forced to shut the windows in order to prevent more animals from escaping. Even with doors and windows closed, it was going to be no easy matter cornering the malnourished, flea-bitten cats.

While Rob and Claire stalked a small yellow creature that looked as cute and innocent as a baby chick, Bill attempted to examine the handcuffed Flossie. His two compatriots held her gently but firmly in place while he looked into her ears, nose, mouth and hair, then studied her arms, fingers and toes. Aunt Flossie was busy calling the poor paramedic every name in the book when Claire and Rob finally nabbed the little yellow cat. Though it fought tooth and claw, they dropped it into the pet carrier and shut the metal door.

"Animal rescue here!" a heavyset woman announced, barging into the room. She put her equipment on the floor and immediately began setting out traps. Baited with food, the small cages would capture the cats alive and unharmed.

"About time we did this," the woman offered as she worked. "Hey, Miss Ross, how you doin' this morning? Gettin' a medical exam, I see. Good, good. We're gonna round up some of your spare kitties, take 'em over to the shelter and see that they get baths, tags, shots, worm medicine. It's just one of those things we need to do. We'll bring you back one or two, how's that? Make sure they can't start any new litters, and you can have a couple of 'em. There you go—I thought that'd cheer you up! Hey, Chief, looks like you caught one already. And is that Claire Ross? Well, I'll be jiggered. You don't look a thing like you did in high school. Remember me— Jane Henderson? I didn't think so, 'cause I was a grade or two younger, but I do recall you giving your senior assembly speech about how Buffalo was important in the Civil War. That was a good speech, and I never forgot it. Okay, let's get to work, how 'bout?"

"Hey, I helped make that presentation," Rob spoke up. "That was my project, too. Mine *and* Claire's."

Jane eyed him for a moment. "You gave a speech about Buffalo?"

"Yes, as a matter of fact, I did." He hooked his thumbs in his belt loops. "For your information, Miss Henderson, the town of Buffalo, Missouri, was founded in 1841 on Buffalo Head Prairie, which was named for a buffalo skull landmark erected by the first settler, Mark Reynolds. During the Civil War, Dallas County was pro-Union, which made it the target of many guerrilla raids. In October 1863, Confederate troops under the command of General Joseph O. Shelby burned down the county courthouse. And in July 1864, Confederate raiders burned the Methodist church, which was being used as the courthouse."

Claire began to clap. "Well done, Chief West. I award you an A plus for excellent memory skills."

"Told you I was smart," he said. "And look at that."

They followed his pointing finger to a cat that had already ventured into one of the traps. As it leaned toward the bowl of food, the cage door fell shut.

"Voilà!" Jane Henderson cried. "Cat number two is down for the count! Tell you what. You two head on outside and see if you can catch any of 'em in the yard. I spotted a few under the porch. I'll work in here, me and Miss Ross. Huh, Miss Ross? You and me."

Flossie glared, red eyed and pinch lipped, at Jane Henderson. "You're planning to kill my cats."

"No, I ain't. Now, who's this over here in the trap? This one got a name?"

"Betsy."

Rob slipped his arm around Claire's shoulders and bent down to whisper in her ear. "Betsy? Betsy and Oscar?"

Momentarily disconcerted by the nearness of the man, Claire couldn't come up with a witty response. All she could think was that to Aunt Flossie these creatures were not wild, stray cats. They were Betsy and Oscar and who knew who else? They were her friends, her companions. Her family. And because of Claire, the old woman was handcuffed in her own house, enduring the humiliation of a medical exam by a total stranger, forced to surrender her precious privacy.

Those thoughts were running through Claire's head at the same moment she was realizing that Rob West smelled just the way he had in high school—like shaving cream and leather and the fresh, wide outdoors. But he was closer to her now, closer than he'd ever been, and in spite of her heavy coat she could feel the steely strength in his arm around her. Near her cheek, his chest spread out like a flat plain that seemed to go on forever, and the geometric angle of his jaw grazed her temple as he hurried her out of the parlor and onto the porch.

"Whew, escaped!" he said, and his breath was warm on her skin. "Good ol' Jane. She's been wanting to catch those cats ever since she started working at the shelter, but I knew how much they meant to Miss Ross. I kept hoping I could somehow talk her into giving them up."

"Not a chance," Claire said, rubbing her bare hands together for warmth. "Rob, I think it's more than an obsession. She loves those cats."

"Maybe so, but she can't take care of them. Look at that group huddled over there near the chimney." He absently cupped Claire's hands between his and blew on them. "Mangy little things. They'll be better off with Jane. She's been fairly successful at adopting out the animals she gets. And she said she'll bring a couple of the cats back over here to keep Miss Ross company."

Claire tried to listen as he went on telling her about the local animal shelter, but somehow her mind was no longer on cats. It was on Rob West. Tall, handsome, brave, generous—and yes, even smart—Rob West. Rob West, who was holding her hands and smelled like heaven and had eyes that could make a woman quiver right down to her toes. Rob West, whom all the girls in school had had secret crushes on. Rob West, who'd quarterbacked the football team and won all those wrestling trophies. Rob West, who hated studying Missouri history and resented working with skinny Claire Ross and somehow still remembered every word of his senior assembly presentation.

But it wasn't really *that* Rob West, either. This one was ten years older and went to church and had lost his wife in a car accident. This one had become a police chief who helped plan the town Christmas parade and caught cats in a little old lady's house. Somehow all the Rob Wests were woven into a single man who was standing here in front of Claire. She knew him. And didn't know him. He was familiar. And a stranger. He was comfortably normal. And overwhelmingly, disconcertingly attractive.

"So you think we can figure out how to use that lasso thing of Jane's?" he asked, turning to Claire so that she was no longer looking at his profile but staring into his blue eyes. "If you came at the cats from one direction, and I came from the other…"

He stopped speaking and swallowed. She blinked. Dropping her hands, he shoved his own into his pockets. She moistened her lips.

"Uh, yes," she said. "That would be good. Surround them."

For a moment he didn't respond. "Did you always have those eyes? That color, I mean. Green."

"Hazel, I think."

"No, they're green."

"Well, they're the same ones I've always had. I don't wear contacts, either. Just glasses for reading." She nodded, trying to think of something else to say that made sense. "And grading papers."

"Okay." He frowned. "Because I don't remember those eyes from high school."

"You probably don't remember anything from high school." She managed the old teasing tone. "Except your speech, I guess. That was pretty impressive, by the way."

"I remember stuff, Claire. I told you I heard everything you said to me." He shifted from one foot to the other. "And I remember your hands, too. Long, thin fingers. You had pretty hands. Still do."

"Thank you." She pushed them deep into her coat pockets and wrapped them around her gloves. "Thanks for…warming them."

"Yeah, well… I guess I'd better go get that lasso thing." As though suddenly remembering he had to be somewhere, Rob turned and barreled back into the house.

Claire let out a breath. This was weird. Rob West was way out of her league. She could tease him. Scold him. Educate him. But she could not—absolutely *not* —desire him. And she knew the way her heart was beating at this moment had nothing to do with the exercise of chasing stray cats or battling Missouri's winter wind. Definitely not.

"That's far enough!" Rob gritted his teeth in concern and frustration as Claire inched her way across a tree limb toward a shivering cat. Did the woman ever listen?

"Hey, Claire, don't go any farther!" He tried again. She had insisted on being the one to go after this cat. At six foot four and a hundred pounds heavier, Rob had reluctantly agreed. "That branch is too thin, Claire. It's not safe."

"Shh!" She scowled down at him, her eyes flashing in the setting sun. They were *not* hazel. "Stop yelling at me, you nincompoop."

"Just try the lasso."

"All right, all right." Spread full-length along the branch, she gripped it with one hand and both knees as she extended the metal pole toward the cat.

Except for this wily black-and-white tomcat, the group gathered at the mansion had finally captured all the felines. Earlier in the day Rob made the welcome discovery that Florence Ross had locked all the doors to the basement and upstairs rooms, confining her living area mainly to the front parlor, the foyer and a single bathroom. After combing the house for weapons, he located the pistol and several caches of ammunition, which he confiscated. Though concerned about her reaction to the cat roundup, he removed Flossie's handcuffs.

Despite the old woman's every effort to deter them, Jane Henderson—along with Bill Gaines and the two firemen—eventually trapped all the indoor cats. About midafternoon, Jane and her crew stacked the humane shelter's van with ten cages. After promising to make regular checks on Flossie until they could return a couple of her cats, Jane drove away. The men begged off, saying they needed to go take showers.

That left Claire and Rob to continue the nearly impossible job of cornering the strays that lurked around the perimeter of the mansion. Climbing trees, falling through the rotting porch floor, negotiating the roof, and racing back and forth, they'd managed to nab six cats. The two indoor ones that Jane's shelter couldn't take made eight. This final tom in the old oak tree would complete their mission.

"The pole isn't long enough," Claire called down from the tree limb. "I can't reach him."

"Just come on down, then. We can leave him."

"Leave him? After all this, you want to leave him here?"

"Claire, it's one cat. Please come down. You're making me nervous."

"Rob, I'm fine—just good ol' Clarence up a tree. What do you care anyway?"

"I care, okay?"

Her face appeared over the limb a second time. Green eyes pinned him, and he felt again an unexpected jolt that zinged down his spine and settled in the pit of his stomach. What was *that* all about? She was right— it was just dorky Claire Ross up in the tree. Skinny ol' Clarence…whose curls cascaded downward like a flow of red-hot lava. Whose lips transfixed him every time she spoke. Whose peach-soft skin just about begged him to caress it.

He couldn't be looking at her this way, Rob cautioned himself. After his wife's death, he had made a conscious decision not to date again, and certainly never to remarry. The painful experience had taught him that he wasn't cut out for the job. Like the Apostle Paul, he had a God-ordained mission that transcended marriage. Rob West belonged to the people of Buffalo. He was their servant, their caretaker, their protector. In a strange sense he was wedded to a town. And quite content with the relationship, too.

Besides, women were a lot of trouble. Sherry had been unhappy with just about everything Rob did. Despite all his triumphs in high school, he learned that in his wife's eyes he appeared a total failure. Sherry hadn't wanted Rob to become a policeman. She disliked the size and condition of the only house they were able to afford after their wedding. She hated the church he had joined, and refused to attend. Most of all, she resented being married.

Though he had dated the vivacious blonde through much of high school and had believed they were in love, he belatedly discovered that Sherry had goals that went far beyond the little town of Buffalo. After graduation, she packed up and headed for college as a theater major, planning one day to move to Hollywood and try for her big break as an actress. When she found out she was pregnant with Rob's child, she reluctantly agreed to marry him, and even though she miscarried the baby, they stayed together through seven unhappy years. Sherry had regularly reminded her husband that he had killed her dreams and ruined her life. He never wanted to do that to anyone again.

"I care because I'm the police chief," he called up to the green eyes that were currently hypnotizing him into a jelly-kneed trance.

"I see," she said, still staring.

Absolutely, he could not let Claire know the effect she was having on him. He squared his shoulders. "I can't have the newspaper printing a story about me letting the high school history teacher fall out of a tree while chasing a cat. It wouldn't look good."

"Oh, right," she said. "Well, excuse me for *not* caring about your precious reputation."

Turning away, she edged farther along the branch toward the cat. Rob swallowed as the slender limb dipped downward. The cat growled, a long guttural emanation that reverberated through the chill air. Claire stretched out the aluminum pole. The noose on its far end slipped over the cat's head. Claire tightened the loop, and the cat leaped.

"Oh, Rob!" Her arm jerked downward as the big tom's white paws and black tail flailed in midair, and she clung to the branch with one hand and her knees. "Rob, he's going to hang. I'm killing the cat."

"Let him go! Drop the pole!" Rob pulled himself onto a lower branch and started climbing the tree. "Just don't fall. Let the cat go."

"But he's caught in the noose! If I drop him, he won't be able to land on his feet. He'll get hurt."

"Forget the cat, Claire. You're the one who's going to get hurt!"

She was trying to lower herself to another branch as the cat squirmed and yowled on the end of the pole. "Help him, Rob! Move him onto a branch, and I'll try to loosen the—"

She lost her grip and toppled downward right into a large empty squirrel's nest that had been built in the crossed branches of the tree. Dead leaves flew outward in a puff of brown dust. The cat dropped to the ground and took off running with the aluminum pole still attached to the noose around his neck.

"Claire, are you okay?" Rob reached for her. The branch under him cracked. "Hang on!"

"*You* hang on!" She scrambled through the leaves to grab him. The branch snapped, and they both went down, sliding through bare limbs and snapping off twigs on their way to the ground.

"Ha! Ha!" Flossie Ross crowed through an open window as Rob rolled off Claire, who was squealing in pain. "Serves you both right! I hope you broke all your arms and legs! And your heads, too!"

Rob caught Claire's shoulders and lifted her into his lap. "Are you hurt? Is anything broken?"

"Where's the cat?"

"He's fine. I can see the pole sticking out from under the porch."

She let out a breath. "I'm okay, too. You?"

"Other than you just about scaring me to death, I'm fine."

Looking up into his eyes, she smiled. "Well, Rob West. It seems we've just completed our second project together."

He couldn't resist stroking his hand down the side of her face. "That is the last time I ever let you climb a tree."

"You can't keep me from climbing trees."

"I'm pretty good at getting what I want."

"Are you, now? Well, I certainly know what I want."

Her words rushed through him with all the force of a dam breaking. When he spoke, his voice came out husky and breathless. "Oh, yeah? What's that?"

Hesitating, she closed her eyes for a moment. When they opened again, he saw that they had gone soft and dark. "Not much, really," she whispered. Her lower lip trembled, and she cleared her throat. "Actually, I was thinking about pizza."

He laughed. "Pizza?"

"Over at Dandy's in Bolivar." She sat up and tugged her cap back down over her ears. "They make the best mushroom-and-onion pizza I've ever tasted."

"Mushroom and onion? Whatever happened to good ol' pepperoni?"

"Fine, we'll order two." Standing, she took his hand and pulled him to his feet. "Go haul that poor cat out from under the porch, and I'll meet you at your car."

Claire was going with him to Bolivar. Rob stared after her as she headed for the open window through which her great-aunt continued to heckle them. Claire Ross was going with him to Bolivar. They would drop the cats at the shelter, and then they would drive to Dandy's and eat pizza. Just the two of them.

It would be like a date. Only, he had vowed not to date again. This was only geeky Clarence, he reminded himself. So it didn't count. Not really.

He watched her standing at the window talking to the older woman, assuring Flossie that she would drop by to check on her tomorrow and that she'd return a couple of cats to the mansion within the week. Claire's auburn curls covered her shoulders, tumbling over her green coat and down her back. Her slim hips and long legs looked just about too good to be true. As she turned to face Rob again, the setting sun flashed in her green eyes.

Maybe just one *sort-of* date wouldn't matter too much. In fact, the more he thought about it, the more it seemed like a good idea. Just two old friends having pizza together and talking. What was the harm in that?

Chapter Three

Claire wiped her fingers on a napkin and sighed as she settled back in the restaurant booth. Nothing like warm toes and a full stomach on a cold winter night. Three hours earlier, she had left Aunt Flossie still hurling insults through the open window of Ross Mansion and had driven home to shower and change out of her filthy duds into clean jeans and a forest green sweater. Half an hour after that, Rob had picked her up in his squad car.

Back seat filled with yowling, hissing cats in small cages, they'd left Buffalo for the twenty-minute drive to the nearby town that boasted a charming courthouse square, a small Christian university and an abundance of quaint nineteenth-century homes. The manager of the Bolivar animal shelter took the cats, promising to restore them to health and try to find them good homes. And then it was pizza time.

"You only ate three slices," Rob said, starting on his fifth.

"Enough, already. I'm as stuffed as that crust."

Chewing, he grinned at her. "You always did like pizza."

Uncomfortable with the ease of his statement, she

knitted her fingers together under the table. They had spent most of the evening chatting about the past—his memories of the football team, her recollections of their different teachers and their mutual reminiscences about the joint history project.

But Claire couldn't deny that it was disconcerting to have Rob West seated across from her in this dimly lit restaurant booth tonight, his blue eyes gazing into hers and his hand occasionally reaching out to touch her arm. No matter how hard she tried to convince herself otherwise, she enjoyed his company. And not just as an old high school friend. There was something about Rob that drew her. A connection, a soul-deep response, a heart yearning.

Of course, he was handsome. No female in her right mind would deny that. Just the sight of the man sent tingles dancing like snowflakes down her spine. Yet what she experienced in his presence went much deeper than mere physical attraction.

With Rob, Claire felt exactly like herself. Not like the woman she wished to become. Not like a dream image of the perfect heroine in her own life story. Just herself. Claire Ross. For some reason she couldn't quite understand, that relieved and comforted her.

And it definitely made her reconsider the man she had been so certain she ought to marry. Had she ever known Stephen as well as she knew the man across the table? Certainly she and Stephen had much in common, and Claire had admired him almost to the point of reverence. Young, highly acclaimed and well traveled, Stephen was a writer—a gifted historian whose books she had read and respected. She had been assistant curator of the museum in which he spent much of his research time, and he'd commended the accuracy of her work there.

They'd spent time together quietly discussing differing accounts of a war, or the influence of some long-dead figure, or the findings of an archaeological dig. Stephen had agreed to attend Claire's church, analyzed the sermons from start to finish and pronounced himself a believer. Though his life hadn't borne much fruit from that point forward, it had been enough for Claire.

She liked Stephen. Loved him, she'd felt sure. When he had asked her to marry him, she'd agreed, convinced that a future with the man made good sense. Their plans perfectly matched the ideal life she had dreamed up for herself in college. She and Stephen would spend their years in the serene and studious pursuit of historical accuracy. They would attend cultural events together. They would travel to the great places of the world and visit important sites. Okay, so they might not laugh much…or tease each other…or chase cats…

Claire sighed and glanced at Rob. He was nothing like her former fiancé, who had bolted off into the blue after a young admirer had made a fuss over his latest book. Stephen, it turned out, preferred hero worship to fidelity. He craved awestruck veneration over mutual respect.

Rob West, on the other hand, was steady. Authentic. And definitely a lot more fun.

He was smiling gently at her now, almost as though he was untangling and reading the web of confusing thoughts that jumbled her mind. To Claire's mortification, she realized he probably was.

"You told me your mom and dad used to bake home-made pizza every Friday night," he recalled. "That's why you didn't come to my games. Because you wanted to eat pizza with your family."

She lowered her focus to her plate. "Those were fun evenings, and my folks still do pizza night when they're in town. But I might have been giving you an excuse. I didn't go to football games because I didn't have anyone to go with. It was a culture, you know, the whole football scene. I didn't have many friends, and we weren't big on all that rah-rah stuff." She paused. "Anyway, I never have understood football."

He leaned forward, his brow furrowed. "You don't understand football? What does that mean?"

"Was I speaking a foreign language just then? No, I don't understand football. My dad never watched it on TV. He was a farm boy growing up, and he didn't care for athletics. I didn't have brothers and rarely went to the games. When I did go, I could never find the ball."

"You couldn't find the ball?"

She stared at him. "Are you going to keep repeating things? The football is brown and tiny, and it's always hidden in some burly guy's arms."

"Yeah, that burly guy is the quarterback. Me."

"How can anyone tell who's who? All the players look alike."

"They have numbers on their jersey backs. Names, too, in the pros."

She shrugged. "Anyway, it's always the same. The teams suddenly burst into action and start running around all over the field, the crowd yells, most of the players fall down and the referees throw yellow hankies everywhere."

"Flags."

"Whatever. Then the football reappears, and the

whole scenario repeats itself. I never can find the ball, so what's the point?"

He sat up straight and put his slice of pizza down on the plate. Then he pointed a finger at her. "You are coming over to my house tomorrow, Claire Ross, and we're watching Sunday afternoon football."

Claire swallowed. Time alone with Rob West. This was not in her plans. Not at all. She unknitted her fingers and then knitted them back again.

"Well, I do have papers to grade."

"And I have bad guys to catch. I've got a methamphetamine ring scuttling around right under my nose, but they'll just have to wait a couple of hours to start playing cat and mouse with me again. You and I are watching a game together tomorrow. That's settled."

"Is this by order of the police chief?"

"It's an invitation."

"It sounded like a command."

"Seriously, Claire. I can't let a red-blooded American girl get by without understanding football. That's not acceptable."

"I'm not a girl." She pushed a piece of crust from one side of her plate to the other. "I'm twenty-eight, Rob. This isn't high school."

"I know that." His eyes darkened. "Are you saying you don't want to come over?"

"Would that be right—you and me alone together in your house? As my grandmother would say, 'There'd be talk among the people.' Besides, I don't care about football."

"How can you say that? You don't understand it, so you don't know how you feel about it. Look, okay? Just take a look at this."

Rob got up and came around the table. Claire barely had time to scoot over before he climbed into the booth, seating himself beside her and sliding the white paper place mat out from under her plate.

"Now, here's the thing about football," he began, pulling a pen from his jeans pocket and drawing a pattern of Xs and Os on the mat. "It's a game, but it's more than that. It's a battlefield, a test of strategy and strength. It's like that float your students are building— chess come to life."

Claire tried her best to concentrate on the place mat and the ink marks and Rob's animated explanation. With the stroke of his pen, players designated with positions such as wide receiver, tackle and linebacker marched back and forth across the white paper field. Yards and downs and penalties appeared and disappeared. Patterns formed, merged, then dispersed as the opposing teams fought to get the ball or to keep it out of the end zone. A foreign culture with its own language, football took on an unexpected mystique. The battlefield analogy resonated with the historian in Claire, and she was intrigued.

But even as she watched the drama unfold, Rob's shoulder kept inserting itself into her line of vision and disturbing her concentration. Large, solid, covered in blue denim, the mass of muscle pressed against her own shoulder—a firm reminder that the presence beside her was all man. He smelled of clean, soapy skin and shampoo. And shaving cream, of all things. Had Rob shaved before picking her up? Why? Did men normally do that sort of thing at six in the evening?

His hands kept reaching into Claire's thoughts, too. Rob had never possessed ordinary fingers, palms, thumbs. Now, ten years later, his hands looked even more amazing to her than they had in high school. They were large and tanned, with long, strong fingers and blunt nails. They had calluses and interesting small scars, and they worked in tandem with their owner's words. Rob didn't just talk—he hammered, pointed, jabbed, pounded and thumped his way through a conversation. Sitting beside him, Claire was poked and prodded, her hand regularly tapped, her wrist touched, her elbow bumped.

Under any circumstances, no one could ignore Rob West, and on this night Claire could hardly focus. Along with his big shoulder and constantly signaling hands, she had to contend with the fact that the long plane of his thigh pushed against hers, demanding her attention. His dark hair gleamed in the lamplight, and his perfect profile sent tiny butterflies circling around in her stomach. She felt as though neon lights flashed around him, blinking the word *Male*. Tall, dark, handsome male. Brave, fascinating, intelligent male. Wonderful, amazing, desirable male.

Forcing the willful word and its accompanying distress from her mind, Claire listened closely enough to manage several fairly sensible questions. Rob answered with infinite detail and more diagrams. Lots more diagrams. As the waiters began shutting down the restaurant for the night, Claire realized her place mat was covered front and back, and Rob's was looking a little like a Jackson Pollock painting.

"So a field goal is worth three points?" she asked. "Why is that?"

"Why? Who cares why?"

"There ought to be a reason."

He studied her face for a moment. "There's not a reason for everything, Claire. Sometimes things are just the way they are. Like you and me. Neither of us planned a lot of what happened in our lives."

"Random acts of circumstance and fate?" She pointed to the place mat. "Or do you believe some heavenly head coach is up there moving things around like players on a football field—planning events, maneuvering us into position, causing things to happen to us?"

"I believe the same as you. God is in control of everything, and He knows everything. But He gives us choices, too. Look at your great-aunt. Florence Ross didn't have to become a crotchety old bat, but she made decisions that molded her character. I'm sure God knew how she was going to turn out."

"I don't know, Rob. Maybe Aunt Flossie didn't choose to become so angry and bitter."

"She chose it. Babies aren't born bitter. Things happen to us, and we decide how we're going to react to them. God gave us the freedom to do what we want, and the ability to respond to whatever happens. I didn't have to get Sherry pregnant. I could have listened to my friend Claire and behaved like a gentleman. I didn't have to marry Sherry, either, but this time I was thinking about what my friend Claire would have said. She'd have told me to do the right thing and accept my responsibilities. Sherry losing our baby was one of those sorrows in life that happen—whether by God's design or the enemy's or just a confluence of events, I'm not sure. But I'm the one who chose how to respond. I imagined what my friend Claire would say—"

"You really thought of me as a friend?"

"Didn't you?" Consternation furrowed his brow. "Didn't you see me as *your* friend?"

Claire lowered her head, thinking. During most of high school she had been so lonely. Her few companions had been in the French club or the chess club or her church youth group. They had done some fun things together—silly teenage stuff. But the one person she had always been able to count on was Rob West.

He showed up for their meetings. He did his part on the project even though he clearly considered it a boring assignment. Most important, though, Rob talked to her. They rambled on and on for hours while combing through history books or painting posters or designing charts. Claire had told him everything about her family, her hopes, her dreams, her faith in Jesus Christ. And he had shared his goals and beliefs, too.

He had never been to church or had a family who deeply cared about him, and it was as if he drank in Claire's words each time she spoke of such things. He teased her and made her laugh and protected her from the taunts of anyone who dared to put her down as a skinny redhead. If friendship meant communication and support and fun, then Rob certainly had been her friend.

"I never really worked it out in my mind that way before," Claire finally said. "But yes, Rob, you were my friend. Maybe my best friend."

His mouth curved into the hint of a smile. "I like that."

"So do I. And by the way, despite not listening to my great words of wisdom as well as you should have, you turned out all right. I'm proud of you, Rob. It's wonderful that you went into law enforcement. And I'm thrilled that the aldermen appointed you chief."

"Really?" He blinked as if stunned. "I mean, that

was *my* goal, but I never thought...it didn't occur to me that anyone else would..." He looked at her. "No one has ever said they were proud of me."

"Are you serious? When I heard about you being police chief, I thought, Well, what do you know? That dimwit Rob West made something of himself after all."

He chuckled. "That's not why I went after the job. I mean, I'm glad you feel good about what I do. But I really didn't give a flip what anyone thought of me."

His expression sobered as he continued. "I should have cared more. Sherry didn't want me on the force here in Buffalo. She would have preferred that I go into business. Be a store manager or run some sort of enterprise. She wanted to live in the city. I'm talking about Los Angeles or New York, you know, where she could have pursued her acting career. But I just couldn't see myself behind a desk full-time, and I'd already made a commitment to the police academy when I found out she was pregnant. I stuck with my plan, but I understand now how selfish that must have looked to her. It caused a lot of trouble between us."

"I'm sorry, Rob."

"Well, a person makes mistakes."

Claire nodded. "You don't have to tell me that. I've made enough of my own."

"Good thing I got right with the Lord, or I'd have drowned in remorse by now. It took me a long time to forgive myself for all the stupid, selfish things I did when I was younger. But once I realized that if God—the creator of the whole universe—could forgive Rob West, then it was a done deal. God had erased my mistakes, and I'd better start letting them go, too."

Claire couldn't help leaning against his arm and resting her head on his shoulder. "That's good advice, Rob. I need to do a better job of following it myself. But I hope you don't regret choosing police work."

"I can't regret it. I know it's what I'm supposed to do. More than anything else, I want to help people. In high school it was all about fame and glory, you know? Quarterbacking the football team, winning wrestling trophies."

"Completing an outstanding history project with your brilliant partner."

He grinned. "That, too. But after a while the hero thing got to feeling shallow. It was what Sherry wanted me for, but not what I wanted for myself. I needed some challenges that really made a difference, you know? Not just pinning some guy to the mat. Or getting a football from one end of the field to the other."

"Though that is fascinating," Claire said, holding up one of the decorated place mats.

"Yeah, all right, I confess. I still like football a lot."

"Okay…and I guess I have to confess I no longer think you're quite as dumb as a Missouri mule."

"Hey, I'm smart, Clarence Ross!" he declared. "I'm every bit as smart as you. Admit it!"

"No way!" She giggled as he grabbed her hands. "What are you going to do, Chief, handcuff me?"

"I might, so you'd better start talking, girl. Say 'Rob West is smart.'"

"No! Let go!" Laughing, she pushed on his chest as he struggled to hold her hands. "I'll never talk. Na na— you can't make me."

"No, but I can do this."

He kissed her on the lips. Hard. Once. And then again—softer, damper and sweeter.

Claire went weak as shock gave way to pleasure. Melting against him, she drifted into the kiss, aware of nothing but the delicious pressure of his mouth against hers, the rough graze of his chin, the tightness of his hands as his fingers threaded through hers. When he pulled away, she hung breathless for a moment, suspended in the vacuum his presence had just filled so completely.

"Oh… Rob…" She leaned against the brick side of the booth, the back of her hand to her mouth. Struggling for air now, she realized she was clutching his sleeve and staring into his blue eyes and wishing with every fiber of her being that he would kiss her again.

"Excuse me, sir." A young waiter stepped up to the booth. "Umm…hey, Chief West. How are things in Buffalo?"

"Hey, Andrew." Rob turned away from Claire and cleared his throat as he shook the young man's hand. "Andrew Rodman, this is Claire Ross. Andrew's been working at Dandy's for a couple years now."

"Three years, sir. Started when I was sixteen. Now I'm a freshman in college."

"Is that right?" Rob raked a hand through his hair. "Time sure does fly. Miss Ross teaches history over at the high school in Buffalo. We had to deliver some stray cats to the humane shelter here in Bolivar and thought we'd get a bite of pizza. Nothing like Dandy's after a long day."

The waiter nodded, his eyes glancing back and forth between the police chief and the schoolteacher. "Well, I hate to bother you, Chief, but the manager asked me to tell you that we're closing down for the night."

"No problem." Rob scooted out from the booth. "We've got to get back to Buffalo anyhow."

Claire pulled on her coat and grabbed her purse and gloves. As she slid out of the booth, she felt as though she were exiting a time machine—a place where time had stopped, the past melded with the present and nothing made sense. Rob West couldn't have just kissed her. That hadn't happened. Impossible.

She didn't want a man in her life again. Not that way. Not for a long, long time. Stephen had practically abandoned her at the altar, and she wasn't about to give away her heart so soon. Certainly not to Rob West. They knew each other well, but they were just buddies. Pals.

As Rob paid the bill, Claire rooted around in her purse on the pretense of needing her lip salve. There was no way she could look at the man ever again. The whole thing was just embarrassing and silly. An accident.

He started for the door, and she hurried after him. Don't look at him, she told herself. Don't look. Don't say anything. Just get in the car.

She climbed into the squad car, and Rob shut the door behind her. They would have to talk, she realized. Two people who had just bared their souls and then kissed each other couldn't sit for twenty minutes in silence.

It felt like high school, but it wasn't. They were adults. She had been engaged. He'd been married.

But the kiss hadn't been any big deal, really. A crazy, impulsive, meaningless thing, that's all.

"So, methamphetamines," she blurted out as he started the engine. "Wow, that's a big deal for Buffalo, isn't it? How did you learn someone was running a ring in town?"

He drove without speaking for a moment. She could see his jaw working.

"Traffic stop," he said finally. "Female ran a stop sign on the square. One of my patrolmen thought she was acting suspicious, so he searched her car. She'd hidden the meth in a pill bottle in her glove compartment. I questioned her at the station, and she told me she'd bought the drug locally. I got a few names out of her. Supposedly her suppliers."

"Did you find anything?"

"Nope. Then we started running across the stuff on a regular basis—traffic stops, domestics. Not just kids, either. Adults. Even some older folks. A real surprise. We're seeing more vandalism and petty stealing, too. The sheriff and the highway patrol are seeing the same thing. Everyone's coming up with identical information. Someone close to Buffalo or even in town has a methamphetamine lab. We just haven't found it."

Claire considered his words in silence for a moment, grateful for the passing time and the neutral topic. "I thought people usually built meth labs way out in the country."

"That's typical. Farmers keep one of the ingredients in tanks on their property—anhydrous ammonia. It's a volatile liquid fertilizer that adds nitrogen to the soil, and meth makers steal the stuff to put in their mix of cold pills and household chemicals. Also, meth has an odor, so they like to cook it in remote areas where no one can smell it. Besides that, it's explosive. They'll often rig up a lab in an old barn or an abandoned trailer. If it catches fire—*boom*. But they'll be long gone before the fire department gets there."

"Hard to believe people would take such a risk."

"Not really. Meth is profitable. It's also highly addictive. A lot of the makers are using the drug, too, so there's strong motivation. People will cook meth in the same room where their babies are sleeping and their kids are running around."

He fell quiet as they rolled into Buffalo and started toward Claire's house. "Two or three times we've found evidence of a lab." He spoke again, as if trying as hard as she had to fill the silence. "Plastic containers, hoses, burners. Personally, I think the dealers are moving around. Staying one or two jumps ahead of me."

"Like a chess game," she said. "Or football."

The corner of his mouth tilted as he braked in front of her yard. "You know, you're pretty smart, Clarence."

She managed a carefree smile as she reached for the door handle. "Well, I hope you catch them soon. And thanks for your help with the cats, Rob. I really appreciate it. I'll be over at the mansion tomorrow cleaning up, so I should have it ready by your deadline. But you're not really asking me to paint the place, are you? I mean, that's too much."

"I thought you were going to be grading papers tomorrow afternoon."

One foot on the ground, she pursed her lips for a moment. "Well, that, too. It's nearly the end of the semester, so I have to give exams and check term papers. That's why I don't have time to paint Aunt Flossie's house."

"Claire, listen. About what happened at Dandy's—"

"I enjoyed learning about football, Rob. It was fun. I'll try to watch a game one of these days. I promise." She started out of the car. "So, good night."

"Claire." His arm shot out, and he caught her hand. "About Dandy's—"

"It was okay. It was fine. Really."

"Look, I'm sorry if I—"

"You didn't. It's just that I have a lot going on. Like Aunt Flossie—I have to take care of her. And my students. The parade. Christmas. Besides, I went through all that with my fiancé, you know, so I'm not going to...to be..."

"I understand."

"Well, I'm not sure you do. Because it was awful, and I'm still angry. I'm not as far along with forgiveness and letting go as you are. I was very hurt. I don't want to be in that kind of place again. Ever. I just prefer to be alone."

"Yeah, like I would ever hurt you." He spoke under his breath. "Okay, this is Chief West signing off. And you do have to paint the outside of the mansion. At least the front."

"Rob!"

"It's in my report. Gotta follow the rules." He winked at her, though there was no sign of a twinkle in his eye. "See ya, Clarence."

Mayor Bloom waved at Rob from across the street. As a large float made of brightly colored tissue paper and chicken wire pulled to a stop between them, a gaggle of squealing, bouncy, ponytailed cheerleaders swarmed it. Crossing toward the mayor, Rob checked his uniform in the bank window. Neatly pressed black shirt and pants, patch on each shoulder, badge, name tag and collar brass with the shiny initials *BPD*—Buffalo Police Department—all in place. He'd made sure his car was washed and waxed to a high shine earlier that morning. Nothing but the best for the Christmas parade.

"How about this weather?" the mayor asked as the two men shook hands. "You couldn't ask for a better day. Sun's shining, sky's blue, temperature's hovering in the midforties."

"Just about perfect," Rob concurred.

"Mrs. Hopper's got the floats lined up in the right order. Don't know what we'd do without Dorothy. I spoke to Claire Ross a minute ago, too. She said things are all set with the parking situation at the school." He paused, eyeing Rob. "She's down there near the chess club float."

"Is that right?" Rob assessed the mayor, who appeared to be wearing the slight hint of a smirk.

"Just in case you were wondering, she's wearing a green coat."

"Aha." Rob made a point of checking his watch. "Well, I guess it's about time to get started."

"Ten minutes ought to do it. Give the cheerleaders time to get situated on the float." Bloom nodded. "Last Monday morning Jane Henderson called me about Florence Ross's cats. I hear you all had quite a time rounding 'em up. I went on over to the shelter and gave them all shots and dewormed 'em."

"I appreciate it, Mayor. That's an important community service."

"Yessir, took care of all ten cats. Did the spaying and neutering during the week. I guess you know Claire came over to the clinic on Wednesday and picked out three of 'em."

"Three cats?"

"Two for her great-aunt and one for herself. Feisty little ball of yellow fluff. She didn't tell you?"

Rob could see where this was leading. Somehow

the mayor had gotten wind of the police chief and the schoolteacher spending time together, and he was not about to pass up the opportunity to pry.

"Haven't talked to her since the day of the roundup," Rob said. "I'm sure happy to hear Miss Ross has a couple of her cats back. That ought to take some of the sting out of her bite."

The mayor chuckled. "I gather she was none too pleased about the raid. Jane Henderson told me Flossie was still squalling when she left. Said she hated to leave you and Claire there to chase down the last of the cats, but you didn't seem to mind. Said you were planning to take a bunch of 'em over to Bolivar?"

"That's right."

"Ol' Dandy's sure makes good pizza. I'll tell you what."

Rob struggled to stifle his ire. One of the blessings of small-town life—and certainly its greatest bane—was the grapevine. Everyone knew everyone else's business, or made it a point to find out. Neighbors checked on each other, and folks spent a good part of each evening sitting on the front porch watching the comings and goings of the community.

For a policeman, this was ideal. If an elderly woman fell while checking her mailbox, no more than five minutes went by before someone found her. Kids had a hard time getting into trouble, with everyone snooping over fences and craning necks to see into distant living-room windows. If someone got a new car, or dog, or wife, the whole town knew about it within the hour. Calls to the police station generally came from friends and neighbors who had spotted a problem, and Rob considered it a privilege to do his part in resolving any disturbance that marred Buffalo's quaint serenity.

But he had no desire to have his own private life strung out like grandma's wash for everyone to see and discuss. He could just about clobber Andrew Rodman right now. No doubt the young waiter at Dandy's had friends in Buffalo, and he had been eager to report that he'd seen the police chief kissing the schoolteacher.

Everyone in town probably thought they were an item, even though Rob had refrained from calling Claire all week. Not that he hadn't thought about her a lot. More than a lot.

In fact, he had driven past Florence Ross's home several times hoping to spot Claire, but it seemed she hadn't found room in her busy schedule to start painting the place. His normal rounds took him down her street, and even though he saw her lights shining on several evenings, he never caught a glimpse of the woman herself. Even when he visited the high school to give one of his regular talks on the dangers of drug and alcohol use, he failed to see Claire.

Yet their kiss played over and over in his mind, and no matter how hard he tried to convince himself it hadn't mattered, he knew the truth. She had responded. The moment his lips touched hers, she had softened, melted, gone supple and breathless against him. She had liked it. He had, too. But they both knew better than to make anything of it. Rob didn't want to date again, and he wasn't about to get married. And Claire had left no doubt of her own feelings on the subject. She wanted nothing to do with romance.

Mayor Bloom's juicy little rumor was about to end right now, Rob decided. He opened his mouth to speak.

"There she is, her own self," Bloom said, pointing to the far end of the float. Claire had just walked around it, her auburn curls bright against the green coat. She was headed their way.

"I invited Claire to ride with us, Chief," the mayor continued. "Figured you wouldn't mind. Her on the committee to represent the schools, and all that. Jane Henderson is coming along, too. The shelter can use the community support. A lot of Mrs. Henderson's funding comes from donations, you know. Everyone's talking about Florence Ross's cats and how you all rounded them up, so I thought it might be a good idea to have the two ladies along. They can throw bubble gum. I brought a whole bucket full of it."

Before Rob could protest, the mayor pushed a plastic pail into his arms and headed for the squad car.

"Hey, my favorite kind," Claire said, stepping up to Rob and dipping her hand into the bubble-gum tub. "I didn't think you remembered."

If he could have thought of something quick and witty, he would have shot it back at her. Instead, he stared like some goggle-eyed boy as she unwrapped the chunk of pink gum and popped it into her mouth. An expression of ecstasy suffused her face, turning her cheeks an even brighter pink as her lips went moist with delight.

"Good, huh?" Rob mumbled. He handed her the tub. "The mayor wants you and Jane Henderson to throw it out the window for the kids. He bought the gum."

Her green eyes clouded for a moment. "Should be fun." She shrugged as they crossed the street toward his car. "Hey, guess what. I have a cat. Remember the first one we caught? The little yellow thing—so scruffy and wild? Turns out he's actually very quiet, and he loves to snuggle. Opie—that's his name."

Rob opened the car door for her, trying not to think about what it would feel like to cuddle up with Claire and her little cat. Trying to remember this was the Christmas parade, and he was the police chief, and…

The pink bubble that emerged between Claire's lips took him by surprise. But there it was, round and shiny and getting larger by the moment. What else could he do but—

"Robert West!" she squealed as he smacked the bubble with his palm. It popped over the tip of her nose and across the side of her cheek like a big spill of pink paint. "I can't believe you did that! Oh, great—it's stuck!"

"Gotcha, Clarence." Guffawing as loudly as he always had in high school when he popped Claire's gum, Rob strutted around to the driver's side of the squad car and climbed in. Hoo, that felt good! Nothing like busting a great big ol' bubble to lift a man's spirits.

Mayor Bloom, already seated, gaped as Claire attempted to peel the sticky film from her cheek. He gave Rob a frown and shook his head. Clearly this did not fit his mental image of two lovebirds—which pleased Rob no end. Claire was peering into the passenger's side mirror when Jane Henderson trotted up, took one look at the predicament and burst out laughing.

"Well, I'll be. You a history teacher and so sophisticated and all. Get on in, girl. I'll help you." Chuckling, she followed Claire into the back seat. "I'd have thought the gum was for the kids, but you never can tell what a grownup'll do. Every now and then I'll take it into my head to climb a tree or go wading in the creek. As a matter of fact, three girlfriends and I once ate an entire pan of brownies by ourselves. It's just one of those things."

"An entire pan?" Claire asked.

"Yep, and I'll tell you what, my husband could have throttled me the day I did that. He came into the house after work—he has a good job over at the gas station on the highway, you know—and he smelled those brownies, but there wasn't even a crumb left in the pan. Boy, he sulked about that for a week, but anyhow...girl, you have got that gum stuck all over the tip of your nose. Lean over here, and let me see if I can...well, Chief, if you'd quit jerking the car around, that sure would help."

Rob glanced in the rearview mirror as he led the parade slowly out into the street toward the downtown square. As Jane Henderson tossed a handful of bubble gum to a group of children standing on the sidewalk, Claire fastened her focus directly on him. They eyed each other for a moment, then a slow grin tiptoed across her mouth. Rolling her eyes at him, she looked away, dug her fingers into the bucket of gum and threw a bunch out the window.

"Nothing like the Christmas parade to put a body into a good mood," Jane commented. "Let me tell you what. I've been at every parade Buffalo's had since the day I was born, and that's saying something. I'm talking about homecoming parades and Easter parades—all of 'em. Yessir. It's just one of those things. But this is the first time I ever got to ride in the lead car with the mayor. Kind of puts a different perspective on things, you know, riding in the front. I've been on more than one float where you're out there in the fresh air and you can near see the whole parade one end to the other if you're up high enough. But inside this car and leading all the floats and the marching bands…well, it's just a little different is all. Not that I don't like it. I do, but you just don't quite get the whole experience…"

Unable to concentrate on Jane's running monologue despite his top speed of two miles per hour, Rob drove with one hand and waved with the other and tried to keep from glancing at Claire in the rearview mirror. Occasionally he obliged the crowd by whooping the squad car's siren in little bursts that made the kids cover their ears and shriek in delight. The mayor called out the names of friends, neighbors and colleagues as the car rolled past. And Claire, in the back seat, threw gum and attempted to blot the sticky residue on the end of her nose. And she tried her best not to look in the mirror at Rob.

Like Jane Henderson, he had been at most of Buffalo's parades, Rob realized as they approached the square with its brick courthouse and festive storefronts. The Christmas celebrations were his favorites—with the marching bands playing carols, floats depicting Christ's birth or a family reading the Bible around a living-room fireplace, and the watching crowd bundled up to their necks in coats and mufflers. But this particular parade might take first place as the all-time, number one best of show.

The reason, of course, was the red-haired, green-eyed, sticky-nosed woman in the back seat. Despite everything sensible, and every good intention in his head, Rob knew he was going to have to find a way to kiss her again. As Jane Henderson would say, it was just one of those things.

Chapter Four

"No, don't open that! Not that!" Florence Ross tottered across the room, her ratty pink bathrobe flying out behind her skinny legs and her hands clawing the air in agitation. "You stay away from there, girl. That's mine. It's my private business!"

"Okay, Aunt Flossie. Relax."

As the early-afternoon sun crept over the parlor windowsill, Claire sat back on her heels and blew out a breath of frustration. Right after the Christmas parade that morning she'd grabbed a sandwich, driven over to Ross Mansion and forced her way inside. Just getting through the front door had been a challenge. But convincing Aunt Flossie to let her throw the piles of newspapers and trash into garbage bags had been a veritable Everest.

No way would the job be finished by the time Claire had to leave that evening. Sunday was supposed to be a day of rest, but Rob West had left her with no choice but to return to the filthy old house tomorrow. Though Claire had told herself that her work on behalf of her great-aunt was something of a ministry, she would much rather have stayed home and propped up her feet. Every move she made turned into a battle of wills with the elderly woman.

"I won't open the chest," she told Flossie, "but I have to clean it. There's an inch of…well, I don't even know what this is. Newspapers cemented onto the top, old food wrappers, and here's a sweater. A blue sweater. It was probably very nice once, too. Aunt Flossie, why have you let this happen?"

"Let what happen?" Flossie grabbed what was left of the sweater—a wad of tangled yarn covered with cat hair—and pressed it against her belly. "I was living here peaceful and happy till you and that—that—"

"Rob West. He's the police chief, and it's his job to take care of people in this town. Including you."

"*Take care* of me? Stealing my guns—my only protection? Hauling off my cats? Invading my privacy? And then he ordered you to come barging in here to mess up my things. You call that helpful? You call that kind?"

"I don't like being ordered around any better than you do, Aunt Flossie. But you and I both know there's no option other than to clean this place. Besides, you've got Homer and Virgil over there to keep you company after I'm gone." The pair of mature male cats—recently neutered by Mayor Bloom, the town veterinarian—lay curled up on the hearth.

"Thanks to the fire department, your fireplace is working again," Claire reminded her aunt as her fingers ticked off the improvements. "A home-health-care nurse came over to treat your flea bites and make sure you have vitamins. I scheduled a dental appointment for you."

"Which I won't go to."

"Yes, you will, if you intend to keep the teeth you've got left. My church donated a stack of clean clothes and a nice warm winter coat."

"Which I won't wear."

"The senior center is bringing you some good food to eat instead of this awful—"

"I happen to be a connoisseur of European cuisine," Flossie huffed as Claire peeled the remains of a frozen-dinner box from the lid of the old chest. "I enjoy Italian food. French. Spanish. Even Greek."

"European cuisine? This was a TV dinner! Lasagna."

"That's Italian."

"How did you cook it?"

"I put it on the fire." She snatched the box and flipped it over her shoulder. "Oh, what do you care?"

Aunt Flossie's question reverberated through Claire. The evening she had been perched high in the old oak tree outside the mansion, she had flung that same question at Rob.

He did care, he'd told her. In his eyes she had read the depth of meaning behind the words. But instantly he'd covered the intensity of feeling with the comment that a newspaper article about her falling out of the tree could harm *his* reputation. He had hidden his emotion just as surely as he'd made certain she knew the mayor had bought the bubble gum on the day of the parade.

Rob said everything so carefully. His words insisted that Claire was simply a friend from high school— nothing more. Yet his eyes, his touch, his face…and his kiss…told a different story.

Claire studied her great-aunt, who was so wrapped up in her own miserable existence that she didn't even know how bad things had gotten. Pretending it was pleasant to live with a horde of feral cats inside a stinking, garbage-strewn house. Believing herself content. Carrying on a futile effort to convince herself that she was satisfied with her lot in life.

Was Rob doing the same thing? Was Claire? And if so, why? What was it about her that caused Rob to build walls of protection so high around his heart? He didn't seem to find her unattractive. She knew he enjoyed teasing her. He recalled their long-ago conversations, and clearly they both still enjoyed talking together.

Maybe the problem wasn't Claire. Maybe Rob was seeing someone else. Maybe—despite their unhappiness together—he was still mourning his wife. Or maybe he had made up his mind to live alone for the rest of his life.

Claire herself had chosen the latter route, hadn't she? Licking her wounds, she had decided to hide her hurt in the haven of her work, her church life, her volunteering and her little house. Now she had Opie. And she was doing her best to make it seem as if that was enough.

But it wasn't. Deep inside, under the layers of defense, a hunger burned in her heart. A need to connect. To touch. To love and be loved. And she knew God had put it there.

It made sense, after all. God had created people in His image, created man because He Himself ached for companionship. Then He made woman so man wouldn't be alone. This urge to reach out and hold another human being was part of her fiber, Claire realized, but she had denied it by hiding away in her comfortable nest. Rob had repressed it by building a fortress around himself. And Aunt Flossie kept people at bay with her meanness and her lifestyle. But God had put His own desire for communion into each of them, and Claire knew it was time to open the door to her heart.

"I care about you, Aunt Flossie," she said softly. She laid a hand on the woman's bone-thin arm. "I really do. I don't want you to be so alone anymore. I can't be happy if you're not."

"I was happy before you came over here and ruined everything!" Flossie barked, jerking her arm away from Claire's touch. She filtered her fingers through her thin white hair and stared out the window. Her lower lip quivered a moment before she spoke again. "Once upon a time, I had it all."

"You can have it all now, too. You don't have to push everyone away. You can have friends. A family. A lovely home and a social life—"

"I don't want those things! None of 'em!" She swatted Claire on the shoulder. "Now get up. Get away from my chest. This is mine. Right here is what I had once. This—and a lot more. I see you eyeing it. You think it's money in there, don't you? That's what you're after. I know your kind. You come in here and pretend you care about me. All you want is my money! Well, you can't have it. So there!"

"I don't want your money, Aunt Flossie, for goodness' sake."

Disgusted, Claire stood and moved away from the filthy trunk. Despite her resolve to reach out to her aunt, she could feel her ire growing again. The Christmas parade and this cleaning job would put her hours behind in grading papers. The last week of school before the winter break began this coming Monday, and she could feel the pressure mounting. There was no way she could have the house painted by Rob's deadline. The whole situation was impossible—and now Aunt Flossie was accusing her of plotting a theft.

"I have my own money," Claire told her aunt. "I'm a teacher with a salary. I bought a house and a car, *and* I have a microwave oven in which I can cook TV dinners. Why would I want your money? What good has it done you? You have to cook your meals over a smoky fire. You wear rags. Your furniture is falling apart. You have nothing, Aunt Flossie. Nothing and no one."

"I have Homer and Virgil!"

"Cats?" Claire set her hands on her hips. "There's more to this world than cats! I admit, there are times all I want to do is hide in my house with Opie. When he crawls onto my lap and starts to purr, I feel wonderful. But people should count for more than cats, Aunt Flossie."

"People? Ha!" Flossie's thin lips twisted into a sneer. "I suppose you're one of those pie-in-the-sky types who thinks people are basically good at heart. People mean well. People care about you. Well, I say that's a bunch of hooey!"

She stood there glaring at her niece, as if daring Claire to defy the accusation. "You know what? I agree with you, Aunt Flossie," Claire replied. "God created us in perfection, but Eden's gates were barred a long time ago. People are fallen and flawed and mean-spirited and ugly. We may do a little good here and there, but basically we're all the same. As rotten as that sweater you're clutching so tightly."

"You think so?"

"Yes, I do."

"Then what are you doing here trying to make nice? Get on home and rot like everybody else."

"Believe me, after today, I'd welcome that."

"You're here because you're afraid of that police chief, aren't you? Afraid he'll make you take me into your house. Afraid of what that might do to your cozy life."

"I won't deny that's what got me over here to round up the cats. But you might remember I came to see you before, Aunt Flossie. I brought you a wreath to wish you a merry Christmas. And despite the fact that you threw my gift into the mud, I came back here today because I do care about you."

"Hogwash!"

"I'm just a fallen sinner, but God forgave me. He's why I come to see you."

"Now, don't be giving me that religious claptrap, girl. I've seen your kind of people. I know about those preachers on television and how they take people's money. Bunch of hypocrites, all of you."

"Maybe so. I have plenty of flaws. But I am a Christian, Aunt Flossie, and that means I've surrendered all my ugliness and sin and failure to Jesus Christ. He took it to the cross, where He destroyed its power to control my earthly life and sentence me to hell."

"Oh, so now you're saying I'm doomed in this life and the next, are you?"

"I'm saying that the Holy Spirit lives in me, Aunt Flossie. He's whatever is good inside me. Whatever's righteous. Whatever is pure and kind and loving."

"Hush with your nonsense! There's not a good bone in your body. You took my cats. Stole 'em away from me. Left me all alone with no one but Virgil and Homer to love. Well, guess what? I don't care! I don't need anyone! I've been alone for more than fifty years—fifty years since they took away my life. Fifty years since they tried to kill me. And I was doing just fine! I've been perfectly happy, and that's all you need to know!"

Claire gazed at her great-aunt and the mounds of detritus still heaped around her. She shook her head. "Who tried to kill you? What are you talking about?"

"Them! Those no-gooders!" She hurled the old sweater to the floor. "They killed him, and they thought they killed me. Killed us both. But I fooled 'em. I'm not altogether dead yet. I have my house…and my cats… and…and…"

Flossie sank suddenly to her knees and covered her face with her hands. Her shoulders heaved, and a strangled sob escaped her mouth. Claire gazed down in confusion at the old woman. What was her aunt talking about? Who were the no-gooders? And who was this person who'd been killed? Despite the mental disorder that had led to her hoarding the cats, until now Aunt Flossie's speech had always made sense.

Claire knelt and slipped an arm around the frail shoulders. "Aunt Flossie, are you okay?"

"Do I look okay?" Fiery blue eyes flashed at Claire. "I haven't been okay for fifty years, and you want to know why? I'll tell you, Miss Nosy. Open that chest right now. Open it up. There you go. What's in it? Tell me what you see. None of that precious money you're after, is there? Hah! Told you! You're not getting a thing out of me. Not one red cent!"

Claire hesitated before prying open the lid. She reached into the wooden trunk and lifted out a stack of letters tied with a length of yellowed lace. The postmarks and stamps were Austrian. The ink, still black and clear, directed the letters to Mrs. Schmidt of Buffalo, Missouri. The return address also bore the surname Schmidt.

"Give 'em here!" Flossie cried. "You can't have those. They're mine. Let me see 'em."

She took the letters and cradled them in her lap. A prickle of excitement ran up Claire's spine. Maybe there was more to her great-aunt than met the eye. "Who wrote those letters?"

"Hans, that's who." Flossie slipped the first letter from beneath the ribbon and opened it. She read for a moment in silence. When she spoke again, her voice was wistful. "After the war, when I was barely eighteen, I joined the USO."

"The USO? I never knew about that."

"Nobody remembers it. I was the youngest of the children, and our folks had died three years before. Flu took the both of 'em, just like that. By the time the war was over, my brothers were already married and busy with their jobs and families, so they didn't pay attention to me. I was gone to Europe for two years, singing for the troops. Entertainment is all it was—just to encourage the boys. The USO trained us, you know, and off we went. Helping out. Doing our part. The fighting was done, but the soldiers were still over there. Rebuilding. Setting things in order. You don't forget your men just because the war is over."

"So you went to Austria?" Claire asked.

"I went all over—how do you suppose I learned to appreciate European cuisine? Educated my palate is what I did. And when I got to Austria, there he was. Hans Fredrik Schmidt. We met in a bakery in Salzburg.

He bought me a cup of tea. He had been studying in Switzerland when Austria was annexed by Hitler, and he stayed in Switzerland, helping the resistance movement from there, until the war was over. Hans came from a good family. Very wealthy and influential, so no one suspected them of secretly aiding the Austrian resistance movement during the war. They were nice folks, took to me right off, thought I was something else. I was, too. I was pretty in those days. Had all my teeth, you know. Good figure and smart and, boy, could I sing."

Flossie hummed for a moment, her eyes misting and her face growing soft. "'Stille Nacht.' That's 'Silent Night' in German. Hans gave me a music box that played it. He would put the key in and wind it up—kind of like the apostles clock he sent over—and we'd sit together in his family's parlor and listen to it."

"Wait—an apostles clock?" Claire asked. "What in the world is that?"

"On the mantel. It doesn't work anymore. Neither does the music box over there."

Claire glanced from the ornately carved clock that she hadn't even noticed to a large, jewel-encrusted case on a nearby table she had just begun to uncover. "Hans sent you these things? After you returned to America?"

"Why not? He loved me. We were two of a kind, really, Hans and I. I'd grown up here in the mansion, and he lived in a big house, too. But we were both country people at heart. We fell in love right away. Didn't take us more than a week. He asked me to marry him, and I said yes. His family couldn't have been happier."

"You *married* Hans Schmidt?"

"Who do you think these letters came from?" Flossie

fingered the envelopes gingerly, as though they might suddenly disintegrate. "He was my husband. People around here still call me Flossie Ross. Dumb sounding name. Flossie Ross, Flossie Ross—like a hissing snake. I've always hated it."

"Florence Schmidt," Claire said. "It's nice."

Flossie grinned, her face folding into the first pleasant expression Claire had ever seen on it. "Yep, that's me. Mrs. Schmidt. Frau Schmidt is how you say it in German. Anyhow, it turned out the USO didn't want married girls. Too much trouble. Hans decided I ought to come back here and set up housekeeping. So after our wedding he packed me up and sent me off. He was going to join me as soon as he got his papers together— no more than six months, we figured."

"What happened, Aunt Flossie?"

"Nothing, at first. Things ticked along as good as that clock on the mantel. I sailed back home. Hans and his folks crated up the very best of their furniture— every fine chair and rug and lamp and painting in that big house in Salzburg—and they sent it over here to me. I unpacked it all, put everything in place and went to waiting for Hans."

She smoothed her hand across the stack of letters. "He wrote me every week. Faithful as the sunrise in the morning. We had us a big plan, Hans and me. We were going to live here at the house, and pretty soon we'd bring his parents over, too. All of us together— one big happy family. There'd be plenty of room. The Schmidts wanted to leave Austria—desperate to get out, really. Folks had turned against 'em after the war, when it came out that they'd been secretly helping the resistance. 'Course, that made them heroes to the Allies, and folks resented that the family had made it through the war with their house and all their belongings still safe and now were being feted by their wartime enemies."

"He never came, did he?" Claire whispered.

"One afternoon right before Christmas I got a telegram. Said there'd been an accident on a road high up in the mountains. The Alps. The car skidded on a patch of ice and plunged off a cliff. The whole family died. That was a lie, too, of course. The Schmidts had a few friends still in Salzburg, and later I got letters telling me the truth. Hans and his parents were murdered. Made it look like a car wreck, but it wasn't. They killed him."

Claire laid her hand over her aunt's. "Who did it?"

"How should I know?" The snarl returned as quickly as it had gone. "I was a twenty-year-old girl from Buffalo, Missouri. I couldn't just sail back over there and sort it all out. What did it matter, anyway? Hans was dead. All I had left of him was this." She swept her hand around the room. "Things. Furniture. And more furniture. Look at that painting over there. The frame is covered in gold leaf. You hear what I'm telling you? I got gold and silver and china and silk and velvet and ivory and more junk than you could ever put a name to. I got stuff I don't even know what it is. Musical instruments. Cooking utensils. That clock on the mantel."

"The apostles clock?"

"Back in Austria, when the hour struck, one of the twelve apostles would come out through a little door. He'd slide right over in front of the nativity scene and bow to the baby Jesus. Then he'd slide back through that other door. A different one would come out each hour. All of 'em bowed except Judas. Don't give me that look, girl. Judas did *not* bow. I saw it myself—all done with cogs and wheels and tiny chains. But I never understood how to wind the old clock. I don't know how to play that crazy-looking guitar over there, either. And I don't give a flip about these paintings. None of it means a thing to me, except that it once belonged to Hans."

"Then why don't you sell some of it, Aunt Flossie? You could take the money and move into a nice—"

"You'd like that, wouldn't you? Then you'd inherit the rest of my treasures when I'm dead and gone." Flossie glared at her niece. "Well, you can't have them! They're mine! Hans gave them to me. They were his, and I mean to protect them."

"Protect them? Aunt Flossie, you've let everything deteriorate so much that most of it is probably worthless. The clock is covered with soot. Your music box is…well, it's been buried under all those damp newspapers so long…"

Claire stretched out her hand and tugged the crusty box off the table. When she turned it upside down, she could see that the key was still in place. She tried to give it a twist, but the key wouldn't budge.

"Stuck. See? It's all worthless," Flossie said. "Just a pile of sorry old junk. And when I die, it'll all be just as worthless as I was. As Hans was. As empty and hopeless as everything in this God-forsaken world."

Claire ran a fingernail along the dirt-encrusted seam around the box's lid as she spoke. "God hasn't forsaken the world, Aunt Flossie. He's here with you. And He's with me, too."

"You think so, do you? Fool!"

"If God had abandoned you, would He have sent me here? We have each other now, Aunt Flossie. My fiancé left me feeling just as empty and hopeless as Hans left you. I never even had the chance to get married before he abandoned me. He found himself another woman—someone prettier, maybe, or smarter. Certainly she was more adoring. I don't really understand what happened. All I know is he canceled the wedding, and for a while I thought I had nothing and no one."

"You *don't* have anyone, girl. Don't kid yourself! You're alone in this world, and nobody gives two hoots about—"

The tinkling sound of the music box silenced the woman. The key had been wound to its tightest point, Claire discovered, and when she lifted the old wooden lid, it began to play. Flossie knelt at her side, and together they gazed in awe at the majestic miniature scene that unfolded before them.

Set on snowy white velvet, a group of enameled porcelain figures clustered around a tiny baby lying in a manger. On either side of the Christ child stood Mary and Joseph, clothed in brilliant blue robes and crowned with halos of clustered diamonds. As the familiar song played, a group of onlookers slowly circled the Holy Family. Shepherds knelt with heads bowed. And the magi, three of them, presented gifts—a cube of solid gold, a teardrop-shaped ruby and a square green emerald. Inside the box lid, painted angels raised their hands as they worshiped amid an array of tiny starlike diamonds embedded in the wood.

"'*Stille Nacht*,'" Flossie sang softly, her voice quavering. "'*Heilige Nacht. Alles schläft, einsam wacht...*'"

"'Round yon Virgin Mother and child,'" Claire joined in. "'Holy infant so tender and—'"

"Who's here?" Flossie broke in.

As red lights flashed on and off, Claire imagined for

a moment that somehow a Christmas tree had magically appeared outside the mansion. But the heavy footsteps on the porch told her it was Rob, and the light came from his squad car.

"Ho, ho, ho! Merry Christmas," he called out, knocking on the heavy wooden door. Before Claire could respond, he appeared in the foyer and poked his head into the parlor. "Hey, Miss Ross. Afternoon, Claire. I saw your car here and thought I'd check on your progress."

Her heart beating far too heavily over the mere sight of Buffalo's police chief, Claire gave an exaggerated shrug. "We're fine, thanks. Aren't we, Aunt Flossie?"

"Better than you, you ol' scalawag!" Flossie shook her fist at Rob. "You're the scoundrel who stole my guns! Took away my cats—"

Before the old woman could scramble to her feet, Claire caught her arm. "Unless you've come here to help out, Rob West, you can just get your sorry hide back to chasing drug runners. My aunt and I are too busy to chat."

Rob's dark brows rose a fraction as his mouth curved into a smile. "As a matter of fact, I did come here to help out. Along with a few other good folks."

He turned his head, put his fingers to his lips and blew a piercing whistle. As the foyer filled with people, he continued. "After the parade, the mayor and I got to talking. It's not too cold this afternoon, and we decided that since the fire truck was already out, maybe we could put it to good use. Several firemen, three of my patrolmen, Jane Henderson and quite a few others have come over to see what we can do for our good neighbor."

As Rob spoke, the mayor took up a position on the third step of the long staircase in the foyer and began to supervise the work. Bellowing instructions, Jane Henderson directed the cleaning crew, ordering those with brooms to start at one end of the marble floor and those with mops and buckets to follow along behind them. Two of the firemen began to work on the fireplace in the adjoining second parlor—a more formal room kept closed behind pocket doors—which primarily had been used by the Ross family for wakes. A group of women wearing rubber gloves rolled up their sleeves and began dumping into heavy-duty garbage bags the mounds of reeking newspapers that covered nearly every surface. Outside, the rest of the firemen hooked up their hoses and started spraying down the old house, washing away the accumulated grime from roof to basement.

Aunt Flossie flew into a rage. "You people get out of here!" she screeched, leaping to her feet and dancing around in a state of near hysteria. "This is my house! These are my things. You can't have 'em. Get out! Help! Where's my gun?"

Desperate to ease her aunt's panic, Claire put an arm around the old woman's shoulder and drew her close. To Claire's surprise, Flossie sagged suddenly, burying her face in her niece's embrace. "Oh, help me. Somebody please save me," she wailed.

"I'm right here," Claire murmured, leaning her cheek against the puff of fluffy white hair. "No one will hurt anything that belonged to Hans. I'll make sure of that. No one will steal it. No one wants to take your things, Aunt Flossie. I don't want anything in this house. It's all yours. Yours and your husband's."

Flossie nodded as tears rolled down her cheeks. Torn between slapping Rob and hugging him, Claire led her aunt toward the kitchen. When she pushed open the swinging door, another surprise awaited her. Expecting the large room to be filled with trash, she discovered that it must not have been occupied in years. The counters were clean, the long wood table was bare and the 1930s vintage refrigerator was still humming. Though the room was chilly and the stench from the rest of the house had permeated it, the kitchen clearly remained locked in a time capsule. After seating her aunt at the table, Claire was preparing to rummage around for tea or coffee when Rob tromped into the room bearing a large thermos.

"Hot coffee, Miss Ross?" he asked. "We've brought enough to float everybody clear to China and back. Here you go."

He set a foam cup on the table before Flossie and then faced her niece. "I hope you don't mind," he said, pouring a cup for Claire.

She rolled her eyes. "Well, now's a fine time to ask," she retorted, taking the offered coffee. "You might have checked with us before you came barging in."

"Us?"

"This is our project. Aunt Flossie's and mine."

"I hate to disagree, but I'm the one who got the ball rolling. I look at it like our Buffalo history project. It's just you and me, Clarence. And Aunt Flossie, of course."

"Just you and me? Then what are all those people doing here?"

"I brought them. Fulfilling my part of the project—like I always do."

Claire glanced down at her aunt, who was sipping gingerly at her coffee. The minute the invasion had begun, Homer and Virgil had hightailed it out to the kitchen, and both cats were now curled up at her feet.

Despite the chilly room and the noise and confusion outside, it was a pleasant scene.

"You come with me," Claire said, grabbing Rob's arm and pulling him toward the door that led to the backyard. They crossed the kitchen to the darkened corner beside the old refrigerator. Claire leaned close enough that he could hear as she spoke just above a whisper.

"I'm talking to you now as the chief of police, Rob," she began. "I've just found out from Aunt Flossie that this house is filled with treasures from Austria. Most of what you see was sent here right after World War II, and its worth is probably…well, it's priceless. I'm a historian, Rob, and I'm telling you right now that nothing better disappear from this house. Your cleaning crew is not to touch one painting—not even the frames. If lemon-spray polish landed on that fragile artwork, it would—"

"Calm down, Claire."

"I'll calm down when you assure me that everything here will be treated with the utmost care and respect."

"Okay, okay." He set his hands on her shoulders. "Relax."

"Historically this is so important, Rob. Not just for my aunt and our family. It's important to Buffalo. Maybe even to the world. I don't know what she has in this house. It could be very significant. The furniture needs to be professionally restored, if at all possible. The lamps have to be taken down, and each crystal removed and washed separately. The rugs that are totally ruined can be tossed, but if there are just a few holes—"

"A few holes? The rugs are shredded and soaked in cat urine. You can smell it all the way in here! Claire, this place is a disaster. I was hoping to get those fire hoses inside and just spray everything right out the door and into a Dumpster."

"What? Are you nuts? There's a clock in the parlor that is amazing...and a music box filled with jewels... and no telling what else. It's all hers, too. It belonged to her husband—to Hans Schmidt and my aunt."

"Flossie Ross had a husband?"

"Don't call her that. We hate that dumb name."

Rob stared at her. "Claire—"

"Just don't let anything happen, Robert West. I'm counting on you to protect those valuable possessions out there."

His blue eyes searched her face. "Claire, what's going on? Do you honestly think it's worth trying to save all the junk in this house?"

"It's not junk. Not under the mess. These are my aunt's treasures. They belong to her." She took a breath, trying to collect herself. "Something happened to Aunt Flossie years ago—a terrible tragedy and loss. Her husband's death started her down this long road of mental illness, Rob."

"I told you she hadn't been born bitter."

"That's right, and I'm going to see that my aunt gets help now. If she wants to keep these things, I'm going to make sure she has them. If she chooses to sell the contents of the house, fine. I want her to be able to live in comfort and health for the rest of her life. Our family should have been caring for her all along, and from this day forward, that's what I'm going to do."

"Why, Claire? Are you doing this out of guilt? Because you don't owe—"

"No!" Claire protested vigorously. "That's not it at

all. I love my aunt. I love the adventurous girl she used to be. I mourn what she could have been. And I care about who she is now. In some strange way, I see myself in her." She looked away from him. "Rob, if I keep going the way I am—refusing to share myself with people, hiding in my safe little world—I'm afraid I could become bitter and hateful just like Aunt Flossie."

"You would never—"

"You might, too, Rob." Cutting off his denial, she met his blue eyes. "I know things didn't turn out right in your marriage. I'm not sure if that's why you've changed, but I've known you long enough to see a big difference. You never used to keep people at bay. You always spoke your mind. You weren't afraid to talk about your feelings."

"I talked to *you* about how I felt. Not to everybody."

"But these days, you won't reveal your true emotions even to me. You're locked away like Rapunzel in a tower."

"Whoa, now. Wasn't Rapunzel a girl? She was the one with all that long hair, and the prince had to—"

"Robert West! Don't try to change the subject." Claire jabbed her finger at his chest. "I am being deadly serious here. My aunt got hurt, so she turned her back on people, and look what happened to her. I've been heading right down that same road…"

"Yeah, you've got your first cat already."

"This is not about cats!" she said hotly. "Quit making jokes and listen to me! You are the police chief, and you're not too dumb to hear what I'm saying. I don't want you to turn out like my aunt and me. You'd better stop pushing people away."

"All right," he said, taking her arms and pulling her close. "Is this better?"

She caught her breath as his hand slid down her back, drawing her against his chest. "Rob, I didn't mean…"

"Didn't you?"

"No, I…"

"I think you meant this," he said, brushing his lips across hers. "And this." He kissed her again, taking time to fold her in his arms and teach her lips the extent of his feelings.

Then he drew back. "Mmm, I wanted to do that again," he murmured. "Claire, listen to me."

"I see you two over there!" Flossie's high voice carried across the kitchen. "I know what you're up to!"

"Aunt Flossie, it's not what you think." Claire pulled away from Rob, eager to reassure her aunt that she had no intention of plotting with him to steal the Austrian treasures. "We were just—"

"Spoonin'! I saw the two of you. I may be a little teched in the head, but I'm not blind. Somebody fetch me some sugar and milk. This coffee is for the dogs."

Laughing, Rob nudged Claire as he passed her on his way back to the cleaning crew. "Keep on preaching at me, Clarence," he said. "I think I'm finally beginning to get your message."

Chapter Five

The moment Claire stepped out of her car she noticed the large pine wreath centered on the moonlit front door of Ross Mansion. Though its ribbon bore traces of mud, the branches were still green, and the silver bells twinkled. No tree lights glittered inside the parlor's bay window and no mistletoe hung over the door, but at least the wreath stood as a symbol of warm wishes to all who might visit the house on this chilly Christmas Eve.

Carrying the large gift she had wrapped in shiny gold paper and tied with a red satin bow, Claire stepped onto the porch. School was over for the holidays, and the townsfolk were preparing their own celebrations, yet she had no doubt many people had dropped by the mansion earlier in the day. In the past week, volunteers had repaired the steps, the porch railings and the porch floor. They had replaced broken windows, hosed down every outside wall and thoroughly scrubbed the parlor and foyer where Florence Ross Schmidt had lived out more than fifty long and lonely years. Every afternoon that she could spare, Claire had joined the work crew, though her job had consisted primarily of calming her agitated great-aunt.

"Who is it? I hope you aren't here to sing carols at me again!" The door opened a crack, and Flossie's face appeared in the silvery light. "I've had about enough caroling to choke on, and as for fruitcake, well… Oh, it's you. What are you doing out on a night like this, girl? Get inside quick, before you freeze to death."

Claire cast a glance at the greenery as she entered the foyer. "I see you decided to use the wreath I gave you, Aunt Flossie," she said as she made an unsuccessful attempt to hug the elderly woman. "It looks pretty."

"I'd tell you one of the other ladies hung it out there, but that'd be a lie. I did it myself. Saw it sitting over there on that table and figured I might as well put it up." She tottered toward the parlor, her cats following the hem of their owner's ratty pink bathrobe. "Bunch of old pine branches… I never did understand the point of such nonsense. But I guess it's all right. Got the fool thing out of the house, anyhow. It stank to high heaven."

"You thought the wreath smelled bad? Aunt Flossie, your house still reeks after all those cats. I'm beginning to wonder if we'll ever get rid of the odor. I imagine the curtains will have to go. And certainly what's left of the wallpaper has to come down."

"Sure, take everything. Leave me with nothing. I know that's what you want anyhow."

Smiling at the now familiar refrain, Claire set the gold-wrapped gift on a lovely mahogany table with a polished marble top. One of the volunteers had taken on the table as a special project, and tonight it fairly gleamed in the firelight that warmed the room with a golden glow. Homer and Virgil resumed their positions on a new rug that someone had bought at the local discount store, and Flossie settled into a chair that had been draped with a thick wool bedspread.

"Well, sit down, girl," the woman said. "What are you planning to do, stand there all night?"

"I just wanted to absorb everything for a moment," Claire explained as she seated herself on the edge of a settee that still needed to be reupholstered. "People have worked so hard here, Aunt Flossie. Your house is really beginning to look like a home again."

"I guess so. It's a bother, though, folks dropping by morning and night. People hammering and sawing. And you—you're the one who took away all my paintings! Why'd you do that? I liked those pictures! They're mine, and I don't want anyone to—"

"I already told you, Aunt Flossie," Claire cut in, taking her gift from the table and handing it to her aunt. "I've sent them to a preservation service for analysis. We need to find out who the artists are, when the pictures were painted and whether they're salvageable."

"Whether they're worth anything is what you mean." She cast her niece a glance of reproach. "Don't think I'm ignorant. I'm not too old to know what you're up to. You want all this for yourself!"

"Now, Aunt Flossie, we've been over this several times already." Claire pulled a sheet of paper from her purse and set it on the table beside Flossie's chair. "Here's the paper for you to sign. A lawyer in town was nice enough to draw it up. It's not a proper will—you'll have to have her help with that. But it does allow you to specify what you want to happen to the house and all its possessions after you're gone. This is a legal document, and all you have to do is fill in the blank here, and sign it."

"Well," Flossie said, crossing her arms. "Sounds like trickery to me."

"It's not a trick. After I leave, you read it over and sign it if you want. Even if you don't sign it, I won't inherit any of your possessions, Aunt Flossie. I'm not your next of kin. My parents and their siblings have that role."

"They all deeded this house over to me. It's mine."

"That's right, and you get to decide what happens to it."

Claire sighed and leaned back on the settee. How many times had she tried to explain this to her aunt? Nothing seemed to dent Flossie's certainty that everyone was out to get her. She was skeptical of the hard work that had gone into making her house fit to live in. She distrusted the people who had given so much of their time and labor without expecting anything in return. And she still believed her niece was conspiring behind her back.

Perhaps this was all part of the mental illness that had plagued Aunt Flossie since the death of her husband. Claire had made appointments with both a medical doctor and a psychiatrist in the nearby city of Springfield, but those examinations would have to wait until after the holidays. She certainly hoped the professionals could come up with a way to ease the fear and unhappiness that resided in her aunt's heart.

"Why don't you open your present, Aunt Flossie?" Claire asked. "Tonight's Christmas Eve. I wanted you to have something special."

Flossie muttered nonsensical fragments of sentences

as she went to work picking at the bow. Sadness crept into Claire's heart as she watched the thin fingers plucking and pulling at the red ribbon. She had no doubt medical and psychiatric care could help her great-aunt. But Claire sensed that the greatest healing needed to occur in Aunt Flossie's soul. After more than fifty years, the woman still clung to her bitterness. She hadn't forgiven those who had murdered Hans and his parents, and the vines of hatred had choked every last fragment of kindness, hope, faith and love from her heart.

"It's a robe," Flossie said, lifting the warm blue chenille garment from the box. She frowned as she examined it. "I don't need another bathrobe. I got one already."

"Yes, but yours is—"

"How come you didn't bring me a fruitcake, like everybody else?" she sneered. "Or a chicken casserole? I've only got about fifteen fruitcakes, five casseroles and now two bathrobes! What would make you think—"

"I don't know, Aunt Flossie," Claire snapped. "I don't know what would make me think you needed something to replace that old pink rag that hangs in shreds from your shoulders. I don't know why fifteen people bothered to bake you fruitcakes. Or why five of them brought casseroles. But most of all, I don't know why you're so determined to think the worst of everyone! The people of Buffalo have reached out to you with love and generosity—"

"I'll tell you why I think the worst of everyone. You said it yourself. They're all rotten." She pushed the gift box and the robe onto the floor. "Rotten to the core."

"At least they're making an effort at kindness. They're not sitting around wallowing in their rottenness. Most of the people who have helped you are Christians, Aunt Flossie. Christians don't practice evil. They don't welcome nastiness in their lives. If they find it, they confess it, ask forgiveness for it and get back to trying to be obedient to Christ."

"Well, la-dee-da. Take your blue bathrobe and go on home. I don't need your sermons."

Rob's words to her the last time they had spoken echoed in Claire's thoughts. She did have a tendency to preach, and maybe people didn't appreciate it as much as she wished. Obviously her sermonizing had turned Rob away. Something had.

Though his last touch had been a kiss and his last words had sounded like a tease, Rob had not made any effort to contact her all week. She thought she understood why. He wasn't willing to surrender his pain. Like Aunt Flossie, he wanted to cling to whatever held his heart so tightly locked away. That was Rob's choice, and as much as Claire now wished she could change him, she knew he had to live his own life. And she would live hers.

"I promise I won't preach at you, Aunt Flossie," Claire said. "I'm through with that. I just want to tell you a little story. The end of a story, really."

"Which story? I'm in no humor for fairy tales."

"This is not a fairy tale. It's the truth." Claire picked up the blue robe and folded it as she spoke. "It's the end of my Stephen story. He was my fiancé."

"The one who jilted you? As far as I'm concerned, that's the end of the story."

Claire swallowed at her aunt's painful words before she could go on. "It's not the end of the story," she said in a low voice. "There's more, and you're going to listen to it."

"Get on with it, then," Flossie said. "I don't have all night."

"Until last week, I didn't want to let Stephen off the hook. Ever. I thought he ought to suffer for what he had done to me. His betrayal hurt me so badly that I wanted him to hurt, too."

"Serves him right."

"But then it occurred to me that my anger, resentment and bitterness wasn't hurting Stephen at all. He's having a fine time writing his books and dating whichever woman currently admires him the most. I'm the one who's been doing all the suffering—isolating myself in my little house, surrounding myself with comforts that don't really help and trying to keep well-meaning people from getting too close."

"I know you think I'm just like you," Flossie growled. "I got your point—and it is a sermon, by the way."

"No, it's not, because it has a happily-ever-after ending."

"You said it wasn't a fairy tale."

"It's a true story. You see, last week when I was over here—"

"Sure, I saw you kissing that man who stole my guns. So you're getting married. Happy wedding bells."

"Married?" Claire gasped. "I'm not marrying Rob West."

"Why not? It's obvious he's sweet on you—grabbing you and smooching you like that. And right in my kitchen, too!"

"Aunt Flossie, Rob is not sweet on me. We haven't

talked for a week. There's nothing going on between us, I assure you."

"No? Hans never kissed me that way till after we were married. So if there's nothing going on, let me tell you what. You better get something going on, or the both of you will wind up like me, sitting in a big old house with nothing and nobody."

"Well, that's my point." Claire shook her head, trying to clear it. "Not my point about Rob. I'm talking about Hans and Stephen."

"Hans and Stephen? They never even knew each other. What kind of craziness are you on about now, girl?"

"I'm trying to tell you that I forgave Stephen for hurting me. I did it the other day, in my house, on my knees, by myself. I forgave him for all the pain he caused me, and I asked God to help me forgive him again when the hurt came back to haunt me. Which it does."

"You saying you want me to forgive that police chief for stealing my guns?"

Claire gave a cry of exasperation. "This is not about Rob! I'm asking you to forgive the men who killed Hans so many years ago, Aunt Flossie. Forgive Hans for dying. Forgive everyone who ever hurt you. Let it go! Get down on your knees and beg God to help you forgive everything that's ever been done to you. Just release it all. Your bitterness won't make anyone else suffer—you can only keep hurting yourself. And hurting everyone who cares for you."

Flossie sniffed as she picked at a string on her bathrobe. "Not much of a happily-ever-after ending," she said finally. "I thought I was getting invited to a wedding."

"Well, you're not. I don't need Rob West or any other

man to make me happy. I like Rob. I do care about him, but I—"

"Oh, you love him. Just admit it."

"I am a contented woman with a good life. Besides, I have you to love now. You can't escape me, Aunt Flossie. I'm here for the long haul."

"Happy day." Flossie eyed her niece from under her scowl. "Well, go ahead and open your present. Might as well get it over with."

"You have a present for me? I didn't expect—"

"Yes, you did. Don't try to deny it." Flossie handed Claire a familiar box. "There. You can have that."

"A fruitcake," Claire said, gazing down at the colorful picture of nuts and candied fruit embedded in a brown cake. "Oh, thank you, Aunt Flossie. I really appreciate your sharing—"

"It's not a fruitcake! Open the lid!"

Jumping to obey, Claire lifted the lid of the fruitcake container to find the jewel-inlaid music box that Hans had given to his wife so long ago. The diamond-encrusted blue enamel sky glittered as she opened the box and watched the shepherds and kings circling the baby Jesus. As sweet music filled the room, Claire shivered at the beauty of the scene.

"Oh, Aunt Flossie," she said softly. "This is too much."

"I figured you ought to have it before one of those people who keep tramping in and out of my house decided to carry it off. You never know what folks will do. They're liable to have stripped me blind, for all I know. I bet you most of those hand-knotted Persian wool rugs are gone."

"They are gone. That's exactly right. Gone to the trash, because they were ruined by the cats." Claire rose from the settee and went to her aunt's chair. Kneeling, she slipped her arms around the frail old woman. "Thank you, Aunt Flossie. Thank you so much for thinking of me at Christmastime. I know you've been overwhelmed by..."

Claire paused at the sight of two glowing green eyes shining out from under a chair near the fire. The eyes blinked once. Then again. Claire pulled back and faced her aunt.

"Aunt Flossie, there's a cat over there."

"Homer and Virgil," Flossie said. "Right beside the fire. Their favorite place."

"Yes, but you have another cat, don't you? It's hiding under a chair behind you."

"It is? Well, poor little thing. Come here, kitty, kitty!" Flossie turned her head and began calling in a high-pitched voice. "Come here, Sweetpea. That's her name. Sweetpea is the yellow one. Is that cat yellow?"

Claire stared at her aunt. "You mean you have more than one?"

"Just a skinny, tiger-striped fella. Came up to my back door yowling his head off last night. It was so cold. Did you ever imagine cats would like fruitcake?"

"Oh, Aunt Flossie!"

"You know, people drop their cats off right here at my house, because they figure I'll look after 'em. Sweetpea showed up today right after lunch when everybody had gone home for the day. She's so pretty. Look at her, creeping up on us like that. See her little white paws? Why, aren't you a sweet girl!"

"Aunt Flossie, you can't have these cats!" Claire said. "No wonder it still smells so horrible in here. Where's the litter box?"

"What litter box?"

"Oh, Aunt Flossie!" Rising, Claire grabbed her purse and pulled out her cell phone. In moments she had dialed the police department. Thank goodness it was Christmas Eve, and no doubt the chief would be taking the night off. At least she had one thing to be grateful for.

"Chief West here," a voice said. "What can I do for you tonight?"

Claire stared at her phone for a moment as though it had betrayed her. "It's me," she said finally.

"Claire?"

"Aunt Flossie has two more cats, Rob. I'm sorry to bother you, but—"

"I'll be right over. Try to keep them in the parlor."

Pressing off her phone, Claire stared at her aunt. The yellow cat had leaped into her lap and was curling up for a nap. How could they deny this lonely old woman her only comfort? But how could they allow the cats to return?

The place still reeked, and despite all that the volunteers had done, it would take months to restore the mansion. Claire had been upstairs only once, and she was thankful to find that the closed door had kept away the cats. But broken windows had allowed bats to take up residence, and piles of guano littered the valuable antiques. If she couldn't keep the cats out, the house would quickly return to its former state. Rob would condemn the building. And Aunt Flossie would have no choice but to move out.

"You can't keep Sweetpea," Claire said gently. She knelt beside her great-aunt. "I know you love cats, Aunt Flossie, but they need proper care. That means shots,

neutering and most of all litter boxes. What happened
to the box we set up for Homer and Virgil?"

"Oh, it's over there where you put it. Someplace…
I don't know."

"It has to be kept clean, Aunt Flossie, or the cats will
stop using it."

"I don't care what they do. Let 'em have the run of
the place." She looked up and squinted at the red lights
flashing outside. "What now? Wonderful, it's your boyfriend come to call. Next thing you know, you'll be
spooning right here in the parlor."

"Aunt Flossie, we were not—"

"That thief. See if you can get him to give me back
my guns." She stroked the yellow cat's head. "Ain't that
right, Sweetpea? We need to have some protection from
all those do-gooders who keep barging into our house."

Claire stood as Rob stepped into the parlor. "I didn't
think you'd be working tonight," she said.

"Figured I'd let the other boys have the evening off.
They've all got families." He shrugged as he turned his
attention to Flossie. "Evening, Miss Ross. Who's that
you got there in your lap?"

"Sweetpea." Flossie glared at him. "Thief!"

Rob chuckled. "You can have your guns back, Miss
Ross, as long as you agree not to fire them inside city
limits again."

"What good is that? How do you suppose those
Union soldiers would have fared if they hadn't had
their guns when the Confederates attacked the town?"

"They didn't fare too well even with their guns,
ma'am. The Rebs burned down the courthouse and the
Methodist church anyhow." Rob winked at Claire. "Isn't
that right, Miss Ross?"

Claire couldn't help smiling at his reference to their project. "That's right, Chief West."

"Oh, now it starts," Flossie said. "The two of you moonin' over each other like a pair of doves. Coo... coo...coo. Cuckoo is what you are. Well, get on with your courtin' and leave me—"

"Aunt Flossie," Claire cut in quickly, "Chief West has come out here to take Sweetpea and the tiger-striped cat to the shelter."

"Felix is his name, and you can't have either one of 'em. They're mine. They came to live with me."

"We'll figure out what we can do about Sweetpea and Felix after we get them over to the shelter," Rob said. "Jane Henderson and Dr. Bloom both need to have a look at them. Let me see that little gal there. Come here, Sweetpea."

Rob lifted the kitten into his arms and ran his hand down the small creature's scraggly fur. Claire's shoulders sagged in relief. Reaching out, she stroked her fingers over the poor animal.

"She put fruitcake out for them," Claire whispered. "There's no telling how many more will wander over here. Rob, I just don't know what to do. Can you smell that awful odor? Already the cats have stopped using the—"

"Wait a second!" Stiffening, he lifted his head and breathed in. "Here, you'd better take this cat."

"Rob? What's going on?"

"Dispatcher," he said into his shoulder radio. "This is Chief West. I'm at Ross Mansion. I'm going to need all the backup I can get. Send my men over here—everyone—and alert the highway patrol and the sheriff."

"Backup?" Claire said. "So far it's just two cats, Rob.

You're not going to need the highway patrol and the sheriff."

"That smell, Claire. It's not just cats. There's another odor underlying it." He studied her for a moment. "You smell that?"

"It smells like just cats to me."

"It's not. That's the odor of a methamphetamine lab."

While Rob watched out the window for his backup to arrive, Claire calmly kept her great-aunt talking, carrying on a conversation about the past. Though he knew it could be dangerous to remain in the house, he had no desire to alert the methamphetamine manufacturers that something was up. If his suspicions were correct, they had grown accustomed to seeing his squad car parked outside, and they had chosen to brazenly continue their illicit activities right under the noses of Buffalo's good citizens. A few minutes ago Flossie had given Rob her permission for the authorities to conduct a search, and as long as she kept up her chatter, he hoped no one would suspect what was about to occur.

Castigating himself for failing to note the odor earlier, Rob wondered where the lab was hidden. It could be in a residence nearby. Or the carriage house on the mansion's grounds. Or possibly somewhere in the old building itself. The basement, perhaps? Or the attic? It was clever of the criminals to choose this spot. The building was centrally located, yet the odor of Flossie's cats masked the smell of the drug dealers' operation.

As Flossie began some sort of harangue about fruitcake, Rob's assistant chief, his corporal and three of his five patrolmen pulled up to the mansion all at the same time and all within five minutes of his call to the dispatcher. Good. His first priority now was to get the two women to safety and secure the site. After that, his men could scour the area for the source of the meth odor.

"Claire," he said, crossing the parlor to the fire. He slipped his arm around her and pulled her aside. "I want you and your aunt to leave the house now. I know how you feel about this, but can I ask you to take Miss Ross home with you? I promise you we'll have her back in here by morning. You won't have to put up with—"

"Rob, it's fine," Claire said. "I'm happy to take Aunt Flossie home with me."

"I ain't goin' nowhere!" Flossie squawked. "This is my house, and I'll be hog-tied and strung up before I let you run me out of it."

"Listen, Aunt Flossie," Rob said, switching to the more comforting name her niece used. "Someplace near your house, people have set up a laboratory. They're making a drug called methamphetamine. It's dangerous, because it can explode. I don't know if the meth makers are inside the mansion or in one of the houses surrounding you. But if they're near enough to smell, they're too close. Now, I want you to go home with Claire until we take care of this problem. Do you understand?"

"No, I do not! This is my house, my property! What are those policemen doing here? Hey!"

"Stop hollering," Claire said, putting a finger to her lips. She helped the elderly woman from her chair and edged her toward the parlor door. "Come on, Aunt Flossie. You and I are leaving now. We'll go to my house, drink some hot chocolate and listen to Christmas carols."

"Not that!" Flossie cried. "Not carols!"

Rob shook his head as he strode out of the room just

ahead of the women. Lifting up a quick prayer of gratitude, he marveled for a moment at the change in Claire.
Just a few weeks before, she had flatly refused to ever
let her aunt inside her own home. Now she welcomed
the opportunity. Claire had accused Rob of barricad-
ing his own heart, and he couldn't deny it. But could
he really let down his walls? And if he did, what would
happen?

Needing to confer with his men, he trotted across the
barren lawn toward the gathered squad cars. The Buffalo patrolmen had run this exercise so many times—
and always in vain—that he knew he would barely need
to give orders. They had the drill down pat, and finally
it looked as if they were about to catch the bad guys.

As Rob greeted his men, the sheriff and several deputies arrived on the scene at the same moment as Buffalo's other two patrolmen. Under Rob's direction and
with the sheriff's concurrence, the deputies formed a
perimeter around the mansion and the surrounding
homes, covering streets, alleyways and yards to prevent anyone escaping. Three highway patrol units pulled
up as Rob ordered his own men to proceed toward the
house.

He opened the door of his squad car for protection
and was watching the operation unfold when suddenly
he saw Claire Ross appear in the mansion's front doorway. Pulling on her great-aunt's arm, she was doing
her best to urge the elderly woman out onto the porch.
Flossie would have none of it. Wrapped up in a blue
bathrobe, she held one cat against her chest and kept
reaching for another, finally breaking loose from her
niece and disappearing back into the house.

Alarm prickling down his spine, Rob called to the

sheriff across the driveway. "In the foyer! It's the home-owner and her niece. I thought they'd gotten out."

"I'll cover you," the sheriff replied.

At that moment one of Rob's men ran up. "We found 'em, sir," he panted. "They're in the basement. Seems they've been coming and going through a window hidden behind some yews. We can see 'em in there—looks like they're already breaking down the lab. I think they're on to us, Chief."

"How many?"

"Six, at least. Five males and a female."

Rob spoke into his radio, narrowing the deputies' perimeter to the yard surrounding the mansion. Then he headed for the front door. As his foot hit the foyer's marble floor, Claire looked up, her face ashen. "I can't get Aunt Flossie out, Rob."

"Leave her to me." Rob strode into the parlor where Claire's great-aunt was seated by the fire again. Two cats were just settling onto her lap as he stepped up, scooped the scrawny woman into his arms and swung around to the door.

"Florence Ross, you are a mean old lady," he said as he carried her out into the foyer. "Mean and selfish. And if you don't start cooperating, I'm going to have to—"

A loud bang resonated through the house. Flossie stiffened in Rob's arms. "It's the basement door!" she hollered. "Someone's breaking in! They'll steal my things! I'm being robbed! Call the police!"

"Where's the basement door?" Rob demanded.

"In the kitchen!"

Setting Flossie back on her feet, Rob rushed the elderly woman and her niece out the front door. As he drew his gun, he intercepted three men who had just exited the kitchen and were hightailing it up the long curved staircase leading to the second floor of the mansion.

"I need backup inside," Rob shouted into his radio as he pursued the men up the steps. "Stop! You three, stop now. Get on the ground!"

Ignoring his orders, they raced up the staircase. Rob knew if they made it into the honeycomb of rooms up there, they would have an easier time eluding pursuers. But bless Aunt Flossie's cold little heart, he thought as the men hit the top landing—she had locked the door to the upper floor.

Trapped, the men had no choice but to turn around and raise their hands in surrender. Two sheriff's deputies pounded up the staircase right behind Rob. In moments, they'd handcuffed the three suspects and led them back down the stairs.

Outside, Rob found that the rest of the methamphetamine makers had been captured, as well. One of the men had cut his arm while trying to escape through a broken window, so an ambulance was on its way. The others—cuffed and shackled—sat staring at the ground as an officer recited their Miranda rights.

"Chief West, I've already called for the haz-mat crew," one of the highway patrolmen spoke up. "I think we should secure the building and stay out of it until they get here."

Rob nodded. The hazardous materials experts would know how to safely disassemble the lab in the basement.

"There were two women in the house," he said, his heart hammering. "Did they…"

"They're out, Chief," his assistant said. "Miss Ross and that redheaded teacher over at the high school?

They exited the building a couple minutes ago. The redhead took Miss Ross off in her car. Told us they'd both spend the night at her house."

Thanking God for Claire's safety—and for Aunt Flossie's—Rob felt the knots in his stomach loosen as he studied the growing crowd of neighbors and other onlookers. He would need to unroll crime-scene tape and set up barricades to keep folks back. What a way to spend Christmas Eve! It looked as if he and his men wouldn't get home until nearly dawn.

"Say, that teacher sure is pretty," the assistant chief spoke up again. "The redhead."

"Her name is Claire," Rob said. "Claire Ross."

"Was she the one you took to Dandy's in Bolivar the other night? I heard you two had a good time."

Rob sighed. People were elbowing each other as the ambulance pulled up to the mansion. Another night in Buffalo, Missouri, where minding one's own business was clearly an alien concept.

Chapter Six

"Not enough singing, if you want my opinion." Florence Ross Schmidt allowed her niece to assist her down the church steps following the community Christmas service. Wearing one of Claire's dresses—Flossie had selected a pink satin print—and high heels only a tad too large, she clutched a black purse between her gloved hands.

"Not enough singing, Aunt Flossie?" Claire asked in wonder. "Only yesterday you were complaining about the carolers who had been to your door."

"It's one thing when people come knocking at all hours. And it's quite another when you get to exercise your own vocal cords."

"You do have a pretty voice. I can see why you enjoy singing." Claire scanned the crowd one last time, but Rob was not among the cheery congregation. She hoped he was all right.

Before the service began, the pews had been abuzz with talk of the previous night's raid. Methamphetamine makers in *our* town, people said, shaking their heads in disbelief. Four men and two women were caught in the attic of Ross Mansion. No, it was six men and one woman, someone clarified. Five men but no women, another explained, and they were in the basement.

The whole town had gone out to watch the excitement, it seemed to Claire. People had been up till all hours, peering over the barricades as the officials conducted their investigation and the hazardous materials crew disassembled the lab. Claire felt thankful it was all over. Now the mansion would be safe, and the odor certainly lessened.

"I always was a good singer," Flossie told her niece as they headed toward the parking lot. "Why do you think the USO took me without a squawk? I could really belt 'em out in my day. Hans used to beg me to sing for him. I learned a lot of his favorites in German."

They walked in silence for a moment, Claire reflecting on her great-aunt's loss and the enormous changes that had been imposed on the elderly woman in the past few weeks. Would Claire have fared as well if her world had been turned upside down?

Flossie had put up a mighty fuss until the moment Rob finally rushed her out of the mansion the night before. After that she had done an about-face. Once inside Claire's little bungalow, she warmed immediately to the rescued kitten, Opie. Meekly accepting the order to take a bath, she had sat for nearly an hour in a tubful of bubbles. Then she emerged in her new blue bathrobe and immediately adopted as her own a rocking chair by the fireplace. Together, the two women drank hot chocolate beside the little Christmas tree while Flossie crooned carols.

Claire had expected a monumental storm over the prospect of attending church the following morning, but her aunt actually displayed a certain girlish eagerness as she selected a dress and shoes. She allowed Claire to curl and style her white wisps, and then they ate breakfast like a civilized guest and her hostess.

"Hans could sing, too, and we made a nice duo." Flossie continued the conversation. Then she shrugged and flipped her hand as if to brush away the past. "But that was all in the old days. What's gone is gone."

"It's okay to keep your memories, Aunt Flossie," Claire said gently as she reached for the car door handle. "Just don't try to live in the past."

"Preaching again." Flossie settled into the passenger seat. "Preach, preach, preach."

As much as she enjoyed the changes in her aunt, Claire would be relieved to send the elderly woman back to the mansion in a few days. Maybe Claire was more cut out for the single life than she'd wanted to admit. Rob certainly had made up his mind in that direction. Despite kissing her—nothing more than a teasing impulse, she realized now—he showed no inclination toward forming any sort of relationship with her. Not even a real friendship. He never called, nor did she. They enjoyed talking when their paths crossed, but she felt certain it would happen rarely now that Flossie was under proper care.

Opening the driver's door, she climbed in and settled her purse beside her. "The turkey I put in the oven is going to taste good," she told her aunt. "I'll mash some potatoes and fix us a salad, too. Will you help me set the table?"

Hands folded, Flossie was staring out the window ahead. "That table you have is nice," she said. "In fact, I like the little house. Two bedrooms. Just right. I think we oughtta swap."

Key halfway to the ignition, Claire paused. "Swap?"

"Trade houses, girl, what do you think? You've had your eye on my place all along anyhow, and I've taken a shine to yours. Why don't you just take the old heap—and all that junk inside it, too. Junk, junk, junk. I don't know what half of it is anyhow, and I sure don't need it."

"But, Aunt Flossie, the mansion belongs to you." The thought of surrendering her precious little nest sent a stab of panic into Claire's heart. "I really do love my home, and you certainly belong in the mansion. I'd be happy to help you fix it up. Some of the furniture is still very nice, and we could make you a little bedroom area, along with a sitting room and a dining table. Besides, you don't want to live without all the things you said meant so much. The paintings will be back soon, and we'll bring some nice carpets down from the upstairs rooms, and the apostles' clock—"

"That old thing doesn't work worth a hoot. Who wants all those apostles sliding around and bowing every hour, anyhow? Not me." She waved her hand in dismissal. "Nope, it's yours. I prefer that nice clock hanging on your wall. Just a dial and a pair of hands. Easy to read, and no Judas popping out every twelve hours to scare the pants off a person."

Though the idea of preserving the mansion definitely excited Claire, she had no intention of surrendering her home to her great-aunt. If she had to live all alone in that imposing space, she might turn into a cat hoarder herself.

"Uh-oh, here he comes." Flossie broke in to her niece's thoughts. "Your boyfriend. Here to grab you and start smooching you again right in front of God and the whole town. Lord have mercy upon us."

"Aunt Flossie, Rob is not my boyfriend," Claire hissed as the man strode up to her car. "And if you so much as—"

"Merry Christmas," the police chief said, peering through the window Claire had just rolled down. "How are my two favorite Rosses this morning?"

"My proper name is Mrs. Schmidt," Flossie informed him, tilting her nose in the air. "I'd prefer to be addressed as such in the future, Mr. West."

Rob's blue eyes turned on Claire, and his brows rose. "Well, it looks like we're off to a good start."

"We are, actually," Claire said. "The church service was lovely—"

"Not enough singing," Flossie put in.

"And I have a turkey in the oven."

"I sure hope your bird can wait a few minutes." Rob opened her door. "Claire, will you and Mrs. Schmidt please come with me? The three of us need to pay a little visit."

"A visit?" Claire protested. "But I—"

"Oh, hush your yapping. No one likes being around a griping woman." Flossie settled Claire's purse strap over her arm as she stepped back onto the parking lot. "I wish you'd assist me to your car, Chief West. These heels just aren't made for winter sidewalks."

Turning a shoe from side to side as if to show off her

ankle, Flossie was actually flirting with the police chief, Claire realized. What had come over the woman? Had getting out of the mansion done that much for her? Or had Flossie actually listened to her niece for once and forgiven those who had hurt her in the past?

"We're swapping houses," she informed Rob as he escorted her to his car.

Wearing a bulky dark blue sweater and a pair of jeans that fitted him far too well for Claire's comfort, he arched an eyebrow as he looked over his shoulder at her. "Swapping?"

"I'm moving into her house," Flossie explained, "and she'll take the mansion. It's what she's always wanted, you know. Had her eye on my stuff all along. But I don't care! Let her have it. Just a pile of junk anyhow. I'll take Homer and Virgil and move into the smaller place. Sacrifices, you understand. They're part of life."

"Hmm, this is an interesting development," Rob said, studying Claire's face across the top of the car as he settled her great-aunt into the front seat. "It'll make the museum plan easier anyhow, I'll give it that much."

"What museum plan?" Claire asked as she slid into the back seat. "And by the way, I have *not* agreed to swap houses with you, Aunt Flossie. That's your idea, and I… What museum plan?"

Rob smiled as he started the car and pulled out into the street. "The Buffalo Historical Museum. Mayor Bloom and I have been discussing it for quite some time. I told him how significant Buffalo was during the Civil War. It was pro-Union, you know, Claire."

Irked at his teasing, she clenched her fists. "I'm

aware of that, Rob. What do you mean about the Buffalo Historical Museum?"

"You see, Mrs. Schmidt, Confederates burned down the courthouse and the old Methodist church," he went on. "And then there's all that important history connected to the railroad. A spur was supposed to come into Buffalo, but it was never built. In anticipation of the increased opportunity, though, people moved here and started businesses and built big houses. Which is why Ross Mansion would make a perfect museum."

"It's a museum, all right," Flossie said. "Full of dead dreams, dead hopes, emptiness. You can do whatever you like with it. I don't ever want to set foot in the place again."

"You'll need to go inside at least once more," Rob said as he pulled to a stop in front of the big old house. "I don't think you'll mind this time."

"But I thought we were going to go calling on someone," Flossie protested. "I was hoping for a slice of pecan pie. That's my favorite. I don't know why nobody asked what I liked before they started bringing me all those fruitcakes."

As Flossie went off on a tangent, Claire clambered out of the car and made a beeline for Rob. "Do not tease me, Robert West," she said, catching handfuls of his sweater. "Does the mayor really like the idea of a museum?"

"Sure, and the aldermen, too. Especially if Miss Ross—Mrs. Schmidt—would allow Ross Mansion to house it."

"Are you serious? How did this happen?" Claire accompanied Rob as he headed for the porch. "This is what I've been dreaming about! When I first came back to town, I spoke to the mayor and several of the aldermen, but none of them showed much interest. What did you do, Rob?"

Laughing, he slipped his arm around her as Flossie stepped into the foyer. "I just mentioned it last night while we were all standing around. Mayor Bloom was out in the crowd, of course, along with most of the aldermen. I told them what you'd said about all the valuable pieces inside the house, about the things from Austria, and about how much a museum might mean not only to your family but to the whole town."

"Oh, Rob..."

"Mercy sakes!" Flossie screeched. "Look at it! Look what they've done!"

Claire stepped into the parlor and gasped. A wonderland of twinkling white lights, chandeliers draped in gold ribbon, swags of pine branches and the fragrance of sweet cinnamon and nutmeg, the room fairly cried out, "Merry Christmas!" A fire crackled on the grate, while Homer and Virgil stretched out before it like a pair of indolent sultans.

"My kitties!" Flossie cried, tottering over to them in Claire's high heels. "Aw, look at you pretty cats! I bet you feel happy today, don't you?"

As her aunt knelt to stroke the pets, Claire felt Rob's arms come around her. Standing behind her, he whispered in her ear, "You missed the best part." Then he turned her toward the bay window, where a huge tree towered to the ceiling. Covered in colorful ornaments, ribbons and gold garland, it glittered with hundreds of tiny white lights. "Jane Henderson and some of the ladies cooked up this surprise last night. Jane and Mrs. Bloom headed the committee. The investigation was complete, so I gave my permission and helped them bring in the tree. They came over here before church to set everything up."

"I can't believe it," Claire whispered back. "All the work they'd already done on the house…and now this room…and the museum, too. Rob, why?"

"I think you infected the whole town with the Christmas spirit."

"Me? I was just trying to keep you from throwing Aunt Flossie out."

"So she wouldn't have to live with you."

Reveling in the warmth of his arms around her, Claire leaned her head back against Rob's chest. Though she knew she shouldn't enjoy his presence so much, she couldn't help herself. Maybe this was all she would have of him—a few hugs and the occasional impulsive kiss— but she would drink it in like cold water on a hot day.

"I can't deny it," she said. "I had the worst attitude."

"God can take the worst and turn it into the best. You taught me that a long time ago. And you showed the rest of the town by tackling the whole Flossie Ross problem head-on."

"Don't call her that, remember? Flossie Ross—we hate that name."

He chuckled. "You two are quite a pair. I think she'll be willing to move back in once we fix a few rooms upstairs just for her. With the museum on the main level, she'll have plenty of company, and no one will let a cat through the front door."

Claire closed her eyes, soaking up his presence and

thanking God for miracles large and small. "You've been wrong about only one thing, Rob," she murmured. Fighting tears, she forced herself to speak her heart. "You said the tree was the best part. It's not. This is."

Silent behind her, he tightened his arms around her waist and rested his cheek against her head. Carrying a cat, Flossie walked across to the table that held the jeweled music box. When she lifted the lid, the notes of the hymn drifted through the room.

"'Silent night,'" Flossie began to sing. "'Holy night. All is calm, all is bright…'"

"Claire, you challenged me to be more open with people," Rob said in a low voice. "To be more open with you. I've watched you change as you opened up to your aunt. And even Flossie changed as she finally let you in. The thing about me is just that I—"

"It's okay, Rob. You don't have to say anything."

"I want to talk. But I don't know if you'll want to hear what I have to say."

Claire struggled to hold back the tears that threatened. "Go ahead and be honest. I'm your friend, Rob."

"You're my friend, that's true. But…" He let out a breath that was warm against her ear. "But, Claire, I love you. I've loved you from the moment I walked into the gym and Mr. Jackson handed me the name of my partner and I saw it was you—a skinny freshman with red hair that stuck out in strange directions and a sharp tongue and a heart that was bigger than any I'd ever known. I loved you way back then, but I was too thick to admit it—okay, I was as dumb as a Missouri mule and twice as ornery. Doing things my own way took me down the wrong path, just as you said it would.

But God saved me and brought me to Him and gave me a reason to live again. And then He put you back into my life. Claire, I know you just see me as a friend, and you've been through all that pain in the past, and you've worked hard to make a new life for yourself, but—"

"But if you don't kiss me right now, Robert West," she said, turning in his embrace and throwing her arms around his neck, "I don't know what I'll do."

Without waiting, she stood on tiptoe and kissed him with every ounce of feeling that had been building inside her for so long. "Oh, Rob, I love you, too. I love you so much I'm about to burst with it!"

"Claire, are you sure?"

"Of course I'm sure. You know I always speak my mind."

"Then I want you to have my heart," he said softly. "Just take it and hold it and keep it safe forever. Will you do that?"

She searched his eyes. "Forever?"

"I want you to be my wife, Claire. I know it's sudden, and I don't mind if you take your time—"

"Yes!" she cried, the tears at last spilling down her cheeks. "Yes, I want to be your wife, now, always, forever!"

With a burst of laughter he caught her up in his arms and swung her around. "Do you mean that? Oh, girl, I've been going crazy over you!"

"Rob, this is too much! I can't believe—"

"Here we go again," Flossie cut in as she hobbled across the room, shaking a finger at them. "Spooning right here in public. Kissing and giggling and whatnot. Let me tell you something, young man. You'd better have honest intentions toward my niece. She's a fine girl, and I mean to protect her from the likes of scalawags and scoundrels."

Claire and Rob stared at Flossie for a moment, and then they swept her into their hug. As the three turned around and around in the parlor, the music box mirrored their movement—shepherds and kings circling the holy infant, so tender and mild. Through Him, promises made would be kept. Miracles begun would end in completion. What was broken would be made whole. And one day, the whole world would sleep in heavenly peace…sleep in heavenly peace.

* * * * *

CHRISTMAS MOON

Gail Gaymer Martin

* * *

"'Twas in the moon of wintertime
When all the birds had fled,
That God, the Lord of all on the earth,
Sent angel choirs instead.
Before their light the stars grew dim,
And wond'ring hunters heard the hymn:
Jesus your king is born!"
—Jean de Brebeuf, traditional carol

To my husband, Bob,
who has given me more than I could ever return.
He is my support, my cheerleader,
my housekeeper, my cook, my laughter, my love.
Thank you, Lord, for this wonderful gift.

Chapter One

"Rose... I want you to marry me."

Rose Danby's spoon clanged into the sink as she spun around to face her employer. She searched his face, expecting to see a grin, but he looked serious. He was handling the joke with the skill of a stand-up comedian.

"So...what's the punch line?" Rose asked.

Paul Stewart faltered. "It's not a joke. I was thinking that—"

"It's not a joke?" She felt her forehead rumple like a washboard. Not that she wouldn't want to marry a man as kind and handsome as her employer, but she was his twins' nanny. "What do you mean it's not a joke?"

His gaze searched hers. "I'm sorry. I shocked you." He moved closer. "It just makes sense."

"It makes sense to you, maybe, but I don't get it."

He glanced over his shoulder before refocusing on her. "Are the twins sleeping?"

She nodded. "They went to bed about an hour ago."

A relieved look settled on his face, and he pulled out a kitchen chair. "Could we sit and talk?"

Talk? She felt her legs tremble and realized sitting

was a wise move. Before she took a step, the teakettle whistled. "How about a cup of tea...while we chat?"

Without waiting for an answer, she moved to the stove and pulled the water from the burner. Talk? What more could he say after his "I want you to marry me" line?

Rose made the tea with as much speed as her shaking hands could manage, then set a mug in front of him and sat across from him with her own. "What's this about?"

He raised his focus from the cup to her face. "I've been asked to take a transfer. Told is more accurate."

"Transfer?" Her world spun out of control. What would she do? She had taken this position more than a year ago after a romantic fiasco. She wasn't ready to find another job. "You mean transferred out of L.A.?"

He nodded, then refocused on the tea.

"Transferred to where?"

"Minnesota."

She felt her breath escape. "Minnesota?"

He inched his gaze upward. "To Little Cloud."

"But why? I don't understand."

"One of our branches is having serious problems. They'll give me two years to troubleshoot or close the place." He rubbed the back of his neck, then shook his head slowly. "That's why I need you. The kids need you."

The kids. What would life be like without his four-year-old twins? Ice edged through her veins. Though she had a huge challenge with Paul's daughter, Kayla, Rose loved the children. Kayla had been born a quiet child, and her brother, Colin, had taken over for her. She mainly communicated through Colin and occasionally her father. But Rose had finally made progress. What would happen if they moved away? Kayla needed her. They both did, and she needed them, but… Her thoughts were a jumble, but one thing was clear.

"I can't marry you, Paul."

Though she spoke the words, the vision of being in Paul's arms rose in her mind. She had dreamed it before, then scolded herself for being so foolish. She was the nanny. The dinner maker. Even the thought of another employer-employee romance made her recoil.

His brown eyes sparked with concern. "But I can't go without you, Rose. I can't find someone to care for my kids and handle a floundering corporation without help."

"You didn't ask me to help. You asked me to marry you. They're different." A deep sigh escaped her. She longed to say yes, but she was a Christian—a woman who knew love and commitment were what the Lord expected for marriage.

She shook her head. "I can't leave Los Angeles, and I can't marry someone who doesn't love me." Old memories tore through her and left her reeling.

"I thought you loved the kids."

"You didn't ask me to marry the kids. I love them with all my heart. The thought of losing them kills me." Tears rolled from her eyes.

He knelt beside her. "Don't cry. Please. I made a terrible mistake asking you to marry me. I know you're a Christian woman, and I thought marriage would be the only way you'd agree to come with us."

Angry at her uncontrolled emotion, she grabbed a napkin from the holder and daubed her eyes. "You're an executive. You're strong and persuasive. Tell them you can't drag your kids that far away. They'll have to listen to you."

"And if they don't?" He rose and rested his hand on the back of her chair.

She lifted her eyes to his stress-filled face, trying to contain the ache in her heart. "They'll listen, Paul. They have to."

Chapter Two

Rose... I want you to marry me.

The words still echoed in Rose's ears two months later as she looked out the patio window of the lovely Victorian house that Paul had rented in Little Cloud. The setting was perfect for the twins—large yard, woods, creek, freedom. She watched them playing in the leaves, still amazed that in October trees had already turned colors.

Since arriving, she'd reviewed why she had finally agreed to come. But the answer was easy. The separation from the children had been dreadful. At night she would look at the moon and tell herself the same moon was hanging over Little Cloud, Minnesota, but the thought hadn't given her comfort as much as it had accentuated her isolation.

The children had become her life. After three weeks of Paul's pleading, she had agreed to relocate, and her fantasies had grown, with herself as mistress of a lovely home in Little Cloud—Paul coming home to dinner and telling her about his difficult day.

Then reality had set in. Things hadn't changed at all.

As always, when Paul arrived home she returned to her quiet apartment. He had kept his promise—their deal, he called it. Not only was the apartment waiting when she arrived, but he'd bought her a new car.

Rose pulled her thoughts back to her task. She unloaded another carton of kitchen equipment and piled the empty box along with the others. She'd discovered the boxes in the back entry, waiting to be unpacked.

Time was fleeting, and Paul was late again. Even if he ate warmed-over meals, she had to feed the children.

Rose set the boxes aside while she checked the casserole in the oven, then called the children inside. They scampered through the doorway with leaves clinging to their clothes and dried grass on their shoes.

"Don't move," Rose said.

Colin stopped, then halted Kayla by the patio door.

"Look at your shoes," she said, heading for the broom. When she returned, Colin giggled.

"Shoes off and shake your jackets outside before you go upstairs…or I'll use this broom to shoo you back outside."

Colin dodged her teasing and even Kayla grinned as they slipped off their things and darted up the stairs.

Rose chuckled at her ploy. She used the broom as an idle threat. The twins would laugh when she grasped it and gave them a warning, but she'd learned they would usually do as she asked.

She swept up the debris and put away the broom. Then remembering Kayla's tangled hair, Rose headed for the staircase. "Kayla, please bring down your brush." If Kayla didn't respond, she prayed Colin would bring it.

In minutes, the children's footsteps reverberated on the stairs, and Colin arrived with Kayla's hairbrush.

"Thank you," Rose said, giving him a quick hug. "Kayla, please come here."

Rose looked at the four-year-old and waited.

"Kayla, please."

The girl didn't move.

Rose's stomach twisted. Since their relocation the child had reverted to her old self before Rose had become their nanny. "Colin, please talk to your sister."

He repeated Rose's request, and without hesitation Kayla crossed the room and sat beside Rose.

She dragged the hairbrush across Kayla's long hair while the little girl sat statue-still. Rose wanted to take her in her arms and hug conversation out of her, but she'd tried that before and Kayla hadn't responded.

The day Rose had arrived in Little Cloud, Kayla had clung to her like moss to a tree trunk, but when it came to speaking, Rose never knew what to expect. She wondered if the child feared she'd leave again.

The thought broke Rose's heart. One day she would leave when Paul had no need for her anymore. A new panic jolted her. What did she have to go back to? She'd forsaken everything to make the move.

As Rose continued brushing Kayla's hair, static lifted the strands like magic fingers. "Look, Colin."

"She looks like a long-haired porcupine."

"I do not," Kayla said.

Rose heard curiosity in her voice. "Yes, you do. Colin's right." Praying it would work, Rose lifted the hand mirror in front of Kayla. "See for yourself."

Kayla giggled. "I do."

The child's words thrilled Rose. "But you're a very pretty porcupine."

Kayla looked at Rose—her smiling brown eyes so like her father's—and grinned.

Rose put down the hairbrush while an unexpected concern filled her mind. Kayla had begun preschool, and Rose prayed the other children weren't making fun of her and the teacher hadn't lost her patience. If so, Kayla could slide back even further. Maybe that's what was happening to her now.

The casserole's aroma filled the kitchen, and in moments the children and she were around the table, saying a blessing before they ate.

Time ticked past, and Rose finally sent the children to bed without seeing Paul. The scenario broke her heart.

The moon had risen high over the trees when Rose finally heard Paul's car pull into the drive. She stood and headed for the kitchen. He stepped through the doorway the same time she did.

"You look terrible," she said, witnessing the stress on his face and the tired look in his eyes.

He dropped his briefcase on a kitchen chair and gave a one-shoulder shrug. "I'm okay. The place is too laid-back for a well-run corporation. I'm trying to get the hang of their politics before implementing changes."

She moved to the refrigerator and brought out his dinner plate covered with plastic wrap. "How much longer will this go on?"

He shook his head and sank into a chair. "I don't know. It's taking more time than I planned, but I hope it ends soon."

"So do I." Rose slid the dish into the microwave and pressed the buttons.

"I'm sorry, Rose. I know this cuts into your time."

Her time? Rose's life revolved around this family. She had no life of her own. She wondered if he really understood. "It's not me I'm thinking of, Paul. It's the kids. They miss you."

"I know they do, and I miss them."

Rose looked at his expression and wished she'd kept quiet.

Chapter Three

Paul's head drooped, and Rose turned away, her heart aching for him. He wanted to be a good father, she knew.

When the buzzer sounded, she pulled a salad from the refrigerator and set the plate in front of him. "Would you like some coffee?"

"Sure," he said, "if you don't mind."

While she filled the coffeemaker, her mind whirred with memories. She recalled the day she'd arrived in Little Cloud. Paul had surprised her at the airport. She'd envisioned him dressed in a dark suit with a conservative tie and his hair immaculately combed as usual. Instead he'd worn jeans and a T-shirt beneath a plaid flannel jacket open at the front. His hair had seemed longer and shaggier. He'd looked as handsome and burly as a Minnesota lumberjack. She'd faltered before gaining control over her emotions. At that moment she had known she was in trouble.

"Rose."

Hearing the single word—her name—stirred her

senses, and she swung around, sprinkling coffee grounds on the clean floor.

Paul noticed and smiled. "Sit with me while I eat."

She worked like a robot cleaning up the spill, then settled into a chair across from him.

Paul drew the napkin across his mouth. "How were the twins today?"

"Something good happened. Kayla spoke to me."

His face brightened. "What brought that on?"

She told him about Kayla's hair static. "I'm thinking I need to do something special with her. Colin spends his afternoons outside searching for all kinds of horrible bugs, while Kayla wants to play. I need to find ways to show her more attention."

"She'll eat that up."

"I hope so."

"How's she doing in school?" Paul asked.

"I haven't heard anything, but I plan to talk with the teacher next week and see if Kayla's communicating."

"Good. Thanks." Paul glanced at his empty plate. "I did a pretty good job."

"You did. You want that coffee now?"

His chair scraped on the tile as he pushed it back. "Sure. Then we can sit in the living room and talk."

Her pulse jumped at his words. "Talk?"

Paul gave a tired grin. "Just talk. I need a friend."

He needed a friend. So did she, but any relationship beyond the boss-employee boundary sent chills down her back.

"You go ahead," she said, "and I'll bring it in."

Paul vanished through the doorway, and Rose stared at the empty space. She poured the coffee and carried it into the living room. Paul had lit a fire, and the warmth beckoned her. She handed him a cup, then settled nearby.

Silence surrounded them, except for the snap of the embers sending up a sprinkle of red and yellow sparks. She watched the glow, waiting for Paul to talk. The longer she waited the more uncomfortable she felt.

This wasn't the first time Paul had asked her to visit before she made the lonely ten-mile trek home. Sometimes she wondered if she'd made a mistake letting him persuade her to relocate. But she couldn't blame him solely. Her heart had made her decision.

"Why so quiet?" Rose asked, wishing he'd say something.

"Thinking about the kids. I know I'm letting them down when they need me."

"You are. I'm not going to soften it. They wait all afternoon for you to come home, then go to bed missing you." She missed him, too, if she were honest.

"I'll do better soon. Promise."

"Promise?" She'd heard that before. She knew he had good intentions, but—

"Please trust me. I'm trying to get things settled."

Trust me. She'd heard that before, too.

They fell into silence again, and Rose relived the hurt and humiliation of nearly two years earlier when she had learned that her fiancé—her boss—was cheating on her. While she was chattering about her marriage plans and spitting out her hopes and dreams, the whole office staff knew about…

The memory caught in her throat. She'd stopped shedding tears. Now she'd hardened herself. That day, she had returned Don's ring and walked away from her plush job. Never again. She'd trusted a man once. She had garnered too much experience, too much doubt and too much humiliation to make that mistake again.

"Sometimes I feel strange, sitting here with you."

"Strange? Why?" He looked at her for the first time since she'd brought him his coffee.

"Many times you've asked me to sit after you get home late and we chat like old friends…and yet I'm your employee."

"Rose, please," he said, grasping the arm of the chair and leaning closer. "You're more like a friend, not an employee. I have employees at the plant."

Friends. Employer. Employee. She gazed at Paul's profile. He was good-looking and stable. She wanted to trust him. His light brown hair shimmered with highlights in the glow from the fire. But she'd let good looks sway her once. Not again.

Rose paused a minute, drawn by the gold and red leaves fluttering to the patio. The children's laughter drifted in from outside. They seemed to love the outdoors and had spent time after school playing hide-and-seek, then switching to tag as they tripped and tumbled onto the broad expanse of lawn. When they bounded from the ground, the leaves attached to their clothing like colorful patchwork.

Looking out, Rose smiled until she recalled Colin offering to show her a snake he'd found. She wanted no part of any creature that didn't walk on four legs or two. That included bugs and spiders.

Rose looked at the clock, knowing she should be doing other things, but none of the options struck her fancy. The fresh air had a greater pull.

She climbed the stairs, grabbed a sweatshirt and

tugged it over her blouse. Back in the kitchen, she stepped through the doorway to the covered patio. A pleasant breeze carried the scent of damp earth and dried foliage to her.

A leaf rake leaned against the house as if calling to her, and she grasped it while the children beckoned her to join the fun. While the twins grabbed handfuls of the dried leaves and tossed them her way, she raked them into a pile. Because of the noise the children were making, Rose didn't hear Paul arrive until she felt him shove a handful of leaves down her neck.

"This is war," she called, gathering her own crispy weapons and charging toward him.

Still dressed in his suit, he captured her hand and held it fast while his other one grasped her waist as if fending her off. She tried to wiggle free, but he kept them close.

When their eyes met, something passed between them. Awareness? Concern? Surprise? Before she could decide, he pulled away with a laugh. "Unfair," he said, dashing across the lawn. "Let me go change."

In a flash he was gone, and the children joined her using their hands while she piled the leaves into a high mound.

When Paul returned, dressed in jeans and a pullover, he brought along another leaf rake and a camera. They took a break to snap photos of the twins, then Paul and Rose with the autumn colors as their background.

Finally they returned to work. But before Rose realized what Paul was plotting, he grabbed her rake and tossed her into the colorful heap. Leaves billowed around her, catching in her hair. They crackled as she shifted to rise, ready to make her own attack, but the children had already begun the job.

With the twins against Paul's back, he tumbled forward and landed beside her with a thwack. The crisp pile crunched beneath Rose's elbow as she tried to move out of the way, but Paul turned his face so close the nearness unsettled her. Before she could escape, the children joined the battle with armfuls of gold and orange.

Playful, Paul became her protector, blocking the children's attack. As he shifted, their noses brushed in the chaos, making her heart flutter like a lone leaf clinging to an overhead bough.

The twins jumped into the fray, and they became a tangle of arms and legs until she and Paul sorted them out. They clamored from the strewn mound, their cheerful voices ringing in her ears.

For once Rose knew why she'd come to Little Cloud. This was home.

Paul stepped back and feasted on the sight of their leaf-strewn clothing. The children's smiles had never been brighter. His gaze shifted to Rose, her cheeks ruddy, her eyes glistening with their fun. His chest tightened.

He'd managed to convince her to come to Little Cloud. He'd called it a deal. Agreement. Contract. Whatever. He had dragged Rose to Minnesota to make life easier for him. He'd given little thought to her needs, and now he'd asked her to be his friend. An unpleasant sensation rattled through him. Had he turned Rose's life upside down only to offer her a business deal?

He studied Rose's slender frame. He loved her broad

smile when the children made her laugh with their antics. He couldn't help but wonder why she'd never married and what had caused her to leave a good paying job and end up baby-sitting for his kids. She'd never told him, and he felt it too personal to ask.

But then, who was he to question anyone? Since Della's death, he'd had to learn to live without a woman. But time had passed, and he felt his mind and heart wakening to a need. His gaze shifted to the children. They deserved a mother.

He grabbed the rake and dragged the thought away along with the leaves. "Let's get this back into a pile, and we can have a bonfire." He had to do something to stop the ache that had grown inside him.

Rose excused herself and headed for the house while Paul tugged at the leaves, drawing in the scent of autumn and a hint of winter's cold. When he'd made a high mound, he lit the leaves and watched the flame grow, crackling and spiraling smoke into the air.

Despite his attempt to forget, his concern for Rose returned again. The children were a handful, yet the dearest kids on earth. But they were nonstop, and so was Rose's life. He had to give Rose a break. She put up with too many long, stressful days.

He thought of his aunt Inez, who'd been so helpful when he first arrived. He'd been blessed to have her so near. Asking her to help again seemed pushing his luck, but he had to do something until his work life calmed down. He would think of something special for Rose.

Chapter Four

Rose walked across the lawn, watching the sparks sail into the sky like fairy dust. "Pretty," she said. As she stood beside Paul, a shiver coursed through her.

"Cold?"

"A little," she said, stepping closer to the fire. She eyed the trees not far away. "When the woods start on fire, remember I warned you."

He laughed and slid his arm around her back, giving her an amiable squeeze. As he let go, Colin bounded toward them with Kayla on his heels.

Paul tousled their heads. "What did you learn today in school?"

"We learned about the Ojibways," Colin said.

Kayla jigged in front of him. "We're going on a trip to the field."

"To the field?" He looked at Rose with a puzzled expression.

"It's a field trip," she said. "They're going to the Mille Lacs Museum next week. I put the permission form on the kitchen counter."

"A field trip. That sounds fun." He paused, then

spoke what seemed an afterthought. "Do you like the teacher? I don't think I've asked." He glanced at Rose.

"No, you haven't," Rose said. She saw him flinch from her biting comment. Usually she felt bad about what she said, but not today. Paul had to face responsibility.

"She's nice," Kayla said as she spun away.

Rose watched the children run off to search for more leaves and tried to forget her comment. The children danced around the flames like the Ojibways they'd learned about in school. Rose drew in the acrid scent of burning leaves permeating her hair and clothes. But she didn't care. She loved the glow of the flames and the feeling of being one with nature and the joy of watching the twins.

"You're quiet," Paul said, closing the distance between them.

"Just thinking how peaceful it is." She brushed a leaf from her hair.

Paul set the rake in front of him and leaned against it while she studied his face. He stared at the curling flames in silence, and Rose wondered what was on his mind.

Finally he shifted. "I've not only neglected the kids, Rose, but I've worked you overtime. I can't thank you enough for your dedication."

"That's what I'm here for." Her response punctuated her situation. She had no life of her own. No friends. No coworkers. No reason for a day off. She'd made some progress at the church, but no friendships yet.

Paul rested his hand on her shoulder and gave it a gentle squeeze. "Still, I owe you some time off. I'll check with Aunt Inez and see if she could take over for an afternoon or two."

"And take her away from her social clubs or church ladies? You can't do that."

Paul chuckled. "I'm sure she'd give up an afternoon. She should be happy to have us so close."

Rose's curiosity was piqued. "I've always wondered how it happens that your aunt lives in Little Cloud."

"It's not really a coincidence. Uncle Lucas was a big honcho with the company. In fact, he helped me get my job with them after I graduated from college. Right after he was transferred here. Aunt Inez hated it."

"She doesn't hate it now."

"No, it's been her home for many years, and she loves the place now."

Rose could understand his aunt's qualms. Even thinking about the cold weather that she could already feel heading their way set her on edge.

Paul shifted toward the bonfire and caught some straying leaves. "My uncle was well respected, and the company flourished, but after he died, things changed. New leadership. New ideas. I don't know."

"So that's why they sent you here. Bring back a Stewart and the company will come to life again."

"Something like that." He reached over and brushed his hand against her cheek. "You have a decoration," he said, reaching up to pull a leaf from her hair. He brushed it against her cheek before tossing it onto the fire.

At that moment Rose enjoyed their closeness, a kind of simple sharing that seemed so warm and intimate. She raised her eyes beyond the drifting sparks to a small twinkling diamond in the heavens and prayed life could feel this good forever.

Rose rested her palm against Kayla's shoulder as she waited to speak with the teacher at the Bright Beginnings Children's Center. Colin hovered nearby, too, and Rose knew he was anxious to have her meet their teacher.

As the other parent stepped away, Miss Gladwin turned toward her with a smile. "Well, now, it's your turn, Mrs. Stewart, eh?"

Rose opened her mouth, but before she could correct the woman, Colin spoke up. "Her name is Mrs. Danby."

"Miss Danby," Rose said. "Mrs. Stewart is deceased."

"Oh." The woman's face took on a puzzled look, and she glanced back at the papers. "Then you are...?"

"The nanny. I care for the children while their father works."

"Nanny?" She gave Rose a curious look. "My word, I thought you were the twins' mother."

Rose waited a moment for her to continue.

She didn't.

"I need to talk with you about Kayla," Rose said, hoping to help her recollect their previous conversation.

"What is this about, eh?" She looked at the children, then back at Rose.

Rose drew up her shoulders and eyed the twins, wishing they'd wander off and give Rose time to talk privately. "She's shy."

"Yes, your son... I mean, Colin mentioned that."

"Kayla's father would like to know how she's doing," Rose said, being more direct.

"Why can't Mr. Stewart come to see me instead of—"

"The nanny?" Rose felt her hand tremble. "Mr. Stewart works long hours. He's planning to meet you when he can find the time." She had said more than she wanted. "I just need an answer. Is Kayla communicating with you or not?"

Miss Gladwin turned her attention toward Kayla. "Why, we get along just fine, eh?"

Kayla gave her a nod and looked at Rose with questioning eyes.

Rose felt her defenses rise. She grasped Kayla's hand and drew her closer. "If you have any problems, please call the Stewart home. We'd be happy to do whatever you suggest."

Miss Gladwin gave her a distracted smile while Rose grasped the children's hands and tugged them out to the parking lot. She unlocked the minivan door, then gulped the brisk air while the children scrambled into the back and clamped their seat belts.

Collecting her thoughts, she got into the van and pulled away. Paul had said the town was different, and it was. Much of it was wonderful. She enjoyed the slower pace, but she wished she hadn't been made to feel that she was nobody.

Paul had given her the apartment and the car. She should be grateful. Instead she felt depressed when she had to leave the cozy Victorian for her empty place. She thought of her friends back in California. She missed them. She missed the warm weather and sunshine, but when she was there she missed the twins. And she missed Paul.

She had no answer and saw no happy ending in sight.

At home the children headed outside to tug the rakes around the yard in hopes of another bonfire. The sun that had seemed warm when she entered the children's center earlier had slipped behind a cloud, and a gray haze settled over the sky and her mood. She watched the children while her mind took her to places she didn't want to go.

The day had dragged. Rose's mind dwelled on her vacillating mind-set. One minute she loved being in Little Cloud, the next she longed to go back to L.A. Her unrest had grown during her visit with Miss Gladwin, who had looked at her like some kind of usurper.

Sometime after dinner, Rose saw Kayla yawn, and looked at her watch. Bedtime again. Her heart ached for the children. She stood and wrapped her arm around Kayla.

"Time for bed," she said, knowing she'd hear groans.

"I want to wait up for Daddy," Colin whined.

Rose used her free hand to tousle his hair.

Kayla's sad eyes caught Rose's. "Me, too."

Each time Kayla spoke to her, Rose's chest swelled with joy. Each day Kayla had expanded her world to include Rose, and hopefully she would also include her preschool teacher.

Rose lifted an eyebrow. "I could sweep you both upstairs with the broom."

They ducked from her grasp with giggles.

"But here's what we'll do," Rose said. "Get ready for bed, then I'll come up and tuck you in."

Colin's eyes narrowed. "But we want—"

"You can keep your light on, and if you hear your dad come home before you're sleeping, you can come down to say good-night. Is that a deal?" As the word left her mouth, she cringed. Her whole life had become a deal.

The children agreed with the second plan and scampered up the stairs. She listened to the sounds above her, feeling a brief sense of completeness before it was barraged by her perplexing unhappiness.

In minutes, Rose heard the side door open, and she headed for the kitchen. When she came through the doorway, Paul stood in the middle of the room, his eyes looking tired.

His caring face triggered Rose's emotions and the tension of the day rushed in like a flood. The dam she'd built for the children crumbled, and the tears poured from her. She lowered her head, hoping he wouldn't see.

"What's wrong?" he said, dropping his briefcase on the floor and rushing to her side. "Is it the kids?"

She could only shake her head, feeling out of control and disgusted with her lack of restraint.

Paul slid his arm around her and pressed her head to his suit coat. She leaned against his firm body, holding her arms against her chest, but longing to wrap them around his protective frame. When she'd calmed enough to talk, she pulled her head away from his dampened suit jacket. "I'm sorry. When I saw you, I fell apart."

His frightened expression tugged her back to reason. "The kids are fine. I sent them upstairs for bed." She wiped her eyes with the back of her hand. "It's me."

He shook his head as if trying to make sense of her words. "What's wrong?"

"I don't know. I'm depressed."

"Daddy!" Kayla bounded into the room, followed by Colin. Both had dressed in their pajamas, and Rose could smell the minty scent of toothpaste.

As disheartened as she felt, Rose was pleased they'd done as she asked and even brushed their teeth.

Paul gave them a hug. "Daddy wants to change clothes, so come upstairs and I'll tuck you in." He beckoned to them, then signaled Rose. "We'll talk later."

She nodded, understanding what it was like to be a parent. Much of what seemed important was held for later, away from little ears.

Chapter Five

While Paul put the children to bed, Rose warmed his dinner, pondering what she should do and why she should do anything at all. The microwave buzzer sounded as Paul returned to the kitchen.

"Hungry?" she asked.

"I'm sorry I was so late tonight," he said. "It's been a difficult day."

"I know. You eat, and I'll start a fire."

Rose left him alone and went to the living room, knowing now wasn't the time to talk. She lit the fire in the grate, but the icy tendrils that crept through her heart couldn't be warmed by heat. She had to leave the cozy house and head across town to her own home—rooms that didn't seem iike home at all.

Settling in front of the hearth, Rose leaned back and listened to the quiet. Soon Paul's steps sounded in the hallway, and he appeared carrying two mugs.

"Coffee," he said. "Yours has cream. That's how you like it, right?"

She nodded, pleased that he remembered. Rose accepted the cup and took a sip. The drink rolled across her tongue and spread an inner warmth in her chest. In silence she studied Paul's face.

He didn't ask questions. He ran his finger around the mug's rim, waiting. The silence lingered, and though she wanted to talk, Rose felt empty of words.

"I don't like seeing you this way, Rose," Paul said. "You've always been so upbeat. Tell me what's wrong?"

Rose drank in his kindness, but what could she say? She didn't know what was wrong.

Paul sipped his coffee without prodding.

"I should be happy, but I'm…miserable."

"Rose, I'm—I…" His words faded while he looked at her with so much concern it broke her heart.

"It's nothing you can do," she said. "I suppose I'm homesick. You know, the little girl goes to camp for the first time and misses her family." The image weighed heavily on her. "Except that's what's wrong. All my relatives live on the East Coast. You are my family. That struck me today. If I did go back to California, I'd be going back to nothing. Sure, I have friends that I miss, but—"

He lowered his eyes. "No apartment. No job. No—"

"No future."

He opened his mouth to speak, then closed it as if he couldn't rebut what she'd said.

Rose hadn't intended him to feel guilty. "I talked with the teacher today."

"How did it go? Is Kayla having problems?"

She shook her head. It wasn't Kayla. Rose was having problems with herself, but how could she explain that? "I think she's okay. She understands Kayla's shy."

Paul's face darkened. "Something's upset you."

"It was silly. Nothing important."

"It upset you, Rose, so it *is* important."

She gave in and told him about the teacher's reaction to her visit. "I felt useless—like I was a woman playing mother to the kids. She didn't want me there."

He closed the distance between them and knelt in front of her. "Rose, these people aren't questioning you. You're a novelty. A new face in town. A nanny. They've probably never heard the term except on TV. That part is probably more interesting to them than anything else."

Rose bit her lip. "Maybe, but sometimes I think I should go back."

"Go back? You mean to L.A?" He rose and sat beside her. "Please don't think about that. I won't let you."

She felt her back stiffen. "This is a job, Paul. I can leave anytime. I have to do what's best for me." Though she'd made the statement, the children came into her thoughts. What was best for them?

"I suppose it is a job," he said, looking as if he'd been slapped.

A job to her? Yes and no. The question was, what was it to him? "I didn't mean it like that. I just—" Just what? She just wanted to be a wife and mother. She wanted…what? She looked at his handsome, worried face and knew what she wanted.

Like a movie, her life played out in her mind's eye— past and present. But what about the future? She'd never been more content in her life than she had with Paul and the twins. She loved the kids. Life didn't seem worthwhile without them. And Paul? She knew the answer. She was falling in love with him. But as hopeless as it was, her mind kept asking—what if?

Paul looked at Rose and waited, one hand on her arm, the other flexing with tension. What did he expect of her? She'd given up everything to follow him, and why? What did he have to offer her? The answer: nothing.

Maybe he should encourage her to leave. If he did, he might be motivated to find a woman—a wife, someone to take care of the house and love his children. His contemplation frightened him. He sounded cold and unloving. He didn't want a relationship like that. But what did he want?

"I've only been thinking about me," she said, "and not what's important. I need to give my problems to God."

His heart sank at the sadness in her voice. "You've focused on us." What was he doing to her? Condemning her to a life of emptiness to keep her with him as a housekeeper and nanny. Using her to make life easier for himself. Rose was a beautiful woman—charming, witty, confident.

He wanted to tell her how wonderful she was, but she wouldn't believe him. He'd already frightened her once with his hasty proposal. Why had he been so stupid?

"You need to spend time on yourself, Rose. I know I work long hours and keep you here longer than—"

He stopped in the middle of the sentence and reeled with the awareness. Though his mind was plagued with company issues throughout the day, his deeper focus had left him longing to come home to this house and the twins. He'd set his mind on doing something for Rose, but what had happened?

She deserved to be pampered. He vowed to do what he could to bring a smile to Rose's face, to make her eyes light up and to make her move to Little Cloud worthwhile.

"It's okay," she said. "I feel better now."

He tilted her chin upward and looked into her eyes. "I want you to feel the best, Rose, not just better." Paul let his gaze linger on her mouth, compelled by an unexpected urge. Confused, he redirected his thoughts. Apparently he'd been without a woman too long.

Paul closed his eyes, wondering what had gotten into him. He'd never survive this deal he'd made unless he stopped looking at Rose as a woman.

"It's Daddy!" Kayla called.

The children darted from the living room while Rose held a print of an oil painting, trying to decide where it would look best. If she were honest, she'd admit she didn't like the painting, but this wasn't her house.

Paul came through the doorway with the twins tagging beside him, both talking at once. "Let me catch my breath." He plopped into the recliner, and his eyes widened. "What's happened in here?"

"Unpacking boxes," she said. "I thought it was time this room looked like a home."

"Looks good." His gaze traveled the room, then focused on the kids.

The pleasure in his face warmed Rose, and she sat on the edge of the sofa. Still holding the painting, she let the children tell their stories.

"What's up? Have you been helping Rose?"

Kayla's head bounced like a rubber ball. "We picked out border and paint."

Paul gave Rose another questioning look. "Border and paint?"

"For their rooms," Rose said. "I'm going to paint during the week, and maybe on the weekend we can get the border up."

"Border and paint," he repeated. "Sounds like an exciting weekend." He gave her a teasing wink.

"We'll show it to you," Kayla said. The twins scampered from the room, leaving a moment of silence.

"I unpacked the boxes that were in the dining room. The photographs of the kids and…your wife are on the built-in shelves. I hope that's what you wanted."

Paul rose and ambled across the room, his gaze scanning the work that she'd done. "It looks good, Rose." He lifted the photograph of Della and looked at it a moment, then turned to her. "I think I'll give this to Kayla, and I have one in my room for Colin." He laid the framed photo facedown. "I think it's time—"

"Changes are good in a new house," Rose said, hoping to ease the tension. She lifted the painting. "I hung some of the artwork, but I wasn't sure about this one."

He shook his head. "I never liked that piece. Della wanted it. Let's just put it away. I hear there's an autumn art and craft show in a couple of weeks. Maybe we could find something new for that wall."

"I'd be happy to look," she said. Change was difficult, but it could be positive. It could turn life from status quo to innovative. She'd had a big taste of that lately.

Paul moved closer, his hands in his pockets. "I'm trying to get my time regulated at work. I don't want to spend every weekend glued to my office chair, and I don't want to disappoint the kids. Count on me for the weekend."

Rose opened her mouth, but her words were drowned by the kids' chatter as they ran into the room dragging the borders, which trailed dangerously under their feet. She watched the exuberance of the twins as they described plans for their bedrooms. Paul slowed them to a walk, and Rose sank into the sofa, her heart full.

Paul stood in Colin's bedroom, reading the instructions on hanging the border. It seemed simple enough. He felt guilty having dumped the painting job totally on Rose. She'd done a good job. He gazed at the soft-blue room that coordinated with the race-car border Colin had chosen. Kayla's room was as pink as her cheeks. She'd picked a design of pink hearts with a smattering of pastel flowers. Rose had guided them well.

The door banged below—Rose had come home from church. His pulse gave a jolt. Too much coffee, he speculated. He set the border on Colin's bed and descended the stairs. The children had already met her in the kitchen, and he could hear them whining about lunch. Paul winced. He could have at least taken care of that. He'd become too job focused. The promise he'd made to pamper Rose had slid from his thoughts.

When he came through the doorway he expected a sharp look from Rose for messing up yesterday by working another Saturday. Instead, she smiled.

"How was church?" he asked.

"Nice."

He wanted to ask more, but her attention turned to other things. She slipped off her jacket, laid her handbag on the counter and began making lunch.

"I'm getting everything ready to put up the borders. Okay?" he asked.

A look of surprise brightened her face. "Sure, if you don't mind helping."

He wanted to hug her. "I should have helped you with the painting. I'll make up for it today."

He hurried away, gathering ladders and water containers to use for dipping the prepasted paper. When he had everything assembled, Rose came up the stairs with a sandwich on a paper plate. She'd thought of him again.

"Thanks. I should have made lunch for the kids."

"It's okay," she said. "Let me change, and then we can decide who does what."

It wasn't okay at all, but he turned his attention to the task and reread the instructions.

Rose returned wearing jeans and a pullover. She stood inside the doorway and leaned against the doorjamb. Though twenty-seven, she looked like a teenager with her slender figure and her hair in a gentle curve at her jawline. The sun's rays shining through the window touched her tawny locks with golden highlights. She seemed as fresh and dewy as her name. He felt old at thirty-one.

"Ready?" he asked. As the question left him, two sets of feet thumped in the hallway, and the twins came into the room.

"Can we help?" Colin asked.

Paul looked at Rose for the answer.

"Good idea," she said. "How about the men hang their border in this room while Kayla and I take care of hers."

"Like a contest?" Kayla asked.

Rose gave Kayla a one-arm hug. "Why not? Last one finished cooks dinner."

"Okay," Paul said, wanting to squelch the idea. Still, he was taller. Hanging border would be a snap.

As Kayla and Rose darted from the room, Paul looked at the wall and drew in a breath. If Rose could do it, he could. "Okay, Colin. Let's get to work."

He looked at his young son and wondered how the two of them were going to hang the border way up there.

Rose closed the bedroom door, anticipating their task. Border at the top of the wall seemed impossible.

"What can I do?" Kayla asked, her cheeks rosy and her eyes wide.

You can give me a huge hug, Rose thought, gazing at the sweet child. In the past days, Kayla had forgotten not to talk. She'd opened like a blossom in spring.

An idea struck Rose. "Here's my idea. Let's put the border here." She held the border at the same height as the chair railing. Kayla would enjoy it at eye level.

"Okay, and I can see it lower," Kayla said.

They became a team. Rose used a yardstick to mark the height, and when she finished, Kayla dipped the border into the water and held an end while Rose smoothed it along the wall. In an hour the job was done, and they crossed the hallway. When Rose pushed open the door, she laughed.

Paul stood on the ladder with border draped over his shoulder. His jeans and shirt were soaked and glue clung to his cheek. He'd finished only one side of the room.

"We're finished," she said from the doorway.

He spun around gaping. "Finished?"

Kayla clapped her hands and crunched down with her giggles. "You look silly, Daddy."

He climbed down the ladder with an expression of disbelief. He pulled the border from his neck and grasped her shoulders with both hands, moving her ahead of him.

When they entered the room, he stopped cold. "You cheated. I thought it had to be on top."

"I didn't tell you where it had to go." She reached up and brushed the gob of paste from his cheek while the children clustered at his sides. "Paste," Rose said, holding up her finger to show him the evidence.

"Looks good. You two did a good job, but if you want to eat dinner tonight, I need some help," he said.

She acquiesced, happy to spend the time with him working on the project.

The twins became bored and wandered away. Rose climbed the ladder while Paul used the one from Kayla's bedroom. Their conversation rolled like that of old friends as they smoothed and dipped, adding each long stretch of border until the end was in sight. One final swipe of the cloth to smooth the last piece, and Rose descended the ladder.

"Looks really good," Paul said, wrapping his arm around her shoulders. "We make a great team." He shifted his gaze to her face. "Do you like it?"

Like it? She loved feeling his arm around her. "I do." Her double meaning skittered through the air.

Paul gave her a gentle squeeze and glanced at his watch. "It's late. How about fast food?"

"What about my home-cooked meal?"

He pressed the tip of her nose. "Tomorrow night?"

"Right." She grinned, knowing he'd wheedle out of their deal.

Chapter Six

Rose sat at the kitchen window, watching the children play in the backyard. That morning when she'd taken them to preschool, frost had clung to a few green plants trying to brave the nippy winds. By the time the sun had risen to its zenith, the foliage lay limp against the ground.

She decided to brave her battle. She'd found comfort and strength at her new church. The Sunday before, she'd left the church feeling guilty as the Scripture reading rang in her head. "O you of little faith… Do not worry about tomorrow, for tomorrow will worry about itself. Each day has enough trouble of its own. Do not judge, or you, too, will be judged."

She had worried, and she had judged Paul. He'd made promises that he'd meant to keep but often didn't. He'd asked her to trust him, but trust had been difficult since Don's betrayal.

Yet when she arrived home from worship, God had answered her prayer. Paul was ready to help with the border. They'd had fun, and she sensed a change in their relationship.

In the past weeks, church attendance had drawn her

closer to God. She realized moping wasn't going to get her anywhere. Until the Lord directed her otherwise, she would continue to be a nanny for the twins, and if Paul came home with a woman, she would have to...

That thought unsettled her. There was one issue she hadn't resolved—her feelings for Paul. He hadn't helped the situation either, because the past week he'd arrived home earlier than expected and even surprised her once by cooking dinner. One evening they had listened to the children relive their trip to the museum. Another night he'd taken them to a family movie. She'd become a part of their lives, but sadly, Rose knew one day it would end.

Through the window Rose saw the children bounding toward the house, then caught sight of Paul. He crouched and clasped the children in his arms. She longed to be there, too, wrapped in his strength and comfort.

She pushed the useless thought aside and looked toward the sky, noticing the sun had sunk below the treetops. Night came fast in late autumn, and the wooded setting only added to her feeling of solitude.

Paul headed toward the house, and Rose moved from the window. "Hi," she said as he entered. "You're home early."

"Sure am."

She recognized his conspiring look. "What's up?"

"Aunt Inez agreed to sit with the kids tonight."

Her heart skipped. "Why?"

"You need a night out. We're celebrating."

"Celebrating?"

"I've finally made progress at the plant. I know what's causing the problems, and today I put together a plan to implement the changes." He shrugged. "I realize it'll still take time."

"And that's what you're celebrating?"

He moved closer. "No, but here's my good news. L.A. is sending someone to give me a hand for a few weeks."

"That should be a relief."

"It is. I'm anxious to spend more time with the kids." He reached out and touched her arm. "But we'll still want you to hang around. The place is too quiet without you."

"You'd get used to it quick enough," she said, wondering if he would miss her. "Where are we going?"

"First to the arts and crafts fair. Do you realize that Christmas will be here before we know it? November's here in four days. Then Thanksgiving. Then Christmas."

Christmas. The word washed over her. "You mean we're going Christmas shopping?"

"If you remember, I suggested a while back we look for a new painting to go behind the sofa."

That seemed ages ago, and she'd forgotten. "Okay, but you said 'first.' What's second?"

"That's a surprise."

Walking beside Rose, Paul enjoyed the closeness. She was a lovely woman. Her smile, her thoughtfulness, her joy—she exhibited so many attributes he admired.

He adjusted the package clutched in his arms. Since they'd entered the Elks Lodge, Rose had already goaded him into buying Christmas decorations, a huge wreath and numerous gifts for the children.

At the end of the aisle Paul spotted a booth selling artwork. He moved closer, drawn by a large watercolor that captured his interest—a wooded setting, a stream and two leaves, stems still locked together, floating along on the ripples. Elusive lines, muted colors, yet a vibrant image. He thought of himself as a leaf floating along life's river, caught on the ripples with no turning back. Yet he drifted alone. The picture filled him with hope. Two leaves glided side by side, their stems bent upward toward the sun filtering through the trees. Hope and completeness, two leaves as one.

"It's beautiful," Rose said.

He turned toward her and realized she was gazing at the same painting.

"It touches me here," she said, resting her palm against her heart. "I see togetherness through the rough spots, a kind of solidarity. I can't explain it."

Neither could he. "I'm going to buy it. It'll look good over the sofa."

"It's perfect." Her smile warmed him.

Paul was amazed at their oneness. So often they thought the same. Yet other times he sensed her wariness—her sensitivity—and he wished he understood.

He paid for the watercolor, then moved on. Within moments Rose stopped at another booth.

"I like candles in the windows at Christmas," she said, surveying the decorative tapers.

Candles in the windows. Rose's exuberance fueled that Christmas feeling that made Paul want to burst into a chorus of "Joy to the World."

Before they moved farther, she turned to him. "Thinking of Christmas, I'd like to take the children to Sunday school, if you wouldn't mind. I think they should have the chance to know what Jesus's birthday really means."

Paul caught his breath—another way he'd neglected his children. "Sure. It'll be good for them."

Rose gave him a pleased look, then moved on ahead. He'd never been given a strong faith upbringing, but

Della had thought it was important, and before she died they'd all been going to church. Paul recalled it had become a comfort. It gave him something to cling to when times got rough. But when Della died, his faith did, too. He agreed. The twins needed a chance to learn about Jesus on their own.

Something to cling to. The words surged through his mind. He'd needed something to cling to these past months. He'd hung on to his problems as if they were treasures. They'd caused him to become even more self-focused, and he hadn't given God a chance to direct him. Had the stress in his life been a reflection of his weak faith? If this was the Lord's way to give him a swift kick, He'd done a good job.

Another booth caught Rose's interest. She shuffled through a display of handcrafted wooden puzzles. "Look. The kids'll love these. I'll buy a couple for Christmas."

He agreed. They were intriguing.

She selected two for each child, and he wanted to hug her for being so generous.

Paul toted the growing mound of packages, and when they arrived where they'd begun, he stopped her. "Are we about finished? Remember, we have one more place to go."

She tilted her head with questioning eyes. "I know." She gave him a wry grin. "I won't ask."

He gave her a wink, but before he moved, he had to ask one last question. "Out of all these gifts, didn't you find one thing you liked for yourself?"

She thought a minute. "I loved those bracelets. The ones with the fused glass beads. They were beautiful, but too expensive for my taste."

"I remember," he said while his gaze darted in the

direction he thought he'd seen the booth. "Do you mind waiting a minute while I find a rest room?"

"Not at all," she said. She reached for the packages, and he handed her a few and then set the others against the exit wall. "I'll be right back."

He had no idea where he was going, but he hoped to find a back entrance into the craft show. As he rounded a corner, he spotted a doorway and maneuvered his way down the crowded aisles to the booth selling stained glass.

In only a minute he found the perfect bracelet, with translucent glass beads in pastel blue and amber, each bead connected with small gold links. It was lovely and fragile like Rose. He paid the money, dropped the package into his pocket and wended his way to the exit.

"Ready?" he asked.

"Can't wait," she said, her voice dubious. Rose returned his packages, and she carried the watercolor.

The night was chilly, and the scent of snow filled the air. They hurried to the car. On their way, he and Rose talked about everyday things, and when Paul reached the town, he followed the signs to Historic Log Village.

"Where are we?" Rose asked.

"Crosslake. It's north of Little Cloud." He spotted another marker and turned. "I think you'll enjoy this. You deserve a little fun."

When the parking lot came into view, Paul pulled into an available slot and opened the door for her. Her smile was illumined by moonlight, and it roused his exhilarated feelings. He paid the admission, and they were each handed a lit candle. Rose sent him a curious look, but once inside the Historic Log Village, the purpose was clear.

Rose grasped his arm and released a breathless sigh. "It's beautiful."

He agreed. In front of them lights flickered in the darkness as visitors were taken back in time to the days of the pioneer settlers. Candles brightened a turn-of-the-century schoolhouse, a restored logger's shack and bunkhouse. Workers were dressed in costumes of the day and offered them cups of cider as they made their way along, learning about the days of the Minnesota pioneers.

"The twins would love this," Rose said, her eyes glinting brighter than the candles. "You'll have to bring them here. They would learn so much."

"We will," Paul said, wanting Rose to share the pleasure.

She paused to sip the cider, and Paul was mesmerized by the shape of her mouth and the soft look of her well-formed lips. To quell his thoughts, Paul swigged down the tart juice.

He disposed of their empty cups, amazed at the realization that had washed over him. For so long, he'd wanted a mother for the children, and lately he'd felt an urge for a companion. Tonight he found one standing beside him. He'd never appreciated Rose's charm and beauty until now.

She turned to face him, the candle flickering a soft light over her lovely face. "Thank you for the surprise."

"You're welcome." Unbidden, he drew her into an embrace. "You deserve much more," he whispered into her hair. She felt fragile against his chest, and a gentle fragrance of fruits and spices surrounded her. Puzzled by his feelings, he released her.

Bewilderment covered her face, probably matching his own confusion. He lifted his gaze to the sky. *Lord, tell me what You want. I need Your direction.*

Chapter Seven

Rose sat in her too-quiet apartment. In the dim lamp-light the moon spread its glow along the living-room rug like silver fingers.

Sleep had escaped her. The evening had been wonderful. The twinkling candles, like fireflies, had danced along in the darkness. The historic buildings, the costumed workers, the tangy cider had made the evening more than memorable. Most of all, Paul had embraced her.

He'd changed so much. In past weeks he'd been arriving home earlier than expected. The children were ecstatic. They had time to enjoy his company before bedtime. Watching them lifted Rose's spirits.

But it was more than that. He'd mellowed. Paul seemed more sensitive, almost as if he were pampering her. She loved it. Yet she distrusted it. They were from two different worlds. He had an education, a position and polish. She'd become employed following one year of business school. She'd never traveled. She'd experienced little. She had so little to offer a man like Paul.

Often Paul looked at her curiously as if he didn't understand why she reacted as she did. She'd never been open with him about her broken engagement and the issues it had caused. The situation had destroyed her trust and confidence. She'd been pitied, and no one wanted pity.

Had Paul pitied her, too? Was he pampering her to motivate her to stay in Little Cloud? She couldn't ask him. She would have to explain too much.

Rose shifted in the chair and reached for her Bible. She scanned the pages until her eyes focused on Proverbs 3:5, 6. "Trust in the Lord with all your heart and lean not on your own understanding. In all your ways acknowledge Him, and He will make your paths straight."

That's what she needed, a straight path. Rose had tried hard to let God lead her, but she fought Him every step. *Lean not on your own understanding.* She would make that her motto.

Rose placed the Bible back on the table and switched off the lamp. The moon guided her steps, but before returning to bed she pulled back the curtain. Tonight she saw a melon-colored moon. The mountains and valleys that created the moon's face were clear, and the moon seemed nearer than its great distance from earth.

Melon moon. Melancholy moon. She gazed upward into the black sky, seeing the lonely orb in a sea of shimmering stars. The stars captured her imagination and drew her back to the candlelight at the log village.

"Twinkle, twinkle little star." The childhood rhyme played in her head.

Twinkle, twinkle little star.

The melon moon is not so far.

She smiled to herself. The moon was nearer than any other heavenly body. Why did it make her lonely?

God is much nearer, she thought. The words hummed in her head.

"Are you coming? We'll be late." Rose stood at the bottom of the staircase, waiting for the children, as she'd done for the past few weeks since Paul's work had become more demanding.

"Why are you leaving so early?" She turned and saw Paul in the dining-room doorway. "The kids haven't eaten yet."

"I know." She slipped her arm into her coat sleeve. "The church is having its annual pancake breakfast this morning. The offering is used to purchase Christmas gifts for needy families." She shrugged her other arm into a sleeve. "Anyway, the kids love pancakes."

"So do I," Paul said.

She felt her mouth fall open. "I know, but—"

"Can only members attend?"

"No." His question shocked her. "I didn't think to—"

"To invite me." He grinned.

Footsteps could be heard pounding along the upstairs hallway, and in an eye blink the twins bounded down the steps.

"We're having pancakes," Colin said, dragging his tongue over his lips and rubbing his belly.

"Me, too," Kayla said, mimicking Colin's actions.

"Me, too," Paul said, aping them both.

"You are?" Kayla's eyes widened. "Are you really coming, too?"

"You don't mind, do you?" He pointed the question to the children, but Rose sensed he was aiming it at her.

"We'd love to have you join us," Rose said.

Paul held his arms extended at his sides and eyed his slacks and pullover sweater. "Is this okay?"

"You'll be the best-dressed man there," she said.

Rose stepped from the house, amazed that Paul had joined them. She'd longed to invite him to church, but she'd felt an invitation was out of place.

Since his help had arrived from L.A., he'd fallen back into his old pattern—home late, no time for the kids, no conversation. She missed it. The long hours were reflected in his tired face.

Paul drove, and as she sat in the passenger seat she gazed at the leaden gray sky, but she didn't let the weather darken her spirit. She grinned, thinking if she'd known all it would take to get Paul to church was a meal, she would have invited him to the Mulligan Stew and Bar-B-Cue they'd held a few weeks earlier.

"I'm pleased you decided to come along. It's good for the kids to see you at worship."

"And good for me." He gave her a tender smile. "I know I've been quiet lately. My mind's filled with details, and I'm so talked out at the plant I'm not in the mood when I get home. But we're making progress."

"I assume the L.A. exec has been helpful."

"Absolutely. Gretchen's top-notch. Wonderful. I respect her immensely."

Gretchen. A woman. Rose hadn't considered he'd been spending late evenings with a female. She stared out the passenger window, trying to control her sudden fear. Paul's long days away, his silence, his withdrawal. She knew the day might come, but she wasn't ready for it.

"She'll be leaving right after Thanksgiving. By then,

everything should be in place. Then it's a matter of training."

"That's good," Rose said, managing to sound sincere while facing her worst fear. A woman had walked into Paul's life—a woman he admired and respected.

They entered the church through the side door, and the enticing aroma of buttery pancakes and grilled sausages guided them to the fellowship hall. Rose tried to push Paul's startling news out of her mind. She was in the Lord's house, and today she needed solace. They joined the buffet line, then found empty seats.

To Rose's surprise, Paul recognized two men from the plant at their table. After they were introduced, she waited for a raised eyebrow or a questioning look.

"You're a nanny?" one of the wives asked.

"She baby-sits us," Colin said, "except we're not babies."

"Me, either," Kayla added.

Rose grinned at the children, thrilled at Kayla's outgoing nature. The change had been overwhelming.

"I'm sort of the babysitter and glorified housekeeper," Rose said, managing a pleasant look while enveloped with a sense of uneasiness. Today she needed nothing else to play with her emotions. She studied the woman's face, but saw nothing but cordiality.

"I never thought housekeeping had any glory in it," the woman said with an amiable grin.

Everyone chuckled, and the chatter continued. Rose wanted to relax, but she couldn't. She forced down the breakfast she, for once, hadn't prepared.

Paul watched Rose with concern. She'd gotten quiet, and he wondered if he'd made a mistake inviting himself to the breakfast, but the reactions of his employees settled over him like a gift. At the office, conversation felt strained, but this morning it seemed spontaneous and congenial. Maybe being in church would create a new bond between them. Believers seemed bound together with special ties. An old hymn lilted into his thoughts—"Blest Be the Ties That Bind." Perhaps those ties were stronger than he had realized.

They ate their breakfast, intermingled with conversation, until the crowd thinned, and Rose motioned toward the doorway. "I'll take the children to their Sunday-school classes. You can meet me upstairs for church."

Paul agreed and followed the worshipers to the sanctuary. Soon Rose arrived, and they found an empty pew. The service began, but Paul's thoughts drifted to his new feelings for Rose. He wished he could put a finger on them. He knew he felt gratitude and—

The truth settled over him. For the first time since Della died, he was looking forward to Christmas. Rose had been the catalyst. They'd become friends. Their lives had become entwined. *Blest be the ties that entwine.* The words twisted in his head.

As they'd spent more time together, Paul had sensed a kind of like-minded spirit they shared. The painting came to mind. They'd both been drawn to it immediately. But it was more than that. He felt comfort in her presence. She exuded compassion and evoked from him a new tenderness.

The congregation rose for the Gospel, and Paul yanked himself upward, aware that he'd been daydreaming.

"Today we will hear a lesson from Paul's letters to the Philippians, chapter two, beginning with verse one." The pastor's rich voice filled the air. "'If you have any encouragement from being united with Christ, if any comfort from His love, if any fellowship with the Spirit, if any tenderness and compassion, then make my joy complete by being like-minded, having the same love, being one in spirit and purpose.'"

Paul's heartbeat accelerated. Hadn't those same words entered his thoughts moments ago—tenderness, comfort, compassion, like-mindedness? He'd been thinking of Rose, but these words applied to Jesus and to faith.

Marriage was about being united, but being united in Christ was beyond his imagination. *Make my joy complete.* Was that what made Christians optimistic in the depths of despair? They found blessings in failure and joy in sorrow? His mind whirred with questions.

He slid a glance at Rose with her chin tilted upward, her eyes straight ahead, her lips curved at the corners. She was beautiful inside and out, and he was blessed to have her touch his children's lives—blessed having her touch *his* life.

Make my joy complete. Rose's face brightened his thoughts.

Snow illuminated by the porch light drifted past the dining-room window. Rose slid the chairs beneath the table and replaced the centerpiece. Everything seemed in order. She'd worked hard to keep Paul's lady friend out of her mind. He hadn't brought her home. He hadn't mentioned anything about her. Rose needed to leave well enough alone until the day came when she'd have to move on.

Tonight the children had settled on the living-room carpet, playing a game while Paul read the newspaper.

The house seemed cozy and comfortable, but not her. She had to drive to her apartment alone.

She drew in a lengthy breath and snapped off the dining-room light. Turning toward the kitchen, she was drawn again to the snowflakes settling on the shrubbery outside the window. She stepped back and gazed at the wintry scene. In the darkness, the minute patterns glided downward like confetti from heaven. White and perfect. Beautiful.

"Are you leaving?"

Paul stood so close behind her, she jumped at his voice.

"I didn't mean to scare you," he said.

He didn't step back, and she stood where she had been, feeling the heat from his body and his breath rustling her hair.

"I was thinking how beautiful it looks."

He rested his palms on her shoulders. "I like looking at the snowfall, but I'm guessing a full week of driving in it will be about all I'll want."

She felt the warm pressure of his hands and struggled for something lighthearted to say. "Everyone dreams of a white Christmas." Another song rippled through her mind. "Did you ever roast chestnuts on an open fire?"

Paul chuckled and gave her shoulders a squeeze. "No, but there's always a first time." He lowered his hands. "If this keeps up, we'll have a white Thanksgiving."

The holiday caught her attention, and she spun toward him. He caught her shoulders again and stood so close her pulse quickened. She stepped back before she could draw in enough breath to speak. When she moved, Paul dropped his hands to his sides.

"Are you planning to have Thanksgiving dinner here?" she asked.

"I thought so."

"Will you want to invite guests? Your aunt Inez?"

"I hadn't given it any thought, but why don't you call her? Invite friends from church, if you'd like."

His offer surprised her. "This is your family's Thanksgiving, not mine."

Paul shook his head. "You're part of this family. Don't forget that." His gaze captured hers as if he'd read her mind.

"Thank you," she murmured, lowering her eyes.

She could hear him breathing, and she waited for him to walk away. When she found the courage to lift her head, she saw that he was studying her face as if searching for something.

Rose watched his hands rise, this time capturing her arms as they hung at her sides. The warmth of his touch rolled down her limbs.

He looked desperate. "If you would just tell me..."

She felt his hands tense against her arms as he drew her closer. Stunned, she searched his face, his eyes heavy lidded, his chest rising and falling in deep breaths. He lowered his head and his lips parted. Paul's mouth neared hers, and her chest ached with the waiting.

"Daddy, Colin won't let me play."

Kayla's voice invaded the room like an alarm signal. Paul jerked backward, and Rose gulped for air.

Kayla bounded toward them with Colin on her heels.

Rose shifted away. In the kitchen she pulled her coat from the back closet and located her handbag. Before she could call good-night, Paul stood in the kitchen doorway.

"I'll see you tomorrow," she said, avoiding his eyes. "I'll give Aunt Inez a call in the morning. I'm sure she'll be pleased." She stepped toward the back door.

"It's probably slippery out there. Are you sure you want to drive into town tonight with this—"

"I'll be fine," she said.

"If you're sure."

As she put her hand on the knob he said her name, and she turned toward him.

"I suppose we should invite Gretchen for Thanksgiving dinner. She's away from home."

"Sure thing," she said, giving the door a push. The wind caught it, and Rose struggled to keep the door from tearing from its hinges. She stepped from the porch into the wet snow. It sifted into her shoes and covered her ankles.

"Be with me, Lord," she whispered, not sure if she were talking about the drive home or about what had happened inside the house.

Chapter Eight

Paul hadn't felt normal since the night he'd nearly kissed Rose. He couldn't stop replaying the moment and asking himself over and over what he'd been thinking. The answer was always the same. Rose and her smiling eyes.

He hadn't been able to loosen her image from his thoughts, not since the night at Historic Log Village when he'd seen her face illuminated in the candlelight. Even before that. Days seemed to meld together like a collage of wonderful moments. Rose had brightened their lives.

But now he had to decide what to do about it.

Struggling with his dilemma, Paul let his gaze drift to the sleeve of photos he'd taken in the backyard weeks earlier. They'd been lying on the table, and he hadn't looked at them since Rose had brought them home.

He opened the packet. Emotion washed over him. He gazed at the twins mugging for the camera, their faces shining in the autumn sunlight, their clothes sprinkled with leaves. He shifted the top photo and, beneath, sat his own picture with his beautiful children beside him.

Next he saw Rose cuddling the twins while love filled her eyes. He paused, afraid to look, afraid to see what was coming. He inched the top photo away and looked. Rose again. Each one touched his heart—her smile, her happiness, her face glowing with contentment. He slid a photo into his shirt pocket and placed the rest back into the sleeve.

Paul stood and moved to the window. Outside, the leaves were gone. Beneath the leaden sky the earth looked cold and hard, but his life had been warmed by a woman who'd been his children's nanny for nearly two years. What would he do now with these growing feelings?

He'd been blind.

The scent of turkey filled the air as Rose removed the potatoes from the burner. She'd been in a daze for the past three weeks, trying to make sense out of Paul. She'd truly thought that he was about to kiss her that night. The ride to her apartment had been a nightmare, between the unfamiliar slippery streets and the events that had brought on a tangle of fantasy, reality and disbelief.

She and Paul hadn't spoken of it since that evening. So often, Rose wondered what might have happened if Kayla hadn't barged into the room. She'd been prepared for his kiss. She longed for it, yet she knew it wasn't meant to be. It could only have added to the confusion already in her heart, especially since she'd learned Paul's friend was a woman. Now she was coming for Thanksgiving dinner.

When the doorbell rang, Rose let Paul answer it. Voices drifted in from the foyer, and Rose's heart lodged in her throat. Prayer had helped her with the struggle. Only God promised to be faithful forever, and Rose couldn't blame Paul. He'd asked her to be his friend— nothing more than that. And she'd realized this woman might also be only a friend—maybe a beautiful, shapely friend, but those were things Rose couldn't control.

"Rose."

She straightened as Paul's voice sailed through the dining room. She could see their shadows moving across the white table linen before she saw them.

"Rose," Paul said again, coming through the doorway. "I want you to meet Gretchen Thomas."

Rose managed a smile.

"Gretchen, this is Rose Danby, my right arm...and my left one, too."

When she saw the woman behind Paul, Rose clamped her jaw to avoid showing her surprise. Rose had expected a young, shapely woman. Instead standing in front of her was a tall, large-boned woman whose hand was extended toward her.

"It's nice to meet you," Rose said, accepting the woman's handshake.

"I've heard so many wonderful things about you," Gretchen said.

Shame washed over Rose as she gazed at the woman's once-blond hair, now streaked with gray. She'd never thought Gretchen would be a woman executive in her fifties, but Rose could only guess that's what she was. "I'm glad you could come. Eating alone on Thanksgiving isn't easy."

"I've had to do it since my husband died," she said. "We were married nearly forty years."

Nearly forty years. Rose did her math. Unless the

woman had married very young, she had to be in her sixties. "It must be difficult."

"We can get used to anything as long as we have our faith," Gretchen said.

"Can I help you do anything?" Paul asked.

Rose shook her head. "We'll be eating shortly. I'm just about ready. You go ahead."

Paul took Gretchen's arm and steered her back through the dining room. Their voices faded to a distant hum.

Ashamed of herself, Rose leaned her back against the kitchen counter and covered her face. "Lord, what can I do?" She'd judged a situation that she'd known nothing about.

Living with distrust and jealousy was destructive. She'd become too involved in the family and knew she needed a life of her own, a husband and children. She'd never have these staying in Little Cloud.

If she couldn't get her emotions under control, she had no choice but to leave. Jan had told Rose she was always welcome if she decided to return to L.A., and Rose truly missed her friend. Maybe this was God's way of pointing her back to California.

While Paul was giving Aunt Inez a ride home with a bag of turkey-dinner leftovers, Rose helped the children with their baths, then convinced them it was bedtime. They grumbled until she teased them about the broom, and they giggled as they obeyed.

The scent of turkey filled the house, giving her a homey feeling. The meal had gone well, and she had finally settled her ragged emotions and enjoyed Gretchen's company. She could see why Paul respected and admired the woman.

She settled on the sofa, recalling her fluttering heart as her arm had brushed against Paul's while they worked in the kitchen. They'd been preparing dessert—he making coffee, she whipping cream. Since the night of the near kiss, they'd become like strangers at a bus stop, apologizing for getting too close and avoiding each other's eyes. The change felt frightening, but it made her think.

Tonight she decided to talk with Paul if she could find the courage and the opportunity. The chance would arise when he returned from his aunt's. In a way she felt better having made the decision.

By the time Paul arrived, the house was quiet. Rose had her legs curled beneath her and a blaze in the fireplace.

"Thanks for the fire," Paul said as he came through the doorway. His coat was littered with newly fallen snow. He slipped it off and shook it, then vanished.

Rose heard the entry closet door open and close, then footsteps as Paul came back into the room. "It's snowing again?" Rose asked, uncurling her legs and rising.

He nodded. "Just a few flakes, though."

Paul settled into a chair by the fire while she remained standing. He grew more handsome every day, and the reality broke her heart. Tonight his light brown hair looked disheveled from the wind, and his close-cut shave had begun to shadow. She longed to touch his jaw and feel the prickles of the whiskers that bristled on his cheeks.

"Are you leaving?" he asked.

She motioned toward the window. "If it's snowing, I

probably should go." But that wasn't what she'd planned to do. Her commitment to talk to him niggled in her mind.

Instead of leaving, Rose returned to the sofa. "Do you have time to talk?" She sat on the edge of the cushion.

"Talk? Sure."

She lowered her gaze, not knowing where to begin. The words clung in her throat, unwilling to leave until she forced them out. "We don't usually talk about personal things, but I want to tell you something so you understand why I react as I do."

"Is this about the other night?" he asked.

It was the first reference he'd made to the incident, but she didn't want to start there. She had too much to explain before that ever happened.

She shook her head. "When I first came here, you said you needed a friend. I certainly needed one. I had no way to make friends, since I wasn't working in the community. But sometimes I'm not sure…" She faltered, knowing she had to back up to start the story where the problem had begun.

When she looked up, Paul was giving her a questioning look. "I hope you didn't misunderstand me," he said. "I never meant anything inappropriate when I asked you to be my friend. I—"

"I know that, Paul." Suddenly she felt foolish. Why confess the humiliating experience with Don? "Never mind. Let's forget it."

He leaned forward. "No, please. I want to hear what's bothering you. I thought it was the proposal or something else I'd said or done. The other night when—"

"It's a combination of things," she said. She sent a

quick prayer that the Lord would help her tell the story without bitterness or embarrassment. She so often felt guilty for what had happened. Yet she had been faithful, as God commanded. Don hadn't.

She began, controlling the old hurt that clashed with the present. She made it brief, and when she stopped she studied his face. "So you can understand why I have a problem with trust…and judgmental people."

"Yes, and thanks for trusting me. I understand now. I know you have a strong faith and high morals. I'll always respect that."

He stood and crossed the floor, sinking beside her on the sofa. "But I wish you'd told me before. You've been suffering in silence, and I've probably stepped on your toes a million times without knowing what you had gone through."

She shrugged. "It just takes me a while to come to grips with most everything."

"You needed a friend you could trust, and then I walked through the door in L.A. and proposed to you without explaining what I had in mind."

"That did undo me. Don had been my boss, and I've promised myself never to mix romance and work."

Paul flinched. "No wonder you were upset."

"And I've never understood how you could propose to someone you didn't know well or didn't care about."

Paul pressed his hand against her arm. "Don't think that, please. I cared very much about you. You were excellent with the twins. They loved you. I admired your ability and respected you as a person. I thought that perhaps—"

"But you didn't love me."

Paul jolted backward, hearing her words. "No, I

didn't, but I…" After what she'd said, how could he ever tell her now that his feelings were different? He'd spent every waking hour thinking of her and the twins, imagining how they were spending the day, envisioning Rose's smile waiting for him when he came home, her gentle voice when she met him at the door.

"You say you respected me, but I don't see it."

"What do you mean?" His pulse tripped.

"If you respected me, you would have known I would never marry a man who didn't love me fully. Not for convenience, not for money, not for comfort or security. I'd rather be single."

"I wish you wouldn't say—"

"I'd rather be childless." She turned to him. "And I want children more than anything else in the world."

Childless? Seeing the look on her face, Paul felt his heart break. He couldn't imagine Rose single and childless for the rest of her life. One day a man would sweep her off her feet, and lately he'd wished he could be the one to do just that.

Chapter Nine

Rose leaned against the kitchen counter and wondered what she was doing. Prolonging the agony was her answer. She'd fallen in love with the children, and worse, she'd fallen in love with Paul.

He cared about her. She accepted that. He'd been kind and generous. He'd included her in family activities and told her she was important to them, but as she'd said the other night, she was his employee. That would never change.

And she would never be available for another man as long as Paul was in her life. So what about marriage and children? The answer hung on a thread.

Christmas was only three weeks away, and she needed to prepare the family if she were really going back to California. The quicker the better, as far as she was concerned. As soon as the thought entered her mind, a knot formed in her chest. *Heavenly Father, please let me hear Your voice.*

She heard nothing but the twins banging something from the front of the house.

Her thoughts drifted back to Gretchen. Rose had

been mortified when her jealousy had caused her to concoct a romance between Paul and the woman. Every time the memory resurfaced—and it did often—she cringed.

Jealousy, distrust and frustration had become her way of life, and they were not the attributes of a Christian. She'd asked God to guide her, to give her courage to leave, then her heart would tell her to stay.

Since Gretchen had returned to L.A., Rose was pleased that Paul had done what he'd promised. He'd been arriving home on time again. She knew it would be good for the children after she was gone.

Gone? Is that what she would ultimately do?

Her only defense had been keeping busy, planning for Christmas and wrapping the children's gifts. She'd hidden them everywhere she prayed the twins wouldn't look. Today she'd put her energy into baking cookies. She'd have a supply that would last through January.

Rose wandered into the living room and put on a CD of Christmas music. The holiday carols filled the room and wrapped around her heart. She checked on the children, who'd decided to conspire in Paul's study about what they wanted to give their father for Christmas. They'd been particularly well behaved in the past week, and Rose assumed their goodness had to do with Christmas.

Though she'd written to Jan that she was giving serious thought to going back and had even received a lively telephone call filling her in on all the news and giving her encouragement, Rose couldn't envision actually walking out the door. The thought made her ill.

Yet the idea persisted. Though she would miss the

twins, the possibility of getting married and having her own children softened the hurt.

Before she left Little Cloud, Rose wished she could be honest with Paul about her feelings. But what good would it do? She'd only embarrass herself and face his rejection. A woman should never fall in love with her boss. The relationship was doomed.

The buzzer on the oven sounded, and Rose's heart lurched. She opened the door and pulled out two sheets of plump sugar cookies. She'd bought decorator frosting, and once she covered the cookies with a white glaze, she planned to let the children help make the designs.

As the new aroma sailed into the air, she heard the sound of two pairs of feet thudding nearer. She watched the doorway, and in a heartbeat the twins appeared.

"More cookies?" Kayla asked.

"I thought you liked cookies," Rose said.

Kayla leaned over the pans and sniffed. "We do, but you've made lots already."

"I'm stocking up." Rose's throat tightened.

Colin eyed the icing tubes. "Can we help put on the decorations?"

"Once they cool." Rose shifted the cookies to cooling racks, then set the sheets in the sink. "Did you decide what gift you want to buy for your dad?"

Kayla nodded.

"What is it?"

Colin plopped his hand over Kayla's mouth. "A surprise, but we need little round macaronis."

His request threw Rose. What would they do with macaroni? "I'll pick some up for you the next time I'm at the grocery store."

"Okay," Kayla said. "Buy a big box. We're going to make something."

"Make something. That's wonderful. Your daddy will love that more than—"

A noise caught her attention, and all eyes shifted to the outside door.

Paul stepped into the kitchen in his stocking feet. "Mud," he said.

Colin pointed. "Rose will get the broom after you."

Paul wiggled his toes. "No shoes. I'm safe."

Rose grinned at their antics.

Paul sniffed the air, then ambled to the table and snatched a cookie. He took a big bite and licked away the crumbs. When he turned, he gawked at the filled containers piled on the counter. "We're having a bake sale?"

"We're stocking up," Kayla said. "And don't eat any more of those, Daddy. We're going to decorate them."

"I'm sorry," he said, meandering across to the counter that held the plastic bins of cookies. "Are you decorating these?"

Rose shook her head and watched him slip out another. "You won't be hungry for dinner."

"Yes, I will. Paul Bunyan can eat a million flapjacks." He grinned. "Or something like that."

Rose eyed him. "Paul Bunyan?"

"Paul Bunyan's a lumberjack," Colin said, peering at Rose.

"I know, but what's that have to do with anything?"

"We're cutting down our Christmas tree tonight," Paul said.

"We are?" The twins whooped and bounced across the floor to Paul's side.

He gave them a hug, then looked at Rose. "Don't worry about dinner. We can pick something up while we're out."

She nodded, having lost her spirit for cookie baking. The Christmas tree. The emotion seemed too much for her.

"You'll come, too," he said, as if he sensed what she'd been thinking.

"No. I think I'll—" She stopped herself. She wanted to decline, but sitting home alone was the last thing she wanted to do tonight.

"You're coming along," Paul said. It wasn't a question.

Rose nodded. "Do we have time to ice these cookies?"

"By all means. I have to change clothes, and then I can help, too."

When he was gone, Rose pointed the children to their task. She put on the glaze, and they decorated. By the time Paul returned, they were giggling at their mistakes and praising their successes.

Paul pitched in, and soon the cookies were finished and spread out over the table to dry.

Within minutes, they bundled up and headed out the door. Paul drove to the restaurant first, and when they'd finished eating, they were on their way. Rose still hadn't gotten used to the miles and miles of forest that lined the roadways. In L.A. a tree off a freeway was a rarity. As she watched evergreens blur past her window, she figured they could have stopped anywhere and laid an ax to a pine or fir.

About thirty miles from town Paul pointed to the sign—Willard's Tree Farm. The temperature had dropped in the past hour, and the mud had frozen. At the tree farm the car bumped along the compact ice and snow as if it were on an old corduroy road. The few flakes that had twirled past the windshield earlier had grown to a full snowfall. Rose hoped they'd dressed warmly enough.

After they parked, Paul pulled a handsaw from the trunk and headed toward the cashier's shed. The kids frolicked beside him while Rose trudged behind, her heart vacillating between sorrow and joy. This Christmas had become so special to her—not because of her leaving, but because of the closeness she felt to all of them.

The attendant pointed out their options, and soon they were trudging across the frozen earth toward the trees. "Douglas fir? Balsam? Scotch pine? What's your pleasure?" Paul aimed his gaze at Rose.

What was her pleasure? She drew in the pine scent that filled the air. This moment was her greatest, surrounded by the people she loved and entertained by the snowflakes flitting from the sky. They caught in Paul's hair and lashes. The children twirled in circles, their tongues sticking out to catch the infinitesimal crystals.

Though the night was cold, Rose warmed at the sight of it all. "I like real Christmas trees with big gaping holes and short needles. The kind I had when I was a kid."

"You mean the ugly kind?" Paul's voice was filled with teasing.

"Beautiful ones," she said, swinging her fist to poke his arm.

With the momentum of her punch, she lost her footing on the slippery ground. She felt her legs sail out from under her, and all she could do was protect her arms and head from being injured. She smacked against the ground on her backside.

Kayla darted forward, concern wrinkling her smooth face. "Help her, Daddy," she cried.

"I'm fine," Rose called out to halt their worry.

"You don't look fine to me," Paul said, coming to her rescue. He reached down, clasped both her hands in his, braced her feet against his heavy shoes and pulled her upward.

She stumbled against him, her breath making a cloud of white mist that mingled with his in the cold air.

When their eyes met, Paul let her go.

"No, Daddy," Colin said in his directive voice. "You have to hold Rose up so she doesn't fall again."

Paul shrugged as if the boss had spoken. He clasped Rose's waist and held her close to his side.

Rose felt enveloped in protection and love. The children romped in front of them, pointing to trees and chattering like squirrels. Finally Rose spotted the tree between the feathering snowdrops. A beautiful tree, almost perfect, with widespread limbs and open places to hang large ornaments.

She slowed and pointed. "That's it. That's a real Christmas tree."

Paul let his arm slide from her waist and moved closer. He read the tag. "It's a Fraser fir. They say it doesn't lose its needles."

"That's what we want," Rose said, thinking of the housecleaning.

The children agreed, so Paul stepped forward, bent low and drew the saw back and forth. Rose watched the tree until Paul called, "Timber." As it tilted, Rose scooted in and caught the fir before it hit the ground.

While she carried the saw, Paul hoisted the heavy tree over his shoulder, and they made their way back to the hut. He had become Paul Bunyan as she watched him walk along, his back so straight he seemed taller than usual, his strong arms balancing the tree on his shoulder. The vision made her ache.

The attendant bagged the fir, and as Paul paid the cashier, she ushered the children to the car. The snowfall grew heavier. In moments Paul joined them, and while he mounted the tree to the car roof, she buckled Kayla and Colin into the back seat. Before she could open the passenger door, Paul stepped beside her and laid his hand on hers.

"I'm glad you came. It wouldn't have been fun without you," he said.

She sensed his sincerity and something deeper in his eyes. The look sent her reeling. "That's because I fell and made you all laugh."

He tilted her chin upward, and she felt snowflakes settle on her nose and eyelashes.

"No," he said, "it's because you're as much a part of this family as I am." His hand slid up to cup her face and he leaned closer and kissed her cheek.

Rose's skin tingled, and his words swirled through her mind as wildly as the snowflakes. *Heavenly Father, why can't I hear You?*

She heard nothing but Paul's breathing.

Chapter Ten

Paul sat in his study, looking out the front windows.

He'd kissed Rose's cheek two days earlier, and he couldn't lose the memory. He relived the moment his lips had touched her face. He'd felt the cold of the snowflakes, but the warmth of her skin had melted his heart.

During the past days he'd faced where his emotions were leading him. He would sometimes pause in the kitchen doorway to watch her. How he longed to sneak up behind Rose, wrap his arms around her waist and kiss her graceful neck…but his dreams stopped there. Until he felt assured Rose would accept his advance, he'd keep his place, as she kept hers.

With possibilities tossing in his head, Paul wandered to the front window and leaned on the casing. He'd always disliked winter, but again today snow drifted down like feathers from a torn pillow. The view from the study inspired him. From the turret he could look out four windows into the wooded landscape across from the house. The bay window would make a perfect location for their tree.

Tonight Rose had mentioned hanging the Christ-

mas decorations. He grinned, thinking about the elec-
tric candle boxes he'd seen stacked on the living-room
chair, and he could picture one in each of the study
and dining-room windows that looked onto the front.
He was curious what else she'd bought that he didn't
know about.

Hearing the telephone jingle, Paul headed toward
his desk, but the ringing stopped. Rose rarely received
a call, so he left the study to see if it was for him.
He heard her voice from the kitchen telephone, and he
paused in the doorway.

"Thanks for inviting me."

Inviting her? His chest tightened, and he waited.

"No. Really. I can't. It's impossible."

Instead of eavesdropping further, he walked into the
kitchen and leaned against the door frame. Rose's face
was flushed, and he knew something had upset her. A
deep urge washed over him, and he longed to hold her
in his arms.

"You're very kind. Yes. Thank you." She hung up the
telephone, and when she turned around, she gave a start.

"Sorry," Paul said. "I thought the call was for me."

She shook her head, a frown furrowing her face.

"Is something wrong?"

"No, not really."

He knew differently, but he hoped she would tell
him. Paul's concern grew. He crossed the kitchen and
touched her arm. "You're annoyed about something."

Her eyes darkened when she looked at him. "I should
be complimented, I suppose. A gentleman from church
asked me to go with him to dinner and the Historic
Home Tour."

His pulse quickened.

She turned away. "I said no, naturally."

Was that natural? She didn't date. She longed for children and marriage one day, but she'd said no. As her employer—her friend—Paul knew he should encourage her to go out with the man, but he couldn't respond to her in either capacity. He could respond only where his heart led him. "You said no because of the children?"

"It's not the children, Paul."

He searched her eyes, wanting to probe. "I was just curious."

"I know," she said, her voice as disillusioned as the last kid picked on a baseball team.

He stood there not knowing what to say and knowing he should say nothing. He shoved his hands into his pockets and wandered across the room to the refrigerator. He stood in front of it, not hungry but yearning for something.

"Why did he call *here?*" Paul asked before he could stop himself.

"I work here. He didn't know my home phone number. It's not listed."

It had been a stupid question. He couldn't look in her eyes, fearing what she might see. Instead, he stared at the floor and dealt with emotions he hadn't felt in years. Frustration, anxiety, jealousy. What would he have done if Rose had said yes to the man?

His mind worked like a calculator, trying to figure which man had called her for a date. He supposed the guy had every right, but it seemed...

His stomach twisted. He had no hold on Rose. She could date anyone she desired. She could do anything she wanted. The possibilities left him empty. Rose had become his life. She was the reason he hurried home.

She was all he could think about. The realization etched itself on his heart.

He'd felt it coming like a gentle breeze—no sound, no drama, only an awareness, an airy dance of emotion that touched him almost imperceptibly. He was falling in love with Rose.

"I'm going up to check on the kids and make sure they're sleeping," she said.

Before her words registered, she had vanished. He stared at nothing while questions filled his mind.

How could he have missed what was happening? He knew he admired her. He'd been grateful and tried to make her happy. But was that love? Could he want a mother for the children so badly that he only thought it was something deeper? A voice said no. Could he be responding to the social pressure of having a wife? No again.

His feelings were as real as the tension growing in the cords of his neck. He moved to the stove and turned on a burner, then filled the kettle and set it on the stove.

He heard Rose's footsteps and paused.

"They're asleep."

Alien sensations sizzled through his limbs, and he didn't know what to do or how to react. He gestured toward the kettle. "I'm making tea."

"That sounds good." She sat on the edge of a kitchen chair and ran her hand across the back of her neck as she stretched her shoulders.

"Headache?" Paul asked.

"A little one. I'll be fine."

Paul watched her a moment until longing spurred him to slip behind her. He used his thumb to massage her upper back, then kneaded her shoulder muscles, working his way up to the cords of her slender neck.

Rose gave a soft moan of pleasure as she relaxed against his hands. She tilted her head back and forth, her silky hair brushing against his fingers.

He struggled to keep himself from running his hands through her locks. The kettle whistled, and he was forced to move away. "Feel better?"

"Thank you. That felt nice."

He focused on making cups of tea while calming his emotions. He longed to tell Rose how he felt. Perhaps he could tonight if he found the courage.

"Let's get comfortable," he said, leading the way. They settled in the living room. Both seemed thoughtful and quiet as they sipped their drinks.

Paul noticed the boxes of candles and remembered their plan. "Are we decorating tonight, or don't you feel up to it?"

Her gaze shifted to the boxes. She shrugged. "It's getting late."

"I'll help you," Paul said—anything to keep her there.

She set her cup on the saucer. "I told the kids they could help me decorate, but I assume they're mainly interested in the tree." She rose and moved to the boxes.

He joined her. "Ready?" His senses were sparked by Rose's nearness. Her fragrance seemed to surround him—the scent of spices and vanilla like the cookies she had baked.

She lifted a box and tore off the wrapper. They worked together freeing the candles, then headed into the dining room and set them in the windows. While he ran after extension cords, Rose finagled a way to fasten them to the windowsills.

When they moved to the study, Paul pulled a Christmas CD from the stack, and the soft music floated through the speakers. When the last candle was attached and lit, they adorned the open banister with green and red ribbons, then attached the wreath to the front door.

"I'll clean up," she said, heading into the dining room. He returned to the study and gathered the empty boxes. Soon Rose came through the doorway with a trash bag, and he dropped the cardboard into it. She knotted the end and he smiled at how organized she was…and how important she was to him.

A prayer entered Paul's thoughts, and he sent it heavenward, asking God's assistance. Rose's sensitivity had become his primary concern. He had to tell her how he felt at the right time and in the right way. He could only pray that she would believe him and forget he was her boss.

Mel Torme's velvet voice filled the room. "Chestnuts Roasting on an Open Fire."

"Remember?" he said.

She searched his eyes and nodded.

"Sounds like a plan," he said, trying to ease the mood. "Dance?"

Her frown returned, and he expected her to push him away, but he persisted. He grasped her hand and drew her into his arms.

The room was lit only by a desk lamp and the soft glow of the window candles. His pulse accelerated.

Rose felt stiff in his arms, but he drew her closer, breathing in her sweet fragrance and feeling the softness of her skin against his. Finally she relaxed and rested her head against his shoulder.

They moved slowly, swaying to the Christmas music, and Paul felt whole for the first time in years.

As the last strains of the song faded, Rose stepped back. Her hand trembled in his, and his gaze was drawn to the look of sorrow on her face.

"What's wrong, Rose?"

She lowered her head, but he'd already seen tears rolling down her cheeks. His stomach tightened as fear slammed against his happiness.

"I've made a difficult decision this evening," she said.

He didn't like the sound of her voice.

"What kind of decision?"

"I'm going back to L.A. It's the only way I'll ever be happy."

Chapter Eleven

Rose's words knocked the breath out of Paul. He gaped at her, making no sense out of what she'd said. "Please don't say that."

"I'm not making idle talk, Paul. I've struggled with this for too long. I believe it's for the best. We can both get on with our lives."

Get on with our lives? What lives? She'd become his life. He opened his mouth to tell her how his feelings had changed and grown, how she filled his life with joy. She'd given him a sense of wholeness, but he searched her serious face and stopped himself from opening his heart.

Rose wouldn't believe him. She would think he'd confessed his feelings so he could keep her there, and she'd promised never to fall for her boss.

The room hummed with silence.

Her misty eyes caught his. She stood so close he longed to take her into his arms again and hold her against his chest to soothe the ache that burned within.

He forced himself to speak. "What will we do? What will the kids do without you?" He captured her arms, his heart ready to speak despite his fears. "What will I do without you?"

She lowered her head and shook it. "Please don't ask me those questions. I'm trying to figure out what I'll do with my own life."

Her life. His heart burned for her, and his prayer rose to heaven begging God for an answer. Did she love him? Could she love him? Questions pressed against his chest like a boulder. He needed time.

"The holidays are here, Rose. Christmas is less than three weeks away. Maybe this is selfish to ask, but could you stay through the holidays?" His hands trembled so wildly he shoved them into his pockets. "Stay for the children. They'll be devastated without you."

He'd be devastated.

His gaze followed the tears that rolled down her cheeks and he reined in the desire to kiss them away. He felt helpless and hopeless. Only God could heal the situation.

Rose inched her chin upward, her eyes wet with tears. "You're right. I shouldn't have said anything now. I should have waited until the holidays were over." She brushed the tears from her eyes with the back of her hand. "I'll stay for the twins."

He rested his palm against her back, almost afraid to touch her for fear he wouldn't be able to stop. "Thank you. This means so much to me."

She looked directly into his eyes. "I'm doing it for myself, too. Your kids mean the world to me."

"You deserve children of your own. I know."

She nodded. "I hope you understand."

"I do…with all my heart."

"We'll have to make the best of it," she said, rallying.

"I feel better now that I've told you. We'll get through Christmas, and then I'll try to explain to the kids why I'm going. It'll give you a chance to find someone to replace me."

Replace her? His body trembled with the thought. "I can never replace you. Don't even think it. You have no idea how much you mean to us."

She stepped back. "Don't make it more difficult. Please. This wasn't a flash decision. I've struggled with it for a long time."

"What will you do?"

She shrugged. "I don't know. My friend Jan invited me to stay with her until I get things together."

She'd already spoken to a friend. Pain ripped through him. She'd really planned this long before telling him. He'd allowed himself to fall in love, and now…

"I'll keep busy," she said. "I want to do some more shopping. I have a few gifts for the kids hidden in the guest-room closet. I've wrapped some during the day when they're at school."

Her words tumbled together, and he made no sense out of them. Shopping? Gifts? How could she talk about those things? His sorrow veered toward anger. "You shouldn't do so much for them."

"Why not?"

He had no answer, except that she was leaving them. In a heartbeat Paul realized he was angry at himself, not Rose. She'd given her all to them. He'd given her so little. *Lord, help me to show my love. I'm lost already.*

"Paul Stewart, please." Rose waited, her ear pressed to the telephone and concern pounding in her head. Then she heard his voice.

"Paul, this is Rose." She swallowed.

"Is something wrong?"

"I'm worried about Kayla. She hasn't gotten up from her nap this afternoon. She's running a temperature, and she's very listless."

"What's the problem?"

"I don't know for sure. Colin seems all right. I called the pediatrician, and he wants me to take her to Emergency if I can't get her fever lowered."

"Emergency?" He paused. "I'll come home now. You'll need help with Colin."

"Thank you," she said. "Be careful. It's snowing heavily over here."

"I'll be careful."

Rose clutched the telephone to her chest long after Paul hung up. She feared she was acting overly concerned. Children got sick—that was part of life. But this time her worry had reached its peak.

Only hours earlier the children had hidden themselves away with the macaroni. They'd needed their safety scissors and glue, and Rose couldn't imagine what they were making.

When she'd noticed Kayla's discomfort, Rose had given the child aspirin. Now she'd given her more with the doctor's orders, and all she could do was wait. If that didn't work, she would bathe Kayla in cool water. Her next concern was not alarming Colin. He'd already hovered nearby while she telephoned the doctor, and he looked worried.

The snow had begun to fall early, and in the past hour it had increased. The wind had picked up, and the flakes were flying at a wild angle, leaving snow piled against anything standing.

Christmas filled Rose's mind. It was only three days away, and its coming meant she would be leaving soon. Though she'd professed leaving would be the only way she could be happy, her heart fought against her decision.

Each time she looked at the children, she was stunned by the emotion that rattled her. She loved them like her own, and the longer she stayed the more she cherished them. She'd thought leaving would bring her happiness, but now she sensed nothing could.

"What can I do?" Colin asked from the doorway.

"You can give me a hug," Rose said.

He plodded across the room, his arms dangling like a chimpanzee, and wrapped them around her neck. She drew in the scent of his laundered T-shirt and the peanut butter and jelly he'd eaten for lunch. Rose knew he was concerned about Kayla, and so was she.

"I have time to play one game," Rose said.

He grinned and ran from the room. Rose trailed after him, in no mood for games today, but she needed to keep Colin distracted as well as herself.

They played a game of concentration, and Rose was so distracted that Colin won legitimately. He jumped around the room, cheering as if he'd won an all-star game. She pushed herself up from the floor and tousled his hair. "Let's go up and see if Kayla's awake yet."

"Is she sick?" His questioning brown eyes, the same color as Paul's, searched hers.

"A little," Rose said, hoping she sounded convincing, "but she might feel better now."

"Did she take her aspirin?" he asked, striding beside her up the staircase.

Rose nodded.

When they entered Kayla's room, Rose's hopes died. Beads of perspiration covered Kayla's nose and forehead.

"Could you do me a favor?" she asked Colin, hoping to keep him busy.

"What?" His gaze was directed at his twin.

"Would you help me run water in the tub? We have to make it cool. Not icy cold, but cool."

He looked puzzled.

"Do you understand? We need to use the water to help get Kayla's temperature back to normal."

"Not cold. Cool," he repeated.

She nodded, then grabbed the thermometer and put it under Kayla's arm. She counted, then checked Kayla's temperature. One hundred and four.

Rose beckoned to Colin to follow her, and they headed for the bathroom. Rose turned on the tap. "Now you check it for me, okay?" she said to Colin, his face so filled with concern it broke her heart. "Remember, not cold, but cool."

Colin placed his hand in the water. "It's good," he said, looking at her as if to make sure he'd done the job well.

Rose felt the water. "Perfect. You're doing a good job." She touched the side of the tub. "When it reaches here, I'll turn it off."

"Is Kayla okay?"

"She'll be fine." *Please, Lord, we need Your help here,* she prayed as she waited for the tub to fill before turning off the tap.

When she returned to the bedroom, Rose slipped her arm beneath the child's neck and called her name. "You need to wake up, sweetheart."

Kayla gave a soft moan, her eyelids fluttering.

"I know you feel terrible, but I want to get you into the tub so you can feel better." She eased Kayla up, her body limp, her arms flopping at her sides. Though Rose was slender, fear made her strong. She maneuvered Kayla into her arms, then straightened her back and headed for the doorway.

Outside she could see the heavy snowfall continuing. She pictured Paul trying to drive the two-lane highway to the house, and she feared for his safety, as well.

When she entered the bathroom, she sent Colin to watch TV, then undressed Kayla and slid her into the tub. The child reared upward when the cool water washed over her, but Rose held her firmly and began to sponge her while sitting on the edge of the tub.

After a while her back ached, and she wondered if she had the strength to lift Kayla out of the water. She reached for the bath towel, and in her peripheral vision she saw motion.

"How's she doing?"

Rose's heart leaped when she heard Paul's voice. "I don't know. I'm praying she's better."

He moved to her side and rested his hand on Rose's shoulder. "If you move, I'll lift her."

She breathed a sigh. "Thanks. Somehow I got her in there, but I wondered how I'd get her out."

While Paul lifted his daughter, Rose wrapped her in a towel, and Paul kissed Kayla's cheek, then headed toward her room.

Rose stood a moment, enjoying the sense of relief that rushed through her. Paul's presence made her strong again. She might be an employee, but she loved them all as if God had meant them to be a family.

The stress of the day caught in her throat and pushed behind her eyes. She drew in a deep breath to calm her thoughts.

Paul glanced over his shoulder, looking for Rose. She looked tired and strained, and he couldn't thank her enough for what she did for the twins. He'd been surprised to see Colin enrapt in a television program. Before he came up the stairs, Colin had reported that he and Rose had played a game, and he'd helped her run the water. She was so good with the children. Like a real mother.

If only... He let the thought fade. Only God could solve what seemed so impossible.

In Kayla's room Paul set her on the bed, wondering if he should leave her in the towel or find clean pajamas.

"Let me," Rose said behind him. In moments she'd taken the wet towel from Kayla and dressed her in a nightgown, then pulled up the sheet.

Paul stood beside her holding the damp towel and looking down at his sleeping daughter. "How's her temperature?"

"It was a hundred and four, but I want to take it again." She tucked the thermometer under Kayla's arm and checked her watch. Then she focused on him. "How was the driving?"

"Horrible. If I hadn't started home when I did, I wouldn't have gotten here. They're announcing travel advisory warnings on the radio, and the snow isn't going to stop for a while. They're calling it a blizzard."

"I saw it through the window," she said. Her gaze fell to her watch. She leaned down and pulled out the thermometer. "One hundred and one." She released a sigh. "Much better."

She cleaned and stowed the thermometer, then turned to him with relief written on her face. "Thank You, Lord."

He nodded. "I can't imagine us trying to get her to Emergency in this mess."

"Let's just hope the fever stays down." She brushed her hair from her forehead. "I suppose I should think about dinner."

He touched her arm and smoothed her hair with the other hand. "Let me worry about that."

A faint smile curved her mouth. "No pizza tonight."

His heart swelled seeing her smile, as meager as it was. "You don't think I can cook? Have you forgotten the meal I made for you?"

"Hmm." She eyed her watch, then gave him a generous grin. "I think that was three months ago. Do you still remember how?"

Paul slid his arm around her back and guided her out the doorway, then gave her a wry look. "But what's in the house to cook? I only have a small repertoire."

She spurted a laugh, the first he'd heard in days.

"Okay, Chef Stewart. I'll play assistant and show you a thing or two in the kitchen."

Paul felt the Lord smiling down, and he sent up a rousing thanksgiving. If nothing more, the horrible day had drawn them closer. If God were willing to move mountains, maybe Rose would realize their ties were not only bound, they were tangled around their hearts.

Chapter Twelve

"You can't go home, Rose. Van or not, you'll be sitting in some ditch with no one to help you."

Rose let her arms drop to her sides. "What do you want me to do?"

He shook his head, amazed at her morality. "I think God would understand if you stayed here tonight. We have the room, and you know—" he prayed that she did "—I would never do anything—"

Rose stopped him. "I know. It's my upbringing. I can't help how I feel."

"Your feelings are good ones, but not very practical tonight." He wanted to hug her for her strength of character.

Her expression turned serious. "It's for the best, I suppose. I should stay close to Kayla…just in case."

Paul stood to stretch his overfull belly. They'd cooked a delicious meal of pasta and vegetables, but everyone's focus was on Kayla's absence from the table.

"While we're stuck here—" he gave her a gentle smile "—why don't we set the tree in the stand? It'll give it a day to spread out so we can decorate it."

"It'll pass the time," she said, but her face showed

her concern. "I hope Kayla's able to help tomorrow." She shook her head. "I tried to get her to eat, and she's still not interested."

"Later maybe." He drew up his shoulders, hoping to cover his own worries. "I'll get the tree, and you get the stand."

Rose stood and headed toward the door. "Where is it?"

"Good question." He glanced over his shoulder. "Get creative."

She laughed again, and the sound was music to him. Colin followed Paul onto the back patio and he let the boy think he was helping. He'd seen worry in his son's eyes, and it broke Paul's heart.

Colin held the door while Paul tugged the tree into the house. By the time he got it to the living room, he was grateful they'd bought the Fraser fir. He looked behind him and saw no trail of needles, just a trail of snow.

Rose hadn't returned yet, but before he left to help her find the tree stand, she appeared, carrying that and a large box.

"What's the box?" he asked, trying to read the red letters on the side.

"Another tree. I hope you don't mind." She handed him the stand and set the box on the floor.

"Another tree?"

"One of those fiber-optic trees that turns all the colors. I thought it would look pretty in the study in the bay window. It'll look beautiful from the front yard."

Paul felt his mouth sag, knowing how his and Rose's thoughts marched side by side. He recalled thinking about the bay window.

After much struggling, Paul settled the tree in the stand, and to his relief Rose declared it straight after his fourth try. He slid from under the branches and strode back to join her. "Straight as a plumb line."

"And now," she said, pointing to the box, "the pièce de résistance."

"You're a pièce de résistance," he said, sending her a wink.

Her smile warmed him. He opened the box and pulled out the fiber-optic tree. Instructions fell to the ground, and Rose rescued them. She scanned the paper. "Do you want to hear this in French, Japanese or English?"

"If you want this put together right, try English."

He led the way to the study with the tree while Rose read the directions behind him. It was easy to assemble, and once it was plugged in, Paul understood why Rose had bought it.

"Wait until dark. We can sit in here and watch the lights change colors."

We can sit in here. The words charged over him like ice water. In three more days she'd be getting ready to leave. The sorrow felt too deep, too cruel to bear.

Rose couldn't sleep, couldn't stop thinking about her leaving. She'd come here first with trepidation, but in only days, she'd realized how much she'd missed them. And they had missed her. She'd grown to love the strange little town more than she would have imagined. While her love had deepened for the children, her world revolved around their well-being and their lives.

Then came Paul. He'd filled her foolish dreams, and even though common sense told her to stand back and protect herself, she hadn't listened. Perhaps she'd listened, but her heart couldn't follow what wisdom deemed right. She'd dreamed that impossible dream.

When she thought about all that had happened, the lovely thoughts dimmed with the knowledge she was leaving. She'd agreed to be Paul's friend, and like a friend, he'd kissed her cheek and danced with her that evening in the study as they listened to the velvety Christmas tune—the night she had told him she was leaving.

That night she'd wanted to forget her decision to leave. What if she never had a husband or children—would she be any less happy than she felt right now, tearing herself away from the only place she'd ever felt complete?

Her thoughts made no sense, and she rose in the dark and walked to the window. The wind bent the trees while heavy snow pelted the house, and though she could see nothing but moonlit drifts, she could trace the familiar outlines. The lilac bush, the wooden bench swing where she'd sat watching the children play in the fall. Bushes and shrubs that had become like old friends.

Though Paul had his faults, she'd grown to admire his strength and fortitude. He'd lost a wife, yet he'd fought to meet his children's needs even when his work had been long and stressful.

And he'd shown Rose love, too. Maybe not the kind she wanted, but—

As the wind shuddered against the window, a loud crack followed by a heavy thud slammed above her head. She spun around, frightened. Fearing for the children, Rose wrapped a blanket around herself and darted into the hallway. As she dashed to their rooms, she heard Paul bounding up the stairs.

"What was that?" she asked, trying to muffle her voice.

"I think a tree limb fell on the roof. Is everyone all right?"

"I'm checking," she said, veering toward Kayla's room. Paul turned left toward Colin's.

Rose studied the ceiling in the darkness. She saw nothing and felt no wind seeping through a broken roof. Kayla slept soundly. Rose touched her cheek, thanking God as her hand touched the child's cooler skin.

She turned back and met Paul in the hallway.

"All's well there," he said, "but I'd better check the attic." He opened a door in the hallway and snapped on the light. A dim bulb lit the stairway.

Rose stood at the bottom and held her breath.

Paul appeared again and descended the stairs. "No inside damage, but if that wind keeps blowing, I'm afraid that limb will slide and tear the shingles off the roof."

"You'll have to call the owner," Rose said.

He shook his head. "I decided to buy the house, Rose. I signed the paperwork the other day. I was going to surprise you at Christmas."

Surprise her at Christmas? She'd been the one to surprise him first with her leaving. His words inched over her, leaving her with questions. Why would buying the house be a surprise for her?

She started to ask, then stopped herself. The whole thing was too sad to talk about in the middle of the night. Too sad to talk about anytime, for that matter.

To Rose's delight, the next morning Kayla appeared in the kitchen doorway.

"It snowed," she said, panning everyone with a glazed look.

"How are you feeling?" Paul asked.

"I was sick."

"I know. Are you feeling better?"

She nodded. "But I'm hungry."

Rose stepped from the counter, knelt beside the twin and wrapped her arms around her. Kayla rested her cheek on Rose's shoulder. "I'm so happy to see you awake, and I bet you are hungry. I was just beginning to make breakfast." She led the child to a chair and patted it. "You sit, and I'll make you something yummy."

"Pancakes." Kayla licked her lips.

"Everyone loves pancakes," Rose said, winking at Colin.

Paul rose and pressed his hand against Kayla's cheek, then kissed the top of her head. "She feels like my regular girl today."

Kayla gave him a goofy look as if she didn't understand.

Paul didn't explain, either. He wandered into the dining room and looked into the front yard. "I can barely see our cars. The snow has drifted six feet high in places."

"Six feet," Rose said as if disbelieving.

"Looks like it," Paul said, returning to the table. "Right after breakfast I need to get up on that roof and check out the tree. We're not going to get anyone out here for days, and I know it's going to tear up the shingles."

"No way," Rose said, giving him her sternest look. "I'll take the broom after you."

The children giggled, but Paul only shook his head. "Okay. I'll let you climb up there?"

If Rose had her way, no one would be climbing a ladder in this weather. "You'll never dig the ladder out in this mess."

"Want to bet?" He stuck out his hand for a shake. "I'm going to get that tree limb off the roof. It's big."

Rose frowned. "Let's talk about it after breakfast."

As the words left her mouth, she realized she sounded like his wife, giving warnings and orders. She had no business telling Paul what he could do. He didn't respond, and she closed her mouth.

The pancakes were consumed as they came off the griddle. Rose poured more batter until she finally heard their groans that they'd had enough. She sipped her coffee, enjoying the rich flavor and accepting that she'd hopefully get the last pancake. Two were left.

As she sat with her breakfast and a fresh cup of coffee, Paul sent the children to get dressed, then sat beside her. "I know you don't want me on the roof. I understand. But I have to check it out. I promise if it looks like it won't rip off the shingles or cave in the roof, I'll leave it be."

"We can call someone and just see when they can get here."

He pressed his lips together and eyed her. "It's a waste of time. Look at the road. You can't see it, Rose."

For the first time she headed for the front window, and realized Paul was right. The road was lost in the drifts of snow. "Okay. You're right."

He chucked her cheek and walked away. She heard him in the back hallway putting on his coat and boots, then the garage door opened.

"Lord, keep him safe," Rose said.

She hurried up the stairs and met the children coming down.

"Colin, I want everyone to stay inside for now until your dad checks out the tree, and Kayla, I don't want you outside at all today."

They each gave a whiny moan and stomped the rest of the way down the stairs. She let it go and continued to her room to dress in something warm. If Paul was going on the roof, she was going to be next to the ladder.

By the time she stepped outside, Paul had scraped a pathway to the garage. He'd been correct. The drifts that leaned against the house were taller than she was. Rose had never seen snow like this except in photographs or movies.

Paul appeared, dragging the ladder. "What are you doing out here?" He looked surprised.

"You don't think I'm letting you climb on that roof without someone here to hold the ladder."

He shrugged. "I can't argue that one."

Paul propped the ladder against the house, then extended it to its full height. Rose shuddered, looking at how high he had to climb. He stepped away and vanished inside the garage. In a moment he returned with a chain saw, attached to a large strap. He slung it over his head, and her heart stopped.

"Please," she said. "That's dangerous."

"I'll only use it if it's necessary."

She held the ladder, bracing it against her feet in the slippery snow, while he climbed. She watched as he moved upward, one rung after another, until he reached the rooftop. At her angle, she had a poor perspective as to where the tree limb was in relation to the ladder, and she sent up prayers, figuring she'd barrage the Lord with petitions until He brought Paul down safely again.

When he climbed off the ladder, Rose shifted away and backed up so she could see. Her heart rose to her throat when she saw the size of the limb that had fallen. Paul balanced precariously on one knee, his foot propped against the slippery shingles.

He pulled the cord, and the saw sputtered and died.

Next time he gave it a stronger jerk, and she watched him teeter until finally he regained his balance, and the saw roared into action.

Rose looked toward the patio door and saw both children with their noses pressed to the glass watching her look toward the roof. She knew she should go to them and waylay their curiosity, perhaps their fears, but she had too many fears of her own.

As she looked back toward Paul, a large piece of limb rolled along the shingles and dropped to the ground, vanishing in the snowdrift. Another one followed, then another. Her prayers flew to heaven, and each time Paul shifted her heart stood still.

Five or six large logs had fallen to the ground, and she tried calling up to him to beg him to let the rest go, but he was persistent and probably didn't hear her with the roar of the chain saw.

With her attention glued to Paul's progress, she caught a motion above his head. She watched in horror as a large mound of snow slid from higher on the roof and, like an avalanche, surged along the shingles, plunging toward the tree limb.

Rose could do nothing. She let out a scream, but it was too late. The snow came so quickly Paul didn't have time to move.

The mountain of white heaved forward, taking Paul and the chain saw with it.

Panic charged through Rose's body as she raced toward his plummeting form. She stopped, her knees weakening as he hit the logs buried in the snow and his frame was embedded in a snowdrift. When she saw the dark blood staining the crystal snow, she couldn't breathe.

Chapter Thirteen

As Rose's knees hit the ground beside Paul, the patio door opened, and Colin lunged toward her.

"Call 911," Rose shouted, praying the boy didn't see the blood spreading across the snow.

Colin halted in midrun.

"Do you know your address?" Rose called.

He nodded and spun around, bumping into Kayla, who was on his heels.

"Kayla, stay inside," Rose yelled as she turned her attention to Paul.

She shifted the chain saw, then cradled Paul's head against her arm. She used snow to clean the wound and saw a deep cut where the chain saw must have struck. Without thinking, she lowered her head and kissed the spot below the cut, and when she pulled away she saw Paul's eyelids flutter, then open.

"Don't move," she said.

"Did you kiss me?" His words ran together while embarrassment and worry rolled over her.

A faint grin curved his mouth, yet his eyes were glazed with confusion. "What happened?"

Before she could explain, Colin shot through the doorway toward them. "Colin, stay out of the snow, please."

The child stopped, bewilderment mottling his cheeks.

"Did you call?" Rose asked.

He shook his head. "The phone doesn't work."

Her heart sank, and she studied the situation for a moment. "Find my purse, and we'll use my cell phone."

Colin didn't move.

"It's probably in the kitchen or maybe in the bedroom where I slept last night." Rose watched him turn again and head inside.

Through the doorway she could hear an argument ensuing between Kayla and Colin until their voices vanished, but she had no time to question why they were at each other.

"Are you going to tell me what happened?"

Her gaze turned to Paul. "You fell off the roof."

"My head hurts," he said, lifting his hand before she could stop him. When he withdrew it, he saw the blood.

"I'm trying to call 911. You'll need stitches."

His concerned expression vanished. "Rose, an ambulance is not going to get through that snow until it's been plowed."

"Then they can plow it," she said, determined to get him help. Again she used snow to wash the wound so she could take a good look. "It's still bleeding badly. I need to get it to stop."

"We have bandages inside. Let me get up." Paul tried to shift, and as he did, she heard him swallow a moan.

"You might be hurt worse than you think," she said.

"And I also might freeze to death. I prefer having a little pain and getting inside."

She forced him back against the snowdrift and kept her eyes aimed at the door. Finally Colin came through with the cell phone. As he approached them, she could do nothing to block the deep red stain. When he saw it, his eyes widened.

"I'm okay, Colin," Paul said. "You go back inside, and you and Kayla can get out a washcloth and towel so I can wash my face."

"And some bandages," Rose added as she pressed the buttons of her phone. Her heart sank when she realized the battery was dead. Her charger was back at the apartment.

She dropped the telephone into her jacket pocket.

"What's wrong?" Paul asked.

"Dead. Not enough power to call out."

"I forgot mine at work," Paul said.

Rose shifted her body, feeling the cold penetrate her slacks. Her legs felt frozen. "I'll have to help you up."

She eased him into a sitting position, recognizing she wasn't strong enough if he needed more support. "Are you hurting anywhere particularly?"

"How about my pride?"

She shook her head, amazed he still had a sense of humor. "Anything else?"

"My leg. Ankle more specifically, but let me try to stand before you panic." He shifted to stand, but she saw the strain in his face.

"Let me get something. Just stay there." She rose and headed for the patio door while both children hovered there, looking fearful.

"Your dad's okay," she said, patting their heads. "He has a cut on his head and maybe a hurt ankle."

Their eyes welled with tears but neither cried, and

Rose was proud of them. "I need two helpers. Kayla, find a blanket somewhere, and Colin, bring in the desk chair. The one with rollers. Then I'll need your help to get your dad inside."

The twins moved like lightning, and before Rose had a moment to think, Kayla returned with a blanket and Colin with the chair. "Okay, you wait here," she said to Kayla. "Colin, come with me."

The child slipped on his boots and coat, then followed her outside. Rose maneuvered the blanket beneath Paul, and then she and Colin pulled it like a sled to the patio doorway. The last few feet were difficult, since Paul had removed most of the snow, but Colin tossed some onto the cement and made their going easier.

Inside, while she held the chair in place, Paul used it to pull himself upward. Once settled, she rolled it into the kitchen and worked on his head wound. She sent the children on errands, hoping to keep them busy as she tackled the worst.

"I'm praying you don't have a concussion," she said, "but I think the butterfly bandages will work for the cut."

"You were right," Paul said. "I had no business up there without the proper equipment. I'm sorry."

She grinned, hearing his apology. "Too late for that now, but thanks. Women do know a few things."

"I never doubted that," he said, giving her a contrite grin.

Once the butterfly stitches were in place, Rose turned on the teakettle. "You need to get warmed up and get out of these wet clothes." She needed to do the same.

The children returned and hovered around them,

their eyes focused on the bandages and the bloodstains on Paul's collar and matted in his hair.

"I'm fine. Really," Paul said as he tried to stand.

She noted a grimace that flashed across his face, and she knew he'd choked back a yell. "Really. You're fine. That's interesting."

"Daddy," Kayla said, "listen to Rose."

"Or she'll get the broom after you," Colin added.

The children had been clinging to his side, touching him and peering at his face, but the broom comment made them laugh, and Rose felt relieved.

"You heard them. No more misbehaving," Rose said. "I'll wheel you into your room and lay out your dry clothes. Then maybe Colin can help you dress."

Paul looked at her with surprise. "Okay," he said, touching the stitches absentmindedly.

She noted the matted blood. "Later I'll help you wash your hair."

He didn't fight her this time, and she rolled the desk chair into the hallway, struggling as the wheels sank into the carpet, but the twins pushed, too, and finally they maneuvered him into his room. She praised the Lord the master bedroom was on the first floor and not up the stairs as the rest of the bedrooms were.

She followed Paul's directions and located his clean clothing, then left him in Colin's hands.

The chill had permeated her, too, and she hurried upstairs, dressing in slacks and a top she'd kept handy. With dry socks and warm clothes, Rose returned to the kitchen and made a pot of hot chocolate.

When she checked on Paul, he was dressed except for his socks. Colin was struggling to pull them onto his father's feet.

Rose gave the boy a hug and took over. "Hold your breath and hang on." She worked the sock up his foot, and with only a couple of reflexive kicks and one good moan when she covered his left foot, Rose succeeded. She stood back and looked at him. "Not too bad. I think you'll live."

His ankle concerned her, and she prayed he had nothing else seriously wrong that they hadn't spotted. The Lord was merciful, and she trusted Paul to His care.

"You don't happen to own a cane, do you?" she asked.

He gave her a wry smile. "I thought you'd carry one in your handbag. You seem to have everything else."

"Daddy, you're silly," Kayla said, hanging on to the arm of the desk chair.

Rose ignored his attempt at humor. "Think of something we can use for a cane." She left him to think while her thoughts headed elsewhere. "How about an elastic bandage? I want to wrap your ankle. It's swollen and bruised."

Colin darted off, and Rose paused, wondering where he was going.

"I think you'll find what you need in the linen closet," Paul said.

Rose and Kayla pushed the chair back toward the kitchen, and Colin met them halfway, carrying a baseball bat. "Here, Daddy, you can use this to lean on."

"Good job," Rose said, grinning at the child's ingenuity.

She found the elastic bandage and bound his ankle and packed it with ice. Then, relieved, she settled back with the hot chocolate.

"It looks as if we're at the mercy of the telephone

company and the road plow," Paul said. "Otherwise we're stranded."

The kids grinned, and Rose realized they didn't mind the problem now that they knew their dad was okay. They had his captive attention until help came.

"Can we decorate the Christmas tree?" Kayla asked.

"Good idea," Rose said. "We'll start it after lunch. Tomorrow's Christmas Eve. We've waited too long."

When they finished eating, the children raced into the living room, and Rose followed. Together they dragged out the boxes Paul had set against the wall. "Now wait until your dad gets in here."

She returned to the kitchen to find Paul standing with his weight against the baseball bat.

"It hurts," Rose said, seeing the grimace.

He nodded. "I'm sure it's just a sprain. I'll probably feel better tomorrow."

"Let me help," she said, stepping beside him.

Paul rested his arm around her shoulder and used the cane in the opposite hand. "It's nice leaning on you."

"Glad I can help." She wanted to tell him she loved having his arm around her for any reason, but she stemmed the words.

He didn't move, but stood there, and Rose looked at him to make sure he was okay.

"I'm fine," he said, apparently catching her frown. "I was just thinking."

"About what?"

"How it felt to be Sleeping Beauty."

"Sleeping Beauty." It took her a moment for the reference to settle. She felt her skin warm at his meaning. "I'm sorry. It was a reflex. Instinctive."

"Mothering and loving," he said, looking into her eyes. "I would have done the same."

"You mean if I fell off a roof?" Her heartbeat pitched, and she tried to move him forward, but he remained glued to the spot.

"You know what I mean, Rose."

His words sent her heart on a journey, and she struggled to put two coherent words together, but found none. Instead she eased him forward, taking slow steps until Paul was settled in the living room.

She put on another Christmas CD, then strung the lights. Paul sat back with his ice-packed ankle and directed the activities as they hung the ornaments. Rose kept her gaze veering toward Paul to make sure he was all right. He seemed to be, and she sent up a prayer of thanksgiving.

When the last ornament was hung, Rose walked across the room to snap off the lamps so they could view the tree in the darkness. As she passed the bookshelves, her heart stood still. In the place Della's photograph had been, Rose spotted a new one. A picture of her that autumn afternoon. Her face was tilted toward the sun and a red maple leaf had caught in her hair. Amazed, Rose wondered why she'd never noticed the photograph before. She dusted the shelves often. Most important, why was it there?

She turned toward Paul, but he was listening to the children's excited commentary about the tree. Later she might ask, but for now, she snapped off the light and returned to Paul's side.

Their "oohs" sounded in the carol-filled room, and Kayla ran into her arms and hugged her tightly.

"Why am I so honored?" Rose asked, touched by the child's unexpected expression of love.

"I love you," Kayla said, "and the snow kept us all here together so you can never go away from us."

Never go away. Did the child know? Kayla couldn't, but had she sensed Rose's sadness? Rose held back the tears that surged to her eyes. "I love you, too," she said, wanting so badly to say she would never go away, but she couldn't say that to the child.

For the first time that day Rose felt the impact of her future loss. This family, this house, these moments would be gone forever when she walked out the door. Tears pooled in her eyes. Glad she was hidden by the darkness, she brushed them away and excused herself to make dinner.

Alone in the kitchen, Rose sobbed.

Chapter Fourteen

Later that evening Rose packed away the ornament boxes, then shooed the children off to bed. Her mind was filled with the messages she'd heard that night— Paul's cryptic comment and Kayla's open expressions of love.

While preparing their meal, Rose had felt tears rolling down her cheeks as she thought about her decision. Was it better to stay in Little Cloud and face a single, childless life or return to L.A. and leave her loved ones behind? Both meant heartbreak.

Rose climbed the stairs and checked on the children. They'd gone to bed with little grumbling, each excited about the tree decorating and overwhelmed by Paul's fall from the roof. Before she returned to the first floor, Rose located a bottle of pain reliever. She knew Paul was miserable, and she wanted him to sleep well.

When Rose returned to the living room, the lamplight blinked and then returned. "Do you think we'll lose power?" she asked.

"Very possible. The weight of the snow on those lines, especially if it freezes, can be dangerous."

"If this keeps up, it means no Christmas service or Sunday-school program," Rose said.

"We'll hold our own. It's Jesus's birthday."

His suggestion touched her. "Here's some medicine for pain," she said, setting the bottle beside his water glass. "You should take it now."

He reached over and did as she said, washing the pills down with water, then closed the bottle.

Rose crossed the room and opened the fireplace doors. "We might as well have a fire," she said, piling some kindling onto the grate, then lifting on two large logs. She set a fire starter beneath the fast-burning wood and waited for the kindling to ignite. As the fire spread, she settled into a chair across from Paul.

The music filled the room, and Rose leaned back and let the tiring day wash from her body. Paul's fall from the roof had been overwhelming. Fear had raced through her, followed by panic. The experience of both phones not working, no access to the roads, being snow-bound in the woods was alien to her L.A. existence. Yet now as she relived the moments she recalled a sense of challenge and adventure. Neither had been part of her California life—except an occasional trying day on the freeways.

Without warning, Paul grasped the baseball bat and stood.

"Don't hit me," she said, eyeing the makeshift cane and sending him a grin.

He didn't respond, but hobbled to the fireplace and lowered himself to the floor, then patted the carpet.

She didn't move, and he patted it again, except she only heard the sound. The lights had flickered and died.

"Let there be light," Paul said from the floor.

The darkness continued, except for the warm glow from the fireplace.

Rose's first thought was the children. Without electricity, the blower would stop on the furnace. "I'll go up and add a blanket to the kids just in case," she said. "Where's the flashlight?"

"Foyer closet," he said.

She fumbled her way beyond the firelight to the closet. Inside she felt the shelf until her hand touched the light. Soon the beam stretched across the carpet, then the staircase as she made her way up the stairs.

Colin had kicked off his blanket, so Rose tucked it in and covered him with a large quilt. In Kayla's room she stood a moment, seeing the child bathed in the moonlight streaming through the window. Rose covered her with the bedspread and tucked it in, then turned toward the light.

Outside, the moonlight bounced off the snowdrifts, leaving the night in a silver glow. Rose looked into the night sky. Once again the full moon hung above her, round and bright like a beacon. In the past months she'd viewed it as a symbol of her loneliness and singleness, but tonight its shimmering aura led her thoughts in a different direction. As its beams brightened the dark earth, it offered rays of hope to the lost. Rose bowed her head. The Lord knew she was lost, and God's voice told her she needed to find her way home.

Paul had watched Rose's flashlight beam vanish into the darkness and now he waited for her return. His chest tightened, aware of the love Rose had for the twins. She thought of them first in every way. His feelings for her had grown beyond his imagination, and he knew he had to convince her to stay with them in Little Cloud. He loved her too much to let her go.

He waited, and in minutes the flashlight rays bounced along the foyer floor as Rose made her way down the staircase. The light swept into the room, with her only a specter behind it.

She came to his side and draped a quilt over his shoulders. Without his asking again, she sank to the floor close to the blaze. "I think they'll be fine. Heat rises, so it's warmer up there than here. Hopefully the lights will be back on in a few minutes."

"Don't be too hopeful," Paul said. "This is Minnesota, not L.A."

She sat a moment until a faint grin curved her lips.

"What are you thinking?" Paul asked.

"Funny you say that. Earlier I was comparing Little Cloud to L.A."

"No comparison," he said.

"No, but I'm not totally convinced one is better than the other."

"Really?" Her comment caused his pulse to skip. "I thought that you were going back because…" His voice faded, having no ending for her reason.

"'Because' has no answer, Paul. I'm a mixture of incongruity. Go. Stay. I said I'm going, but my heart is fighting me all the way."

Her admission hit him in the solar plexus. "Then why? Why would you leave if you don't have a reason?"

"I have a reason. I—I don't understand it."

Paul felt her shudder. "You're cold." He drew the quilt over her shoulders and drew her closer. "Explain this to me, Rose. Please."

The embers crackled; otherwise there was silence.

Paul didn't push. He fought his desire to direct the conversation, to beg her again to change her mind, to remind her of the loss the children would have, to confess he'd grown to love her. Instead, he prayed that God's will be done. Paul couldn't make change happen without the Lord's blessing. He'd learned that these past months while going to church and by reading the Bible he'd bought weeks ago.

He'd seen changes in the children. They came home from Sunday school singing songs about Jesus. They talked about their mother in heaven with a new kind of comfort he had been unable to give them. Perhaps a comfort he had never experienced until now.

Rose had led them to the Lord through her strong faith. She had led them into a new world, a complete world he hadn't felt in years.

She stirred, and Paul felt her draw in a deep breath, then release a deeper sigh. He stood on the edge of anxiety, longing to understand. Then she shifted closer.

"It's difficult to explain this, Paul. You know the things that hurt me in the past—that gave me a dislike of gossip, a fear of being rejected again and a horror of being pitied again. I feared even you pitied me."

He opened his mouth to speak, but he sensed she had more to say and he swallowed the words.

"I realize it wasn't pity. You were motivated so much by the love of your children. Your proposal, your pleading for me to come to Little Cloud and your begging for me to stay."

"Rose, it was that, but now—"

She pressed her hand on his arm. "I was motivated by the love of your children. I adored them, but…" Her voice faded, and her body trembled.

"But…?" He held his breath. What did she have to say that was so difficult? He lowered her head to his shoulder and nuzzled his chin against her hair. He longed to open his heart, but he sensed Rose had to speak first before he told her the truth about his feelings.

"I loved your children from the beginning. Dear Kayla with all her problems, and Colin with his need to control. They are dear to me, but something else kept me here when wisdom told me to leave."

Paul lifted his head and captured Rose's chin in his palm. He turned her head toward him. "What kept you here?"

"My heart."

He stared at her, bewildered by her meaning. Her eyes searched his and her meaning struck him as pure and perfect as a snowflake.

"I fell in love with you."

Her whisper brushed past his ear, and the words washed over him. "You love me?"

"That's why I have to leave. I didn't believe it at first. I tried to think it was only my imagination. I admired you and respected you—especially how much you adore the twins."

"I've always admired and respected you, but I realized that—"

"Then when I heard that your L.A. executive was a woman, I realized how envious and untrusting I'd become. I thought—"

"Gretchen? Gretchen's like a mother to me."

"I know that now, but when I heard they'd sent a woman, I concocted a romance in my mind. When she was coming for dinner on Thanksgiving, I thought that you were bringing her home to—"

"To introduce her as my lady friend?"

Rose nodded. "I'd misjudged it all, and I knew that I couldn't stay here without ruining my life and yours."

"But Rose, you can't ruin my life now unless you leave. You're what makes life important to me and to the kids."

"You're too kind, Paul. I understand, but I felt I had to tell you." Exposed in the firelight, tears glistened in her eyes.

Paul leaned nearer and kissed away her tears.

"Dearest Rose, I'm not just being kind. I've loved you for so long. One day it all struck me. Our lives aren't complete without you. I was afraid to tell you how I felt because I'd already bungled with my proposal. I knew how you felt about employer-employee romances, and I feared you'd think I was manipulating you to stay."

"Please don't say that now, Paul."

"Don't say it? I have to tell you how much you mean to me. I've asked God to help me find a way to show you."

She lowered her head, then as if struck by a new thought she raised it. "When did you put out the picture of me? The one on the shelf?" Her hand gestured toward the cabinet.

"A while ago. I'd had the photo, but needed a frame."

"I hadn't noticed," she said.

"I hoped you would. You looked so lovely that day. I knew even then that you were special to me. It took me a little longer to realize the woman I'd dreamed about was right under my nose."

"But we're too different. That's part of the problem. You're educated. You've traveled. I'm only—"

"You're only wonderful. You're a born mother.

You're a tender woman with love in your heart. You're beautiful, Rose. You're wise and intelligent."

Her eyes searched his as if trying to believe.

"You kissed me today. I had hoped that it meant what I wanted it to, that there is hope for us."

A bewildered look settled on her face, and Paul prayed that God would help her to understand and believe. "Don't pull away from me now. Believe me. Trust me."

"But you're my boss. I work for you."

"Rose, you're fired."

He tilted her mouth upward, her lips full and pliant, and he lowered his mouth, drinking in her softness and warmth. He'd been alone with no desire for a wife, only the longing for a mother for his children until Rose stepped through the doorway. Then life changed.

He drew Rose closer, deepening the kiss. Rose yielded to his mouth, and she raised her hand to his cheek and brushed the stubble of his whiskers.

At that moment Paul experienced the deepest love that only God could give.

Rose gazed into his eyes. "Let me think, Paul. I'm overwhelmed. I need to grasp all that's been said tonight."

"Trust me, please. I love you."

She nodded, then stood and turned on the flashlight. "I'll help you to your room," she said.

Paul rose and grasped her arm as they followed the beam to his room. After he'd climbed into bed, Rose and the light vanished while Paul lay in darkness.

Chapter Fifteen

The morning light filtered through the window, and Rose sat on the edge of her bed. All night she'd relived Paul's words. He said he loved her. She felt amazed. Part of her wanted to believe and part of her couldn't.

She opened her Bible, asking God's wisdom. She remembered Paul talking about the Scripture that had moved him to realize how much God loved him. She flipped through the pages, scanning Philippians until she spotted the verses Paul had mentioned. "If you have any encouragement from being united with Christ, if any comfort from His love, if any fellowship with the Spirit, if any tenderness and compassion, then make my joy complete by being like-minded, having the same love, being one in spirit and purpose."

When they'd talked, he'd mentioned that human love could be guided by the same qualities—tenderness, comfort, compassion, fellowship and like-mindedness with one spirit and purpose. Wasn't that what she and Paul had done?

In so many ways their relationship was based on the qualities in those verses. Could God have blessed them with this special love? She loved Paul, and she prayed that God would help her accept the truth.

Rose bowed her head, and as her prayer rose to the Lord, she was struck by reality. Whether Paul loved her or not, she knew what she had to do. She rose in the chilly room, dressed and headed to the kitchen, grateful for a gas stove. By the time breakfast was ready, the children and Paul had joined her.

"How's your ankle?" Rose asked, afraid to look in Paul's eyes.

"I have a good nurse," he said. "I'm feeling pretty good. I might go out and see if I can move some of that snow."

"Don't push yourself," she said.

After breakfast they bundled up, and the twins charged out the door to make a snowman. Paul followed, but paused beside Rose, worry filling his face. "How did you sleep?"

"Not well, but I'm fine. I read the Bible this morning, and I've made one decision."

"A decision?"

"I'm not leaving. I'm staying here even if I'm the kids' nanny forever."

Paul grasped her hand and brought it to his lips. "They'll grow up too fast, Rose. Nannies aren't forever. Mothers are."

He turned and stepped through the patio doorway.

Rose's heart tripped. His words were true. *Nannies aren't forever. Mothers are.* She cleaned the kitchen, then made her way to the hidden gifts and wrapped the last of them. Finally she wandered down the stairs with a load of packages to put under the tree.

"Rose, come outside."

"Come and see what we made."

Kayla's and Colin's voices drew her to the patio door. They beckoned, and she grabbed her coat and hurried outside. When she saw their surprise for her, she faltered.

A snowman stood in the yard, adorned with mop-top hair. Rose recognized her flowery silk scarf at its neck and her broom in its hand.

"You made a snow lady," Rose said, grinning at their ingenuity.

"It's a snow mommy," Kayla called.

"A snow mommy." Rose's voice was a whisper. She hid her tears behind her laughter, wiping her eyes with her fingers.

"Look," Colin said. He pointed to a strangely shaped red spot against the snow mommy's chest.

Studying it, she saw it was an apple carved to make a heart.

Kayla giggled. "It's you, Rose. We gave it a heart because hearts stand for love, and you love us."

"I do," Rose said, crouching and opening her arms to the children.

They came barreling toward her, and with their exuberant embrace, she tumbled to the ground as they toppled over her.

"And we love you," Colin said between giggles.

She hugged the children, fighting the tears that rolled from her eyes.

Paul stepped to her side and offered his hand. "Me, too," he said softly in her ear as she stood.

Rose brushed the snow from her slacks, feeling Paul's arm wrap around her shoulders.

"This is serious now," Paul said, brushing his lips against her hair. "We have to talk."

* * *

Paul descended the staircase, pleased that the electricity had been restored earlier in the evening. The children had gone to bed filled with excitement that tomorrow was Christmas Day, and he felt his own kind of anxiety.

He crossed the foyer and looked into the living room, where Rose sat on the floor beside the fireplace in the same spot they'd sat the evening before. The room was lit with the fire's glow and the glint of the tree lights.

His stomach tightened as he entered the room. Rose turned to face him and patted the floor beside her. He stood over her looking down at her slender frame and watched the firelight glint in her tawny hair.

Tonight she looked relaxed, not stressed, as she'd been so often in their crazy mixed-up relationship. Employer-employee-friend. What had he asked of her? Yet she'd come through as the dearest friend in the world. The dearest woman in his life.

He sank beside her and took her hand. "You're staying."

"I am."

He brushed his finger across her cheek. "Do you know that I love you?"

"The kids love me. I saw that today." She lifted his hand to her lips and kissed his fingers.

"And what about me?" he asked.

"I love you. I told you last night."

He stood and drew her up into his arms. "I love you, Rose. The kids love you and I do. You've given us more than anyone could expect. Your time. Your concern. Your love. You've made our lives complete."

He held her against his chest, his arms wrapped around her waist, her lips so near he could taste the mulled cider they'd drunk earlier. "You've made me whole, and now it's your turn. I want you to be my wife."

Her eyes searched his. Then her lips curved into a smile and she closed her eyes, then opened them. "This isn't a dream?"

"It's the whole truth. The beautiful truth. Remember once I promised you anything to come to Little Cloud. Tonight I'm promising my love."

Rose took him by the hand and led him to the window, where the Christmas moon spread its silver light over the snow, and pointed. "You promised me that once. Remember?"

"I guess I did promise you the moon."

"But you gave me even more. You gave me the sun and stars. The whole universe."

Rose looked into the heavens, then back at Paul washed in the silver glow. The man in the moon shone down on them, just as Rose knew God had smiled down on them and guided their paths.

Paul reached into his pocket and pulled out a small box. "It's not a ring. We're still snowbound, but it's an early Christmas present for you."

Rose's heart skipped as she took the box. When she opened it, the gift amazed her—the bracelet she had admired weeks earlier. He'd bought it that long ago for her. "It's beautiful."

She dangled it in the moonlight, admiring the fused translucent glass. "Is this an engagement bracelet?"

"If you say yes."

"I do," she said.

Paul wrapped her in his arms, and his lips touched hers. She rejoiced in the wave of happiness that rolled through her. After the long struggle, God had given her the gift to trust and to believe there was one man who truly loved her.

"The kids," she said once their lips had parted. "What will they say?"

Paul didn't answer, but kissed her again.

Torn wrapping paper spread across the living-room floor. Two new bicycles stood beside the tree, while wooden puzzles, new clothes and games sat nearby. While Christmas music drifted from the speakers, Rose held the macaroni-edged picture frame in her hand. The twins had used markers to color the pasta and Paul had bought the frames. She gazed at the photograph of Paul and the children that they must have taken from the sleeve of photos. They'd given Paul one of her with them in the leaf pile. Their homemade gifts touched her heart.

"Rose and I have one more gift for you," Paul said.

The children dropped what they were doing and looked at him with curiosity.

Her pulse tripping, Rose shifted beside Paul, and he wrapped his arm around her waist. "Last night I asked Rose to be your mother and my wife."

Their gazes shifted to Rose's face.

Rose felt tears welling in her eyes. "I said yes."

"Yes," Colin said, jumping up and bounding toward them.

"Our real mommy?" Kayla asked. "Not a snow mommy."

"Snow mommies melt," Rose said, crouching down to hold Kayla in her arms. "I don't melt. I'll be here forever."

Kayla's eyes widened. "Forever."

Forever, Rose thought, holding the child in her arms. Forever, like the promise of the amazing Christmas moon.

* * * * *

YULETIDE PROPOSAL

Lois Richer

For Barry,
with love and celebration for 30 amazing years.

O God, You have declared me perfect in Your eyes.
—*Psalms* 4:1

Chapter One

"Hello, Brianna."

The past ten years had been kind to her former fiancé.

Though Brianna Benson scrutinized Zac Ender's lean, tanned face, she found no sign of aging to mar his classic good looks. Even more surprising, his espresso eyes still glowed at her with warmth in spite of their past.

"Good to see you," Zac continued, inclining his head to one side, a smile flirting with lips that once, long ago, she'd kissed. He bent slightly to thrust out a hand, which she shook and quickly released.

"Good to see you, too," Brianna replied.

Zac had always bemoaned his height because an incident in his childhood to his knee left him unable to play basketball. To extra tall Brianna, Zac's height was an asset not often found among the boys she'd known in high school.

That was only one of the things she'd once loved about him.

"How are you?" he asked.

"I'd be better if you hadn't called me out of a session with one of my clients," Brianna grumbled. She'd been back home in Hope, New Mexico, for two months. She'd been the psychologist at Whispering Hope Clinic where the high school referred their students for counseling for almost that long. So why had Zac waited until today, at ten past eleven, to renew their acquaintance?

He leaned back on his heels, studying her. "You look great."

"Thanks. You're director of education, huh?" Brianna's nerves skittered at the way he studied her. Why was Zac back in Hope? More important, why was she reacting to him like some teen with a crush? "I didn't realize you'd given up teaching."

"I haven't given up teaching. Just changed my focus to administration." His unblinking stare rattled her. "It's been a long time." He said it as if they'd parted the best of friends when actually she'd run away from him on the morning of their wedding.

She raised one eyebrow. The only defense she could summon to battle the emotions he raised was disdain. "That's why I'm here, Zac? To reminisce?"

"No." His head gave a quick negative shake. "Of course not."

Frustrated that her traitorous pulse was doing double time, that her palms still tingled though she'd released his hand, that yet again she couldn't control something in her messed up world, Brianna sighed.

"So would you please tell me what is so important that I had to leave work on my busiest clinic day to come here?" she asked, except she really didn't need him to tell her because she knew with heart-sinking certainty that it was Cory. It had to be. She'd expected returning to Hope would give her troubled son the fresh start he needed to turn his world around.

"Let's discuss this in private. My office is this way." Zac stood back, waiting for her to precede him.

The warmth stinging Brianna's face had nothing to do with the late-September heat outside and everything to do with the curious eyes of the office staff now fixed on her. She walked past Zac toward the office at the rear of the hall. As she passed, her nose twitched at the familiar pine scent of his aftershave. Some things never changed.

"Have a seat." He sat down behind his large, austere desk only after she was seated. That was Zac, manners all the way. His mother's influence. If only her mother had been like that—caring instead of trying to force her daughter to give up her dream for a business she detested.

You can do anything, Brianna. You just have to believe in yourself.

Zac's words echoed from those halcyon days. But there wasn't much else to remind her of the shy, geeky boy who'd tutored her through junior and senior year so she could win a scholarship to college. Even his bottle-bottom glasses were gone, revealing the hard straight lines of his face. This mature Zac was confident and completely at ease.

"I don't want to say this, Brianna," he began, tenting his fingers on his desktop.

Her fingers tightened on the arm of her chair.

"Your son, er, Cory." He paused.

"Zac, I know who my son is." She steeled herself. "Get on with it, please." Her heart cried at the thought of Cory messing up this last opportunity.

"He was on drugs in school today."

"What?" Brianna gaped at him in disbelief. This was the very last thing she'd expected.

"Yes. In fact, Cory was so wound up, he hit another student in the hallway. Or tried to. Fortunately he missed and passed out on the floor." Zac's voice dropped forcing her to lean forward to hear. "I was really hoping drugs would not be one of the issues here."

What had she brought her son home to?

"Cory doesn't do drugs."

"He took something today." A touch of irritation dimmed Zac's dark brown eyes.

"Is he all right?" She breathed a little easier at his nod and began summoning the courage to go to battle for her son—again—when Zac continued.

"He's a little groggy, but the school nurse assures me the drug has almost completely worn off."

"Cory doesn't use drugs. I mean it, Zac." Brianna held up a hand when he would have spoken. "You've seen his record. He's made a lot of mistakes, but drugs are not one of them."

"Yes, Cory said that, too." Zac leaned back, face inscrutable.

"He did?" She narrowed her gaze. "When?"

"When I talked to him a little while ago."

"Without me present?" she asked sharply.

"I was acting as guardian for the child, Brianna," Zac defended. "Not as an enforcer, or policeman—to give him a penalty. I need to get to the bottom of this, and Cory provided some perspective." He paused. "What I'm going to tell you now is off the record."

"Okay." Brianna nodded, confused.

"I believe Cory was tricked into taking something. He said someone gave him a drink. I discussed his symptoms with a doctor friend who works with emergency-room overdoses in Santa Fe. He suggested Cory may have been given a powerful psychotic." The name of the drug made her gasp.

"That's a prescribed substance!"

He nodded. "The police tell me they haven't seen it in town before."

In spite of the word *police,* something about Zac's attitude reassured her, though Brianna wasn't sure why. "What happens now?"

Zac was silent for several moments. His steady brown gaze never left her face.

"Are you suspending Cory?" she demanded.

"Not at the moment."

"Then—" She arched her eyebrow, awaiting an explanation.

"I've been through this before, Brianna."

"Through what?" She'd expected anger from Zac. Loathing. Disgust. Something different than this—understanding. "You mean you've seen drugs in school before?"

"Yes." Zac nodded. His jaw visibly tensed. The words emerged in short clipped sentences. "Several years ago I taught a student who was also given drugs without his knowledge."

"Oh." She waited.

"Jeffrey had a lot of difficulties at home and at school. The high he got from that one time made him feel he'd escaped his problems, I guess." Zac shook his head, his voice tight with emotion. "It wasn't long before he became addicted."

"I'm sorry," she said to break the silence. Zac clearly struggled to tell her his story.

"Jeffrey called me the night before he died." Zac licked his lips. Beads of moisture popped out on his forehead. "I think he was looking for a reason to live, but I couldn't talk him out of committing suicide." His ragged voice showed the pain of that failure lingered.

"How sad." She ached for the anguish reflected in Zac's dark gaze. He'd always been determined to help students achieve. This tragedy would have decimated him.

"Jeffrey was the brightest kid in the school." Zac's mouth tightened. "He'd already been accepted at Yale. He had his life before him, but because someone slipped him that drug, his potential was wasted."

Brianna didn't know what to say so she remained quiet, silently sharing the grief that filled his eyes and dimmed their sparkle. Suddenly the earlier awkwardness she'd felt didn't matter.

"It's okay." She offered the soothing response she often used at the clinic.

"It's not." Zac's shoulders straightened. His chin lifted and thrust forward. "It's not okay at all. That's why I have to nip this in the bud now."

"Nip this—I don't know what you mean." Dread held her prisoner. Something was going on behind that dark gaze. Would her son be expelled? Would Zac punish her son because of what she'd done?

"I refuse to allow drugs to ruin another young life. Not Cory's. Not anyone's." Zac blinked. His eyes pinned hers. "I'm going to need your help, Brianna."

"My help?" She gaped at him. "I'll certainly talk to Cory, get the whole story and help him understand how easily drugs can cause damage we never expect. But what else can I do?"

"More. A lot more, I hope." Zac rose and began pacing behind his desk, his long legs eating up the distance in two strides. Nervous energy. He'd always been like that. "Let me explain. I came here—actually I specifically chose Hope because school test scores are rock-bottom, the lowest in the state."

She listened attentively as he haltingly told her of the purpose he'd set for himself since Jeffrey had died. Zac spoke of making a difference, of helping kids find their own potential so that drugs weren't even a consideration. His words reminded Brianna of his youthful eagerness to teach when they'd both been students at college, when their goals had been the same—to help kids uncover their potential.

"You must have seen the test scores in the files of the students you've counseled at the clinic," he said.

"Yes." Brianna nodded. "Pathetic."

"Last year was my first year in this job and it was an eye-opener. I found a major lack of initiative, total boredom and a host of other issues. But I never found drugs."

Brianna grew engrossed in his story of trying to create change until she glanced at her watch and realized she didn't have much time to see Cory before her next appointment.

"I'm sorry it's been so difficult, Zac," she interrupted, rising. "Though I don't know the first thing about combating drugs in schools. Education is your field." His slow smile and those bittersweet-chocolate eyes, glittering with suppressed excitement, made her pause. "What?"

"You know a lot about motivating people, Brianna. You always did, even before you started practicing psychology. Inspiring people is in your blood." He held her gaze with his own. "I doubt that's changed."

Surprised that he'd harked back to a past that could only hold painful memories for both of them, Brianna frowned.

"Remember when there were no funds for our school choir to go to that competition?" Zac's grin flashed. "You were the one who roused everybody and got them to pitch in and raise money for the trip."

"You want me to raise money?" she asked dubiously, confused by his excitement.

"No," he said and continued as if she hadn't interrupted. "When Jaclyn's sister died, you were the one who made a schedule to ensure her friends would be with her during the first hard days after the funeral. You were the one who helped Jaclyn solidify her goal for Whispering Hope Clinic, and you were the one who kept that dream alive even though your other partner left town."

"It wasn't just Jaclyn's goal. Jessica was my dearest friend. I vowed to keep her memory alive by making sure no other kid ever went through what she suffered because of a lack of medical help. That's why I came back to Hope, to help kids," she said.

"I know." Zac smiled. "You're an encourager, Brianna."

What was with the trip down memory lane? It sounded as if Zac was praising her, but that couldn't be. Brianna had jilted him!

"You're a motivator who inspires, and you're very, very good at it. I've always admired that about you."

Admired her? Brianna bristled, irritated that his

memory was so selective. The words spurted out without conscious thought.

"If you admired me so much, how come you betrayed me the night before our wedding?"

That was so not the thing she wanted to say to Zac Ender after ten long years. Brianna clapped a hand over her mouth and wished she'd never answered his summons this morning.

"I—wh-what?" Zac's face was blank, his stern jaw slack.

Brianna had to escape.

"Look, I have to go. I have another appointment." She grabbed her purse and headed for the door. "Perhaps we can talk about this again another time," she murmured.

"Count on it."

The firm resolve behind his words startled her into turning to look at him.

"We're not finished, Brianna."

She wasn't sure whether that was a threat or a promise and she didn't want to consider either at the moment. For some reason she couldn't figure out, Zac still got to her. She needed time to get her defenses back up.

"I'll talk to Cory," she promised and left.

Brianna breathed deeply as she headed back to the clinic. Once there she paused a moment to study the exterior of the building that housed Whispering Hope Clinic and to remember how the dream had started. Jessica's cancer had been diagnosed too late because of a doctor shortage in Hope. As they watched the disease decimate her, Jessica's sister, Jaclyn, Brianna and their friend Shay had made a pact to one day return to this little town in New Mexico and open a medical clinic for kids to ensure no child ever went without help again. Jaclyn was now the pediatric physician at Whispering Hope Clinic. Brianna was a child psychologist and hopefully Shay would soon join them to offer physiotherapy.

Brianna's mother had never understood how deeply Jessica's death had affected her daughter, or how that death had prompted Brianna to volunteer in the hospital's children's ward. But it was there Brianna had learned to listen. That's what she'd been doing on the school steps one afternoon with Shay and Jaclyn. A teacher had later commented on her ability to encourage, and then urged Brianna to consider becoming a counselor. Desperate to escape her mother's expectation that she take over the family business, Brianna focused on her own plan—attend college, get her doctorate and return to Hope to keep her vow. Her mother's refusal to help her reach that goal sent Brianna to seek help from the smartest kid in school, Zac. Once she'd thought he loved her but his perfidy had sent her away from Hope and she'd struggled to achieve her goal on her own.

Now that she was finally back in Hope, fulfilling the dream she'd cherished for so long, Brianna could not afford to get sidetracked by handsome Zac Ender.

Zac ran every evening after sunset, when the community of Hope was nestled inside their houses with their families around them. Usually he used the lonely time to review his progress in reaching his goals. But tonight his thoughts wandered back ten years to a time when he'd been so certain life couldn't get any better; when Brianna Benson said she loved him and he'd loved her.

Zac knew now that he'd been deceiving himself. What did he know about loving a woman? He hadn't had a father growing up, nobody to teach him anything about relationships, especially how to be the kind of husband Brianna needed. He'd always had a social disadvantage. Those first few years after the car accident that had killed his father had left Zac so badly injured he'd had to endure ten years of surgeries just to walk again. Maybe that's when the lingering feelings of abandonment had taken root; maybe he was a loner because he'd never had a role model to show him how to become a man who could open up to a woman, to expose his deepest fears and his worst scars and trust that she would still care for him in spite of everything. Maybe that lack of inner harmony was why he never felt God had any particular use for a man like Zac Ender.

But for that tiny space in time ten years ago, Zac had believed marriage to pretty Brianna was the answer to his prayers. Then, her long, coffee-colored curls had framed her heart-shaped face. Her perfect white smile had engaged everyone and her hazel eyes had sparkled gold glints in their green depths as she'd cheered him on. Zac had bought into her dream that he could finally shed his inhibitions and open up to people as she did, without freezing up. For a little while he imagined it was possible to shed the inner lack of confidence which had branded him a laughingstock from the first awkward day his health had improved so much he'd finally been granted permission to quit homeschooling. He'd walked into Miss Latimer's seventh-grade math class full of excitement and found he couldn't answer a question he'd studied two years earlier. Instead he'd stuttered and stammered until Miss Latimer had called on someone else. Even now, all these years later, the sting of the other kids' snickers and scorn still caused a mental flinch. As time passed, Zac had accepted their branding of the nerd who never fit in.

But in college, Brianna tantalized him with a self-concept that hinted at the possibility of him becoming poised and able to communicate in any situation. Though Zac had improved his communication skills thanks to Brianna's tutelage, he now recognized that back then, inside, in the recesses of his heart, he'd never outgrown being that ashamed, embarrassed kid who couldn't use words to express what was on his mind. Secretly, even then, he'd always feared that one day the vivacious, energetic and exuberant Brianna would realize he could never be the outgoing husband she wanted, that God simply hadn't made him that way. The day her dad told him Brianna had run away from their wedding, the bubble of Zac's pretend world burst.

Now, ten years later, Brianna had changed, and not just by cutting her hair into a pixie style that framed her face and made her eyes the focal point. Zac had changed, too. He knew who he was and exactly what his failings were. He *was* a nerd and he didn't fit in. God didn't mean for him to be a missionary or a minister. He didn't gift Zac with social abilities. Zac still struggled to speak in public. Certainly God didn't expect him to express his faith publicly, other than by attending church. Zac had no illusions about God ever turning him into a public figure. But Zac had a plan. And he'd done what he planned, gotten his degrees, advanced his career. He'd set very high goals for himself. None of them included romance. He had no intention of failing twice.

But now Zac had reached all his objectives save one. It was time to climb the final rung and prove to the world that nerd or not, Zac Ender wasn't a failure. It was time to make his move from delivering education to formulating curriculum. To do that, he needed success. He'd chosen Hope High School as his proving ground.

Success in the only field he was good at was achievable, particularly if he could get Brianna's help.

Zac thought he'd feel awkward with her today. But after the first few moments he hadn't. It seemed natural to seek the opinion of the school division's psychologist about a matter relating to school issues. He'd kept things cool and businesslike between them. No emotion, no harking back to their past mistake.

Until she'd made that comment "How come you betrayed me the night before our wedding?"

Zac jogged up his driveway and made his way to the back deck. He stretched out, gasping for breath as her words played over and over. Finally, when his breath evened, when he'd settled into a patio chair with a bottle of water and still no explanation for her comment arose, he decided it didn't matter.

Their past was over and so was any relationship he'd had with Brianna. It was the future he had to focus on. He didn't intend to waste a second of it rehashing who had done what. She'd come home to Hope. At the first job opportunity Zac intended to leave.

In the meantime he would seek Brianna's help for the school, he'd work toward straightening out her son, but he would not allow any of his old feelings for her to take root. He couldn't. Because some things never changed.

Ten years had proven nerdy Zac Ender was still not the man Brianna Benson wanted.

Chapter Two

"I'm leaving now, RaeAnn—"

Brianna stopped midsentence, surprised to see Zac in her office doorway.

"Hi." He grinned.

"Hello. Uh, I'm just on my way to the nursing home. Mom needs..." She frowned. "Did we have an appointment?"

"No." Zac turned, picked up something and carried it in. "Since you declined my offer of lunch, twice in the past two days, I might add," he reminded, one eyebrow arched, "I figured you must be too busy to go out, so I brought lunch to you." He set the basket on her desk and began unloading it. "Voilà."

Wonderful aromas filled the room, catching Brianna off guard.

"Uh, that's really nice, Zac." She blinked. "But—"

"I'll drop off whatever your mom needs on my way back to the office. Okay?" He stood waiting, looking every bit the professor his friend Kent always called him.

"But—"

"I really need to talk to you, Brianna. Today." Clearly Zac wasn't leaving.

Brianna decided it was best not to argue given that everyone who was still in the waiting room had probably seen or heard his arrival. Hope wasn't a big town. She could imagine news of his visit to her office would spread like the flu that currently kept Jaclyn so busy. If the intense scrutiny the townsfolk gave her now was what Zac had to endure after she left, Brianna was amazed he'd ever returned.

Why *was* he back? It couldn't be just the failing students. According to the television reports, there were failing students all over the country. Why had he chosen to return to Hope?

"Have a seat." Zac pulled forward a small table and snapped a white tablecloth in place.

"Where did you learn to do that?" She stared as he set the table with a flourish.

"I ran out of funds before I finished my PhD so I waited tables." He grinned. "Why do you look so surprised? As I recall, you always told me I had to get out in public more to develop my poor communication skills."

She had, many times. But Brianna did *not* want to hark back to those days and be reminded of the many other things they'd said to each other, especially their promises. So she waited until he'd finished, took the seat he indicated and accepted the plate he offered.

"This is about Cory, isn't it? I did talk to him and he still denies deliberately using drugs."

"I know. We'll get to that," he promised. "For now let's eat."

She took a bite. Chicken salad—her favorite.

"This is really good. I've been to all the food places in town and I never saw this on the menu." Brianna savored the hint of lime. "I haven't had a decent chicken salad since I left Chicago. So where in town did you get it?"

"I made it," Zac answered.

"You?" She stared in disbelief. "But you never cooked." That was a stupid thing to say. In the past ten years, Zac had probably done a lot of things he never used to, just as she had.

"The cook at the restaurant where I worked couldn't read. I taught her. She taught me how to make stuff like this." He shrugged. "You used to eat chicken salad a lot in college. I figured you might still like it."

"I love it." As thoughtful as he'd always been, Brianna mused as she bit into a roll. She frowned, then held it up, looking at him with eyebrows raised. "This, too?"

"Nope. Sorry." He shrugged. "Just not that talented."

"Thank goodness." She made a face. "I was beginning to feel intimidated."

"Hardly." He poured a cup of iced tea from a thermos he'd brought. "Nobody intimidates Brianna Benson."

Brianna stared into Zac's face, unsure of whether he'd meant that as sarcastically as it sounded.

"How is your mother, by the way?" he asked.

"Fine." Brianna let his previous comment go. Zac was always sincere. If he were trying to get a dig at her, he'd do it openly. "She told me you've stopped to see her several times."

"I go to the nursing home a few times a week to visit Miss Latimer. She was so good to Mom before she died that I try to repay the favor." For a moment Zac peered into a distance as if remembering the sweet gentle mother who'd encouraged him through countless surgeries after a car accident that had killed his dad and left five-year-old Zac with multiple injuries. "How is your father?" he asked. "I haven't seen him lately."

"Dad's doing better since his heart attack. He visits Mom a lot." Brianna didn't add that she didn't understand why her father went so faithfully when it seemed all her mother did was carp at him.

"I'm sure he's glad you're back."

"I guess. It seems weird to be living at home again, but Cory does the yardwork and I try to keep the house up. We're managing." She finished her salad and sipped her tea, scrounging for the courage to ask the hard questions. Finally she just blurted it out. "Why are you here, Zac?"

For a moment she thought she saw regret rush over his face. Which was silly. Granted it had been years, but she'd pushed into adulthood with Zac and grown to understand him. He was the type of man who never regretted his decisions. He thought through everything, weighed the pros and cons and made his choices only after he'd done a complete analysis. He didn't have regrets.

So what did he want with her?

"What did you mean when you said I'd betrayed you?" Zac looked straight at her and waited for an answer. A frown line marred the perfection of his smooth forehead.

"It doesn't matter. Let's forget the past and deal with now." Brianna took control of the conversation, desperate to avoid delving into the past again. "You want to find out who is giving out drugs and stop the spread of them in the school. I get that."

"Oh, I want a lot more than that, Brianna." Zac's voice oozed determination. "I want the students in

Hope's schools to shake off their apathy and start using the brains God gave them. I want them to begin looking at the future with anticipation and eagerness."

"But—" Brianna closed her lips and concentrated on listening. When Zac became this serious it was better to let him just say it.

"Do you know that less than one percent of the students graduating from Hope High School go on to college?" Zac huffed his disgust. "And no wonder. They have no interests. There's no choir, no debate club, no science club, no language club. Everything's been discontinued. And regular class attendance is a joke. *That's* what I want to change."

Brianna blinked at Zac's fierce tone. "Okay, then."

"And I want you to help me do it."

"Me?" She could say no more because he interrupted again.

"I am not a motivator, Brianna." Determination glittered in his eyes.

"That's not true," she said firmly. Zac had motivated her time after time when he'd tutored her to win a college scholarship and all through the courses that followed. *You can do anything you want,* he'd repeatedly insisted.

"If there were even a spark of interest, I could work with that." He frowned at her. "But throw drugs into the mix and the challenge expands exponentially. I need a big change, something that will grab the students' attention."

Brianna didn't know what to say. Zac sounded so forceful, so determined. Intrigued by this unexpected side of him, she decided to hear him out.

"I know you haven't been here long, but think about

the kids you've seen at the clinic." Zac's brown eyes narrowed. "Have you spoken with any who are excited about their future?"

"Uh, no."

"No." Zac's cheeks flushed with the intensity of his words. "The world is theirs for the taking but they don't care. They're completly unengaged. Truthfully, so are most of their teachers. They don't want to be, but you can only live with apathy for so long before it seeps into your attitude." He exhaled and stared straight at her. "What we need is something to ignite interest so kids, including Cory, can get excited. That's the only alternative I know to the pervasiveness of drugs."

Brianna blinked. Wow. The old Zac had not been a man of words. This was the longest speech she'd heard him give and his passion was evident.

Of course she knew all about Zac's teaching ability, not just from firsthand experience when he'd patiently tutored her, but she'd seen it while they'd studied for their undergrad degrees. Over and over she'd witnessed the way he'd throw himself into explaining a subject. In those days he'd never accepted her praise or seen his ability to instill interest as unique, but it was his skill as a teacher that had taught her to focus on what she wanted and channel her energy into getting it. He called her a motivator back then, too, but he'd been an encourager for her.

If only Cory could find someone like—

Zac.

In a flash of understanding Brianna realized that Zac was exactly who Cory needed to help him find his way. She'd worked hard to be both mother and father to her son, but she'd failed him somehow. Still, this wasn't the time to stand by and let drugs or anything else ruin his chance to begin again. Brianna needed help.

But Zac?

Brianna had thought she knew what it took to raise a child properly—exactly what she'd always yearned for. Love, and lots of it. But the older her son became, the more Brianna's doubts about her parenting ability grew. Love wasn't breaching the growing distance between them. She was failing her own son.

Still—Zac as Cory's mentor? He wasn't even in the classroom anymore. Brianna spared a moment to wonder why Zac, who had teaching running through his blood, had chosen to move to administration.

"Will you help me, Brianna?" Zac's face loomed inches from hers.

The earnest tone of his voice made her blink out of her memories.

"Uh, help you—do what exactly?" Every sensitive nerve in Brianna's body hummed when he leaned close. In ten years she hadn't given as much thought to their past as she had since seeing Zac the first day in his office. And she didn't like the feelings it brought. "Look, Zac, I don't think—"

Brianna stopped. How did you tell your ex-fiancé you didn't think it was a good idea for you to work with him because he still made you feel things?

Her heart raced, pitter-pattering like any high-school junior's did whenever she saw the local heartthrob. She was nervous, that's all. After all, this man was asking a lot of her, and he'd betrayed her once.

"Listen, Brianna. Last night I learned that Eve Larsen had overdosed on drugs." Zac tented his fingers.

"Jaclyn called me in for a consult." She frowned. "What has that to do with Cory?"

Zac sat back, shifted, and then finally lifted his gaze to meet hers.

"Until Cory's incident I had no idea that Hope—that the school—that *we* had a drug problem."

"Maybe you don't."

"It's the start of one. Hear me out, Brianna." Zac stared at her as if she had something smeared over her face. "I've worked where the schools become infested with drugs. They creep in and then take over if nobody stops it. Once they're in place, it's desperately hard to get rid of a drug problem and loosen their grip on the student population. Believe me, I've tried."

"So?"

"So when Cory's case was thrown at me, I knew I couldn't ignore it, not when I'm responsible for the rest of the students. He's a very smart kid, Brianna, but he needs a challenge, something that tests his current beliefs about the world. He needs to be forced to use that brain." Zac paused, his glance holding hers. "As I understand it, so far Cory's been involved in misdemeanors, petty stuff—minor theft, nasty pranks, breaking his curfew—the kind of things that have repeatedly sent him to juvenile court."

"Yes." She was ashamed to hear Zac say it.

"And before you moved here, his last act was to join a gang. Not exactly the remorse a judge is looking for, which is probably why he gave Cory until Christmas to clean up his act and threatened him with juvenile detention if he doesn't."

"That's what the judge said to me," Brianna admitted.

"So you thought you'd move here, and Cory would

turn around." Zac leaned forward, holding her gaze with his intense one. "I'm very afraid that Cory's not going to find the challenge he needs in Hope, Brianna. Not the way the school is now."

Brianna sat back, concern mounting as she absorbed the impact of Zac's words. She understood what he wasn't saying. She'd arrived at Whispering Hope Clinic believing her work here would be much easier than her old job. But in the past few weeks she'd begun to question her ability, to wonder if she'd ever get the response she needed in order to help these kids.

"I know a little about drugs," she murmured. "I did some practicum work with kids who were using. For most of the clients I saw then, the best I could offer was a listening ear."

"Don't you want to do more for Cory, much more?" Zac remained quiet, waiting for her to assimilate what he'd said.

In that silence, Brianna recognized the depth of his concern. His brow was furrowed—fingers clenched, shoulders rigid. The Zac she remembered only worried when something was out of his control.

"Do you think the drug situation in Hope is so bad that Cory's future is out the window?" she asked, nerves taut.

"Not yet." Zac shook his head.

"Then what are you saying?" she asked, holding back her fear.

"I'm saying that without something to counteract the drugs—and soon—there's potential to ruin a lot of lives, including Cory's. I'm asking for your help to create that counteraction."

"How?" she asked cautiously.

"I'm not sure yet. That's the problem." Zac dragged a hand through his short hair, a familiar gesture that showed his frustration with having to go outside himself and his resources to accomplish something. He glared at her, his eyes intent. "When it comes to administration I'm the best you'll find."

"And humble, too," she teased. Zac glared. "Sorry. Go on."

"I can set the rules. I can find f-funding for programs. I can insist the teachers go beyond the usual to meet student needs..." The stutter proved Zac was moving well out of his comfort zone with his plea for help.

"But?" she prodded, confused by his words and his manner. Belligerent but beseeching.

"But I can't get inside their heads." His eyes glittered with suppressed emotion.

Suppressed emotion? Cool analytical Zac?

"I insisted the board hand over student counseling to Whispering Hope Clinic, to you, because the kids need somebody who's engaged in their world, not a visiting counselor who will listen to them for an hour here or there, then disappear. They'll see you on the street, in the café, at the grocery store. And they'll know you are interested in them because that's who you are. You're a genuine nurturer, and they'll recognize that." He exhaled heavily.

"Thank you," Brianna murmured, surprised by his generosity.

"I'm the authority figure. But you—you're outside the school system, new in town, fresh from the big city. They'll accept ideas from you. That won't be a problem."

"A problem for what?" She felt totally confused.

"For getting rid of the apathy that shrouds Hope. You don't carry any baggage about Hope."

"I don't? You're dreaming, Zac." Brianna glared at him, hoping to remind him of their past.

"I meant preconceptions about these kids that would block you from seeing potential in them." Their gazes locked before he looked away. "Knowing you, I'm pretty sure you're brimming with ideas of what you want to accomplish in your practice. Innovation. Change." He nodded. "That's what I want, too."

Brianna now had an inkling of where Zac was going with this and she didn't like it. She did not want to work with him. She did not want to rehash all her old feelings of regret and rejection and get bogged down in them. Mostly she didn't want to go back to those horrible hours and days after their almost-wedding when she'd struggled with the rightness of her decision to leave Hope and Zac.

"Just spell out what you want from me, will you, Zac?"

"Okay, I will." He inhaled. "I need a plan to get these kids motivated. Hope isn't like it was when we grew up here, Brianna." He hunched forward, his face as serious as she'd ever seen it. "These kids aren't gung ho about their future."

"Not all of our peers were when we were growing up, either," she reminded.

"Maybe not, but the vast majority of this generation of Hope's kids have stopped imagining bigger or better. I want you to help me change that."

Brianna stared at him, amazed by the passion in his voice.

"Aren't you going to say anything?" he grumbled.

"I don't know what to say," she admitted. "It's a

laudable goal and I wish you success, but beyond that, I don't see what I can do. I've already got a lot on my plate," she reminded. "I've barely started at the clinic."

"You'll be busy there. Because you represent hope." He nodded. "That's exactly what I want to give these kids, including Cory. Hope." His voice dropped, his eyes melted. "Please, Brianna. Help me do that."

She'd said that to him so many times in the past. *Help me, Zac.* And every time Zac had patiently helped solve her issue—whether it was schoolwork or peer issues. He even let her bawl on his shoulder when her mom's controlling threatened to destroy her dreams, though she'd been too embarrassed to tell him the truth about the rift between her and her mother. Yet through all her problems, Zac had always been on her side.

Until the day before their wedding.

Brianna veered away from that, back to the present.

"You have to get back to work and so do I. Let me think about it, Zac." When he would have protested she cut him off. "You've obviously been considering this for a while, but it's all new to me. I don't know that I can take on something else until I've got my world settled a little better."

"What's your primary objection?"

"We have a past," she said bluntly.

"So?" His chin jutted out.

"You must remember we seldom agreed on how things should be done."

"I remember. And I remember we made it work anyway." A crooked smile tipped his lips. His grin made her blush.

"Yes, well." She coughed, searching for composure. "You'd want to be rid of me after our first argument. I can't afford any negativity. This is my career and I've worked really hard for it." She tried to soften her words. "It simply wouldn't work, Zac. I'm sorry."

"You could make it work, Brianna. You always had ten irons in the fire and you never had a problem." His voice dropped to a more intimate level as his gaze searched hers. "The past is over. There's nothing between us now, after all these years. What happened when we were kids isn't going to affect me now. How about you?"

His words stung, though they shouldn't have.

Nothing between us after all these years.

Her fingers automatically lifted to touch the chain that held the engagement ring he'd given her one Christmas Eve, hidden beneath the fabric of her blouse. She recalled the many times she'd been down, on the verge of quitting, and had touched that ring, mentally replaying Zac's voice encouraging her to focus on what she wanted and go for it. He didn't know it, but he'd gotten her through so many hard times.

"Don't say no, Brianna. Next weekend is Homecoming. It could be the kickoff for a new plan. Think about it until tomorrow," he begged. "That would still leave us a week to plan something."

"Why does inspiring these kids mean so much to you?" she asked curiously.

"Because of Jeffrey." His voice was raw.

She frowned, not understanding.

"I failed him." Zac's tightly controlled voice held fathoms of pain. "I don't want any more kids on my conscience."

His anguish wrenched Brianna's heart, but the thought of working with him made her knees knock.

"All I can promise is I'll think about it." Brianna rose.

"Good enough." He rose, too.

"Thank you for lunch. It was very nice." *Nice?* It was the most interesting lunch she'd ever had. And that's what worried her.

"You *can* help, Brianna." Zac touched her arm, and then as her skin burned beneath his fingertips, he let his hand fall away. He gathered and stored his things. "Please consider it seriously."

Brianna nodded, handed over the package for her mother when he insisted and watched him leave. Her caseload at the clinic left little time to think about what Zac had said until later that night when, after another argument about his curfew, Cory finally went to bed. She tried to talk to her dad but surprisingly he encouraged her participation with Zac.

"Let the past go, Brianna. Otherwise it will eat you to death."

If it were only that easy.

When he retired and she was alone, Brianna pulled out all the arguments and pieced them together in her head.

Zac made a good case, but despite his intensity and passion, she had a hunch he hadn't told her all his reasons for wanting this project. And forget what he'd said about their past being over; their past was a minefield of things not said. Resentment stirred like a boiling cauldron inside her. Zac, no doubt, carried his own grudges. Sooner or later he'd want to see her pay for running out on him.

Brianna ached to forget the past, but seeing Zac again revived the sense of betrayal she still felt, made worse since Jaclyn had announced her pregnancy. She and Kent were building their future. What was Brianna's future? Cory would grow up, leave and she'd be alone.

She knew love like what Kent and Jaclyn shared

wasn't for her. She'd given that up when she'd left Hope ten years ago. That's why she married Cory's father, because it didn't involve her heart. But she was finally doing the one thing she'd dreamed of all her life—counseling kids. She would not be swayed from that goal.

Like a movie, the night of their rehearsal dinner replayed in her mind.

You're right, Mrs. Benson. We'll stay in Hope for a while. Brianna will work in your interior-design store, maybe even take over for you.

With those few words Zac had derailed her dreams, broken every promise he'd made her and destroyed her faith in his integrity. He hadn't known all the details of her battles with her mom, but he had known that Brianna never wanted to return to the store when she'd left after high school, despite her mother's determination that she do so. And yet, he'd promised her mother Brianna would do the one thing she'd always fought against. He'd betrayed her.

Now he wanted her help.

How could she say yes after he'd destroyed the trust she had in him?

How could she say no when he was trying to help kids—kids like Cory?

Sighing, Brianna pulled out her Bible and read a couple of chapters. But they were just words. God, as usual, seemed far away. Still, ever hopeful, she reached out.

"What do I do, Lord?"

The empty silence left her aching with the familiar feelings of heavenly abandonment. Where was God when she needed Him?

It was going to be another sleepless night.

Chapter Three

There were very few times in his life that Zac regretted his actions. Yesterday's plea to Brianna ranked right up there.

He stabbed the button on his phone that paged his secretary.

"Tammy Lyn, would you get me the number of that counseling outfit in Las Cruces, please?" Zac would find his own solutions. Because somehow, he was going to get that state job.

"I will. And I have Brianna's office on line two. She wants to see you between her appointments tomorrow. Do you have a time preference?"

She was going to refuse. Zac was surprised by the rush of disappointment that swamped him. Had he really been looking forward to working with his former fiancée—the one who'd caused him so much embarrassment?

And why *had* Brianna run away on their wedding day? Zac wasn't sure he believed her mother's explanation that Brianna had realized she was too immature for marriage.

"Zac?" Tammy Lyn's impatient reminder snapped his daydream.

"Sorry." He swallowed, firmed his voice. "Three o'clock. I've got that board meeting at five."

"Okay, we'll try for that." Tammy Lyn clicked off the intercom.

Zac wondered how Brianna would phrase her refusal. She'd probably try to poke around in his brain first, wanting to figure out what he hadn't said yesterday. Guilt made him shift uncomfortably.

He hadn't told her his goal of attaining the state job when she'd questioned his reasons for asking for her help. And he should have. Initiating a program to motivate kids that resulted in higher test scores would certainly improve his chances of getting a job developing curriculum, which sounded pretty selfish. But truthfully, influencing education at a state level seemed to Zac the only viable way he could make lasting changes in student achievement, and do it without the people skills he lacked. Still, when Brianna found out state education was his ultimate goal, she would probably assume he was using her.

Aren't you? the nagging little voice in his head demanded.

Yes, he wanted her help to change things in Hope. But her son would benefit from the changes here. So would a lot of other kids. It had been incredibly difficult for Zac to return to the scene of his biggest shame, to the place where he'd spent a year enduring whispers and gossip about their broken relationship. But he'd come back because of the vast changes that were possible here. If only he could engage these kids.

On the surface, seeking Brianna's help seemed stupid. After all, she'd walked out on him, shattered the love he'd had for her when she left him standing at the altar. That love had crumbled to nothing during a year of public humiliation while he fulfilled the teaching contract he'd so stupidly agreed to. But now, ten long years later, they were both back in Hope and the truth was Zac missed the camaraderie they'd once shared when Brianna had been his best friend.

Zac was finished with love. That year in Hope had made him determined to never again take the risk of giving his heart to someone, to never again risk such public humiliation. He'd spent years honing a protective shell that kept anyone from getting too close.

But now he and Brianna lived in the same town, shared the same friends and had a mutual interest in seeing the school do well. Ten years later Zac didn't want her love. He wanted her help.

Persuading her wasn't going to be easy.

"Zac?" Tammy Lyn's intercom voice cracked through his thoughts. "The person you wanted in Las Cruces is out until next week. Sorry. If you could give me that stuff for the board meeting tomorrow I could format it and distribute it today."

"You'll have it as soon as I'm finished," he promised. Mentally steeling himself for Brianna's negative response, Zac blanked out everything and got busy with his notes for the board meeting. They had to be letter perfect because he was lousy at ad-libbing.

Getting that state job would be the culmination of all he'd worked for. That it might ensure nobody in Hope ever said "Poor Zac" again was an added bonus. At state level he could make curriculum more relevant and help kids learn. That was Zac's primary goal.

If he had to do it without Brianna's help, so be it.

* * *

Brianna walked up the stairs to the district school office the following afternoon with her throat blocked. This was probably the wrong thing to do. She was a gullible fool. But she was going to do it anyway.

Two minutes later she was seated in Zac's office where he had hot tea and some coconut cookies waiting.

"You're not going to tell me you baked these, are you?" she asked, trying for levity to crack the tension in the air.

"No." He smiled as he poured out two cups. "Sorry."

"Thank you." She accepted her tea, sipped it, inhaling the fresh orangey scent that was her favorite. He'd remembered—another surprise.

"Have a cookie."

Brianna accepted one and chewed on it while he talked about people they knew who were returning for the Homecoming weekend. But eventually the small talk became punctuated by too-long silences. It was time to get to the point.

"I've been thinking a lot about what you said, Zac," she began.

"I shouldn't have asked you." For a brief moment his eyes grew clouded. But then he blinked, and the impassive expression was back in place. "I understand why you have to say no, Brianna. People would talk if we worked together and the gossip—" He rolled his eyes. "Let's just say I don't want to go through that again."

"I'm not concerned about gossip." She frowned.

"Then it's working together that bothers you." Zac rubbed his chin. "I thought—hoped that after so many years we'd be past that and able to concentrate on what's best for the kids, but—"

"It's not the past, either," Brianna sputtered, frustrated that he kept butting in.

"Then it's me. I understand your hesitation." He leaned forward, face earnest. "Forget about it. I'll manage."

"But—"

"No, if you have hesitations, you *should* say no." He sat there, silent, as if he didn't know how to proceed.

"Actually I was going to say yes," she said in her driest tone. "But I think you just talked me out of it. I mean, if you no longer need me—"

Zac's eyes widened. His Adam's apple moved up and down as he gulped. He blinked. "Pardon?"

"I said I would help you. If you want me to." His attitude confused her and she hated feeling confused. "Are you regretting asking for my help, Zac?"

"Uh, no. Not exactly." His carefully blank expression irritated her.

"I know you think I let you down—before." She met his stare. "I won't do that again. I promise."

"This isn't about the past," he murmured.

"Maybe not, but our past certainly weighs into it." She needed to get the guilt out in the open, to deal with it and maybe, finally, be free of it. "You can't deny we have a history."

"I'm not denying anything." His head went up and back, his shoulders straightened. "We made plans." He shrugged. "They didn't happen."

"No. They didn't." Because he and her mother had spoiled that. Suddenly it seemed pointless to discuss the past. "So?" Brianna poured herself another cup of tea just to keep her hands busy. "Where do we start?"

"With Homecoming?" He pulled forward a blank

pad and wrote the word across the top in his scratching script. "It would give us the most bang for our buck if we announced a new plan at the Friday-morning assembly. Some parents will probably show up for that so this way they'd learn about our plan at the same time as the kids."

"Whatever our plan is," she added in a droll voice.

"Yeah. Maybe we could put a float in the Homecoming parade." He doodled on the pad.

"A float? We only have a week to organize it. And why a float? What's the purpose?" Brianna didn't mention that her brain had been whirling with ideas ever since he'd asked her to help, because it was also whirling with confusion at how he'd pushed everything they'd shared into the past. Was it so easy for Zac to forget that he'd once said he loved her?

"Forget about the time left." He leaned back in his chair. "Forget about everything but that some kids need your help. Now, I know you've been thinking about this because you couldn't help yourself. You're compelled to get in there and nurture these kids to do better." He grinned. "So how shall we start?"

They brainstormed ideas. It was slow going at first, but gradually Brianna relaxed enough to let her thoughts roam freely. Finally the idea that had been hidden at the back of her brain burst out.

"Your world." She stared at the scribbles he'd made on the paper, then lifted her head to stare at him. "It's called 'Your World.'"

"Okay." He wrote that down then waited. "Meaning?"

"How do you want your world to look?" She smiled as his face tightened. "That's straight from your lips,

Zac. Get kids thinking by giving them a glimpse of what could be, beyond Hope, beyond what is now."

"Good." He tapped his pen. "How do we start?"

"First we need board approval. And a budget. You'll have to get the teachers on board with this, too," she warned.

"I can do that."

She was surprised by how easily Zac accepted her ideas, but she didn't stop to think about it because thoughts kept mushrooming in her head. "Remember Billy Atkins?"

"Billy. Sure, I remember." Zac nodded. "He runs the local newspaper."

"And he's still a phenomenal artist judging by the mural on the side of his building. I think you should have the entry wall, the one you see the moment you enter the school, painted a startling white." She grinned. "And then ask Billy to paint a globe on it with the words *Your World* across the top. Dad could probably help if we needed him."

"Okay." Skepticism filled his face. "What do we do with this globe?"

"This is where you have to be flexible, Zac." She paused, inhaled, then told him the gist of her idea. "Every kid gets a chance to write what he wants to see in his world on that wall." She didn't stop even though his face blanched. "If this is going to work, the students have to believe someone will listen to what they write, listen to what they want. You and the staff must accept their ideas, whether or not you agree with them. You have to be genuine. I will not be part of this if you or the board intend to veto the suggestions they make."

"There are certain things we can't allow," he said stiffly.

"Of course." She nodded. "So you say that to the kids. No vulgarity, no cursing, no inappropriate remarks about teachers. But don't get hung up on the negatives. You want genuine responses that the students are willing to work to achieve."

"And if we get the other?" he asked.

"You have that painted over and wait for a new suggestion." Brianna paused to watch his face. "Be prepared, Zac. It might not go as well as you hope at first. But I think, if given a chance, students will have some remarkable ideas about the way they want their world to look. Some ideas may be quite easy to achieve. But nothing can be discounted just because you think it's too difficult or too far out," she warned. "Every idea deserves consideration."

Zac wrote as fast as she talked, nodding from time to time. When he finally looked at her, a glimmer lit his eyes.

"It might work," he said in a dazed tone. "It just might work."

"It will work, but only if no one judges or criticizes. Your World is all about possibilities."

"What do we do once everyone has contributed?" He laughed and shook his head. "I know what you're going to say. Start working on them. Right?"

"Yes. We'll need a committee of students who are willing to prioritize and a teacher or two who will agree to sit in on their meetings. Sit in on," she repeated firmly. "Not run. This is an initiative by the students."

"Maybe you can think about doing that," he suggested.

Brianna shook her head. "I'm here only to help brainstorm ideas."

"Any more of them?" Zac asked, one eyebrow arched.

"I'd forget about announcing anything at the rally."

"But—" He stopped, looked at her and said, "Go on."

"This might be hard to do in the short time left before Homecoming, but if the board agrees to the plan and you can recruit some people, I think a float in the Homecoming parade is a good idea." He didn't interrupt so she continued. "A great big globe with the words *Your World—How do you see it?* floating down the street will get a lot of attention. No explanation. Nothing. You, the teachers, the board—you all remain silent until the plan is announced on Monday. By the time Monday comes and the wall is ready, everyone in the entire town will be talking."

Zac nodded, jotted a few more things on his paper. By the time he leaned back in his chair, he'd lost the tense air she'd seen when she arrived.

"This is exactly what we need. A little excitement, a little mystery, something out of the ordinary." His eyes met hers sending a little tingle down Brianna's spine.

She was not prepared for his next question.

"Would you be willing to be the spokesperson for Your World at the board meeting?" Zac held up a hand to interrupt her refusal. "You think on your feet. You're good at public speaking. You can present this idea in a way that will grip the board far more than anything I say. They'll listen to you, Brianna."

"They won't listen to you?" She frowned. That didn't sound like a good start.

"Yes, they would. But I'd rather present the information about drugs and the threat to our schools." He met her stare. "I want them to have a clear picture of what could happen if we don't initiate this program."

"You're the negative, I'm the positive, which will make them more inclined to see this as a solution, a way out," she mused. "Good idea."

"You'll do it?"

"Not so fast. By presenting this, I'm the one who'll take the heat if something goes wrong or if the plan fails." She paused. "Or is that the point?"

"I never thought of that, but it works for me." He chuckled at her dark look. "You won't take any heat, Brianna. I'll make sure of that. Anyway, I have a feeling they're going to embrace this idea. It will give everyone a kick start to make changes."

"When's the board meeting?" Brianna asked.

"Tonight."

"What?" She gulped. "Zac, I need time to prepare."

"No, you don't. You always excelled at speaking off the cuff. I doubt that's changed." He stacked his papers together. "Be here at seven. I'll rework the agenda so our plan will go first."

"Zac, I—" Brianna panicked. What was she doing? She hadn't been back in Hope that long. She didn't even know who was on the school board. What business was it of hers to make a suggestion like this to people who'd probably see her as an interloper after so many years?

"Brianna." Zac's hand covered hers and sent a shockwave up her arm.

"Yes?" She refocused. His dark eyes gleamed with something—hope?

"This is for the kids—for Cory." His fingers tightened against her skin. "Don't think about anything else. Concentrate on the kids."

Her free hand lifted to touch the outline of her ring lying under the collar of her blouse. The old Zac, the one she'd remembered, had smiled like that and made her think of possibilities, and infused her with courage when she most needed it.

The tingling in her arm magnified. Brianna drew away from his touch. What was it about this man that he could still get her to react with nothing more than a smile and a touch?

"You can do it, Brianna."

There it was again, that encouragement she remembered so well.

"They're just people," he said quietly. "Parents like you who want their kids to succeed. We can help them, if we work together. If we get the town working together."

How many years had she prayed, begged God to let her help kids, to give her the knowledge and grace to make a difference in the world? Her old job had denied her that opportunity. She'd felt useless, a cog in a machine that ground up and spat out those who didn't conform. She'd done her best to help, but this would bring her the chance she'd longed for every time she'd pushed herself a little harder to finish her doctorate. This was why she'd clung to Zac's ring and savored his past words of encouragement even when he was no longer in her life. Now he was telling her she could make a difference in Hope.

"Okay. I'll do it." Her nerves evaporated.

"Thank you."

"On one condition," she added.

"Brianna." Zac sighed. "What condition?"

"Just listen." She had to stand firm on this. "I have

Cory, my mom in the nursing home and my dad healing from his heart attack. I also have my work. All of
them take my time, time I'll have to cut back on to help
you. So I want your agreement that if and when you
see a time and place where you can get involved with
Cory, you will."

"Cory? But what would I do?" Clearly Zac was not
enthralled by the prospect.

"I don't know. But there must be something." Brianna leaned forward. "Cory's on the wrong path and I
need help to turn him around before his appointment
with the judge at Christmas. I've agreed to help you out,
Zac, now I want your promise you'll do what you can
to find some common ground with Cory."

"I don't know what I can do," Zac murmured.

"You'll think of something." Inside she was desperately afraid he'd refuse, but she stood firm. "That's my
condition, Zac. Take it or leave it." She waited, hoping
he'd say yes because she really wanted to be a part of
Your World, to make a difference, to see lives changed
because of something she'd helped create.

"All right. If there's something I can do, I'll try."
That was all Zac said, but it was enough.

His secretary paged him then, so Brianna left. As she
drove back to work, she realized Zac's project was her
opportunity. If she could just find the right words, share
her vision with the school board, maybe she could finally help kids as she'd longed to since she'd left Zac—
and this town—so long ago.

"Please don't let me screw this up," Brianna prayed.

Chapter Four

"**D**ad, why is Mom so insistent I revive her store? It's been closed for years." Fresh from a disastrous visit at the nursing home, Brianna flopped into a chair. "I don't understand her obsession with that place."

"Nor did I until last year." Hugh Benson sank into his easy chair, his face sad. "I learned the whole story after a private investigator visited us. You see, your grandfather passed away last year. According to his will, his assets were then distributed to his descendents—Anita being his daughter."

"A grandfather? In Iowa? But you never told me—" Brianna frowned at him.

"I never knew. Your mother told me when we were married that her father was dead. That's all I ever knew until last year when your mother told me her father inherited a furniture store from his father. Anita grew up there. She worked in that store from a very early age, loved it and learned every facet of what went on. You know how adept your mother is at business. As an only child, she expected to one day run the family business herself."

"Of course." Brianna recalled her mother's keen business sense. "She'd have been very good at it. She always had a flair for interior decor."

"Yes." Her father looked grim. "Well, Anita stepped in to manage the place when her dad had his first heart attack. She was only eighteen and did well, except she made a mistake. Her error cost the company money and her father was furious. A little later, when he was forced to retire, he refused to give Anita any control because of that mistake. He said she wasn't smart enough or capable enough to carry on the business he'd inherited from his father."

"Poor Mom. That must have hurt."

"Yes, even more because he put some distant cousin in charge and made Anita one of the hirelings. The cousin made bad mistakes but no matter how Anita pleaded, her father wouldn't recant. Anita was desperately hurt and left Iowa after her mother died. Her father told her not to come back so she didn't. She never spoke to her father again. The bequest he left her was the smallest in his estate, smaller than the least employee's. He punished her to the end."

"So to get back at him, Mom created her own business to pass on to me," Brianna guessed, glimpsing the past with wiser eyes. "That explains so much. But why didn't she ever tell me?"

"Would it have made a difference?" her father asked, his face grave.

"You mean would I have given up my goal of psychology?" she asked. "No. But at least I'd understand why she was so determined that I stay. She was ashamed and embarrassed and determined to prove her father wrong by building her own business. Except I couldn't be part of it." Hindsight explained a lot.

"So now you know." Hugh Benson's pencil flew across the page, his caricature of Cory coming to life. "You said you came back to Hope to help kids. So that's why you're helping Zac present this Your World plan tonight?"

"Yes." Brianna sighed. "I'm not sure about working with him, though."

"Because?"

But Brianna could not, dare not answer that. Not until she'd sorted out the miasma of conflicting feelings that took over whenever Zac was around.

Outside, a short beep of a car horn sounded.

"That's Jaclyn. We're going out for a quick supper before I go to the board meeting. I know you're going back to see Mom. Cory's eating at his new friend's house but he's supposed to be back in a couple of hours." Brianna grabbed her bag and her jacket. As she slipped her feet out of slippers and into her sandals she felt her dad's stare. "What?"

"I thought—hoped you might stop by the nursing home later tonight. You know the truth now. Maybe you two could make up." There was no condemnation in his quiet voice but that didn't stop Brianna feeling a ripple of guilt.

"It's too soon for that, Dad." She grabbed the doorknob. "Mom was pretty upset today." She winced, remembering her mother's angry diatribe.

"Brianna." Her dad's firm tone insisted she hear him out.

She inhaled and waited.

"Your mother had a stroke." He sounded angry.

"She can't do the things she wants to do and her temper flares. She gets uncertain mood swings and frequently can't express herself the way she wants. Cut her some slack, will you?"

All the past hurt, all the angry words and bitter remarks she'd endured came flooding back. Brianna couldn't stop the rush of anger.

"I've been cutting Mom slack my whole life, Dad. I figured that maybe, after all these years, she might have learned to do the same for her one and only daughter. But I guess I still embarrass her." Stung by the chastisement in his eyes, she left, quietly but firmly shutting the door behind her before she walked to her friend's car.

"Hey, Brianna. I'm starv—" Jaclyn took one look at her face and turned off the car. "What's wrong? Cory again?" She frowned, shook her head. "No, wait. I know that look. It's your mom, isn't it, Brianna?"

"I'm a fully accredited psychologist, Jaclyn. I've dealt with all kinds of people. Yet, I can't seem to deal with my feelings toward my own mother." Slowly she unclenched her fingers as she relayed what she'd learned. "It explains why, all these years, she's been so driven. But why couldn't she have just told me?"

"Old grudges die hard." Jaclyn frowned. "Now, what are you going to do about it?"

"Keep trying to rebuild our relationship." Brianna couldn't keep the bitterness of the past inside any longer; she had to let it out. "My mother is the reason I left Hope. Well, her and Zac."

"I'm your best friend, Brianna." Jaclyn frowned. "Isn't it about time you finally explained why I never got to wear your mother's choice of that delightful flounced fuchsia bridesmaid dress down the aisle for your wedding?" She giggled at Brianna's gagging sound but quickly sobered. "You're only about ten years late explaining."

"It was always too hard to talk about. I wanted to forget it." She gulped, forced herself to continue the sad story. "Remember the rehearsal dinner?"

"Like I could forget that—all eleven courses." Jaclyn grimaced.

"There weren't eleven!" Brianna argued. "But my mother did have to make her only daughter's wedding an extravaganza."

"Go on."

"After the rehearsal dinner I hadn't seen Zac for a while so I went looking for him. He and my mother were by the hotel pool." Brianna bit her lip. "I overheard them talking. He accepted her offer of a teaching job in Hope for two years. Without even talking to me, he accepted."

"But how could—?" Jaclyn's furrowed brow smoothed. "Oh, I remember now. Your mom was elected chairman of the school board that year, wasn't she?"

"Yes. And she had the store, of course." Brianna swallowed hard. "I heard Zac tell her he was worried about supporting me. Remember I couldn't find a job that summer. As my mother said many times, I returned to Hope with a useless undergrad degree." Bitterness ate another hole inside.

"She never understood how much psychology meant to you, did she?"

"She always said I should get over Jessica's death, like it was a skinned knee or something." Brianna bit her lip. "It hurt so badly to lose her. I couldn't just forget her or that her death might have been prevented if better medical care had been available in Hope."

"Nor could I," Jaclyn murmured.

"Anyway that night Mom preyed on Zac's fears." Brianna needed to get this out and let go of it. "She convinced Zac we should stay in Hope by guaranteeing him a job and telling him that I'd have work in her store while he taught. She said we'd be able to save faster for our PhDs."

"Baloney." Jaclyn snorted. "She was always after you to take over her store. She couldn't accept your refusal so she decided to bribe your fiancé to get her way."

"Exactly. I couldn't believe Zac agreed with her that I should work in the store. He knew as well as you did how useless I felt in that place. I was never into home decor. I had no knack for furniture styles or placement. Still don't," Brianna admitted. "The only thing I enjoyed about that store was the fabrics, hence my love of quilts."

"Did you talk to Zac about it?"

"I tried on the way home after the party. I asked why he'd accepted the job without talking to me. He was surprised that I was angry about it. He thought I'd be glad that we wouldn't have to go into a lot of debt for our degrees." She squeezed her eyes tightly shut and inhaled to ease the stress of those horrible moments. "He said I'd probably end up reconsidering my decision to do a doctorate anyway once we had a family."

"Shades of male machismo." Jaclyn's face tightened.

"No. He wasn't being macho. I don't think he honestly believed I was as committed as he was." Brianna sighed. "I was stunned by what he said. Weeks of him falling in with my mother's suggestions and not standing up for me—I'd been having doubts about getting married and I told him so. But he apologized, convinced me that he loved me, that he only wanted what was best for us."

"So you decided to go through with the wedding."

"Yes. But I was furious. When I got home, I told my mother I knew she'd gone behind my back to coerce Zac into accepting that job." Brianna tried to make her friend understand. "She knew we'd planned to get jobs in the city where we could still take night classes because I'd gone to great lengths to explain our plans to my parents. Zac and I had put months of thought into it because I'd insisted we have our game plan in place before we ever came to Hope for the wedding. She knew that plan and she deliberately ruined it."

Jaclyn squeezed her shoulder in sympathy. "Tell me the rest."

"Eventually my mother admitted asking Zac's mom to say she was too ill to travel for the wedding so we'd have to come here to get married. It was all part of her plan. Zac and I, we were just pawns."

There was nothing Jaclyn could say.

"I asked her why she'd done it. Do you know what she said?" The protective barrier she'd maintained for so many years was breached as tears welled. Brianna made no attempt to stop them. "My mother claimed she'd done it to help me. She said Zac told her he was worried I'd never be able to support myself, that he felt I was holding him back. She said Zac's mom was afraid I might derail his goal to get his PhD. My mother insisted she couldn't stand by and watch me lose him. The way she put it, I began to believe she was right, that for Zac's sake I needed to stay and work in the store."

"Oh, Brianna. I wish you'd called me."

"I wish I had, too. But I was so confused. And Mom just kept piling it on. I was a weight on Zac's back, but she said she would rescue me. She would make me assistant manager at her store. I'd run things and she'd take a break once in a while."

"That wouldn't have happened. She always had to be the boss." Jaclyn bit her lip. "Sorry."

"Don't be. It's true." Brianna swallowed. "Anyway, she said I had to prove to Zac that I didn't need him to be responsible for me, so he wouldn't feel I was—let's see, 'a chain around his neck' was the way she put it. She said that maybe then he wouldn't resent me."

Jaclyn made a face. "And Zac? You did talk to him about it?"

"After my argument with my mother I called him. He said she was right, that he had been worried but he wasn't now that he had the job. He said it was better to stay in Hope and save." Brianna pursed her lips. "He even suggested we consider moving in with one or the other of our parents to cut costs further."

Jaclyn groaned.

"I was reeling." Brianna tried to smile. "All our plans were out the window. I just wanted him to reassure me. But Zac was really worried about the financial aspect of both of us returning to school. He even said he was glad I was willing to do my share. As if I was some kind of leech!"

"He was probably just nervous. Zac was never great with words," Jaclyn reminded.

"He repeated over and over that he was glad I'd *finally* be working," Brianna sputtered. "And he kept babbling about getting his PhD as soon as possible.

He sounded as if he thought I'd ask him to give up his dream."

"He used to bore us to tears with that PhD dream sometimes, didn't he? But I'm sure he loved you," Jaclyn consoled.

"Well, I wasn't so sure. And the more my mother talked to me, the less sure I became. She played me like a fiddle, Jaclyn." Brianna sighed. "I finally decided she was right, that I was holding back the man I loved and that I needed to give up my own dream to help Zac. So I agreed to work in her store."

Jaclyn frowned. "But you didn't stay, Brianna. You left."

"Yes." Brianna couldn't stop her tears. A bitter smile rose from the cauldron of bitterness simmering inside. "Zac phoned me the next morning to tell me of my mother's suggestion that we cut our honeymoon short so I could start work early, as thanks for the elaborate wedding that I never wanted."

Jaclyn's face expressed her disgust.

"I told him in no uncertain terms what I thought of that. He sounded hurt. He was only trying to help make it easier for me, he said. It would be a sacrifice but sometimes sacrifices were necessary. I told him I felt I was making all the sacrifices and he said that he was sacrificing, too, by having to put off his doctorate. We argued a bit, made up and I hung up. Then my mother appeared with a list she'd made of my future duties and responsibilities at the store and a contract."

"A contract?" Jaclyn lifted one eyebrow.

"She said I'd need to sign a contract for five years to make sure she wasn't left high and dry if I changed my mind. Five years!" Brianna straightened her shoulders.

"I knew then how it would be, how she'd grind me down until I gave up my plan to become a child psychologist. And I knew Zac wouldn't be strong enough to stand up to her, either. You see she was right about one thing."

"Right how?" Jaclyn glared at her. "Explain."

"I'd been worried for some time that I was holding Zac back. He was so much smarter, had so much to offer. I slowed him down because he spent so much time helping me, time he should have spent on his own work." Brianna dashed away her tears. "If we'd married and I got stuck in her store, Zac would have felt compelled to stay those five years, too. I didn't want him to lose his dream because of me."

"That woman!" Jaclyn sputtered.

"It wasn't just Mom." Brianna felt the weight of it dragging her down. Wasn't confession supposed to make her feel better? "By then Zac was completely under her spell, convinced that giving up our plans to teach in Hope was his opportunity. I was afraid Zac would eventually turn against me if I objected too much and I couldn't stand that. I loved him and I wanted him to be happy. I thought he would be if I wasn't there so I packed a bag and snuck away."

"I would have helped you if I'd known."

"I know. But then Mom would have caused problems for you." Brianna paused. "Dad saw me leave."

"Really?"

"When I was in the cab, I looked back and saw him standing there. He was crying." Brianna dabbed at her wet cheeks with the tissue Jaclyn handed her. "I wrote him later that when I did get married I'd make sure he walked me down the aisle, but that didn't happen. After Craig proposed, he insisted we marry quickly. He was sick and he wanted me to be able to stay at his house and care for Cory without any improprieties. I was afraid my mother would talk me out of it if she knew, so I married Craig with nobody there. But Craig betrayed me, too."

"How?" Jaclyn asked, her beautiful face sad.

"Craig died three months after we married. That's when I learned he'd known all along that he had a terminal illness." Brianna stared through the windshield remembering the gut-wrenching dismay when she learned the truth. "He knew he didn't have long to live, but he never told me. He pretended he was getting better. Maybe he thought I would have left if I'd known."

Jaclyn's hand covered hers and squeezed.

"I wouldn't have left," Brianna whispered. "Craig was wonderful to me in those horrible weeks after I left Hope for Chicago. He took time to help me find a place to live, helped me find a job. Cory was Craig's pride and joy but neither he nor his first wife, Cory's mother, had family. He had no one to help him. He adored that boy but I saw how hard it became for him to care for him. I wanted to help because I loved Cory, too."

"But you didn't love Craig?"

"No." Brianna smiled, sadness filling her heart. "I wish I could have. He was a wonderful man. But there was never love between us. We were just good friends who married a few months after we met to give Cory a home. At least I thought that's what we were. But when I learned the truth, that he knew—" Brianna bit her lip. "I might not have been so decimated if Craig had prepared me. But he never said a word and suddenly at twenty-three I was a widow and a mother, responsible for this little boy, no clue how I was going to do it and all alone. I was at my lowest when I phoned you for help."

"I'm glad you finally did. That's what friends are for." She wrapped her arms around Brianna and help on tight. "I wish I could have come."

"I know. But you sent your mother instead, and she was wonderful to me. I'll never be able to thank her or you enough." Brianna clung a moment longer then drew back. "Anyway, all of this was to say my dad razzed me about going to see Mom tonight."

"You should go," Jaclyn insisted.

"I can't go to the nursing home again," Brianna admitted. "Not for a while."

"Why not?"

"Today she said I made her ashamed." The lump in Brianna's stomach hardened. "It hurt so much. I don't want to live with that pain again, Jaclyn. I'm done with trying to be the obedient daughter I'm supposed to be. It didn't work for her and it doesn't work for me." Briefly Brianna explained what she'd learned about her grandfather.

"I understand." Jaclyn reached out and started the car. She shifted into gear before facing Brianna. "But you can't go on hating her, either. You've got to find a way past it. And you've got to do the same with Zac. Didn't you say he wanted you to work with him?"

"He's got this idea that I can help him shake up the school."

"About time that school had a good shake-up," Jaclyn said, steering into the restaurant parking lot. "Couldn't hurt your career to be at the forefront of change, either, could it?"

"No," Brianna mumbled.

"Then?" Jaclyn lifted an eyebrow. "What's the problem?"

"The truth?" Brianna climbed out of the car.

"Always."

"I don't know if I can work with Zac." That admission wasn't easy.

"You probably can't," Jaclyn agreed, walking with her to the front door. "Until you let go of your resentment of him. You were young. You both made mistakes because you didn't trust each other. It will take some heavenly healing and help for you to start again, Bri." She rolled her eyes. "Listen to me—the pediatrician advising the child psychologist."

"No, the best friend advising her dim-witted school buddy. Thanks, pal." She stopped Jaclyn before they went inside and hugged her. "Did I tell you I'm so happy you and Kent are having a baby?"

"Me, too. But I want you to be happy, too, Brianna. And you aren't going to be until you make peace with the past. So think about it. Okay?" She waited for her friend's nod. "And I'll pray for you to find a way to mend things with your mom. And Zac." Then Jaclyn tugged her inside the café where they chose their favorite Mexican food.

Brianna enjoyed the meal. But her thoughts kept straying to Zac.

Would the past interfere with working together?

When Jaclyn dropped her off at Zac's office, she went inside only after whispering a prayer for the right words, and after reminding herself that she was doing this for Cory, not Zac.

Chapter Five

Later that night Zac rapped on Brianna's front door, excitement zinging through him. She opened the door, her hair tousled, her feet bare, her face weary.

"We got it," he said simply. "Your World is a go."

Her smile dawned slowly, starting in her eyes, which glowed green in the cast of the house light. The grin moved to light up her entire face, transforming her weariness into beauty.

"Come in, Zac." She waved him to a chair, then flopped down on the sofa across from him and tucked her long legs under her. Her eyes sparkled. "So? Tell me what happened after I left."

"Lots of good discussion." Zac glanced around, remembering how the expensive knickknacks in this living room had always seemed to get in the way of his gangly teenage elbows and feet. Most of them were gone now rendering the room less glamorous but immensely more homey.

"Meaning?" Brianna leaned forward impatiently. "Did they approve everything?"

"Yes." He grinned, sharing the success. "Your speech

was brilliant, by the way, especially the part about saving money in the long run. There was so much interest, I had to caution several board members to keep the plan quiet for now."

"Good."

He explained the budget that had been allocated and told her the few worries he'd heard.

"It all sounds quite positive," Brianna said, then frowned. "Oh, do you want some coffee? Or something?"

"I'm coffee-ed out, thanks." Silence stretched between them, leaving Zac feeling as he had the first time he'd come here—awkward. Nothing new about that feeling. He opened his mouth to rehash more details of the meeting but Brianna spoke first.

"So Your World is on its way." She nibbled her bottom lip, studying him from beneath her lashes.

"Yep."

"And Cory? Did you think of anything you could do with Cory?" Her eyes stretched wide with expectation.

"Not yet." Zac felt like a heel because he hadn't actually given it a thought. He'd been too busy concentrating on that board meeting. "What is it you expect?" he asked cautiously.

The telephone interrupted her response. Brianna picked it up, her face losing its joy as a querulous voice cut across the peace that had filled the room.

"It's quite late, Mom. Are you sure—yes, yes, okay. I'll bring it right away," she promised. She hung up the phone, tense lines marring the beauty of her face. "I have to go out."

"Now?" he asked. A sound on the stairs drew their attention. In a second her face changed, that sad hurt transformed into a mask of unconcern.

"It's okay, Dad. Go back to bed. Mom can't sleep. She wants me to bring over a pattern. She's really getting into this knitting thing, isn't she?" She smiled at him. "I think it will probably help strengthen her hands. Since the stroke she's had problems."

"Hello, Zac." Greetings exchanged, Mr. Benson turned back to Brianna. "You don't want me to go?"

"No. I'll do it. Cory's in his room, in bed I hope, so nothing to worry about there. I won't be long." She waited until he nodded and left, then she turned to face Zac. "I'm sorry. I'd like to talk to you more about Cory, but I have to go to the nursing home."

"Okay." The slide of emotions across her face bothered him. For some reason he didn't understand Zac knew he couldn't let her go alone. "I'll go with you."

"You?" She blinked. "Why?" she asked simply.

"I need to do something to wind down." He shrugged. "If you don't want me to go with you, I can always go for a run I guess."

"Actually, I'd be glad if you came." Relief made the gold sparkles in her eyes glitter. "I'll have to find the pattern she wants first, though."

"Maybe I can help." He followed her to her mother's office but jerked to a halt in the doorway, remembering the one time Mrs. Benson had found them studying in here and the angry scolding she'd laid on Brianna.

"It should be—yes, here it is." She removed a piece of paper from a file, copied it on a nearby copier and slid the original back into its folder in a drawer. The drawer slid shut without a sound.

"I wish my home office was this neat," he said, studying the immaculate room. "This looks like a show place."

"That's because no one uses it." Brianna glanced around.

"Why not? As I remember you always loved to do craft stuff."

"Not in here. This is my mother's room." A pained look washed across her face before she glanced away. "I'm ready."

Once he'd handed her into his car, Zac quickly drove to the nursing home and parked in the empty spot nearest the door. They walked inside without speaking, but he couldn't help thinking what a shame it was that the bright room with its many windows was still off-limits to Brianna.

Zac spotted Miss Latimer, his mother's old friend, sitting in her wheelchair. To give Brianna privacy with her mom he told her he'd catch up with her in a minute.

"Hey, Miss Latimer. How are you?" Zac bent over so the old woman's cataract-covered eyes could see him.

She inhaled, blinked and her face creased in a huge smile. His heart felt a burst of warmth that even though his mother was gone, someone was glad to see him.

"I'm very well, Zachary." She patted his hand. "Thank you for asking. You're rather late tonight. A board meeting?"

"Yes. How do you keep up on all the goings on in Hope?" he asked, amazed as usual by her sharp memory.

"Clean living." She winked at him, then launched into a tale of the most recent happenings in the nursing home.

Zac tried to focus on what she was saying but it grew steadily more difficult because of the racket coming from a room down the hall.

"Isn't it dreadful? She's horrid to that girl," Miss Latimer murmured, leaning close.

"Who's horrid to whom?" he asked.

"Anita Benson is horrible to her daughter, Brianna."

"Oh." He tried to pretend he couldn't hear the vitriolic comments.

"That woman has always ridden roughshod over other people's feelings, but lately she's grown worse. Poor Brianna can't do anything right."

"I guess it's part of her stroke issues," Zac temporized, shrinking at what he heard.

"Huh! Anita uses that as an excuse for her poor behavior." Miss Latimer snorted her disgust. "She was always a bully, but nobody's ever had the courage to say it to her face." She stopped and pursed her lips as a diatribe of complaints echoed down the hall. "Poor girl."

A harried nurse raced toward the room but soon came scurrying back out, her face flushed and her lips in a tight angry line. Zac cringed as those few residents still about stared. Poor Brianna.

"Maybe there's something I can do," he said quietly.

"By all means, Zachary, go." She squeezed his hand. "Brianna's such a sweet girl. It's too bad she's always had such a difficult time with her mother."

She had? Zac didn't remember that. Back in the old days, Mrs. Benson had always been very nice to him, though now he thought about it, they hadn't gone to Brianna's elegant home to study very often. He couldn't remember why.

"We'll visit another time," Miss Latimer promised.

"Yes, we will." He squeezed her hand. After a moment's thought he stopped to buy something at the gift shop that was just closing then strode down the hall, battling his nervousness as he broached the room. This was none of his business. But he felt sorry for Brianna.

"Mother, stop making a scene. This *is* the pattern you asked for," Brianna said calmly.

Zac tapped his knuckles against the open door then stuck his head inside. With her hands clenched at her side, he guessed Brianna was anything but calm.

"Hello, Mrs. Benson." He walked in, pulled the small box of saltwater taffy from his jacket pocket and held it out to the red-faced woman. "I brought you a gift."

"A gift? Oh, you lovely man." Mrs. Benson reached out and took the package. "I love sweets. Now that's the kind of thing you should have thought of," she said, tossing a glare at her daughter.

"No more visiting tonight, Mrs. Benson." The nurse stepped into the room and held the door, motioning for them to leave.

"I guess we have to go now. I'll see you tomorrow, Mom." Brianna ushered Zac out the door while the sticky taffy she was chewing prevented Anita Benson from arguing. "Thank you, Zac," she murmured once they were in the hall. Her lashes fanned across her embarrassed pink cheeks. "I—uh—" The words died away as her cheeks grew even pinker.

"Not a problem," he said. "Anyway I had a chance to say hi to Miss Latimer. Remember her?"

"Math." Brianna cast a quick look around, obviously relieved when she didn't spot her former teacher. "My worst subject. Oh, yes, I remember her."

"I loved math." Zac shrugged at her glower as they walked across the parking lot. "Well I did. Miss Latimer was such a great friend to my mom during her illness that it's my pleasure to visit her whenever I can." He unlocked the car, held the door until she was seated inside.

Zac walked around the car, searching for another subject. "I recognized that deep, rich blue of your father's in the painting in your mom's room. Nobody else gets it quite that shade."

"Yes." Brianna smiled. "The smaller one beside it is Cory's."

"I didn't realize he painted." Zac had been surprised by the delicate touch of the watercolor of Mrs. Benson caught in a happy moment.

"He didn't but Dad's been coaching him." Brianna fell silent.

"He's a good teacher." Zac studied Brianna, noting she'd inherited her mother's amazing eyes, though Brianna's now looked infinitely tired. The confrontation with her mother seemed to have drained her. He pressed a little harder on the accelerator to get her home more quickly. "How is Cory doing?"

"He's made some friends I'm not too keen on," she mumbled. "They've eaten at our house for the past three nights. Not that I care about that, but they never seem to go home unless I tell them to. It's odd."

"Sounds like it." Zac wondered if they were the source of the drugs.

"Day after tomorrow is the Homecoming parade," Brianna reminded him. "Is the float ready?" Her gorgeous eyes narrowed when he didn't immediately answer. He avoided her searching gaze. "It's not finished," she said with disgust.

"I'm working on it." Zac's frustration at his ineptitude with that stupid float surged.

"So what's the problem?" Brianna demanded as he pulled into her driveway.

"If I knew that, I'd fix it. I don't know," he admitted. He got out, met her at the hood of his car.

"Zac!" Brianna's eyes shot daggers. "The Your World project depends on kicking off with that float. I thought you agreed."

"I do. It's just—I'm not mechanically inclined, Brianna. The globe won't balance." Annoyed, Zac followed her to the front door, waited while she unlocked it.

"You're the one who asked me for help, Zac. If you don't want to do this—" She left it hanging, as if he'd deliberately messed up.

"I *do* want to do it. I just don't know how." He'd been going to leave but instead followed her inside to defend himself, forcing his tone to stay even though inside he fumed at the way she'd turned this on him. "Maybe we have to go with a smaller idea."

"So my idea is at fault. That's what you always did when something didn't work the way you wanted. You blamed me." Brianna's glare would have put a frost on the desert.

"I'm not blaming anyone." Zac inhaled and let it out slowly, searching for a way through this minefield. "I'm just telling you that I've had some problems." He tried to explain the issues with keeping the globe spinning but quickly gave up. Sometimes being a nerd was absolutely worthless. "I don't really know anything about making a globe spin," he admitted.

"Then why on earth did you agree—"

"Hey, do I need to put on my referee suit?" Cory, sprawled on the sofa, flicked on a lamp, a half sneer on his face. "What's going on?"

"Nothing," Brianna said, her voice sharp. "You're supposed to be in bed."

"The float for the Homecoming parade is what's going on, Cory." Zac raised an eyebrow at Brianna. "It's not that big a secret," he said. He turned to Cory. "Unfortunately when it comes to the mechanics of fixing things, I am a complete moron."

"Maybe I could help." Cory glanced at his mother.

"Oh, son, I don't—"

The little sparkle of excitement that had flickered in Cory's eyes for a fraction of a second snuffed out. Zac had to intervene.

"Maybe you could help, Cory," he agreed. "I'm pretty sure there's a short somewhere. How are you with wiring?" He ignored Brianna's attempts to catch his eye. "How about tomorrow after school? Could you take a look then?"

"I guess." Cory risked a second look at Brianna. "If Mom's okay with it."

"Why wouldn't she be? She just finished nagging me to get the thing going." Zac ignored Brianna's tightened lips and hiss of anger. "I'll pick you up after the last class. Okay?"

"Sure." Cory rose. "I'd better get to bed. Don't fight anymore, Mom." He winked at Zac before he took the stairs to his room two at a time.

"What are you doing?" Brianna demanded in a low voice.

"I'm trying to help Cory. Did you see the way his eyes lit up when he offered to help?" Zac touched her arm. "He wants to do it, Brianna. If he can't, I'll find someone else, but he was being generous offering his help. At least give him the chance. Besides, it will keep him away from those friends of his you don't like. For a bit, anyway."

Brianna was quiet for a long while, her hazel eyes studying him. Finally she nodded.

"Maybe you're right," she murmured with a sigh. "Maybe I've made him feel unneeded by trying to protect him too much. Maybe I should have included him more."

"Brianna." Zac touched her shoulder, his fingers tingling at the warmth of her skin. "Don't beat yourself up about this. You're a mom and you naturally try to protect your kid."

"Yes, but—" She bit her lip, her face troubled. "I'm not sure—"

"You asked me to do something with him," he reminded. "So let me try this. At the very least we'll get to know each other a little better." Zac drew his hand away, surprised by his yearning to wrap his arm around Brianna's shoulder and draw her close, to comfort her and erase the worry etched on her face. "Trust me."

Brianna didn't say she trusted him.

All she said was, "Tomorrow after school, then. Don't forget."

Zac said good-night and walked out to his car, speculating on exactly why he'd offered to help Cory. Maybe seeing how Mrs. Benson's tirade had deflated Brianna made him want to ease her world a little. It was embarrassing how much Brianna Benson still affected him.

The woman had talked to him on the phone on their wedding day mere minutes before she'd left town without a single word of explanation! And now she had him in knots again with crazy feelings he didn't understand and couldn't seem to control.

Irritated, discomfited and frustrated by his topsy-turvy reactions, Zac grit his teeth when he heard her call his name. He stopped and turned, one hand on the door handle of his car.

"I just wanted— You look kind of green, Zac." Brianna peered into his face. "Something you ate?"

If only a remedy was that simple. Take an antacid and get rid of this ridiculous response to her.

"Zac?"

Worry filled her pretty face. That was the most special thing about Brianna. Always concerned about everyone. Heart of gold. Which is probably why her mother's repudiation wounded her so deeply. If only he could— Zac regrouped.

"I'm fine. Did you forget something?" He was determined not to fall into the same old habit of wanting more than he knew he could have. Brianna was nothing but an old friend.

That wouldn't, couldn't change, because he couldn't let it. The shame of the past had ensured that.

"I just wanted to say thanks." Brianna reached out but her hand froze midair. She licked her lips as if she had second thoughts. "For going with me to the nursing home."

"You're welcome." When she said no more, Zac climbed in his car and drove to his lonely house where he sat in the dark, struggling to make sense of what had just happened.

Why was it that the beautiful woman he'd once proposed to, the one who'd run away rather than marry him, still only had to smile to make him start dreaming about what ifs? Hadn't he learned anything in ten years?

There was no point asking God for relief. If Zac had

learned one thing in all those years, he'd learned God didn't have time to be bothered with his insecurities. So he kept his mask of invincibility intact. He wasn't the kind of person who could open up, reveal the pain she'd caused and ask for an explanation. That vulnerability risked getting hurt and Zac wasn't about to go there.

Brianna was off-limits as anything more than a colleague and maybe a friend.

Losing everything they'd shared hurt, but Zac figured that God must want it that way or He'd have changed things. That nothing had changed, told Zac he was still a cog that didn't fit in God's wheel.

"This was a great idea, Brianna." Zac flashed her a grin as he filled another bowl with chips. "Getting us all together after Homecoming, I mean."

"Thanks. But I couldn't have done it if you hadn't picked up snacks. Today was wild in my office." She ignored the way his smile made her pulse skitter and concentrated on refilling the cheese tray.

"Homecoming is usually a crazy time for everyone." Zac reached in front of her, speared a cube of cheese and popped it in between his lips.

"Speaking of Homecoming—" Kent leaned against the doorjamb "—awesome job with the float, guys. I had a hundred people ask me what Your World means."

"That's exactly what we want, anticipation building until all is revealed on Monday." Brianna shared a look with Zac but quickly looked away.

"We have Cory, his friends and their dads to thank that the float operated at all." Zac inclined his head.

She noticed her son looming on the bottom step and

stifled her misgivings. His friends? Brianna hadn't realized Zac had so much help.

"You did a great job. Thank you, son."

"You're welcome." Cory grinned at Kent. "It was a pretty easy fix. I wouldn't ask him—" he inclined his head in Zac's direction "—to work on your truck, though. Mechanics aren't his strength."

"Dude, I so already knew that." Kent smirked at Zac as he high-fived Cory.

"Are you going out?" Brianna asked her son with a quick glance at the clock.

"Yeah. I'm meeting the guys at the café." Cory's brows lowered as if he expected her to object.

"Have fun. And be home on time," she reminded, refusing to mention his curfew aloud.

"Yes, Mother." The door slammed behind him.

"Hey. Did the party move in here?" Nick Green, their friend who'd turned his quarterback skills into a professional career in the NFL strolled into the kitchen. He looked around, shook his head and grabbed the bowl of chips. "Not enough room," he said before he disappeared into the family room.

"Hey, Nick, hold up. I want to know how you came up with that last play of the game. It was pretty slick," Kent said, leaving the room.

Brianna watched through the windows as Cory greeted his friends. After a quick backward glance at her he hurried away.

Lord, please keep him safe.

"Brianna—"

"Yes?" Zac's touch on her arm jerked her back to awareness. She flinched at the spark his touch engendered and saw him blink.

"Sorry." He stepped back.

"It's okay." She forced a smile. "I guess I zoned out for a minute."

"Brianna, what's wrong?" Zac glanced from the window to her. "Did Cory do something?"

"Not that I know of. Yet." She picked up the tray she'd been arranging, wishing she had avoided these moments alone with Zac.

"I want to thank Cory for his help with the float in a concrete way. Would it be okay if he came for dinner one night? Kent comes over most Wednesdays when Jaclyn works late. I usually barbecue steaks." Zac blinked. "Would Cory like that?"

"You don't have to invite him." But she was glad he'd offered. Maybe Zac could get Cory to take an interest in something other than the two boys he called friends. "But, yes, I'm sure he'd love a good steak. I don't cook it often because I'm not good at grilling."

Was this the help for her son that she'd been praying for? A Proverbs verse she'd memorized in youth group long ago flickered through her mind. *If you falter in times of trouble, how small is your strength.* It seemed she was constantly faltering, and her strength was diminishing with every day.

"He's going to be okay, Brianna." Zac had moved to stand behind her and now his breath brushed her ear. "Cory's nobody's fool. Relax. Give him a chance to prove himself."

"Have some faith. Is that what you mean?" She smiled, nodded and motioned toward the other room. "I'll try. Let's go catch up on what everyone's been doing."

Brianna pretended to enjoy the rest of the evening.

She listened to her old friends tease one another, found out their friend Shay expected to return to Hope within six months and realized that Nick wasn't just her old pal anymore. He, like Shay, was famous, though unlike her, he seemed unchanged by it. Shay seemed much more reserved, and she wondered why, but Brianna's thoughts kept returning to Cory.

One by one her friends eventually left after thanking her for the evening. Zac remained behind to help with clean-up. When he caught her glancing at the clock for the third time in five minutes he took the dishes from her hand, put them in the dishwasher then turned her to face him.

"What time was Cory supposed to be home?"

"An hour ago." She could hide her worry no longer. "He's not supposed to break his curfew, Zac. That's one of the judge's conditions."

"Cory knows that. He'll be here soon." Though kind, his words did nothing to comfort her.

"He's never broken it before by more than a couple of minutes." Brianna stared at him, knowing she had to ask, but wishing it was someone else. Anyone else. She did not want to need Zac. Yet she did. "Will you help me look for him? Please?"

"Sure." There was no hesitation. Zac grabbed his jacket and his keys. "We can take my car."

"Just let me tell Dad what we're doing so he can phone me if he hears from Cory." Relief made her feel light-headed as Brianna raced up the stairs and explained to her dad. She returned to find Zac had finished the cleaning. Everything sparkled. "You didn't have to do that."

"No big deal. Ready?" He handed her into his car.

They drove all over town but found no sign of Cory or his friends.

"It's after midnight," she said. Panic lurked in the back of her throat. "Something's wrong."

"Nothing in town is open now," Zac agreed. "Hope isn't exactly a night spot. Maybe they went out of town."

"For what?" Brianna heard the anger in her voice and modulated it. This wasn't Zac's fault. "I don't know why they would do that, but I guess we can check." She was bowed down with the knowledge that this child she had promised Craig she'd protect was in trouble.

Ten minutes later the headlights of Zac's car caught three figures trudging toward town. Anger vied for relief. As soon as Zac pulled to the side of the road, Brianna reached for the door handle.

"Brianna." Zac's hand on her shoulder stopped her. "I know I have no business telling you this, but I'm going to say it anyway. Don't yell at Cory in front of his friends, even though he deserves it. You can bawl him out later. For now, just listen."

She glared at him, but she knew he was right. Cory would only be embarrassed if she did the mom thing in front of his friends, and they didn't need any more conflicts to add to the strain already building between them. She'd wait until they were home.

Brianna inhaled and opened the door. The trio stood next to the right front fender. Cory looked at her with a mixture of shame and a tinge of defiance. The other two acted nonchalant.

"Need a ride?" It cost Brianna a great deal not to embrace Cory, so great was her relief at seeing him healthy and alive.

"Yeah. Thanks, Mom." He got in the backseat with

his two friends. "Thanks, Mr. Ender. We would have never all fit in Mom's little car."

"What were you doing out here?" Zac asked after a sideways glance at Brianna. He turned around and headed back to Hope as the kids explained that they'd hitchhiked out to an old mine they'd heard about.

"But by the time we were ready to come back, we couldn't catch a ride. Seems like everything around Hope dies at night." That was Adam, the kid Brianna had dubbed the ringleader. His tone was scathing. "Where I come from there's life after nine."

"Where is that?" Zac asked.

"L.A. Man, that place always has something to offer."

"We'll drop you at home," Brianna said. "Where do you live?" The two boys argued to be dropped off in the middle of town but Brianna refused, insisting they be left at home. She heaved a huge sigh of relief when the two were gone and glanced at Cory, expecting an explanation. But his head was down. Probably embarrassed in front of Zac. He should be. She vacillated between anger and relief.

Zac drove them home, saying nothing to break the silence. Brianna waited until he'd pulled into her driveway.

"Go inside, Cory. Wait for me in the living room." She looked straight at him, expecting an argument. Cory said nothing, simply got out of the car, thanked Zac and went inside. Brianna turned to Zac. "Thank you for your help. I really appreciate it. I would never have thought—"

He chuckled and shook his head. "I guess you have to be a guy to think of some things. Don't worry about it. I was happy to help. I'm just glad we found Cory safe and sound."

"Yes." Her fingers curled against the door handle. She needed to get out of this intimate atmosphere before she said something she'd regret. "Just let me know when you want Cory to come over for dinner, will you?" She pushed open the door and met his gaze. "And thank you. Again."

"My pleasure. And thank you for the party. It was good to see everyone again." Zac looked confident, competent and totally in control.

Everything Brianna was not. But, then, Zac didn't have a son to raise.

"Well, good night." She closed the door and walked inside the house, praying desperately for heavenly help with a situation she felt incapable of handling. "Please, God, give me the words to say to Cory."

Another verse popped into her head.

You will keep Him in perfect peace whose mind is fixed on You.

Was that what she was doing wrong? Not spending enough time focusing on God?

Tonight, right after she read the riot act to Cory, she was going to spend an hour reading her Bible. The answers to reaching her son had to be there.

And maybe she'd also figure out how to deal with her escalating responses to Zac.

Chapter Six

"We're not going to leave you to eat alone, Brianna, so come on." Zac stemmed his irritation that she would rather eat alone than join him and Cory.

"But—"

"Kent can't make it tonight so it will be just the three of us." He saw her hesitation and pounced. "I know your dad is eating with your mom tonight. I met him on my way here, and he told me about the home's October Harvest Meal."

Brianna glanced from him to Cory.

"Come on, Mom. It'll be fun."

"If you're sure I won't be in the way." When they both agreed she wouldn't, Brianna finally accepted the invitation. "I'll have to catch a ride with you, though, Zac. My car is in the shop."

"Again," Cory muttered, rolling his eyes.

"It's not that bad." Brianna got in the front seat of Zac's car.

She wasn't sure about allowing Cory this privilege so soon after he'd messed up with his curfew, but she'd done her best to point out the seriousness of his bad choices and he'd seemed to pay attention. For this one evening she was not going to worry about Cory. She was going to relax and try to enjoy herself.

And it was fun. Especially because Cory dropped his macho act and allowed himself to be the kid he was.

"For a first-time griller, you did an awesome job, Cory." Zac savored his steak with appreciative eyes. "It's not everyone who can get a rare steak done perfectly. This one is."

"You did all the work. But thanks." Cory hid his burning cheeks by bending over his plate. But a minute later he glanced up to the plaque on the stone wall next to the barbecue. "What does that mean?" he asked.

Brianna read the words silently.

When He has tested me, I will come forth as gold.

"That's a very special verse my mom taught me years ago when I had to have a lot of surgeries." Zac smiled at him. "Sometimes I got really grumpy so one day my mother read me the story of Job. Do you know it?"

"Sort of." Cory leaned forward, his interest obvious.

"Well, to recap, Job had a lot of problems. He lost his family, his wealth and his health, but he didn't lose his faith, even when his friends tried to convince him he'd done something wrong." Zac pointed to the plaque. "That's what he said in the middle of all his trials. *When He has tested me, I will come forth as gold.* So I try to remember Job's faith when I get tested."

"Tested? You mean God tests you?" Cory's eyes widened.

"Of course. Faith in God means being strong." Zac shrugged. "That's what God's tests are all about. He needs us to learn how to keep doing the right thing, trusting in Him no matter what."

"Oh." Cory concentrated on his meal.

Brianna did, too, mulling over what Zac had said. Was that the reason behind the hardship she struggled with? Was God testing her faith?

If so, she figured He must be disappointed. She hadn't had to endure years of surgeries as Zac had, though she had endured years of her mother's controlling. Still—she decided to think about it more later, when she was alone.

Once they'd finished their steaks, grilled potatoes and the Caesar salad Brianna had made, Zac surprised them with his grilled dessert—chocolate melted over sweet sliced peaches on a bed of crushed cookies.

"Wow!" Cory's pupils expanded. "I never knew guys could cook like this."

"Really?" Zac frowned at him. "Don't the guys you know eat?"

"Yes, but—" Cory glanced at Brianna.

"In my opinion, taking care of yourself is a basic skill every guy and girl ought to know," Zac said firmly. "If you can't even take care of yourself, how can you become an adult who has to be responsible for others?"

It was clear to Brianna that Cory had never considered this. After they'd cleared the dishes and stored them in the dishwasher, Cory wandered off to a spot in the yard where he sat down and stared at the plaque.

"Thank you for that," Brianna murmured. "It seems your words really hit home with him. Finally."

"Sometimes we have to hear things from a different person to get them through our thick heads." He offered her a mug of steaming tea and she took it, even though the evening retained much of its heat. "How do you think Your World is going to go over on Monday?" he asked.

"Zac, are you seriously worried about this?" Brianna could see by his furrowed brow that he was. "Why?"

"I have a lot riding on this project."

"You do? But you said you're staying behind the scenes." As Brianna studied him she felt her body tense. He wasn't telling her something.

"I guess I've never really explained to you why I want this project to make such a difference here," he said, his voice grave.

"You *said* you wanted to challenge the students' apathy." She raised one eyebrow. "Was that a lie?"

"No, of course not. I do want that. Very much. But I have a second reason for wanting to see success in Hope's schools." Zac inhaled, then gazed directly at her. "I want to get into curriculum development, Brianna, at the state level."

"Ah." Understanding dawned. Her stomach took a nosedive. "And to get that job you need a big success in Hope, success you want to achieve with the Your World project, so the folks in the state offices will see that your methods succeed, right? I get it."

Here she'd been entertaining thoughts of tenderness toward him, and it seemed Zac was using her. What a fool!

"Brianna—"

"Hope's failing schools are all part of your big plan. You were telling the truth when you said that's why you came back."

"Yes, but I wasn't trying to use you, Brianna," Zac rushed to reassure, dots of red coloring his prominent cheekbones. "I thought this would be good for your practice, too."

"Really? I think you thought giving Whispering Hope Clinic, me, the contract for school counseling was a way to make me so grateful I'd willingly help you with your big idea." She bit her lip to contain the words but they spilled out anyway. "It's the same old, same old, isn't it?"

"No," he objected, but it was a weak objection.

"Yes." Brianna set down her cup of tea, unable to swallow the very drink she'd been so happy he'd brewed moments before. "Back when we were to be married, you couldn't manage to be honest enough to tell me you'd accepted my mother's job. Now you can't be honest about your reasons for this project. I suppose you won't like hearing that Your World is actually causing a lot of problems at the clinic." Fury burned deep inside. Duped again. How dumb was she?

"What do you mean?" Zac stared at her.

"I mean that I've been working hard with several teens, trying to get them to see beyond their current circumstances to what the future could hold for them. But I'm fighting their parents every step of the way. They don't want their children to leave town any more than my mother wanted me to go way back when." She rose. "In fact, Eve Larsen's parents have been to see me twice, asking me to stop encouraging their daughter."

"Why would any parent object—"

"I can give you several reasons. They need their daughter in their business. Second, they think her goals are too lofty to succeed and, even if they weren't, they're worried about the expense. So you see, any benefit in my practice that I might have expected from

Your World has already been negated by the Larsens bad-mouthing me all over town. I don't expect it to take long before other parents join their objections."

"I'm sorry. I didn't realize—"

"Exactly the point, Zac. You didn't realize. How could you? You were so focused on your own goal, you never gave a thought to what your scheme would mean to me or anyone else. But then it's always been all about you, hasn't it?" She grabbed her purse and sauntered toward the gate. "Stupid me. I thought you'd changed." She cut off the words, unwilling to admit she'd hoped things could change between them. "Cory, come on. We're leaving. Thanks for dinner. We'll walk home. I need the fresh air."

Though Cory gave her several speculative glances on the way home, he didn't ask any questions, choosing instead to disappear into his grandfather's studio in the garage where the two of them painted until bedtime. Brianna went into Cory's room to say good-night and praised his latest watercolor, a pretty picture of Zac's backyard.

"Good night, honey," she said as she hugged him, amazed as always that she was the mother of this amazing child. "Church tomorrow morning, don't forget."

"Yeah." Cory peered at her. "You're pretty steamed at Zac, aren't you?"

"Yes." There was no point in pretending otherwise. "Why?"

"Because he didn't tell me the truth." Bitterness flowed inside. "I've known Zac for a long time. I thought we were friends."

"Sometimes people make mistakes, Mom." Cory's

blue-eyed gaze held hers. "You always told me that God expects us to forgive and forget."

"Yes, I did. And I will. But I'm not there yet, son." She brushed his sandy brown hair off his forehead. "You're old enough to know that sometimes we have to work things through before we can find forgiveness in our heart."

"Is that what you're doing with Grandma? Finding forgiveness?"

"I'm trying, son. I'm trying. Have a good sleep."

Brianna wandered downstairs and found her father sipping a cup of cocoa.

"Warm night for that, isn't it?"

"Probably." He grinned. "But sometimes a cup of hot chocolate is exactly the medicine a body needs. Want some?"

"Yes." She accepted the steaming mug he handed her. "And, no, I don't want to talk about it," she hurried to say, seeing the speculation in his eyes.

"Okay." He led the way to the back patio where they both flopped onto comfortable lounge chairs around the pool.

Brianna sipped her chocolate as she struggled to figure out why she kept being disappointed in people. She needed to unload on someone so finally she blurted out, "Why doesn't God care about me, Dad?"

"Where did you get that idea?" he said, his voice calm in the dusky silence.

"I got that idea from all the bad things that keep happening to me." Again Brianna felt a surge of bitterness take hold.

"What makes you think you should be immune from

bad things?" Brian Benson demanded. "Did someone promise you perfection?"

"No. But—" She frowned. Put that way she sounded childish. "So many things in my life have gone the opposite to what I expected," she admitted.

"Then maybe your expectations were wrong." He set down his cup and turned to face her. "Everyone's allowed to lapse into self-pity sometimes, Brianna, but if you stay there, you're heading for trouble."

Self-pity? She wanted to reject that, but maybe he was right.

"Honey, you have to trust the future to God. He has plans for you, though it might not seem like it now. You can't let the present problems obscure the future."

Brianna smiled. Wasn't that exactly what she'd been telling her clients? The old adage "Physician heal thyself," mocked her. She'd been pushing the kids she counseled, and their parents, to look for possibilities, and here she was doing what they did, letting current problems confound her.

"The thing is, it's called a 'faith walk' because you have to have faith to walk it," her father continued. "You can't know the answers ahead of time, no matter how much you want to. Believe me, I have my own whys that I'd like answered. But God doesn't owe me any answers." His voice grew serious. "Long ago I said He was Lord of my life. A servant doesn't ask the master why he has to do things. He just does them, trusting that the master has a good reason."

His words bit deep into Brianna's soul. That's what she'd been doing. Asking God to justify Himself to her.

"The Bible says the same thing a little differently. It says the clay doesn't look at the potter and say, 'Why did you make me into this kind of a pot? Change me. Make me that kind.'" He chuckled. "My dad told me that and it's stuck with me. Whenever I want to ask God why, I think of myself as a pot on the potter's wheel, one eye wide open, peering at the master potter and telling him how to make me. It makes me feel ridiculous every time."

"I can imagine." She watched while her father stretched, stood, picked up his cup and bent to brush his lips against her forehead. "Good night, Dad."

"Good night, honey." He walked to the back door, paused and then peered through the gloom at her. "Maybe it's time to start thinking about what God is trying to teach you."

Alone in the night, with the moon creeping into the starlit sky, Brianna felt ashamed of her attitude. Yes, it had been hard to raise Cory without his father, hard to learn after Craig's death that he'd known he would die soon and hadn't told her. It was hard to keep encouraging kids when the parents fought her so hard. It was more than hard to see her mother and be subjected to her verbal abuse every time.

Last Sunday's sermon echoed inside her head.

God never promised you a rose garden, but He said He'd be there to help you deal with the thorns.

Brianna resolved to change her thinking. She was still angry at Zac, and she'd have to work to get over that, but she'd also learned a lesson. Zac wasn't considering a future here in Hope. He had plans to move on, plans that made her silly daydreams of what might be futile.

Better to face that now before her heart got in any deeper.

* * *

"You are as close to God as you choose to be."

The minister's words hit Zac with the impact of a steel brick.

"Intimate friendship with God is a choice, not an accident," the pastor continued.

Wait a minute. Did that mean these feelings of uselessness that had plagued Zac for years—that was *his* fault? That God hadn't given up on him?

"If you want a more intimate connection with God, first of all you're going to have to learn to share your feelings with Him. All of them." The sermon seemed specially chosen for Zac. He couldn't have ignored the words if he wanted to.

"God doesn't expect His kids to be perfect. None of the great Biblical figures were perfect. If that was a requirement, none of us would attain His friendship. But God does expect your honesty, even if that involves messing up a million times. Even if it involves complaining and arguing with Him. Read the Psalms. David often accused God of unfairness, betrayal and even abandonment. He said, 'I pour out my complaints before Him and tell Him all my troubles. For I am overwhelmed.' David never pretended everything was okay between God and him."

Zac considered his attitude. He'd always believed he didn't possess the qualities God required in order to use someone, that he was a misfit and therefore unfit for God's work. After all he didn't have the same glib ability as his friends to talk to others about ordinary stuff, let alone about godly things. But that wasn't what the pastor was saying.

"If you read the Old Testament, you'll find God was

very honest with His children. He got so fed up with
Israel's disobedience in the desert He told Moses He
would keep His promise regarding the Promised Land,
but He refused to go one step farther. God was sick
and tired of his kids!" The man joined the congregation's laughter. "I see some of you parents can relate.
So don't worry, God can handle your honesty. He can
handle your anger. But if you're going to be honest with
God and others, you have to be honest with yourself.
You have to open yourself up to others being honest
with you."

And that was his stumbling block, Zac knew. He
just couldn't let go of the fear that if he were honest, if
he let someone see inside to all his cracks and weak-
nesses, they'd make fun of him. That's what terrified
him, that people would see his insecurities and mock
him as nothing but a teacher who couldn't even master
his own issues. How could he help others?

Whatever was said next, Zac missed as he kept turning the issue over and over in his mind. Why was the
deep intimate kind of honesty so hard for him?

When the service ended, he saw Brianna greet Jaclyn
and Kent, but though the couple waved, Brianna kept
her head averted and soon left with Cory. She was still
mad at him and he didn't blame her. He hadn't been
honest with her about Your World just as he hadn't been
honest all those years ago when he'd latched on to her
mother's offer like a life preserver.

It was time—past time—to apologize to her.

Zac hurried out the door and searched the parking
lot. He saw Brianna pulling away in her father's car.
She didn't even glance his way though Zac saw Cory
turn and wave.

"What's the rush, professor?" Kent stood behind him, peering down the street. "You missed Brianna."

"Thank you for that astute observation." Zac regretted the frustrated response as soon as he said it, but apparently Kent didn't take offense. He simply grinned. "I was hoping to apologize to her," Zac muttered.

"For what?" Kent's grin slid away. "You did something really stupid, didn't you?"

"Yes," Zac admitted freely.

"So make it right," his friend ordered before he loped back to his wife.

Yeah. Make it right. But how?

Honesty increases the level of intimacy. But if you're going to be honest with God and others, you have to open yourself up.

Open himself up—to Brianna? Could he do that again and risk leaving himself unprotected? Could he risk not doing it and losing Brianna's help?

Zac trudged the short distance to his home, struggling to dislodge the minister's words. But the words before the benediction hung in the back of his mind like a chant he couldn't ignore.

If you want to be close to God, then learn how to trust Him, no matter what He asks you to do.

Zac ate his lunch without tasting a thing as the inward battle raged.

Trust God?

That was the root of his problem.

Zac didn't trust anyone.

"These colors don't go together. If you'd stayed in the store and learned from me, you'd know that. I can't understand how you could be so stupid."

"Neither do I, Mom. Neither do I." A wealth of bitterness suffused her as Brianna gathered her array of quilt patches and stuffed them into her bag. She said a quick goodbye then left the room, tears overflowing the moment she stepped over the threshold. She felt rather than heard her father follow her and, for his sake, tried to regain her calm.

"Your mother loves you, Brianna. In spite of what you think."

"That was love?" She shook her head, her eyes clouded by tears.

"That was frustration." He wrapped an arm around her shoulder and squeezed.

"Dad, it's obvious that she hates me."

"No, she doesn't. She loves you very much. She just can't express it. She never learned how." He wiped away her tears. "Try to imagine her world. She wakes up and she's here, alone. She doesn't always remember why she's here or where we are. She doesn't know what's going to happen to her. She can't get the words she needs to communicate, to express what she wants. Everything has changed and she's confused and angry and hurt and scared. And, yes, she takes it out on you. But that doesn't mean she doesn't love you."

"Ha! You heard what she said. Being called *stupid* is a strange form of love." Brianna gulped. "I've made quilts for years, and sold many of them to people who claimed I have a knack for blending colors and textures. I paid for my schooling that way. But my own mother can't see any potential in my work. What kind of love is that?"

"She does love you," her dad insisted.

Brianna sniffled her disbelief. She pressed away from him, her eyelashes damp and stuck together.

"I stayed away all these years because she wanted her disappointing daughter out of her life, so I wouldn't ruin her success. I came back because you said she wanted me here, but that's not true. She doesn't want me here. I'm still the bad daughter who wouldn't become part of her business." Her lips tightened. "I've had it, Dad. I'm sick of being put down so she'll feel better. It's better if I don't come here anymore. Less upsetting for both of us."

"No." Mr. Benson clasped his daughter's shoulders and forced her to look at him. "Your mother does not hate you, Brianna. She never has."

"I don't believe you." Brianna saw Zac coming toward them from down the hall. She blew her nose and thrust back her shoulders. "And I don't want to talk about this anymore."

"I do, but we'll have to discuss it later. I'm going back in to make sure Anita's settled. I'll see you at home." He hurried into the room just as his wife called for him.

"I need to talk to you, Brianna." Zac stood in front of her, blocking her exit.

"Isn't it amazing that even after all those years of her running him ragged, Dad still worships the ground my mother walks on?" Brianna muttered as she glared at him.

"I don't know." He frowned. "Did you hear me?"

"I don't want to talk to you or anyone right now, Zac." She walked around him, down the hall and out into the parking lot. "I just want to get out of here."

"I'll take you for a ride."

"I'd rather be alone." She strode away, furious that

he thought he could just waltz back into her life after using her to get his big master plan under way.

"I'm not going away and you won't shake me until I say what I came to say." Though she ignored him, he kept pace easily, modulating his steps to hers.

The afternoon was warm and it wasn't long before Brianna began to perspire. It was clear that Zac wasn't going to be brushed off so easily. Tired, cranky and fed up with her life, she jerked to a halt and wheeled around to face him.

"What do you want?" she demanded. "Today's my day off. I'm not available to give you counseling about your new goal. Or anything else. I need to figure out how I'm going to get to Las Cruces and pick up Cory's birthday present before his party tomorrow. So whatever you need, you'll have to handle it yourself."

"I could take you."

"No, thanks." She glared at him. No way did she want to spend the afternoon tied in knots because of Zac Ender.

"Please, Brianna. Just listen." He gazed at her, his dark eyes serious. "I'm sorry. I mean that sincerely. I apologize for not telling you what I was planning. At first I didn't even think about it mattering to you, and then later—"

"Later I stupidly fell in with your plan, like the idiot I am, and you decided not to give me the consideration of telling me the reason you sucked me into the whole thing. Is that what you're saying, Zac?" She loaded the words with as much scorn as she could, still stinging from her mother's rejection.

"Not exactly what I meant." Zac frowned, hesitated,

but after a moment, nodded. "But if that works for you, then, yes, that's what I'm saying."

"Some apology." Brianna hissed a sigh from between her teeth, glaring at him in utter frustration. "Just like before. When are you going to figure out that all you have to do is be honest, Zac? I would have helped you anyway because I care about helping the kids in this town. What would it have cost you to tell me the truth?"

"A lot." He shrugged. "I don't open up to people easily. You know that. You know that I'm a klutz at human relationships."

"That's your favorite song, isn't it? I can't help it. That's the way God made me." She moved so her face was inches from his and glared into his eyes. "It's baloney, and you know it. You aren't a klutz when you forget about your silly preconceptions. It's when you get the focus off of others and on to yourself that you mess up."

Chapter Seven

Zac flinched, decimated by her diagnosis of his problem. But more than that, with that simple touch on his arm, she'd reached past his self-imposed barriers to reignite that part of him that was not immune to her.

He was tired of this age-old reaction to Brianna, the fizzling spear of tenderness that flamed whenever he looked at her, then shot straight to his gut, doubling his nervousness in spite of his determination to remain unflappable. He was tired of his inability to erase the blaze of feeling he'd had ten years ago. Mostly he was tired of always trying to measure up and feeling like he constantly fell short.

He spared a moment to wonder if God was fed up with him.

Zac inhaled and forced out the words he should have said weeks ago. "I don't want us to be at loggerheads, Brianna. We have to work together. I screwed up. I didn't tell you my plans when I asked for your help and I should have. I'm sorry and I apologize."

There. He'd said it. There was nothing else to say. He turned and walked toward his car.

"That's it?" She grabbed his arm and drew him to a halt. "That's all you have to say?"

"What more do you want?" Anger that she kept pushing him bubbled inside. "I messed up. Again. Is that what you wanted to hear?"

"No. I'd like to hear why you're doing Your World." Her beautiful eyes impaled him. "What's the big draw working at state level?"

Zac studied her, searching for the best way to explain because he knew she wouldn't let it go. "Curriculum, which I've always wanted to be involved in."

"I get that. But that's not all of it," she challenged. "Be honest with me, Zac."

"Curriculum is primarily office work. Developmental."

"Uh-huh." Brianna's sandal-clad feet were planted, her stance combative.

"In curriculum I won't have to do any public presentations," he finally blurted out.

"But—you've always been so great with kids. You used to live to get in the classroom and make education come alive. You're willing to give that up?" The green of her eyes darkened to a forest tone. Her mouth formed an *O.* "You will, won't you? To avoid public speaking."

"Yes," he agreed, wondering if he looked as small as he now felt.

"But you're not required to do a lot of speaking now."

"Assembly tomorrow," he reminded her, dread dogging his spirit. "The parents will be there."

"So what? They're mostly people we went to school with."

"Exactly." He could imagine what they'd think when

nerdy Zac Ender stuttered his way through an explanation of Your World.

"Most parents' concern is that their kids do well. They're not going to be focused on you as much as the program." Brianna craned her neck forward, scrutinizing his face. "You're really that bothered?"

"Yes," Zac assured her, embarrassed by the admission. "If you remember, I was never that good at presentations, and trust me, I have not improved with age."

"Yes, but—" She spluttered, obviously at a loss. "But I've seen you with the kids. You're not nervous when you're with them."

"Sometimes I am, but it's easier to hide it with kids. Not so easy with adults. Especially ones who knew me in the good old days." He shrugged. She wanted honesty? Okay, let's see how she handled him baring his soul. "I freeze up, Brianna. I get tongue-tied and I don't make sense, even to myself. Who wants to listen to that?"

"But you can't just opt out. Not now." She gave him a speculative glance. "Your World is *your* project. You have to be involved. Publicly involved," she emphasized.

"I will be." Humiliated and embarrassed, Zac wanted this conversation to end. "Forget my problems. What I wanted to do today was apologize for not telling you my plans. Now that I've done that, I'll go and let you enjoy your afternoon."

He'd almost made it to his car when she spoke again.

"Is the offer of a ride to Las Cruces still on?"

"Sure." He turned, studied her face, wondering if she would accept his help because she felt sorry for him.

"My car is still in the shop, and I'd really like to pick

up Cory's birthday gift." She must have read something on his face because after a moment Brianna shook her head. "Never mind. I'll think of something else."

"I'll take you. I can pick up a book on South America that's waiting for me." Zac realized he welcomed the afternoon away from town. And with Brianna? "Do you have to be home in time to make dinner tonight?"

"Dad will eat with Mom, and Cory's on that youth-group riding outing. They're having a fire and picnic after so he won't be home till eight or so." She wore a funny look that told him she expected he'd change his mind. "Why?"

"Just thinking. Let's go."

But Brianna didn't move. "Are you sure you want to do this?"

"Yes." Though Zac expected some leftover tension to tinge their afternoon, once they were on the highway Brianna told him she accepted his apology.

"I understand this curriculum job is a big deal to you and that you don't want anything to ruin it," she mused, peering out the windshield at the golden swells of the hills. "So I'll forgive you this time. But, Zac, you have to be honest with me. I refuse to work with you on Your World anymore unless you tell me the truth."

"Okay." He glanced from the road to her, knowing by her tone that there was something else Brianna wanted to say. "And?"

"I don't believe your issues with public speaking are something you can't overcome."

"Overcome how?" Not that Zac intended to change his mind about moving to Santa Fe for curriculum work, but he wanted to hear Brianna's thoughts on defeating the bugaboo that had haunted him for years.

"You won't like what I'm about to say," she warned with a sideways glance at him.

"I'll handle it," he told her in a dry tone.

"Okay." She studied him for a moment. "In my experience, issues like yours stem from an overfocus on yourself."

"Hey!" Zac twisted his head to frown at her.

"I warned you that you wouldn't like it. Now let me finish." Brianna waited for his nod before continuing. "The most effective public speakers, the ones we love to listen to, aren't thinking about themselves when they speak. What they're concentrating on is their audience, on getting their message across. They've got something to say and they're focused on making a point, not on whether their audience will notice if they stumble or make a mistake or pause too long. It's the message, not the messenger. But because they are so good at getting that message to us, we say they are good public speakers."

"You're saying I'm getting in the way of what I want to say." His lips pinched together. The truth hurt.

"Yes, but it's more than that." Brianna looked at him, visibly debating her next words.

"I won't melt from criticism. Go on," he told her.

"If you could forget about what you feel like and focus on what your listeners feel like, on how they're accepting what you have to tell them, you'd forget to be so self-conscious."

"You make me sound selfish." He glanced at Brianna and knew that was exactly what she meant.

"Because I think it is selfish to worry more about yourself than the message." She opened her handbag, a turquoise satchel she usually looped over one shoulder.

That was the thing about Brianna—she knew how to make a point. She could carry off a vibrant color like turquoise because she herself was so dynamic. Little things like speaking to a crowd of people didn't affect her. Oblivious to his scrutiny, she pulled out a small notepad and began writing on it.

"In the presentation tomorrow, for instance, you have to make sure the students realize that no idea they have is unworthy of writing on the board. You need to ensure that they and their dreams are valued. That has to be your primary focus."

"I *was* having a relaxed afternoon," Zac grumbled. "Now I'm getting all uptight about tomorrow and that speech."

"But that's the thing—you're not giving a speech. You are simply explaining how a new program is going to work." Brianna shook her dark head at him, her eyes twinkling. "It's not a lecture, nor do you have to defend anything. You're just explaining and you've done that with students for years. Haven't you?"

"Yes." But admitting that fact did nothing to untie the knot in his midsection. So he turned the focus on her. "What did you think of the sermon today?"

Brianna was quiet for so long Zac was ready to change the subject.

"What the pastor said about friendship with God, that was interesting." She averted her head and stared out the side window. "That God wants—even welcomes—frank honesty from us—I guess I've never thought that way. He said genuine friendship is built on disclosure. God wanting to be friends is a different perspective for me."

"Because you don't like to think of God as a friend?"

Zac found himself curious about the wan look filling her expressive eyes.

"It's not that. I guess I've never thought that it was perfectly okay to blurt out what you really feel. To anyone."

"That's why you never told me about the problems between you and your mom." Zac watched her shift and knew his guess was on target. "Because you had to hide your feelings?"

"Because it was embarrassing. I didn't want my friends to hear her rant." She frowned. "I was raised that talk to God should be reverent. To think that it's okay to tell Him you feel cheated or disappointed in Him, that's odd to me."

"Do you feel cheated and disappointed?" Zac asked quietly.

"Yes." Brianna looked at him steadily. "Yes, I do."

"Why?" Zac recalled the minister's words that a block to true friendship was often hidden anger or resentment.

"I don't understand why He doesn't answer prayers, why He allows certain things. If I were God I would never let children die from starvation," she said, her voice hard. "I wouldn't let people who cause misery and suffering go scot-free and I wouldn't make the innocent suffer. How can I build a friendship with God when He allows this?"

Zac recalled the years after she'd jilted him and the months after that he'd wasted asking why. He'd drifted from God in the intervening years, but he'd finally learned to face himself and all his faults. The lesson had stuck. He was determined to share it now. Maybe, for once, he could be the one to help her.

"Anger, frustration, bitterness—those kind of feelings are natural," he assured her. "You, as a psycholo-gist, must know that giving voice to them and releasing them is the first step toward healing. You were talking earlier about honesty. Isn't it the ultimate honesty to tell God exactly how you feel?"

"I suppose. But what good does it do?" she de-manded. "It changes nothing."

"Not if you leave it at that." Zac shifted in his seat, slightly uncomfortable with how personal this conver-sation was becoming. He wasn't the kind of Christian that God used to help other people, but he couldn't leave Brianna floundering in her anger.

"So?" She frowned at him, waiting.

"The thing is, you have to not only realize but also accept that God acts in your best interest, always, even when it's painful and you don't understand. The pastor said worship is about holding back nothing of what you feel. If God didn't want to hear what we really thought, He wouldn't have allowed Psalms to be in the Bible. It sounded like he was saying that expressing doubt is the first step to building a rapport with God."

The tip of Brianna's pert nose scrunched up as if she thought he was full of hot air.

"It's a process, and I'm no expert," Zac told her. "But He said that every time you trust God's wisdom and do as He asks in spite of your misgivings or lack of understanding, you make the relationship more real. So I guess it boils down to whether we are willing to trust Him or not." Trust again. Something sadly lack-ing in his own life.

"Trust?"

"Yeah. Something I find hard to do." He dredged his brain for the applications he'd studied ten years ago and still struggled to implement. "If we're truly followers of Christ, we follow Him. Meaning we do as He asks. But not because we're afraid of Him, or from guilt or fear of punishment, but because we love Him. And because we love, therefore we trust that He knows what's best for us—in spite of our perceptions of the current state."

Brianna studied him through narrowed eyes.

"What?" Zac felt his cheeks burn at the intense scrutiny. "Why are you looking at me like that?"

"Did you just hear yourself?" she said, a smile tipping her mouth at one corner. "You didn't stutter or stammer or mess up your message. You got it out with clarity and conviction."

"I wasn't speaking in public."

"What difference does that make? You were trying to get something across and you did it because you weren't focused on yourself or how you felt, but on what you wanted me to understand." She leaned forward, her face serious. "If you could just see yourself with the kids, Zac, you'd realize that you do the same thing with them. That's why you're such a great teacher."

"Thanks, but I'm nothing special."

"I give up," Brianna said in frustration. "If you won't see the gift you have, I can't make you."

As he took the exit ramp that led to the mall they'd decided to visit, Zac considered Brianna's words. The gift he had? That was Brianna the nurturer. But all the same, on the drive home he'd treat her to dinner and then ask her help with what he planned to say tomorrow. Maybe she could keep him from totally embarrassing himself in front of the entire school.

And after that he was going to do some serious thinking about his spiritual relationship.

* * *

"I've got several things to pick up." Brianna stood inside the mall doors, shifting uncomfortably under Zac's scrutiny. "Shall we meet in a couple of hours?"

They agreed on a time and a place then Brianna set off to collect the gifts she'd chosen for Cory. Fortunately the store had a clearance on the game system she'd planned to purchase, which allowed her to add a couple of the games that Cory was crazy about. She'd save those for Christmas gifts.

Since Brianna completed her shopping well before the appointed time, she strolled through a quilt store, pretending to envision a new project. But in fact she couldn't dislodge the picture of Zac's face when he'd told her his thoughts on faith. She'd never seen such openness from him before. The strength of his convictions seemed so clear.

Yet he still feared public speaking.

Was part of that her fault? Because she'd left so quickly the morning of the wedding, she hadn't considered what Zac would have to endure. The first thing she'd ever learned about Zac Ender was how much he hated being the focus of anything. She'd attributed that to the years he'd been a patient, with his mother and medical team constantly watching his every move. So to endure a year of gossip and ridicule while he taught must have been desperately difficult.

She owed him an apology. She'd been so immersed in her own pain that day, she hadn't realized how running away from the wedding would affect him.

Brianna shuddered at the thought of harking back to the past again. Yes, she still resented Zac's betrayal of their dreams, their future. It festered like a sore that had never really healed. How could he have given them up so easily? Why hadn't God done something to stop it?

But though she'd asked many times, God still gave no explanation.

Brianna glanced at the clock in the window of a bookstore. Fifteen minutes until she joined Zac. Time enough to go in and see if there was something that could help her find answers to the soul-deep questions that plagued her. She added a devotional book she'd heard Cory mention the youth group using to his birthday gifts, but saw nothing for herself.

"Please help me understand, God," she begged under her breath in a desperate plea as she wandered between the shelves. Nothing. Too embarrassed to ask for help she decided to check out.

"Is that everything for you?" the clerk asked.

"Yes, thanks." Brianna set her items on the counter, wishing that just this once God would have answered.

"I hope you found what you needed," the clerk said as she bagged the items. "I didn't mean to ignore you. It's just that we've got some new stock and I'm trying to get everything shelved before my boss comes in tomorrow morning."

"No problem." Brianna hurried away, not wanting to keep Zac waiting. Maybe on the way home she could find an opportunity to apologize to him. Maybe if she did, she'd finally learn why he'd given up on their dreams.

"You look like your mission was successful." Zac took her packages. "Do you need more time? I could put these in the car?"

"No, thanks. I'm finished." She glanced around. "I could use a coffee, though."

"How about if we do the drive-through thing and take it to the park. It's a gorgeous day." Zac waited for her nod then walked with her to the car. "Hey, we could head out to see the hot-air balloons." He pointed to a poster stuck to a light standard. "Today's the last day of the festival."

Brianna drew on the hazy memory of an afternoon spent with Zac, watching the beauty of the multicolored balloons as he explained how the air filling them lifted the colorful balls with baskets attached high over the white gypsum dunes. Peaceful, relaxing. It was just the thing she needed on this Sunday afternoon.

"I haven't been out there in years," she admitted. That long-ago Saturday had been one of a very few her mother had allowed her to take off from work at the store. She and Zac had left home early, spread a blanket on the hills and huddled together in the cool air to wait for that breathless moment of lift-off when the balloons became airborne.

"Me, neither. Let's go." Zac hummed a tune as he loaded both their parcels in the back of his car.

The crystal clarity of the atmosphere and the heat of the autumn sun offered the perfect opportunity to admire miles of the desert sky. They arrived and found their favorite spot. Brianna blinked at the quilt Zac dragged out of his car.

"You're still using this old thing?" she asked, fingering the threadbare corners she'd so painstakingly stitched for his Christmas gift in their senior year of college.

"Quality never grows old," he said with a wink and chuckled at her droll look.

His laughter brought back so many memories of days

they'd laughed and giggled, making the hours of studying so much fun. She'd forgotten the joy of those times,
or maybe she'd let it get tarnished by anger and frustration. Now Brianna released that and resolved to enjoy
the moment.

As they sat on the hillside, she couldn't stop taking
little peeks at Zac as he sipped his coffee and watched
balloons dot the horizon in front of them.

"Tell me." Zac pointed to the bold colors laid out in
a panorama before them. "Did you ever see anything
like that in Chicago?"

"No." She kept her head averted. "But Chicago had
other assets."

"One of them being your husband, I suppose." His
voice dropped. "What was he like?"

Zac sounded so—intense. Brianna risked a quick
look at him, found him staring at her with those dark
riveting eyes. His curiosity was probably as natural as
hers was when she thought about all the years they'd
been apart. It couldn't hurt to tell him. In fact, the words
came easily. Of all the betrayals, it was Craig's that she
found easiest to forgive.

"Craig was my friend, a real friend when I needed
one most."

"How did you meet?"

"Actually I met him and Cory on the train in Las
Cruces the day I left home. Craig wasn't feeling well
and poor Cory was teething. While Craig rested, I kept
Cory entertained. He was such a cute baby. I felt so sad
that his mom had died in childbirth. He never knew
her." Which was only part of the reason Brianna now
felt such responsibility to ensure Cory got the love and
support he needed. With Craig gone, there was only her.

"Go on." A tinge of diffidence underlay Zac's voice.

"Not much else to tell, really." Brianna remembered the train trip as if it were yesterday. "As we traveled, we talked. Craig told me about a job in a friend's office, another doctor. He helped me get it. He also helped me find a place to live once we arrived in Chicago. As thanks, I babysat for him. We got to know each other. A few months later I agreed to marry him."

"Why?" Zac's mouth was tight.

"Craig needed someone to help him with Cory." She shook her head, a smile of regret clouding her memories. "I didn't know at the time, but Craig was terminally ill with cancer. His treatment left him incapable of caring for Cory. We weren't in love or anything. I agreed to marry him so I could look after Cory full time. He died a few months after we were married."

"I'm glad for Cory." Zac's voice emerged low and intense. "If not for you, who knows what would have happened to him. He's very lucky you were willing to give up your life for him."

"It wasn't exactly like that," she said, brushing off his compliment. But in actual fact, it had been for the first while. "Of course, at first it was difficult. Cory had a tough time teething. There were a lot of late nights."

"It must have been hard for you to be widowed with an infant." Zac touched her arm, his brown eyes soft with empathy. "Why didn't you come home? Surely your parents could have helped."

"You'd think so, wouldn't you?" Instantly Brianna's soft memories hardened into a ball of resentment. She couldn't speak for a moment, so great was her fury.

"What happened, Brianna?" Zac's soft pleading was her undoing.

"Does it matter?" Her joy in the afternoon dissolved, Brianna jumped to her feet. "Can we go now? It's been nice, but I don't want to be too late getting home. I don't want Cory to go out with his friends again tonight."

Zac rose without comment and folded the old quilt. He walked with her to his car and unlocked it. But before she could get inside, he laid his hand on her arm, his fingers curling against her skin, leaving a trail of heat.

Brianna stared at him, waiting for his condemnation.

"I'm sorry, Brianna. Really sorry. If I'd known you needed help, I'd have been there." He studied her for several moments, and then with a last touch, he opened the car door.

She couldn't get over his words, or the way he'd said them. Tender. Comforting. Not at all condemning. And that's when she knew it was time.

"Zac." She turned to face him when they were back on the highway. "I've waited too long to say this, and you probably don't care anyway, but I'm really sorry I left the way I did. I've been so wrapped up in my own side of things all these years, that I never really thought about what it must have been like for you. And I should have. Hope isn't kind to its citizens sometimes."

As she spoke, she saw a mask fall over his features, hardening them. His voice grated when he turned to glance at her.

"Why did you leave like that?" he asked. "You owed me better than that."

"Yes, I did." She admitted it freely. "I should have—"

"No." He held up a hand to stop her. "You know what? Don't say anymore. It doesn't matter now anyway. The past is over and as it turned out, it was the best thing for everybody." The accelerator inched up before he lifted his foot and visibly let go of the strain that had contorted his mouth into a tight line. "Let's just forget it."

The words killed her apology quicker than anything else could have. Zac thought it was best that she'd left? Then he certainly couldn't have any feelings for her now. Maybe he hadn't then, either. He made it sound as if their love had never been anything more than two kids with a crush on each other and yet to her it had been so much more. Brianna had never loved anyone as she'd loved him.

When Zac asked her if she wanted to listen to music, she agreed, glad he chose fast upbeat music that quashed the intimacy of the moment.

They stopped for an early dinner at a small roadside restaurant. Seated across from him on the patio, Brianna realized they had been here once before, during their Christmas break. They'd been so happy then, newly engaged, planning their marriage and eager to escape everyone to share some alone time.

Her old engagement ring lay under her shirt, pressing against her collar bone. Its presence reminded her of the way Zac had looked at her that night—adoringly. Now nothing on his chiseled face bore anything remotely resembling tenderness. Apparently no fond recollections of their shared past in this place bothered him or he wouldn't have chosen it. But Brianna was deluged by a ton of memories—of the big barrel cactus beside her that had been draped in tiny Christmas lights and the way Zac had nudged her behind it to share a quick kiss under a sprig of mistletoe.

For a moment utter loss overwhelmed her. Why had

she let their love go so easily? Why hadn't she fought for him?

"So how is Cory doing?"

Zac's words snapped Brianna out of her daydream. "Pardon?"

"I take it those friends of his haven't disappeared."

"No, and I'm getting more worried every time he goes off with them." She played with her water glass while wondering how much to confess. "Lately I've begun wondering if they were the source of the drugs. Cory won't say who gave him that drink, but the way they act—" She shook her head. "Maybe I'm just too suspicious."

"Maybe you're right to be concerned."

Brianna hoped Zac would remember his promise to engage Cory, but when he said nothing, she decided to leave it for tonight. She suspected he'd become fixated on giving his upcoming speech.

During the ride home they talked of inconsequential things. Brianna was glad when they finally pulled into her driveway.

"Thanks very much for taking me to Las Cruces, Zac," she said as he trailed behind her into the house. "I appreciate it. And dinner. And the balloons."

"No problem." He stood there, as if waiting.

"Would you like to come in for a cup of coffee?" she asked, wondering if there was something else he wanted to say.

But he shook his head.

"Thanks, but I need to get home. I missed my run yesterday so I'll catch up tonight." His eyes searched hers until he finally looked away.

"Okay. Well, thanks again." Brianna waited, but it seemed Zac wasn't finished.

He scanned the room, and then finally, when she was about to speak, asked, "You will be there tomorrow, for assembly. Won't you?"

"Sure. If you want me to." She grabbed her bag and pulled out her day planner. "I have a meeting with Eve Larsen's parents but I think I can still make it."

"More complaints?" Zac asked, one eyebrow tilted.

"Eve's talking of becoming a doctor," Brianna confided. "She's asked Jaclyn all kinds of questions, even shadowed her on the job for a couple of hours to get a better idea of what is involved. With a little emphasis on study, I don't see why she couldn't attain that goal."

"But her parents don't agree?" Zac asked, frowning.

"Her father wants her to stay here so she can continue to work in their restaurant. Help is expensive." Eve's situation was so similar to Brianna's as a teen that she frequently had to remind herself not to make comparisons. "They'll ask me to try to dissuade her or at least lead her in a different direction. I'll lay out a few of the issues she'll face, of course, but that girl has a dream. Why shouldn't she at least try to pursue it?"

"I understand the parents' concern, though. They must be really strapped right now." Zac frowned. "Things are a little better in town since the mine opened, but how can they make up for all the years and lost business while Hope was in a decline?"

"I hope you're not going to tell me to kill Eve's dream," Brianna said. She heard the sour tone in her voice and tried to modulate it. "She wants out of Hope, Zac. She realizes she made a mistake, that drugs aren't the way to go. She's pouring herself into a new dream.

She wants to show her parents that she's not a little girl anymore. But if they won't accept her goal, I don't know that I can help her, or them, anymore."

"I see." Zac looked at her for several moments. "Well, if they come to me, you know I'll support you. I'll even do some checking to see what funding there might be for someone in her situation. My whole focus is to get students to dream bigger. Clearly that's what you have Eve doing. It's what we need to get all the students to do."

"I believe Your World will be the first step for a lot of them," Brianna agreed. "All you have to do tomorrow is get the parents to see that."

"No pressure. Thanks," Zac said in a dry mocking tone. He lifted a hand and left.

Brianna watched him drive away, then lugged her packages upstairs to her room. She tucked Cory's gifts in her closet, noting that she'd inadvertently acquired Zac's book with her own packages. She set it aside to return to him. So much for avoiding him.

Another surprise waited. When Brianna removed Cory's book from the plastic bookstore bag, she found another much smaller booklet underneath it. She remembered there had been a stack of this title on the counter, but she hadn't intended to purchase one. Still, according to the receipt she had bought this tiny book.

She glanced at the title. *Knowing God.* Was that really possible?

She had about a half hour before Cory or her dad would return so Brianna sat down on her bed and began reading. The first words hit her straight between the eyes.

Pain is God's way of rousing us from spiritual lethargy. Problems aren't always punishment, sometimes they are wake-up calls from a God who is mad about you, not at you. He's trying to get you back into fellowship with Him. Read Jeremiah 29:13.

Intrigued, Brianna grabbed her Bible and read the passage. Basically it said that when she was ready to get really serious about knowing God, He wouldn't disappoint. Well, she was serious about it now. But what did it mean for her life? Her mother, Cory, work issues, even her difficulties with Zac—all of that was because God was trying to get her attention?

He had it!

Ready to read on, Brianna paused, recalling her desperate prayer for help in the bookstore. A fizzle of excitement started in her stomach and worked its way up to her brain.

God had answered her prayer! He'd led her to this book. Perhaps this little book could help her discern the Bible for her situation. A seed of hope sent out a shoot of hope.

Maybe if she studied hard enough, dug hard enough, God would finally show her why her life was in such turmoil.

And maybe then her brain would finally accept that Zac could never be a part of her life again.

Chapter Eight

"L-Ladies and gentlemen, teachers and students." Zac glanced around the room, searching for Brianna's face, needing the confidence her gorgeous eyes would impart.

She wasn't here. In a flash the same nemesis of fear that had dragged at him for most of his life, clawed its way to his throat, blocking it.

"I—ah, that is—"

Desperately, Zac scanned the crowd again. But Brianna was not present. Every eye in the room was on him, waiting. He had to continue.

Zac licked his lips, breathed a prayer and dove in to explain Your World. By the time fifteen minutes had lapsed, he knew his presentation was an unmitigated disaster, and so did everyone in the room. But he was determined to make sure the students understood the concept.

"Are there any questions?" he asked. To his surprise, Cory's hand went up. "Yes, Cory."

"Can we write anything on the board?"

"Within bounds." Zac peered at the young man, wondering why he'd asked the question. He listed the absolute no-nos again then went on to encourage all the students to take an active part. The ho-hum response he got was not encouraging, but there was little else he could say. No one seemed interested in Your World now, and for some reason that made Zac furious at Brianna. She'd promised to show. Where was she?

As the students left the room, he gathered his notes and left the platform. Brianna met him outside the door.

"Sorry I'm late," she puffed, obviously short of breath. Her hair was disheveled, too, the usual wispy curls out of place. "How did it go?"

"Even worse than I expected, which means it was bad." He pursed his lips, edged past her and walked out of the school, annoyed that she tagged along beside him.

"I'm sure it wasn't as terrible as you think, Zac."

"Really?" His temper flaring, he threw his suit jacket and his notes in the backseat of his car, then whirled around to face her. "Do you ever keep your promises and show up when you're supposed to?"

"That's not fair!" Brianna's green eyes widened with shock. She took a step back, her gaze narrowing. "I was working," she reminded him. "Doing my job."

"I guess that's as good an excuse as any." He yanked open the driver's door.

"Hey! What exactly did you expect me to do?" she demanded, grabbing his arm so he couldn't escape.

"Help me." The plea sputtered out on its own accord, and Zac felt a fool for having uttered it. All he wanted to do was leave, but Brianna's wounded stare forced him to explain. "You could have answered questions, clarified points—something."

"But you never told me you wanted me to do that," she protested. "You said I should drop by. Or at least that was my impression." Her forehead wrinkled. "I can't remember exactly what you said, but you knew I had a parent conference this morning, because I told you."

"You also said you'd be here." Zac clamped his lips together. What was the point of repeating that? She hadn't been bothered to make the effort. He was stupid to have thought she would care about his presentation enough to attend. "Look, I messed up and I'm in a foul mood, Brianna. I'm sorry. It's not your fault and I don't mean to take it out on you, it's just that I had such high expectations for this whole thing and now—" He left it hanging. His phone bleeped. He looked at it. "I have to go. I have to do a teacher evaluation this afternoon."

"But—"

Zac pretended he didn't hear as he got in the car and drove away.

His miserable presentation had only proven what he'd always believed—God had a tough time using someone like him to make a difference.

"Cory, do you think you could run that over to Zac?" Brianna pointed to the purple bag on the counter, then checked on the pan of chicken breasts browning in the oven.

Her father would be here with her mother shortly. There wasn't much time to make everything perfect, and it needed to be or her mother would be sure to point out her failure.

"Aw, Mom!" Cory glared at her. "The guys are coming soon for my birthday."

"I'll make sure they don't run away until you get back," she teased. "Take your bike. It won't take you long."

"What is this, anyway?" he asked, jiggling the bag.

"A book Zac special ordered. I took it with my packages by mistake yesterday." She raised her eyebrows at him. "Would you mind hurrying? I want you to be here when Grandma and Grandpa arrive."

"You didn't tell me Grandma was coming." He glared at her.

"I didn't know. Grandpa decided this afternoon to bring her." Brianna endured his angry look for a moment before asking, "Cory?"

"Yeah?"

"Were you at Mr. Ender's presentation this morning?"

"Yeah." His voice was hesitant.

"It was bad?" she asked, watching his face.

"Like really bad. I asked a question just so he could explain some more, but it didn't do much good."

Cory hunched his shoulders as he looked at her. "What's his issue anyway?"

"Zac doesn't like being in the spotlight. Never has as long as I've known him."

"You went to high school together, right?" Cory glared at her. "Kent told me that you and your friends were close. You've helped people with problems like Mr. Ender's before. So why don't you help him?"

"I'd like to, Cory. But Zac's had this problem for a long time. It's not going to disappear easily. It's kind of like you when you were afraid of heights. It took a while for you to realize you didn't need to be afraid. Zac is going to have to figure it out his own way." She felt a little strange about saying that but it was true. She could not give Zac what he needed. "So no one really got what Your World is all about?"

"The principal made an announcement after lunch and talked about it a lot. He said he wanted to clear up questions, but I think it was to cover for Mr. Ender. Anyway, I think everybody understood." He fiddled with the bag. "How long till Grandma comes?" Cory had formed a special bond with his grandmother, one which Brianna constantly worried over. She didn't want her son to catch her mother's negative attitude toward her.

"She should be here soon. Better get going," she urged.

"I'll be right back." Cory raced out the door. A second later she saw him speeding down the driveway.

Brianna watched him with a lump in her throat.

"I know you're there, God. Please make this a happy day for Cory. This one time, don't let Mom spoil it."

Ten minutes later her parents arrived at the same time as Cory's pals. Conversation was awkward, especially after Brianna's mother chided the boys about their manners. Brianna tried to cover, but all the same she heaved a sigh of relief when she saw Cory ride up. She almost choked when Zac appeared behind him.

"Mom!" Cory burst through the door. "I invited Zac to my birthday dinner." He returned Brianna's glare with a grin. "He told me to call him that. Anyway, he said he was going to eat leftovers so I invited him." Cory's facial expression made it clear that he thought leftovers were a fate worse than death.

"Great. Welcome, Zac," Brianna said cheerfully, inwardly chagrined. "Well, dinner's ready so let's eat." Her new plan to avoid Zac as much as possible was going up in smoke, especially after her father insisted Zac sit next to Brianna.

Her father said grace, then turned to his wife. "Isn't this a wonderful meal for our grandson's birthday?"

"I hope you enjoy it," Brianna said before her mother

could denigrate her work. "There's plenty for everyone. Help yourselves."

Despite attempts to circumvent her mother's criticisms, the meal progressed with negative remarks about everything Brianna had worked so hard to create, followed by anecdotes about how her mother preferred to serve the item. Cory's friends snickered a couple of times while Zac interrupted to offer his compliments on the food.

Cory seemed oblivious to his grandmother's complaints, his eyes fixed adoringly on her. From time to time Brianna's mother reached out to brush his hair off his forehead or pat his shoulder and he grasped her hand, the bond between them obvious. Brianna felt like an outsider.

Brianna had always baked and decorated her son's cake herself, rejecting the perfection of a bakery cake, as her mother had always done, for homemade love. This birthday was no exception. She carried the painstakingly decorated chocolate layers to the table with candles blazing, leading everyone in the birthday song. She loved this child so much.

"Mom makes the best birthday cakes, Grandma. Wait till you taste it. It's triple chocolate." Cory blew out the candles. "I'll cut you a piece."

"No, thank you, dear. I simply can't tolerate sickly sweet things. But Brianna knows that. I'm sure she's prepared something else for me."

In fact Brianna hadn't because she'd never known her mother to refuse anything sweet. So she sat there, with everyone's eyes on her, wishing she could sink through the floor.

"I'd love a piece, Cory." Zac's voice cut across the

strain. "Chocolate cake is my favorite. I can't bake it and I never buy it because I'd eat the whole thing myself. But it's your birthday and I'm splurging. Make it a big piece." He held out his plate.

Cory's friends echoed that response, and soon most plates were heaped with Brianna's chocolate confection. Except her mother's.

"It's really good, Grandma. Couldn't you try a little piece?" Cory begged.

"No, thank you, dear. I'll just watch you all enjoy it. I understand that your mother forgot about me. After all, she doesn't see me much, does she?"

On and on the complaints went. Brianna tried to ignore them but her father's pleading look forced her to return to the kitchen and scour the fridge for something for her mother. She scooped out a bowl of raspberry gelatin.

"Perhaps you'd prefer this," Brianna said setting it down in front of her mother.

"No, thank you. We have that every day at the home. Don't fuss about me," her mother said in a suffering tone. "I've gone without many times."

There was simply nothing to do but try to enjoy the rest of the evening. Cory loved the biking gear his pals gave him. He looked intrigued by the book on surfing, which Zac offered. He yelped with excitement when he opened the game system Brianna had chosen. But his biggest response came from the check his grandmother gave him.

"Five hundred dollars?" he squealed. "Wow! Thank you." He hugged her and she hugged him back. "I can do a lot with this."

"Honey, remember the rule." Brianna had always

insisted Cory put birthday money into a special account, half for future schooling, and half to save for something special. But as she noticed the speculative gleam in her mother's eyes and the way she looked from Cory to herself, Brianna let it go. Later she'd have a talk with her son. "That's very generous, Mom and Dad," she murmured.

"Actually, that's from your mother. My gift is out here. Follow me." Her dad, his grin a mile wide, proudly led the way to the back porch and when everyone was there, swooped the blanket off a lump which turned out to be a restored remote-control airplane.

"Cool, Grandpa." Cory's jaw dropped.

Brianna couldn't help but smile when her father hunkered down to explain things to Cory and his friends. He looked ten years younger.

"It doesn't look very sturdy, Hugh," her mother whined. "It will probably crash the first time he flies it."

"It's a wonderful gift, Dad," Brianna said, delighted when her father's dimmed joy returned. At that moment she couldn't take one second more of her mother's negativity. "I'll get us all something to drink," she said, and hurried back to the dining room, wondering why she'd ever thought coming home would work.

"I'll help you clear." Zac spoke from directly behind her. With an ease that spoke of his previous job in a restaurant, he stacked the dirty dishes while she stored the leftovers. "I'm actually pretty adept at making coffee, too," he offered.

"Go for it. Strong and black," she muttered, inwardly seething at her mother's behavior.

"It's a nice party," Zac said as he set aside the extra napkins with *Happy Birthday* printed on them. "You have a knack for creating them. You're also a very good cook. That chicken was amazing."

"Thank you." Brianna sighed. No point in punishing Zac because her family was so messed up. "Thanks for giving Cory that book on surfing in Hawaii. Maybe something in it will finally spark some interest in him."

"He sure asked a lot of questions when he returned my book." His hand brushed hers as he helped load the dishwasher. His touch set off a chain reaction in her nerves.

"I guess I picked it up with my packages. Sorry." She closed the dishwasher door and edged away, wishing Zac didn't always have this stupid effect on her. "But that wasn't my only mistake yesterday. It seems I also bought a book without knowing it."

"Oh? Any good?" He leaned against the counter and watched her, which made her even more uncomfortable.

"Actually, yes. It's got me thinking about a whole new perspective on God."

"That's a good thing. Isn't it?" His dark eyes followed her as she pulled out cups for the coffee.

"Yes, it is," Brianna agreed, swallowing hard. Why did Zac still have to be so good-looking? She put the mugs on a tray, added the cream and sugar and drinks for the boys and her mother while she struggled to come up with a way to ask what was on her mind. Finally she just said it. "Zac, have you given any thought to doing something with Cory?"

"No." His relaxed look disappeared. "Not yet."

"I'm not trying to push you, but I am getting really concerned. There was an odd smell in the garage last night. I think someone was smoking something. Aside from those two—" she jerked a thumb over her shoulder toward the porch "—Cory doesn't seem to have made any other friends. When I ask, he won't talk to me about it." Brianna watched Zac's long lashes droop down, hiding the expression in his eyes. "I'm really worried about him getting into trouble," she whispered. "Cory's got to turn things around and he only has until Christmas to do it. I can't stand by and let the judge send him to detention. I just can't."

Brianna hated that she sounded so desperate. She was a child psychologist. She was supposed to know how to deal with kids. She should certainly be able to motivate her own son.

"I'll come up with something," Zac promised, his soothing tone smoothing her irritation. "Don't worry about it."

"He's my child," she whispered. "I can't help worrying."

Zac's eyes narrowed as his gaze met hers, but he nodded as if he understood. He studied her for a few more minutes before he spoke, his voice quiet but determined.

"I need to apologize for losing my temper with you. It wasn't your fault I was terrible at that presentation. I shouldn't have taken my anger out on you. But my lousy performance proves one thing."

"It does?" Brianna frowned. "What does it prove?"

"That I should not be in the forefront of Your World. Any more public stuff and I'll take a backseat. Agreed?"

"But, Zac, that was one time. You can't give up—"

"Hey, Zac. Come and look at this." Cory's voice echoed through the house.

"I guess we'd better get out there." Zac picked up the tray and headed for the porch.

Brianna followed more slowly with the coffee and

a pitcher of iced tea, her heart whispering a plea to the only One who understood how much she wanted to help Zac, Cory and any others He set in her path.

"This movie is awful."

Mentally, Zac totally agreed with Cory's assessment.

"Why don't we shut it off and make some dinner," he suggested, glad when the boy quickly surged to his feet. "I'm starving."

Their night together two weeks after Cory's party wasn't off to a great start. Zac knew he had to do something. Since Cory had asked him numerous questions about grilling and other cooking skills, Zac decided to show him how to use the barbecue to cook meat, veggies and even dessert.

"You could make this on your own," he suggested later when the boy had cleaned his plate.

"I don't think I could make this."

"Practice makes perfect," Zac assured him. He reminded Cory of how easy it had been to prepare everything. "You could give your mom a break from cooking. She'd like that, wouldn't she?"

"I guess."

Zac heard something unsaid in that weak response, so he probed for more information.

"Doesn't she want you to cook?"

"She'd probably like it. She's kind of tired lately." Cory didn't look at him.

"Is she sick?" Zac held his breath waiting for an answer. How stupid was that. As if Brianna's health was his issue.

"No. I think it's about work. I heard her talking on the phone to some parents last night. It sounded like they were really mad at her." Cory carried the used dishes to the counter and began stacking them in the dishwasher.

"I wouldn't worry. Your mom is very good at negotiation. She used to talk my mom into lots of things when we were kids." Zac smiled at the memories.

"I heard you were friends with her." A bitter tone kept Cory's voice surly. "Of course my mother never told me about it. I didn't even know I had grandparents until we were moving here."

"Some people don't like to talk about the past." Zac wondered why Brianna hadn't bothered to tell her son about her own childhood.

"Mom never talks about the past. She changes the subject when I ask." Cory leaned against the counter as he spoke. "I think she kept everything a secret from me deliberately."

"Maybe she did," Zac defended. "But I'm sure she was only doing what she thought was best for you. After all, she's a single mom trying to raise you and do her job. It can't be easy."

"I guess not." Cory poured himself a glass of water and sipped it. "After my dad died, she took as many courses as she could from home, so she could stay with me. I remember getting up once for a drink of water. It was really late. She'd fallen asleep on top of her books." He took the utensils Zac handed him and began drying. "When I went to school, she went to college. But she was always home before me and if I had a sick day, she stayed with me and caught up her stuff the next day."

"Your mom sounds like she did a lot to give you the best life possible. You are the most important person in her world, Cory. That's why she's tried so hard to make a good life for you." Zac wondered what was beneath the boy's comments.

"Maybe." Cory dried the items, stored them in the drawer, then returned to his water.

"Maybe?" Zac frowned. "You don't think your mother loves you?"

"Yeah, she does. But—it doesn't make sense," Cory blurted out when the silence stretched tissue thin.

"What doesn't?" Zac dished out two cones, handed one to Cory, then led the way to his patio.

"Having me to look after, it was hard for her. I could see that. But now I realize she didn't have to do it all herself. I have a grandmother and a grandfather! They would have helped her, I know they would." Anger brought red dots of color to his cheeks.

"Cory, you don't know what happened back then," Zac interrupted but Cory wasn't listening.

"Everybody had somebody for Christmas. A family. An uncle, an aunt, grandparents. We never did. Mom and I went to church like all the other families, but we always came home alone."

Since he'd done the same thing after his mother's death, Zac's heart ached for the hurting boy. "I'm sorry."

"So am I, but so what? Mom could have changed that and she didn't." Cory's bottom lip jutted out. "If we had moved here when I was starting school, I'd have had a family for all the special times. I'd be like all the other kids. I'd have fit in. Instead I'm the oddball."

"Well, living here didn't help me much," Zac confessed, suppressing his reticence to try and help Brianna's child. "We moved to Hope when I was five, after my dad died in a car accident. But I never fit in. I was the oddball around here for years."

"But then what? You finally figured out how to fit in?" Cory frowned at him.

"No." Zac did not want to list his insecurities, but for the first time since he'd met Brianna's son, he saw real interest flare in the kid's eyes. He couldn't ignore the opportunity to engage him, because Brianna had asked him to do just that and there was no way Zac would let her down.

"Then?" Cory prodded.

"After a while I figured out that it didn't matter what other people thought about me, I had to be myself." Zac shrugged. "So I did my thing and eventually I found some friends. Kent, your mom, Jaclyn, Nick Green, Shay Parker. We learned that each of us had something special to share with the others."

"Hokey." Cory tilted his nose in the air.

"Maybe." Zac shrugged. "The point is I was still a nerd, Cory. But with my friends, that didn't seem to matter so much because we cheered on each other, helped each other reach our goals."

"You didn't cheer on my mom while she worked on her goal to be a psychologist." Cory glared at him. "You couldn't have. Because I never even heard of you till we moved here."

Zac hesitated. He did not want to get into the past. With anyone. If he told Cory the truth, the kid might start to think his father had been second best or worry he was second best. Neither were true. Brianna had dumped Zac and by doing so, made it clear to everyone that he didn't meet her expectations.

The sting of that still burned.

"You're not going to tell me the truth about the past, either, are you?" Cory snorted his disgust. "Because

I'm a kid who can't understand. Everybody thinks kids don't deserve to know the truth. Well, I know the truth. Grandma told me you and my mom were going to get married but my mom messed it up."

Aghast that Brianna's mother had spoken to Cory about the past, and maligned her daughter in the process, Zac gulped as he searched for a way to end this.

"That's not exactly right, Cory. Your mom and I were engaged in college but we broke up. That was a long time ago. People change. Things change."

"Why did you break up?" Cory's eyes bored into him.

"Our past is between us—private." Zac had to end this, and fast. Revealing personal details was not part of helping Cory. "If you want to know more you should ask your mother. She will tell you what she wants you to hear." He almost felt sorry for the grilling Brianna might have to endure from this kid.

"You think she'll tell me about your past? Like she told me about my grandparents? I doubt it." Cory's mutinous face reflected his scorn. "I'll ask Grandma. She doesn't think I'm a dummy. She always tells me the truth."

"Does she?" Zac asked quietly, then left it hanging, hoping those words would raise some doubts in Cory's mind. "It's getting late. I'll walk you home. I missed my run today."

Cory trailed him to the door, pausing to graze one finger over the book on South America. "Are you planning on taking a trip there or something?"

"Yes." Zac held the door open and waited for him to walk through. "Actually I'm hoping to use my Christmas holidays for a trek down the Amazon. I need to do a little more research first, though. I like to really study a place before I go there. Gives me more appreciation for it."

"From the look of all your pictures you've gone to lots of places," Cory mused, trying not to sound too interested.

"Quite a few." Zac listed several treks. "Haven't done the South Pole yet so that's on my list of to dos." Because Cory seemed interested, he told the boy a little about the places he'd seen. "I want to go back to Hawaii, too. I love it there."

"I knew some kids in my old school that went to Hawaii. They had awesome pictures." Was there a hint of longing in the boy's voice? But he said nothing more and they soon reached his home.

"Well, thanks for sharing my dinner, Cory. Sorry the movie was a bust."

"That's okay." Cory raced up the three stairs to the house and yanked open the door. "I'm not big on horror flicks anyway. See ya."

Zac turned to leave.

"You rented a horror movie to show my son?" Brianna emerged from the side of the house, lips pursed tight, fingers taut around a small metal weeding tool. Her short hair curled in damp wisps around her gorgeous face.

"No!" Startled, Zac regrouped. "I mean, I did, but I didn't know it was horror! Cory didn't tell me that when I asked him what he wanted to see. Anyway, we shut it off because it was boring."

The steely sparks in her change-color eyes lost a bit of hardness. She sighed.

"Sorry. I didn't mean to jump. I'm just a little on edge today."

"Cory said you were getting flack from some parents." He watched the tiredness bow her slim body. "The Larsens again?"

"And two others whose kids are beginning to talk about doing something with their lives other than maintaining the family business." She stared at him as if to remind him that she had done the same thing when she was their age. "What am I supposed to do? Tell the kids to forget their dreams?" Brianna made a face as she shook her head. "Forget I said that. Everything is supposed to be confidential."

"I can look it up in their records," he reminded her, glancing around. He couldn't prove it, but he had a hunch Cory was somewhere close, listening to them. "You look beat. Want to go for a milk shake? I'm buying."

Brianna blinked, her eyes huge below her spiky bangs. "A milk shake?"

"Pearson's still serves them, you know. With real whipped cream." When it looked as if she'd refuse, he leaned nearer and murmured, "I need to talk to you. Privately."

Brianna caught on immediately.

"A milk shake sounds excellent." She glanced behind her, nodded and said, "I'll make sure Dad doesn't have to go out again so he can stay with Cory."

"I'm not a baby, you know." Cory's indignant tones burst through the open window. "I don't need a babysitter."

"I'll be a minute, Zac. I'll bring my notes for Your World, too." She winked. "You can tell me what you think of my latest ideas."

"Great." Zac waited as a short discussion inside whispered through the walls. A few moments later Brianna walked through the door, a sweater in one hand and her bright turquoise bag in the other.

As they walked away from the house, Zac kept the conversation going with mundane comments but once they were a block away, Brianna laid a hand on his arm.

"You want to talk about Cory," she said.

"Yes." He couldn't help but notice how quickly she removed her hand. "Am I that obvious?"

"Well, you haven't asked me to go for a milk shake in quite a while," she teased then quickly sobered. "What's wrong?"

"Not wrong exactly." As usual, the words deserted him. He pointed toward Pearson's. "Let's get our drink and take it to the park. We could talk there without anyone overhearing."

"Okay."

Once they were seated on a park bench, Brianna turned to him, expectation lighting the green of her eyes to a translucent glow. This was not going to be easy.

"Brianna, this is absolutely none of my business and it isn't easy to ask, but—" Zac exhaled "—do you think it's possible Cory resents you?"

Chapter Nine

"What did you say?" Brianna's jaw sagged.

She'd imagined a thousand scenarios for this "date" with Zac, and not one of them even came close to this.

"I said—"

"Never mind. I heard you. But I don't understand why you would think my son would resent me." Anger bubbled up at the injustice of it. "I've never done anything but my best for Cory."

"I don't doubt it." Zac fiddled with his straw. "And I am not accusing you. It was something Cory said. He'd been asking questions about our past relationship. He said your mother told him we were engaged but our breakup was your fault."

"Oh, no." She felt the blood drain from her head. *How dare she!*

"Then he got into memories about all the Christmases you two spent alone when you could have been here, sharing them with his grandparents."

Brianna listened as Zac related Cory's comments, trying to hide her pain. She worked so hard to keep her precious boy away from the misery her mother had imposed on her own life, and now Cory thought she'd cheated him out of a family? He resented her for saving him from the very things that had marred her own life?

Betrayal burned deep. Despite her best attempt, Brianna couldn't stop the tears from welling or dribbling down her cheeks to her chin.

"I'm sorry," Zac murmured. "I never wanted to hurt you. I just thought that if you knew—" His words faded into the shadows of dusk.

Brianna sniffled, glad that the sun had gone down, that here in the dark, no passersby would see her weeping. Because she couldn't stop.

"It's not fair," she mumbled.

"Oh, Brianna." Zac's arms came around her, and he hauled her against him, cupping the back of her head in his hand and drawing it against his shoulder. "I'm so sorry. I shouldn't have said anything."

"Yes, you should have." She dragged one hand across her face to erase the tears and leaned back just far enough to glare into his eyes. "Just because it hurts doesn't mean it isn't the truth. I have kept Cory away from Hope, deliberately. I had to."

"But, why?" His face conveyed his confusion. "Would it have been so terrible to come home for Christmas? Or invite your parents to Chicago?"

She reared away from him, incredulous that he could even ask.

"You've heard my mother, Zac. She can't stop criticizing me."

"Now, yes, it is bad," he agreed. "But that's her disease talking."

"No, that is my mother talking. That's how she's always been." She saw his disbelief and laughed, though there was no mirth in her eyes, only misery. "Why do you think I wanted so desperately to escape this place after high school? Why did you imagine I begged you to tutor me so I could get a scholarship? I couldn't stay here, work in her store and get ground down anymore. I had to get away."

"You never told me this before." He frowned, fiddling with the curls at the nape of her neck as he tried to puzzle it out. "You never said a word. We were supposed to be married and you never confided any of this."

"Of course not. Do you think I wanted your pity? Your mother was perfect." His touch disconcerted her into saying more than she meant to. "Why did you think I never wanted to come home to be married?" Brianna demanded.

"I don't know." Zac looked into her eyes, searching for answers. "Why didn't you?"

"Because I knew she'd take it over," Brianna blurted out. "And she did. It wasn't our wedding. It was her chance to show off."

"That's why you changed everything from the small simple affair we'd originally decided on?" He sighed at her nod. "I thought it was because you regretted opting out of a big wedding."

"I never wanted a big wedding and I didn't change anything. She did," she murmured, edging her head away from his fingers. It was that or lay it against his shoulder and she didn't have the right to do that. Not anymore. She stared at him, glad the lamp overhead was dim enough to offer some protection from his searching eyes. "I just wanted to be married to you. I wanted us to be happy."

Zac opened his mouth to say something, but closed

it again. Brianna let out her pent-up breath, realizing in that moment that she wanted him to say he wished they'd gone through with the wedding. But Zac didn't say that.

Instead he accused, "We should have talked about all this back then. You should have told me."

That was not what she wanted to hear. Brianna edged away from him, struggling to regain her composure.

"Like you should have told me about the job she offered you, preferably before you accepted it."

"Yes," he admitted. "I should have. But at least you learned about it. I didn't know about your mother and I should have. We shouldn't have had any secrets, Brianna."

Bitterness suffused her soul.

"No," she whispered, "we shouldn't have. But we both did."

"I didn't." He met her glare and frowned. "You're hinting at something but I don't know what. Why don't you tell me why you left? Be honest."

For a second, for one silly moment, she'd let herself imagine that Zac still cared about her, that they could recapture the feelings of the past. But she knew that wasn't true. The past was dead and gone, and just because she was weak and leaning on him now didn't mean anything had changed.

"I am always honest. Are you?" She shifted so his arms fell away from her, unable to bear his nearness and the memories it evoked.

"What does that mean?" he demanded with indignation.

Don't go there, Brianna. The pain isn't worth it.

"Forget it, okay? This is about Cory. I have to help

him or he'll ruin his life." Resolve firmed her traitorous response to him. "I am not going to let that happen. You asked me why I didn't come back home. The truth is I never wanted to come back, except to work at Whispering Hope Clinic. If I could have kept my vow to Jessica and done it somewhere else, I would have. But she died here and I promised her I'd come back, help other kids through the pain of their worlds." She gulped. "My past is something I never want to return to again. But I'll tell you this, if I had to do it all again, I would do the same thing, to protect Cory."

"Have you no good memories of Hope?" Zac asked softly.

"Not enough to outweigh the misery." She refused to give in to the soft, squishy feelings that begged her to remember blissfully happy times in Hope—happy because Zac was there. "Coming home back then— I fell right into my mother's hands. And nothing has changed since except that now her focus is Cory. She'll do everything she can to alienate him from me, including cast doubt on my ability to parent. But my job is still to protect Cory."

"I think you're going to have to explain your decisions to him. He doesn't understand why you did it and he needs to. Plus, he's very fond of his grandmother," Zac reminded her.

"Of course he is." Brianna smiled bitterly. "She gives him everything he asks for. He has no boundaries with her."

"It must be hard for you to watch how she is with him." Zac's quiet words showed her he understood more than she'd expected.

"I'll live. The thing is, I have to walk a fine line between telling him the truth and destroying the relationship he's building with her. I don't want to do that, but neither do I want my son corrupted. Cory only has till Christmas to prove himself. I've got to ensure he does that without any more screw-ups." She rose and tossed her half-full cup in the trash. "Thank you for telling me, Zac. I have to think about it for a bit before I talk to Cory. It's delicate."

He, too, rose and walked beside her down the street without speaking. The entire time they'd been seated on the bench, people had been walking past. Brianna had no doubt that by tomorrow the entire town would be speculating on whether they were getting back together again. Let them. Right now she had to concentrate on her son.

"I'm glad we talked, Brianna. I think we should do it again. What you told me tonight raises a lot of questions about the past—our past." Zac stopped at the end of her walk, studying her through the gloom. "There are so many things I don't understand."

"Join the club." Like why he'd sided with her mother against her. Like why he'd been so willing to abandon everything they'd planned. Brianna pushed away the past, its questions and the pain. Time to move on. "Thanks for your help," she said. "Good night."

Zac nodded but said nothing. He stood in place, watching until she'd mounted the stairs. But as she drew the door closed behind her, Brianna thought she heard him murmur, "Till next time."

She fingered the ring at her neck as she closed the door on Zac and the rush of hope his words brought. There could be no next time for them, except as coworkers. She walked upstairs. Cory was in his room, hunched over the book Zac had given him.

"How was the milk shake?" he asked, his eyes hooded so she couldn't read his thoughts.

"Okay." She decided to say nothing about the mess surrounding her. Not tonight. "Is your homework finished?" she asked as she bent to brush a kiss against the top of his head.

"Yes, Mother," came the droll response.

"Good work. Good night, sweetie. I love you." She waited a second but Cory didn't respond with his usual "love ya." And that hurt. Before he could see her tears, she walked out. But in the security of her room she finally broke down, weeping her mother's heart out to God.

Even when she'd tried so hard to do the right thing, she'd hurt Cory. And praying about it brought little solace.

Her Bible lay open on her nightstand. The words leaped out at her.

Lord, why are You standing aloof and far away? Why do You hide when I need You the most? Why have You forsaken me? Why do You remain so distant? Why do You ignore my cries for help? Why have You abandoned me?

The hurt and anger poured out of her soul toward heaven in a torrent of misery. Desperate to find some relief she picked up the book she'd been reading and looked over Job's words.

But He knows where I am going. And when He has tested me like gold in a fire, He will pronounce me innocent.

The book's claim that some hardships in life were to

test and mature faith, part of a normal friendship with God, reminded her of Zac's garden plaque. She glanced at the book. *Will you continue to love, trust, obey and worship God though you have no sense of His presence?*

"I'm trying," Brianna whispered. "I'm trying so hard to trust Your promise that You will never leave me. Please help me."

Worn out, Brianna sat in her window seat remembering the feel of Zac's arms around her in the park. As she stared up at the stars, old familiar feelings for Zac, which she'd thought long dead, welled up anew; familiar feelings that had made her want to run to him, throw herself into his arms and try to recapture the love she'd once found with him.

But he didn't want that. He'd said it was better they'd separated.

There was no going back. So why didn't that weak spot in her heart understand that just because Zac comforted her, just because he said and did nice things for her and her family, didn't mean he cared about her? Just because her heart skipped a beat whenever he appeared, just because she thought of him constantly, didn't mean anything could come of it.

The past was over.

So why couldn't Brianna let it go?

Troubled by the things he'd heard tonight and by the questions Brianna's comments had raised, Zac stretched out his run until his lungs burned and his knees ached. But tired as he was, he could not rest.

Had Brianna's life at home really been that bad? He'd envied her high-school popularity so much, Zac had never really looked beyond her lovely house, her successful parents and her seemingly perfect life. But now bits and pieces of past conversations with her mother in the weeks before their wedding brought new questions.

Brianna has no sense about color so of course I had to choose the bridesmaids' dresses.

I hope you won't mind, Zac, but I changed the order for the wedding cake. Brianna just doesn't understand how to coordinate anything.

The comments piled up in his mind, little things he hadn't paid much attention to back then, but should have.

When they'd begun college, Brianna's style had blossomed into autumn shades of rust and orange and turquoise. Those colors reflected her vibrant personality. He'd always wondered what prompted the change, though he'd never asked. Now he wondered, was it because she'd finally escaped her mother's dominance?

His overpowering response to Brianna tonight shocked Zac. He'd wanted the right to confront her mother, to shield her from the pain, to protect and help her. But that way of thinking was dangerous. Because their past was over.

Yet tonight, for a moment when he'd held her in his arms, Zac had desperately wished it wasn't. He'd wished he had the right to kiss her, to help her with Cory, to be part of her family and help ease the burden she carried.

Stupid.

Zac made himself a cup of calming tea. He sipped it outside on the patio and watched the stars. He tried to think of everything but Brianna. But despite his attempt to relax, Zac found himself more on edge than ever.

Brianna didn't want him. She'd made that clear ten years ago.

Zac had thought God had done the same thing. Though he still went to church, though he talked a good line to Brianna, it was all a facade to hide the loneliness in his heart. Tonight that barren emptiness welled up more powerfully than ever before, threatening to consume him. He still envied Brianna her family, even with the trouble they caused her.

Better than being alone.

Zac tossed out his tea and hurried back to his office. Work would ward it off. It always had before. Surely if he could focus on the next step to his goal, he could get his mind off the ache in the middle of his gut that came from wanting what he couldn't have.

But hours later Zac still hadn't dislodged the memory of Brianna's tears rolling down her downy-soft cheeks, or the weary sigh she'd breathed into his neck.

Or the realization that it had never felt more right to hold this woman in his arms.

"Look, Peter, my job is not to squash your daughter's dreams. My job is to help her understand herself so she'll find meaning in her world. I'm sorry you're not happy with my counsel, but the fact that Eve is even thinking about her future is a huge growth step from where she was a month ago." Brianna watched her former schoolmate's face harden and inwardly sighed. *Me, again, God. Please help.*

"We can't afford her dreams," came the bitter response.

"You don't have to. Right now they're just dreams. They may change and she'll have to figure a way to achieve them. For the moment she's still exploring." She struggled to sound empathetic but authoritative. "But

I caution you that to keep disparaging her dreams only expands the rift between you. If you could just listen to her, encourage her to talk, share her hopes—"

"Share them? Don't you get it? I'd give my heart for my kid to get her dream. But it just isn't possible." Peter Larsen jumped to his feet. "You can't counsel our kids to do what you did, Brianna, to abandon their families."

"That's not what I'm trying to do," she finished, wincing as the door slammed shut.

Almost immediately the phone rang.

"Brianna, you need to come to my office. Now. Right away." Zac sounded disturbed.

"I wish I could but I've got two more parent meetings this morning."

"It's urgent. It's Cory."

Oh, no.

"Is he hurt?" Panic grabbed her.

"No." Zac's voice sounded hard. "He's fine. It's not that."

"Then it will have to wait. I promise I'll come as quickly as I can, Zac. That's the best I can do." With that she hung up, but through her meetings she remained concerned by the angst in his tone. Peter Larsen had been a sprinter in high school, but surely even he couldn't have gone from her office to the division office to complain so quickly.

Brianna pushed everything but her work aside, using every mediation skill she'd learned to calm the angry parents while still supporting their children's goals and dreams. By noon she felt deflated and certain she'd made little progress.

"Zac Ender called twice," RaeAnn announced. "He said he'd supply lunch if you could get over there now."

"Call and tell him I'm on my way, please." But as she drove over, Brianna felt utterly unprepared to meet with Zac so soon after that evening in the park. No one was in the main office so she walked directly to his door and stepped inside. "What is so urgent?" she demanded, sinking into an armchair.

"This." Zac pointed to the television mounted on the wall. He pressed a button on the remote in his hand and a picture of the globe board at the school appeared.

"You had a camera installed?" she asked.

"The school board had a security system put in," Zac confirmed. "Yesterday afternoon the last camera was installed. Watch."

For what seemed ages the picture never changed. Then three shadowed figures appeared. After some whispering, one stepped forward and scrawled something across a corner of the white board in huge black letters.

"'Your World sucks,'" Brianna read. She frowned as the figure turned away, but in that moment she glimpsed the insignia on one corner of his jacket. "I think I know that crest from somewhere," she murmured, trying to remember.

"Yes, you do," Zac agreed in a grim tone. He backed up, zoomed in and replayed the footage, honing in on the figure.

"Cory!" Brianna gasped.

"And his two friends." Zac played the video once more, but there was no doubt who was responsible for the graffiti. "He's ruined Your World."

"But—when?" she asked, gutted by the knowledge that her child had deliberately sabotaged her. "How?"

"This tape is from last night. It's time stamped

around the time we were talking in the park." Zac's bleak expression spoke volumes.

In that moment Brianna understood how deep his disappointment went. He'd invested Your World with his hopes for that state job and now it seemed all was lost. She knew why. In the present apathetic climate, other kids would pick up on Cory's negativity and ruin whatever chance there had been. Her anger toward her son flared. To deliberately do this when Zac had been nothing but kindness—this time Cory had gone too far.

"What should we do?" he asked.

"Call him in," she said, her voice hard. She checked her watch. "Lunch should be over. Phone the school and get him in here. Have the principal drive him if you have to, but get Cory here now to explain himself."

"Just Cory?" Zac's wide brown eyes expressed his surprise.

"He was the one who wrote on the board. He pays the price." Brianna was done with pussyfooting around her son's issues. Maybe if she acted now, she could stop this from reaching the judge in Chicago. "Do it, Zac." She waited till he finally picked up the phone and dialed, though her knees were quaking at the stare he set on her.

"What is the price Cory is going to pay?" he asked in a tentative tone when he'd completed his call.

"You're the educator, you decide. I'll go along with your judgment." She sat down to wait. "But you should know that I am way past giving Cory another second chance without insisting on stiff repercussions for his actions."

"Be sure, Brianna, because we have to present a united front to him."

As if he were their child. The words hung unspoken in the room.

"Whatever you decide is fine. Clearly what I've tried hasn't worked. You'd better come up with something before he gets here." Because Zac kept giving her funny sideways glances, Brianna pulled out a file she'd shoved in her handbag before she left her office and pretended to peruse it.

At last Zac broke his stare and worked on resetting the video.

Less than five minutes later Cory sauntered into the room and asked, "What's up?"

"You are," Zac said. "Sit down."

Brianna found no anger in Zac's tone, saw nothing on his face to give away his thoughts. Only deep disappointment darkened his eyes, though no one but she would recognize that because she'd seen it before, the morning of his botched presentation.

"What are you doing here, Mom?"

"I asked her to come, Cory. I thought she should see what you were up to last night."

At Zac's words, a deep rich red suffused Cory's face. He looked away from her, shuffling his feet against the carpet.

"Just another reason to be ashamed of me, huh, Mom?" Cory's head lifted. He glared at her, his blue eyes icy with anger and frustration.

"I have never ever been ashamed of you, Cory. I always thought you were God's gift to me. But today—" She glanced at the television. "Today I'm very ashamed. Of myself. I thought I'd done a better job raising you."

Cory frowned, as if he hadn't expected her to shoulder the blame for his misdeeds. "But—"

"The proof is right here." Zac flicked the remote and they all watched as Cory defaced school property.

Brianna felt sick. How had it come to this? How could God be in this?

"Your tests show you have a high IQ, Cory, but I'm beginning to think they're wrong. I'm beginning to wonder if you're actually very stupid."

Brianna's head jerked upward at Zac's strong words. But she remained silent as his eyes chided her to remember her promise.

"Thanks a lot," Cory said.

"I'm serious. What kind of bright person, who is supposed to be making an effort to change themselves so they don't have to go into detention, damages school property? That's a criminal offense," Zac reminded. "Do you *want* to be locked up?"

"That's not going to happen." But Cory's bravado slipped just a little.

"Really? If I call the police now, you will be charged and put in jail. That will be the last straw as far as the judge in Chicago is concerned. I doubt he'll wait till Christmas to rule on your case." Zac shut off the television. "So I guess you've just run out of options."

"Mom?" Cory pleaded, staring at her with those doe-soft eyes that sent a dart straight through her heart.

"This isn't on your mom, Cory. This is on you and you alone. Your two friends were there, but they didn't deface the board. You did. And I have the video to prove it." Zac stared straight at Brianna, challenging her. "Your mother and I have agreed that I must decide your punishment. Brianna, go back to work. I'll talk to you later."

She rose hesitantly, but knew there was no other choice. It had to be done.

"Straight home after school," she said to Cory. "No friends, no television, no phone. Clean up your room and get your homework done before I get home. You may not go to the nursing home with your grandfather. You may not go anywhere."

"But, Mom!"

Brianna turned her back and left Cory sitting there, the hardest thing she'd ever done.

Zac stood by the door, holding it open. She paused long enough to study his implacable expression. His fingers touched hers for an instant, transmitting warmth and something else—hope? Then she walked away, leaving her son in her former fiancé's hands.

Jaclyn met her at the doorway of Whispering Hope Clinic. She took one look at her face, grabbed her arm and drew Brianna into her office. She quickly closed the door and said, "Something's wrong. Spill it."

So Brianna told her the whole awful story.

"I'm failing everyone," she muttered, bitterly ashamed of her uncontrollable world. "Cory, my clients, the clinic, my mother. Especially God."

"That's ridiculous." Jaclyn poured a cup of strong black coffee and set it before her. "Listen to me, Bri, and hear me well. You haven't failed anyone. You're doing your job here at the clinic and doing so well, you have more clients than you can see. The kids love you."

"Because they think I go against their parents." As she'd always rebelled against her mother, Brianna mused.

"Because you really listen when they speak," Jaclyn corrected. "Because in talking to you they find hope for the future. Because you care. Kids can spot a fake a mile off. They wouldn't be here if they thought that was you."

"Thanks. I appreciate the encouragement." Brianna blinked when Jaclyn pushed her back into her chair.

"Stay. I'm not finished." Jaclyn sat down across from her, her lovely face serious. "You never failed your mother, Bri. Not ever. You tried to do as she wanted, but your heart lay elsewhere. You followed it and that's a good thing. Look how God is using you here at Whispering Hope. I'm no psychologist," she said with a funny grin. "But I'm going to hazard a guess that your mother is being so miserable to you now because she realizes all the years with you that she's lost. And as far as Cory is concerned—don't get me started. Nobody, and I do mean nobody, could have done a better job of loving that child. But sooner or later, his choices are his own."

"I guess you're right. It just hurts that he'd deliberately sabotage me that way."

"Of course it hurts, but you trust Zac, don't you?" Jaclyn's stare was intense.

"With Cory, you mean? Yes, of course." The certainty was there in her heart. Zac would do what was right for her son. He couldn't help himself because that's who Zac was.

"Then you have to trust that somehow he'll reach Cory. Zac has a way with kids—you've always known that." Jaclyn waited for Brianna's nod. "Relax. Let him handle this. Support him in whatever he decides and stop stewing over it."

"I'll try." Brianna chewed her bottom lip. "I still feel like I've failed God, though."

Jaclyn was silent for a long time.

"I should get back to work." Brianna set her cup on the desk. "Thanks for the pep talk."

"I want to say something else." Jaclyn cleared her throat as her eyes grew moist. "You won't know this, but when I first came back to Hope I had a terrible time trying to accept that I couldn't work my way into God's favor." A wry smile lifted her lips. "I tried hard, believe me. Worked myself flat out."

Brianna waited, wondering where this was leading.

"One day I was reading in Psalms and I found this verse. It's been very precious to me ever since." She slid a tiny Bible out of her pocket, thumbed through the pages and paused. Her eyes met Brianna's. "It's the fourth chapter. Just listen," she whispered. She inhaled then read, "'O God, You have declared me perfect in Your eyes.'"

You have declared me perfect. Brianna couldn't wrap her mind around those words. She was perfect in God's eyes?

"Amazing, isn't it? God loves us so much He wipes out our sin," Jaclyn said quietly. "To Him we are perfect."

The phone buzzed. RaeAnn announced Jaclyn's patients were waiting. So were Brianna's.

"You always amaze me, Jaclyn. Thank you. But now I've really got to get to work," Brianna said. She smiled. "Some kids need my help."

"So do your mom and Cory, and even Zac," Jaclyn said softly as she hugged her. "And Zac might be the neediest of all. See ya."

Having mulled over the verse in every spare moment

throughout the afternoon, Brianna considered Jaclyn's last words as she walked home that evening.

Zac needed her? Really?

She picked up her pace, anxious to get home and prepare for another parents' assembly at the school this evening. Zac had been there for her today. She didn't know what he'd said to Cory, but she'd been at her wits' end and he'd offered to help. She'd accepted his help because she didn't know what else to do.

Tonight she'd help Zac however she could, because she owed him. But that was as involved as she could get with him. There could be nothing between them and it was time she stopped leaning on him.

Her heart had tricked her into believing it was possible to build a relationship with this man again, but her brain kept repeating that Zac hadn't trusted her once. He might not again.

As she fingered the ring lying against her collarbone, the one Zac had given her so long ago on a very special Christmas Eve, Brianna knew she had to suppress her longing to regain his lost love.

Because she wouldn't survive losing it a second time.

Chapter Ten

"Good evening everyone. Uh, welcome." Zac gripped the edges of the high-school podium and gazed at the assembled group of parents, his mouth as dry as the desert. All the public-speaking courses he'd taken were worthless. He still felt like a guppy out of water when he stood in front of people.

"Uh." He gulped, feeling his palms sweat. "We, er, I promised you that after implementing Your World we'd gather again to discuss any questions you might have. Th-that is the purpose of our meeting tonight."

Mentally wincing at his poor presentation, Zac explained the steps he hoped to take over the next few weeks as the program continued to unfold. He chose to read primarily from his notes, desperate not to look a fool in front of all these people. But the more he read, the more nervous he became and the more he lost his concentration and began making silly errors.

"So, in effect, we've maximated—er—" As muffled laughter broke out in the group, Zac's whole body went tense and he could not get the next word out. Everyone was staring now—gawking at him, the spectacle in their midst.

"Actually, Zac, I don't think we've quite maximated yet." Suddenly Brianna was there at his side, grinning at him as if they'd planned this interruption. "In fact, I don't think we've even come close to tapping the potential our teens have hidden inside." She winked at him. "Can I have a turn now?"

Relief swamped him but he didn't let it show.

"I suppose. But only if you follow my notes," he managed, pointing to the sheaf of papers atop the podium.

Brianna glanced at the stack of notes, rolled her eyes and gave her head the tiniest shake. She leaned into the microphone and whispered, "Not a chance. Those notes are maximated."

The room erupted in laughter. The tension broken, parents smiled as she went on to detail the next phase. Zac would have preferred to leave her to it but Brianna prevented that by deferring to him on several points and including him in a question and answer session, which could have become nasty given the Larsens' and other parents' outbursts. Zac staunchly defended Brianna, glad when she coaxed them to admit that their children were benefitting from the goals of Your World. By the conclusion of the meeting, the situation had grown almost jovial as parents sampled the coffee and cookies Brianna had thoughtfully provided. Zac knew the evening was a success because of her.

"Thanks for bailing me out," he said when everyone had left them to tidy.

"I didn't bail you out." Brianna stopped what she was doing and frowned at him. "Weren't you watching? Didn't you see those faces when you began to talk about the goals and dreams that have gone up on the Your World board? Those people ate up your words of encouragement, Zac. Hope was visible here tonight. Because of you." Then she squinted at him. "By the way, when did the kids start writing their dreams on the board?"

"I saw it on the tape after I sent Cory home." Zac grinned. "They wrote right over Cory's graffiti. I phoned to tell you but you weren't taking any calls. Come on. You can see the board for yourself." He held open the door, waited till she'd exited the auditorium then switched off the lights. "I'll tell you, when the video showed Eve take the pen and actually write on that board, my heart was in my mouth. That took a lot of courage in the face of her parents' objections. Look." He motioned to the board and held his breath.

"I came in the staff entrance so I never saw—" Brianna moved closer to him to take a second look. She read off several of the comments. "Isn't it fantastic, Zac?" she whispered, touching his arm as she stared at him, her eyes filled with awe.

"Yes, it is." Zac bent and kissed her on the lips. "It certainly is," he repeated, stunned by emotions that swamped him.

For one infinitesimal second Brianna had kissed him back. Now she stepped away.

"Why did you do that?" she demanded, her voice choked.

"I don't know. Excitement, I guess." Zac shrugged, pretending nonchalance. "No big deal. Sorry."

Now he was lying. Because kissing Brianna was a big deal to him. He'd wanted to kiss her even before that night in the park. And now that he had, he wanted to repeat it.

But Zac had seen that glint of green fill Brianna's

eyes before. He knew she was suspicious of him. He was going to have to tread carefully if he wanted to find out exactly why she'd left Hope the way she had.

"Aren't you excited?" he asked. "There's your client's dream." He pointed to Eve's signature.

I want to be a doctor.

"I s-see it."

"Are you crying?" He frowned at the stream of tears flowing down Brianna's cheeks and caught one on a fingertip. Something about it did funny things to his heart—squeezed it so tight it hurt. He'd wanted her to be happy, not weeping. "Brianna?" He tucked a finger under her chin and lifted it so he could see into her eyes.

"Tears of joy," she whispered. "Eve struck a chord in my heart the first time I saw her high on drugs and miserable. Maybe because she's in the same sort of situation I was. She carries so much guilt for wanting to be free of her parents' demands, for not being what they want. She was afraid to dream of anything for herself. But now, she's taken the first step toward independence." Brianna accepted the tissue Zac handed her, and smiled at him through her tears. "It's amazing."

"So why does that make you cry?" He didn't get it.

"Because I've finally achieved the goal I set myself way back when Jessica died, the one I started when you agreed to tutor me in high school. I've been able to truly help a child and it feels wonderful." She started crying all over again, and there was nothing Zac could do but wrap his arms around her and hold her while she soaked his shoulder.

Tenderness crept through him. This precious woman had carried such a heavy load for so long. He thought of the long nights she must have spent when Cory was a baby, teething, sick, tummy upsets. He remembered Cory had mentioned falling and breaking an arm when he was in kindergarten. How frightened Brianna must have been. Who had she called to share her fear? Who had she leaned on when he began getting in trouble?

He knew the answer. Tall, vivacious, strong Brianna—she would have hidden the weak moments and pretended she was in control.

"It's okay," Zac whispered, his breath moving the short wispy strands on the top of her head. "You're not alone anymore."

She stilled. The muscles in Zac's arms protested as she edged away from him to stand separate.

"Aren't I?" she asked in a voice so soft he almost didn't hear.

Those hazel eyes studied him with an intensity that made him nervous. There was that hint of something painful in the look she laid on him. And then it was gone. The old Brianna was back in charge.

"What happened with Cory this afternoon?"

"I read him the riot act. Then I gave him a job he'll have to do until Christmas break. He reports to me." Zac shoved his useless hands in his pockets and shrugged. "I hoped I made him face a few hard truths." He frowned at her. "Why didn't you ask him?"

"I did." Brianna arched one eyebrow. "All my son would tell me is that the two of you talked, he's being punished and you are both going to a male Bible study on Wednesday evenings."

"Oh, yes. I forgot to tell you about that. Cory has a lot of questions." Zac felt his face heat up remembering Cory's very personal question about Zac's faith journey. "His faith questions are bigger than I can deal with. Besides, his two buddies have agreed to come along."

"To a Bible study?"

"I guess they want answers, too." Zac gave her a wry look. "One thing I've learned in working with students is that when you don't have the answers, you go somewhere you can find them. So we'll go to a Bible study about Peter, the disciple who was a bit of a misfit." Zac tried to look as if the prospect of studying the subject with Cory didn't scare him silly.

"Does Cory feel like he's a misfit?" The diffident way Brianna asked showed her insecurity.

"Yes." Zac watched her wince. "I think that's part of the reason he's angry at you for not coming to Hope earlier. He thinks that if he'd grown up here, he would have fit in with the other kids. You have to talk to him, Brianna. Explain at least some of your decisions. Otherwise his mind will make up what he doesn't know."

"I'll do it tonight."

"Good. Would you like me to be there?" he asked.

"You? Why?" Her eyes opened wide.

"In case you need help. Or something." It sounded lame, even to Zac. But to his surprise, Brianna nodded.

"Actually I'd really like it if you were there. Lately Cory and I seem to butt heads on everything. Maybe if you were there to act as a buffer, he'd be more open." She smiled, a genuine smile that lit up her green-brown eyes and stretched her mouth wide. "Thank you, Zac."

"No problem. Let me lock up, then I'll give you a ride. Your car is still on the fritz, isn't it?"

"Yes." Brianna sighed. "And apparently not worth repairing. Just another expense I've got to figure out. I'll wait for you outside. I could use a bit of fresh air before, well—" She made a face. "You know."

"Be positive." As Zac hurried to notify the caretaker that he was leaving, he realized he was looking forward to facing Cory's issues head-on. Maybe with Brianna's help, they could explain the past to the boy, and maybe, just maybe, Zac would find out exactly what had derailed their wedding without having to question Brianna. He didn't want to hurt her by dredging up the past, but he did want to know the truth.

For years Zac had rationalized that their breakup was God's way of preventing him from making the biggest mistake of his life because God knew he wasn't the right husband for Brianna. Brianna was bold, vivacious and outgoing. He was the exact opposite, and if they'd married, he knew he would have held her back. Brianna was a people person and though Zac wanted to be, though he'd tried to be for her sake, he knew that she'd have stifled her outgoing take-charge attitude, would have held back from taking the limelight in order to save him from exposure to the public focus he hated.

He wasn't the man for her.

But that didn't mean he didn't still care about her. That's why he couldn't stand by and watch another student, especially Brianna's son, fail. The graffiti, Cory's latest self-destructive behavior, had forced Zac out of his comfort zone and into a Bible study in order to reach the troubled youth.

And all those silly yearnings for Brianna that haunted him would have to be quashed while Zac tried to help her son.

Brianna held her mug of peppermint tea against her cheek and breathed a prayer for help as her son flopped on the sofa.

"This looks a lot like some television intervention,"

Cory mumbled as he looked from her to Zac. "What's going on?"

"I'm worried about you, son. You have only till Christmas, just a few months until the judge in Chicago reviews your case. I'm afraid he won't like what he sees. Vandalism?" Brianna glanced at Zac, hoping she was saying the right thing. "What's wrong, Cory? And please tell me the truth."

"You want the truth?" Cory's face turned red. His eyes narrowed and his hands clenched against the sofa cushions. "Okay. The truth is that I had grandparents and you never told me. I should have known."

Brianna was about to defend herself when she saw Zac shake his head. She inhaled and focused on Cory, waiting for him to let out all his resentment and bitterness. He blamed her for the rift with her mother and laid the blame for the breakup with Zac squarely at her feet. The pain of his words bit deeply, but Brianna refused to give way to it. The wound had to be cleansed before it would heal.

When Cory finally fell silent, Brianna wasn't sure how or where to start. But Zac did it for her.

"Is that all of it?" he asked in a stern tone. "Have you finished dumping all your misery on your mother now?"

"For the moment." Cory's lips pinched tight in fury.

"Good. Then you can listen for a while." Zac leaned forward so his face was only inches from Cory's. "What happened between your mother and me ten years ago is none of your business."

"But—"

"You had your say. Now you listen." Zac waited for the boy's reluctant nod. "Yes, we got engaged in college. Yes, we planned to marry. We didn't. It doesn't matter to you what happened. That's our business. Maybe one day your mother will tell you. Maybe she won't. That's up to her. All you need to know is that she had her reasons for leaving Hope."

"But why not come back?" Cory asked, his voice modulated, pleading as he stared at her. "Did Dad know you had parents here?"

"Your dad knew all about me when we married. Everything. I never lied to him or kept secrets from him." *But he did from me.*

Brianna opened her mouth, then saw Zac frown. She knew he was right. This wasn't the time for that truth. But it was time for another. She had to broach the crux of Cory's unhappiness.

"What I should have told you is that I never came back because of my mother."

"Grandma? Why do you hate her?" Cory demanded, his tone accusing.

"This isn't a debate, Cory," Zac warned. "Your mother is confiding in you because you asked for the truth. The question is, can you be mature enough to hear the truth without jumping to conclusions or judging her?"

After a dark glare at Zac and several moments of contemplation, Cory exhaled. "Go on, Mom," he said in a quieter tone. "I'm listening."

"Your grandmother had a store years ago."

"I know. She told me all about it. It sounded amazing." Cory's eyes glowed with excitement.

"It was amazing. I used to go there every day after school to help." Brianna closed her eyes, pushed back the flood of memories and concentrated on explaining. "My mother was fantastic at what she did. I admired her very much. But I didn't have her gift. I was lousy at what she did. Probably because I wasn't interested in home decor. I always wanted to work with kids. When I told her that, she wouldn't listen. I tried to explain that I wanted to become a psychologist, but she couldn't accept that. She convinced Dad not to support me to go to college."

"But, why?" Cory frowned.

Brianna explained what she'd learned about her own grandparents.

"Gosh, this family is full of secrets," Cory grumbled.

She stared straight at the child who filled her heart and soul with meaning. She loved Cory so much.

"Anyway, it was very important to me that I leave Hope to get my education so I could one day come back to work in the clinic." She told him all about Jessica, how close they'd been, the deep painful loss she'd felt when they'd learned the illness might have been treated successfully if it had been diagnosed earlier. "We'd planned that clinic in high school, Jaclyn, Shay and I. A clinic for kids. Helping kids was my dream."

"You've always said that. Grandma didn't understand?" Confusion filled Cory's face.

"Think about your Grandma, son. Even now she's very determined. In those days she was almost driven by her desire to make a name for her store. But I wasn't good at the things she was, even though I desperately wanted to be."

"Oh." Her son frowned.

Brianna took Cory's hands in her own. After taking a deep breath she reached out with her heart to her son.

"I tried so hard to be the daughter she wanted, Cory. But I couldn't make her dream mine. She wouldn't support me. So I persuaded Zac to tutor me so I could win a scholarship to college. And I did. We went to the same college and that's where we decided to get married."

Brianna deliberately did not say they'd fallen in love and she knew Zac noted the lack. She glanced at her former fiancé once and found his intent stare fixed on her. That's when she knew she had to tell the whole truth, for Zac's sake as much as for Cory's.

"But then you decided not to get married?" Cory prodded, his face confused. He glanced at Zac then back at Brianna.

"Yes." This was going to be hard. "The night before our wedding, my mother offered Zac a job at the school. She had it all arranged that we would stay in Hope after we were married. Zac would teach, and I'd work in her store. When I wouldn't agree she told me I was holding Zac back, that he'd never get the degree he dreamed of."

Zac's eyes widened. "But—"

"She told me a lot of things and I believed her," Brianna whispered, begging him to understand. She turned back to Cory. "I believed that if I didn't do as she asked, I'd lose Zac, that he'd grow to hate me. I was scared and filled with doubts. I didn't want to hurt him and I sure didn't want him to regret marrying me or grow to resent me. But I wanted so badly to keep my vow to Jessica."

"And so?" Cory prodded when Brianna got caught staring into Zac's troubled gaze.

"I finally agreed I'd work in the store. I loved you, Zac. I wanted you to be happy. That teaching job seemed to make you happy. So I agreed to give up our dreams." Brianna felt the old pain rise up inside. The words flowed out. "What else could I do? My mother wanted me in that store, and you went along with it," she whispered sadly.

"Because we needed the money." Zac frowned. "It was only going to last two years. We could have saved a good chunk and—"

"Two years wasn't enough for her. I knew it wouldn't be."

"What do you mean?" Zac demanded.

The time had come. She had to tell him the truth and trust he'd understand why she'd made the choices she had.

"Brianna?"

"The morning of our wedding," she whispered. "Do you remember when you told me you thought we should come back early from our honeymoon as thanks for the wedding I never wanted?"

"I remember you laid a strip on me for even suggesting such a thing."

"Anyway, right after we hung up my mother came into my room. She had a contract."

"A what?" Cory's forehead wrinkled in confusion.

"A contract. For me to sign to guarantee that I wouldn't leave her high and dry." She licked her lips. "It was a contract for five years."

"Five years?" Zac glared at her. "She said two—"

"I know. And you believed her. You wouldn't listen to me when I warned you. You rode roughshod over every protest I tried to make." She gulped. "You wouldn't believe me over my mother."

"But I never meant—" Zac stopped and simply stared at her.

"You didn't suspect she persuaded your mother to say she was too ill to travel for the wedding, did you?"

She smiled at Zac's start of surprise. "Of course you didn't. You never clued in that everything was arranged before we got there. The job, all of it. My mother figured if she could keep you in town, I'd have to stay because we'd be married. So she dangled the teaching job in front of you, and you bit."

"Why didn't you tell me?" Zac's mouth tightened.

"Because you didn't trust me. That's why I left before the wedding." Brianna faced Cory. "I knew we'd never get out once I got involved in my mother's store. I believed that after five years, Zac would hate me for killing his dream. I wasn't strong enough back then. I didn't know how to fight my mother and I knew I couldn't live in a marriage filled with hate. So I left." Brianna focused on Cory who was staring at her as if he'd never seen her before.

After a few moments he blinked and the anger was back. "But later?"

"Yes, I always planned to come home eventually. But then your dad died and you got sick. You were really sick, Cory. I was alone and scared and didn't know what to do. So I phoned home to ask my mother for help." The tears Brianna had kept suppressed spilled out in spite of her best efforts. She dashed them away, angry that still, after so many years the memory could wound so deeply.

"So she came?" Cory asked hesitantly.

"No." Brianna paused, inhaled and gathered her strength. "My mother told me that I'd chosen you and your dad over her and now I was stuck with my choice. She hung up on me."

Nobody spoke for the longest time. Brianna used the moments to gather her composure.

"What did you do, Mom?" Cory's voice was very quiet.

"I called the two friends who'd always stuck by me. Jaclyn couldn't leave but she asked her mom to come help me. Shay sent me some money to live on until your dad's estate was settled. I managed." She cleared her throat and looked Cory straight in the eye. "And I kept on managing. You were my sunshine, my rainbow and I had to make sure your world was okay. I suffered a lot from my mother's criticism when I was growing up, son. It was really hard for me. I never felt loved and I didn't want that for you. So I did my best to raise you with all the love I had. After my mother hung up on me, I vowed I would never come back here. And I didn't. Until the day my dad wrote and asked for my help. I couldn't refuse him."

Silence fell as her child digested her words. But Brianna wasn't finished.

"I deliberately kept the truth from you, Cory. Maybe I shouldn't have. I don't know. All I know is that I had to protect you the best way I could. Back then I didn't know how my mother would react to you, but there was no way I was going to risk her hurting you." She gulped. "So I stayed away and kept my secret. I never told you about them. I managed the best I could."

"But I love Grandma." Cory's face hardened.

"Of course you do. And she loves you. You make her smile." Brianna touched his cheek. "You're a wonderful, thoughtful grandson and you should be in each other's lives. I'm glad you make her happy."

"But you don't want to be in Grandma's life?" Cory looked confused.

"Maybe one day I'll be able to but right now it doesn't

work," Brianna said simply. "She's my mother and I love her, but I can't seem to do anything right around her. You've heard how she talks to me. You've seen the way she gets upset whenever I'm around." Shamed that Zac had to witness this, she continued in a low voice. "I don't want her to have another stroke, so I stay away. You and Dad visit her. She loves that."

"But you're her daughter," Cory protested.

"I know, honey." She smiled as she brushed his hair off his forehead.

"There must be something—"

"There is. We can pray about it." She leaned forward and kissed his cheek. "I love that you want to help, son, but, please, for my sake, don't talk about this with either Grandma or Grandpa. It would make them sad, and I don't want to do that. Okay?"

Cory was silent for a long time. He studied Zac for several moments, then glanced back at her, as if he were trying to visualize them ten years ago. Finally he nodded. "Okay."

"Thank you. I appreciate your listening and under-standing." She rose and pulled him into her arms for a hug. "It's late. You'd better get to bed."

"Yeah." Cory looked at Zac. "Why did you come here tonight?" he asked.

"To support your mom. She hasn't had much of that lately. Now that you've got your answers, maybe you can change that." Zac held Cory's gaze with his own until the two came to some mutual unspoken under-standing.

"Good night." Cory walked to the stairs and took them two at time, pausing at the top. "Hey, Zac, can I ask you something?"

"I guess." Zac turned to face him. "What?"

"The other day I was telling the guys about the traveling you did and all those pictures you have." Cory sat down on the top step. "They were pretty cool. In my old school they had a travel club. Do you think we could have one here, too? If you showed those pictures, I bet that would drum up some interest."

"A travel club?" Zac glanced at her.

"I think it's a great idea." Brianna smiled her encouragement. "Cory, honey, why don't you ask some of the kids at school if they're interested? Maybe if you got a travel club formed, you'd be able to plan a trip somewhere."

"Hawaii, that's where I want to go." Cory jumped to his feet. "I could learn the hula." He swiveled his hips, humming a Hawaiian song as he went to his room.

"Well. His emotions run the gamut in such a short time. I'm exhausted." Zac's face was stretched tight. "I wonder if my mom ever felt like that."

"Often, I'm sure." Brianna gathered up her teacup as she debated her next words. "Thank you, Zac," she finally said.

"Glad to help." He met her gaze and held it but she couldn't read his expression. "It was...enlightening."

"I probably should have talked to you about this before."

"You probably should have," he agreed in a grating tone. "Like perhaps the day of the wedding, maybe right before you took off out of town?" A tic in the corner of his cheek gave away his anger.

"You still don't understand," she whispered, and turned toward the kitchen.

"No," he said, grasping her elbow and forcing her

to turn to face him. "You don't understand, Brianna. I get the part about your mother, though I still think you should have told me."

"But?" There was more to come and she knew it.

"What I don't understand is how you could have so little trust in me. You were far more important to me than any stupid degree. I would have given up anything to make you happy." Zac slid his finger around her throat, caught the delicate silver chain in his fingers and drew out the diamond ring he'd given her. "Did this mean nothing to you?"

"Why do you think I've kept it all these years?" she burst out, furious at him.

"I don't know. Why don't you tell me?" Zac murmured as his other hand grasped her and held her fast.

"Why?" Brianna demanded bitterly. "You said yourself that our breakup was probably for the best. You should thank me for running away."

"Yeah, I probably should. So—thanks a lot," he said through gritted teeth. Then he kissed her. But before she could react Zac was walking out the same door her father had just walked through.

"What was that about?" her dad asked glancing from Zac to her.

"My mistakes," she whispered. "I sure have made a lot of them." Strangely she didn't feel the least bit upset about that kiss. Even more strangely, she wondered when it would happen again.

Chapter Eleven

"You've been avoiding me," Kent said.

"What are you talking about?" Zac replied.

"You, professor. What's up?" Kent set a hip against Zac's desk.

"Work. I haven't been avoiding you. I'm busy. See?" He spread his hands above the papers on his desk and waited for Kent to excuse himself, but his buddy didn't or wouldn't take the hint.

"What is that mess?"

"It's Brianna's mid-November report for the board regarding Your World." He shuffled the papers, searching for an item she'd missed.

"I heard there are a bunch of new clubs forming. Seems like you two have conquered the apathy in the school. How is Brianna? Haven't seen her for a while, either. The two of you are like recluses." Kent slouched in a chair and kicked the heel of his boot over one knee.

"We work, Cowboy." Zac held Brianna's notes up to the light. "What do these scribbles say?" he asked himself.

"You can't phone her and ask?"

"I don't want to call her." That admission cost Zac.

"Because?" Clearly Kent would not give up easily.

Exasperated, Zac told Kent what he'd learned about his almost-wedding day and Brianna's reason for her disappearing act.

"She's a widow but she still wears my ring on a chain around her neck. Explain that."

"Ask Brianna, not me," Kent remarked.

"Not going to happen." Frustrated, he glared at Kent. "I've got to get through this. Can we talk later?"

"No." Kent straightened. "It's Saturday. You need a break, and I need your help. You may recall Thanksgiving is next week, then comes Christmas?"

"So I've heard." Zac gave up and leaned back in his chair. "Help with what?"

"Decorating the church for Christmas. You volunteered for that, remember?"

"Vaguely." A dim recollection filtered through Zac's brain.

"Our mission today, yours and mine, is to take the girls to the Christmas farm and gather enough props to decorate the outside of the church, ready for the live Bethlehem production." Kent checked his watch. "We leave in half an hour. You in?"

"Girls?" Zac studied his friend suspiciously. "And by that you mean?"

"Jaclyn and her helper, Brianna. Problem?"

Zac opened his mouth to object, but one look at Kent's resolute expression changed his mind. "You won't leave until I give in so let's go." He rose, grabbed his jacket and led the way out of his office.

Maybe this was the opportunity he needed to finally face Brianna. It was foolish, but he missed her. The hours moved so slowly when he didn't get to see her hazel eyes brighten with amusement, or darken when she was irritated with him. He missed her voice and the way she constantly encouraged, made him feel as if what he did mattered. It had taken these weeks for his anger with her to fade away. Now all he felt was loss.

"You're too quiet." Kent unlocked his truck and waited while Zac climbed inside.

"Be warned that this may not go well. Our last meeting was a little—testy."

"When you kissed her." Kent grinned at his blink of surprise. "Brianna talks to Jaclyn. Jaclyn talks to me. You should try that, buddy. Or maybe just go with the kissing."

"Not a bad idea. Except—where would a relationship between us go?" Zac snapped his seat belt as Kent started the engine and reversed, steering out of the lot and toward Whispering Hope Clinic. "I'm counting on my work here to get me into state education. Besides, now I've learned what was really behind Brianna's decision to leave Hope—lack of trust in me. She didn't even tell me the truth about her relationship with her mother! That's pretty hard to accept."

"Is it?" Kent let the truck idle as they waited for some kids to cross the road. His blue eyes pinned Zac. "Isn't the real reason you accepted that job offer her mother made was because *you* didn't trust Brianna?"

"That's what she said, too. I don't get what either of you mean." Zac glared at him.

"Come on, professor. The rest of us figured there were issues between her and her mother in high school. You were closer to Brianna than us. You must have had an inkling something was wrong," Kent insisted.

"Well, I didn't. I thought she had the perfect life. Call me clueless."

"I've called you worse," Kent joked, then grew serious. "Even so, why wouldn't you have talked to your *fiancée* about her mother's job offer?" He shook his head. "I get a job offer, I know I'm talking it over with Jaclyn long before I decide anything. You guys were on the verge of marriage. You didn't think maybe you should get your almost-wife's input?"

"Brianna couldn't find work, remember?" Frustrated with having to defend himself, Zac repeated the things he'd told himself for ten years. "Going back to school was expensive. We needed the money. Staying in Hope so she could work in the store made a lot of sense."

"Made sense to whom? And at what price—the cost of Brianna's dignity, her dreams?" Kent shook his head. "I think it all boils down to trust. You didn't trust her enough."

Zac opened his mouth to argue then stopped. In a way Kent was right. He *had* been afraid—that if he didn't get his doctorate he wouldn't measure up in her eyes, afraid that he'd never get to be more than nerdy Zac. Most of all, he'd been afraid Brianna would ask more of him than he would be able to give.

It was that last one that stuck in Zac's brain as they drove to the clinic. His PhD wasn't the issue. Putting it off until both he and Brianna had enough funds to return to school would have cost him some time back then, but he would have achieved his goal eventually.

The real truth was Zac had refused to acknowledge his own doubts before the wedding. He'd glimpsed security in that job and clung to it. The real truth was Zac had been terrified by Brianna's girlish dream of the two of them forging into the future with only each other to depend on. The real truth was he hadn't believed in Brianna enough so he'd grabbed the easy way, just as her astute mother had known he would.

"I didn't trust that she was as committed to her dream as I was to mine," he confessed aloud, stunned by the truth. "I didn't trust that her warnings about her mother's manipulations were in my best interest. I didn't trust her."

"So what we have is the two of you heading for marriage and neither fully trusts the other." Kent scowled. "Doesn't sound like a recipe for happiness to me. I'd say it's a good thing you two didn't get married."

"That's what I told Brianna a while ago," Zac admitted.

"But did you mean it?" Kent pulled up to the clinic and switched off the motor. "The thing is, Zac, lack of trust is a disguise for plain old fear. Fear burrows into the deepest part of you. It infects everything you think, every interpretation you make. It weakens you so much you begin to withdraw rather than take a risk. You keep to yourself, you don't get involved. You see where I'm going here?"

"Sort of." Zac frowned at him.

"Fear is insidious. People laugh, you assume they're laughing at you. Next time you see them, you don't smile. They don't smile back. Pretty soon you expect the worst of everyone."

Zac frowned. Was that what he did?

"Fear is what got between you and Brianna, Zac. And it's still getting between you and others." Kent's earnest tone begged him to hear the truth. "You have to overcome your fear that you'll draw negative attention, that you'll be on display and people will laugh. You have to give people a chance to see the real you."

Trepidation crept up his spine and closed around his skull. Let them see the real him? The insecure part that yearned to be loved? The thought terrified him.

"Stop worrying whether you'll say the wrong thing or give the wrong impression and recognize that everyone is struggling just as hard as you to figure out the path God has set." Kent frowned. "The idea is for us to help each other along the way, not to go it alone."

Zac mulled that over until Kent's chuckles drew him out of his introspection. "What's so funny?"

"Look at our ladies. I specifically said we would be walking over rough terrain." He inclined his head. Jaclyn and Brianna emerged from the clinic, both wearing high heels.

"You expected hiking boots? Fashion is king with those two." Zac watched them lock the clinic door, wave, then saunter toward the truck. His heart thumped an extra beat when Brianna's gaze rested on him.

"Our Bible study got me thinking," Kent said. "You're the reverse of Peter. He blabbed whatever came into his head, but you think too much about what you're going to say. Be honest, Zac. Speak to Brianna from the heart."

Easy to say. Hard to do. Zac got out of the truck.

"Hi, guys." After kissing Kent, Jaclyn stood on tiptoe and brushed her lips against Zac's cheek, her smile welcoming. "I'm so glad you could come. Will you mind squishing in the backseat with Brianna? I'd do it but the baby makes me carsick when I sit in the back."

"No problem," Zac agreed, slightly unnerved by Brianna's intense scrutiny of him.

"Great." Jaclyn beamed. "Cory's coming, too. He should be here in a minute. It's too bad we only have bucket seats in front. You and Brianna will be squashed." She accepted her husband's help to ascend the truck.

"Cory?" Zac glanced at Brianna.

"Oh, yes," she said, her voice tight. "He was talking to Mom about how she used to decorate the church inside and out, and now he thinks he's going to direct us to create the same result."

"Good for him." Kent waited until Zac and Brianna were seated in back. He stood waiting for Cory, who came across the lot at a run and flung himself into the backseat. "Everybody okay? Not too squished back there?"

"We're fine," Brianna said quickly.

Fine? With Brianna seated so close to him, Zac found it impossible to mull over his best friend's words. He couldn't help but inhale the soft sweet gardenia scent of her favorite soap, or brush against her bright red quilted jacket when the truck bumped over road construction, or notice the flattering length of her knee-high boots as she eased her long legs into a more comfortable position. She was gorgeous.

"Do you have enough room?" he asked. Brianna's hair brushed his chin as she nodded. She kept her eyes focused forward.

"So, Cory," Kent said, "what have you been up to?"

"Library. Research." He shot Zac a look. "I made a really dumb mistake, so for payback I have to write some essays. I have to do two per week."

"What's the topic?" Jaclyn asked.

"Hawaii."

Zac could feel the heat of Brianna's stare. When he turned his head, he saw a funny little smile tug at her mouth.

"Very clever. He wouldn't tell me what his punishment was," she murmured, for Zac's ears only. "Hawaii is all he talks about now. Getting him to do even more research on it has kept him busy, and his friends are just as engaged."

"It's an awesome place." Zac had planned to take her there for their first anniversary. Instead he'd gone alone.

For the rest of the ride Cory deluged them with facts about the islands. They also learned that he'd persuaded one of his two friends to help with the church decorating. When they finally reached the Christmas farm and Zac climbed out of the truck, he felt oddly reluctant to have the ride end.

"Will you be able to load as much stuff as I want?" Cory asked, glancing from Zac to Kent.

"Uh, how much do you want, exactly?" Kent was careful to ask.

"A lot. Grandma gave me a list. It's pretty big."

"Honey, did you check with the pastor about this?" Brianna looked worried. "There must be a budget."

"There is. Grandma found out and wrote it all down. The pastor said nobody else had offered so we should go ahead and get whatever we see fit. Okay?" Cory was almost dancing with anticipation.

"Okay." Brianna nodded and he raced off. Kent and Jaclyn were close behind. Jaclyn shared Cory's vision for the decorating and was eager to help.

"So? Where should we start?" Zac studied Brianna's glowing eyes and bright cheeks.

"In the coffee shop? They're serving mulled cider." She shrugged. "Let's let them do all the hard stuff."

"My kind of volunteering." Zac walked with her to the entrance, found it bustling. "How can Christmas be just five weeks away?" he asked, amazed by the number of people present. "Seems like only days ago we started Your World."

"I know. And now it's taken off." Some of the glow left Brianna's eyes. After telling him what she wanted she hurried to claim a table before someone else grabbed it.

Confused by her reaction, Zac purchased their drinks along with gingerbread cake with whipped cream and carried the tray to the table. Something was wrong.

"What's up?" he said, when after several minutes Brianna hadn't touched either.

"I've lost Eve Larsen as a client. She said her parents refuse to let her see me anymore. They've had to lay off another employee and Eve will have to fill in the slack at the café." Brianna fiddled with her cup. "There's no way they could pay for even one year of college now. They're barely staying afloat."

"I'm sorry." Zac didn't know what else to say.

"So am I. But I can't blame them. She's not even finished school yet. Their priority has to be providing a living for the family." Brianna lifted her head, pretended to smile. "Eve said she's not letting go of her dream, just putting it on hold, for now. But even if she eventually found funding, I'm not sure she could abandon her family when they need her so badly."

"I'll do some checking into funding. And there's always a scholarship." When she didn't return his grin

Zac sipped his cider and tried to decide on a way to broach his apology. Finally he just blurted it out.

"That day at your house— I'm sorry I blew up."

She looked at him, her face sad, her eyes shadowed. Then suddenly her shoulders went back and her eyes began to glow green with anger.

"You know what, Zac? I've had it with apologies," she said in the "tough mom" voice he'd heard her use on Cory. "I apologize for the past. You apologize for the past. We're always saying we're sorry. I don't need apologies anymore."

"Okay." Her vehemence surprised him. "What do you need?"

"Answers. Why did you go along with my mother and give up all our dreams?" She leaned forward, her face inches from his.

In that moment Zac knew there was no more hiding, no more pretending. He owed her the truth.

"I was scared," he admitted.

"You were scared?" Brianna blinked. "Of what?"

"You. You and me. That we wouldn't last. That I wouldn't be good enough for you. You're so strong, Brianna. You're outgoing and you get up there and inspire people and I, well, I don't. I get tongue-tied and flustered and the right words never come out. I figured you'd want me to change, to become someone more like you, and I knew I couldn't do it. I will never be like you." Haltingly Zac admitted the feelings he'd kept bottled inside for so long. "I envied you all through high school, you know. You were always so popular. You had everything I wanted. Even when we were making wedding plans, I couldn't believe you'd actually marry me. When you left I realized I'd secretly been waiting for it to happen."

"You didn't trust me, that I loved you as you are," she whispered sadly.

"Just like you didn't trust me," he countered, and reached out to brush a finger against the silver chain just visible at her throat. "We both let our secret fears ruin what we could have had." Zac withdrew his hand. He didn't know what else to say.

"I did love you." Brianna met his gaze and didn't look away. "I loved you very much."

"Why me?" He needed to know.

"Because you loved me as I was. Because with you I was enough. I didn't have to change anything about myself." A funny smile appeared. "I didn't have to pretend with you."

"And yet you did," he reminded. "You pretended your mother's choices about the wedding were okay. You should have told me they weren't."

"I know."

"And I should have listened to you. I shouldn't have pretended I was okay with you not being able to find a job. I was worried sick that we'd get into some kind of massive debt like my mom had because of my surgeries," he confessed. "Every day I watched how scrimping to get out from under that debt load stole her health. I vowed I'd never let that happen to me. That's why I was so quick to agree to your mother's suggestion. I saw a way out."

"You never told me that. And you should have." After several moments, Brianna shook her head and sighed. "So where does that leave us?"

"As friends?" he asked, his insides quaking at making such a bold request. "Friends who don't keep secrets? Friends who trust each other enough to tell the truth no matter what? Friends who'll be there for the other one whenever needed?"

"Yes." Brianna smiled shyly. "I'd like that, Zac. Friend." She held out her small hand.

Zac shook it with a rush of relief. But the moment his fingers touched hers, he wondered if friendship was going to be enough for him.

It would have to be, he decided. Because he wasn't husband material. That was the one thing their breakup had taught him. He would never be any different than he was now. A nerd. An oddball. He didn't want her to be ashamed of him. Of course, knowing that didn't negate the root of love that had snuck back into his heart. Brianna was still the only woman he cared about.

But acting on those feelings? No. Too much time had passed. She'd moved on.

Besides, he didn't dare tell her his feelings and risk her rejection. His throat clamped closed and his palms began to sweat as memories of his year of embarrassment and humiliation flooded in. He could not, would not, go through that again.

After they finished their snack, they headed outside and toured the Christmas lot. Brianna chose several things she wanted to decorate her house with. She paused beside a huge potted poinsettia.

"This is my mother's favorite flower," she murmured. She fingered a petal, lost in thought.

"How's it going with her?" Zac asked, hating that she'd lost her happy glow.

"I don't see her much," Brianna admitted. "Things always seem to go south when we get together and somehow, great psychologist that I am, I can't seem to stop it." She gave a self-effacing laugh. "All that education I worked so hard to achieve—wasted."

"I doubt it. But maybe what you need is a new approach," he said.

"Going to fix my mom as you fixed Cory, Zac?" Brianna teased. "He's like a different kid. What did you say to him that day in your office anyway?"

"Not a lot." Zac didn't want to betray Cory's confidences. "I laid out some cold hard facts and he manned up."

"Well, you did a great job," Brianna said. "I told you years ago and I'll repeat it now, you have a very special way with kids, Zac. I wish you weren't so set on leaving the best part of education for a desk job in a room where no kid will get the benefit of your gift."

"I don't know about any special gift, but I am still aiming to transform kids' lives. I'll just be doing it through curriculum," he defended.

"I know. And you'll be a success there, too." A small sad smile lifted her lips. "But it seems such a waste of a God-given talent. You start talking to a kid and before you know it that kid is responding, opening up, seeing potential in himself and possibilities. I wish you'd realize how much of a difference you make when you're with them one-to-one." She grinned, shook her head. "Never mind me. What I really wanted to say was thank you for taking an interest in Cory. He told me he has to report to you on several fronts."

"He's a good kid." He knew her mind wasn't on the task though because she moved from one display to the next without choosing anything. "So what else is bothering you?"

"Cory's working really hard to get the travel club going, but the other kids scoff at his dream of a group trip to Hawaii at Easter. I wish there was a way to snag their interest." She sighed. "But then I'm a mom. I just want to fix everything in my kid's world."

"Brianna, you always want to fix everything in everyone's world," he said, cupping her cheek in his palm. "That's what makes you so good at what you do."

"Why, Zac, what a lovely thing to say." She snuggled into his palm for a sweet moment.

The way she smiled at him sent Zac's heart into overdrive.

"Hey, Zac?" Cory's voice interrupted the moment.

"Hey. How's it going?" Zac dropped his hand, summoned a smile and tried not to resent Brianna's son for interrupting them.

"Good. Kent and Jaclyn are discussing some props. I was wondering if you could help me with something." Cory glanced at Brianna's feet. "You don't have to come, Mom. We men can handle it. Besides, it's rough ground, and you might trip."

"Thank you for your consideration, son," Brianna said, tongue in cheek. "I did want to check into getting a live tree for Christmas. Shall I meet you at the main building in half an hour?"

They agreed, and she wandered off.

Zac looked at Cory. "What's going on?"

"I wanted to ask you something and I didn't want her to overhear." Cory shuffled his feet.

Zac waited.

"It's about Mom," he said in a hushed tone.

"What about her?" Zac watched Brianna's red jacket move in and out of the booths surrounding the area. "Is something wrong?" he asked turning his focus back on Cory.

"She didn't tell you." Cory looked straight at him. "She's lost seven clients. Now some of the parents are trying to convince others to get keep their kids away from Whispering Hope Clinic."

Zac sucked in his breath and tried not to let his anger show. Brianna had gone above and beyond to encourage these kids, to get them thinking about their futures. And some selfish parents were going to ruin all her work? No way.

"What did you have in mind?" he asked Cory.

"Some kind of event that would show everyone the good she's done." Cory's blue eyes begged for help. "Please? I don't want us to have to leave Hope, but more than that, I don't want my mom to have to leave Whispering Hope Clinic. She loves her work there."

"Give me a couple of days to think about it, Cory. I'll come up with something." Zac had lost sight of the red quilted jacket. "Let's go over to those booths. I want to take a look at the ornaments."

"Why? I thought you were going to the Amazon for Christmas?" Cory stared at him.

"So? I'd still like to have some Christmas decorations up. I might even decide to have a party. I'd like something really nice." He was babbling. Thankfully Cory didn't seem to notice as he led the way to a booth with blown-glass ornaments.

"Mom loves these," the boy told him.

That was good enough for Zac. He ordered a grouping and paid to have them shipped.

"You're sure getting in the Christmas spirit." Cory blinked at the amount the clerk quoted.

"Yes, I am," Zac agreed. For the first time in years warmth filled his heart. Brianna thought he had a God-given talent.

He wandered through the stalls with Cory, thinking about that conversation with Brianna. Kent had been right, as usual. He did need to be more open. Look what it had got him—being friends with Brianna.

He liked the sound of that.

But a niggling little voice in the back of Zac's head reminded him of his accelerated pulse when his hand had cupped her face, warned him of his regret that he hadn't been able to pull her into his arms and hold her, as he'd once had the right to do.

Was friendship with Brianna going to make him regret they didn't share more?

Chapter Twelve

"I don't know why I ever agreed to do this."

The day before Thanksgiving, fear crept over Zac's handsome face. Brianna knew she had to do something to shock him out of his self-consciousness.

"You agreed because you're a wonderful friend who is trying to help Cory," she whispered. She stood on tiptoe to kiss him on the mouth. "Now go and show those kids the glories of Hawaii."

He nodded, turned and walked away as if in a daze.

"Some of you are considering joining the travel club," he said when the room had quieted. "I thought you might like to see just a few of the wonders you'll find if you go to Hawaii."

The room darkened. Brianna sat down at the back, prepared to intervene if Zac needed her. Instead she became transfixed by Zac's stunning pictures and by his easy commentary. Several times he had the room giggling, sometimes he commanded total silence, but not once did he lose his train of thought or stumble. This was a man bent on sharing his love of the islands. His passion infused everything he said. At the end of the presentation, Cory's sign-up table had a lineup.

"You did a fantastic job," she praised Zac when the cluster of kids around him finally left. "I think it was the cliff divers that sealed their interest."

"Those pictures are pretty good," he agreed, shutting down his computer.

She touched his arm to draw his attention.

"I wasn't talking about the pictures, though they are awesome. I was talking about you. You reached out and grabbed the kids' attention when you spoke. You had them eating out of your hand." She smiled. "That's one more reason you should be back in the classroom. You're God's gift to this school."

"That's twice you've called me God's gift. I'm getting a swelled head," he joked, a flush of red heating up his neck.

"Well, you can only be God's gift if you let Him use you," Brianna said. She studied Cory's almost full sign-up sheet. "All right! Let's go celebrate. My treat."

"Thanks, but can't do it, Mom." Cory shoved his papers in his backpack, hurrying to join the two friends waiting for him by the door. "We're doing a project together."

"Okay. See you at dinner," she called. She turned and found Zac studying her. "What project are they working on with him?"

Zac shrugged. "I have no idea. Whatever it is, he's very excited about it. I can't believe how he's changed."

"That's thanks to you."

"He did it himself. I just gave him a push."

"I hope they're not up to something bad—" She squelched the thought. "I'm sure they're fine. You do realize he's going to want you to act as chaperone when they get a trip to Hawaii organized." She frowned at him. "What?"

"Brianna, I'm covered in scars from the surgeries," Zac protested. "I don't want the kids to see that."

"So wear a T-shirt. Or don't. After the first glance, they'll be too busy taking in the sights to notice you." She waited. "Well?"

"You're very pushy, you know," he teased. "I'll think about it. Okay?" He lifted his laptop. "Did you mean it about that treat?"

"Sure. Why?" she asked, curious about the determined look on his face as they walked through the school.

"I want to discuss something with you."

"Okay." Ten minutes later Brianna ignored the coffee she'd been craving to stare at him, amazed by his genius. "A student fair," she repeated.

"A Your World fair," Zac corrected. "The last day of school before Christmas break. For students to showcase what they've learned. Here's what I've got so far."

Brianna listened, applauded his ideas and suggested a few of her own. It was a great idea that would maximize the students' successes. That was the thing about Zac. He was always looking out for the students. That's what made him a top-notch educator. If only he could realize his own potential.

"The last day of school before Christmas break?" she asked.

"Yes." Zac grinned. "Two reasons for that. The kids will go out on a high, and the parents will have the break to think over the results achieved. Maybe that will quash the nay-saying that's going on now."

"You heard," she said, embarrassed that her failures had reached his ears. He was probably regretting ever giving the school counseling contract to Whispering Hope Clinic.

"I hear most things," he said, studying her with a serious look. "There aren't many secrets in Hope anyway."

"I guess not." Brianna wondered if Zac knew that the old flame she'd carried for him had reignited. Did he guess that the feelings she used to have for him had grown and multiplied? Had she given herself away?

"So you're good with a Your World fair?" he asked.

"It's a great idea. It won't hurt for the state folks to hear about this, either, will it?"

"I never considered that, Brianna." Zac frowned at her. "This is for the kids and the parents."

"Oh, I know. But it can't hurt you to have them witness your success." She smiled to hide the fact that she hated to think of Zac leaving Hope. He'd become an integral part of her life.

"*Our* success." Zac pushed away his coffee cup. "And someone would have to tell them. I, for one, don't intend to do that. This should be a town-wide celebration." He checked his watch. "I need to get back to the office."

"Okay." She followed him outside then impulsively stopped him with a hand on his arm. "Listen, I know it's a bit late and you probably already have plans, but I was wondering if you wanted to come over tomorrow for dinner. I'm not the world's greatest chef but I think I can guarantee most of our Thanksgiving dinner will be edible. Unless—"

"I'd like to come. Thank you." He said it so quietly she blinked.

"Oh. Great." Surprised by his enthusiasm, Brianna got lost in his amazing eyes.

"What time and what can I bring? Brianna?" Zac shook her arm.

"We won't eat till later in the day," she mumbled, embarrassed that he'd caught her staring. "Come when you like and bring whatever you want. Or nothing at all. We'll have plenty of food."

"I know how to make an awesome salad," he offered.

"Perfect." Nonplussed by the intensity of his gaze, Brianna waved. "See you tomorrow."

"Yes. Thanks."

Brianna glanced back once, found him still watching her. Her stomach fluttered. Heat suffused her face. She suddenly had the urge to skip down the street.

I'm going to need some help here, God, she prayed as she walked home. *Zac's a nice guy, but he wants to be friends. I want more but he plans on leaving. Help me?*

As soon as she arrived home, Brianna changed clothes, then grabbed the book and her Bible and began searching for answers. The first words she read stole her breath.

Relationships are always worth restoring.

She'd already restored her relationship with Zac. It wasn't exactly the relationship she wanted and it would take time to rebuild the trust, but they'd made a start. She was also working to reestablish her relationship with God. So what—?

Her mother.

Immediately a sense of guilt and frustration filled Brianna. How could she possibly restore that relationship knowing that her mother had been integral to causing her unhappiness?

Forgive.

She didn't see the word on the page. Rather it was a soft sweet whisper in her heart.

Forgive. Start afresh. Restore.

Only with her mother?

Or could God possibly intend that her previous relationship with Zac could also be restored?

Giddy, scared and filled with questions, Brianna prayed.

"Let's eat everyone." Flushed and looking slightly off balance, Brianna waited as her father pushed her mother's chair to the table.

Cory sat on one side, her father on the other. Zac took the place next to Brianna, which wasn't a hardship. Lately he wanted to sit beside her more and more. Anything just to be near her.

"Dad, would you say grace?"

"Yes, of course. Let's join hands."

Brianna blinked. Zac reached out and grasped her hand in his. He loved the way her hand fit into his. His gaze caught and held hers. He smiled. Brianna smiled back.

"Happy Thanksgiving," he whispered so softly no one else could hear.

Her father started praying, but when he said, "Let a spirit of thanksgiving and love pervade this house on this day," Zac tightened his fingers around Brianna's. He wished he could make it so.

Because that was exactly what he wanted for her here in her old home. A spirit of love. A time when she would finally be appreciated for all she was. If God gave him the opportunity, he was going to make that happen. Brianna was a special woman who devoted herself to helping others. It was way past time her mother saw that others appreciated her daughter.

Zac felt her gaze on him. Her smile made his stomach twist.

Oh, Lord, I am crazy about this woman.

Brianna withdrew her hand on the pretext of passing food.

"Mom, this smells so good. I'm starving."

"Thanks, honey. I hope you enjoy everything." Cory's comment brought a soft glow of joy to Brianna's face, quickly doused by her mother's complaint that the turkey was too dry.

"I don't want to contradict you, Mrs. Benson," Zac said quietly, "but I think this turkey is cooked to perfection. And when loving hands prepared it, that makes it taste all the better. Don't you agree?"

Mrs. Benson's mouth formed an *O* of surprise. She glanced around and quickly nodded. "Yes, that's true. But the potatoes—Brianna always makes them too soft."

"I'm sure that's because Cory likes them that way. You probably did the same kind of thing, made food her favorite way when Brianna was a child, didn't you?" Zac asked smoothly. "I know my mom did. I guess that's what mother's do. They go all out for their kids, because they love them."

And so it went. For every complaint her mother voiced, Zac countered with another about family or love. Determined to stop this woman from ruining Brianna's Thanksgiving, by the end of the meal he thought he might have succeeded. Mrs. Benson's complaints had dwindled to almost nothing.

"I hope everyone left room for pie," Brianna said, rising to collect plates.

"I'll have to wait awhile," Zac told her as he gathered up serving dishes. "Everything was so good, I ate too much dinner."

"Me, too, Mom." Cory grinned. "I think I ate the most potatoes. They were so good."

"Everything was good," Mr. Benson said. "It was a delicious meal, honey. Don't you think so, dear?" he asked his wife.

"Well—" Mrs. Benson began to say something, glanced at Zac and nodded. "Everything was very tasty, Brianna. You did a good job."

"Thank you." Brianna's hazel eyes stretched as she stared at her mother. Finally she gathered herself enough to say, "You and Dad go relax with Zac. I'll just clean this up."

"Don't be silly. I'm helping you." Zac took the dishes from her hands as he glanced at Cory. "We all are. You did the cooking, we'll do the cleanup."

"Zac's right, Mom. We can do it. You take a break. Stay there." Cory poured her a cup of coffee, added cream the way she liked it, then grinned. "C'mon, Grandma. You can show me the right way to load the dishwasher."

"You mean you don't know?" she asked, frowning at him.

"No clue," Cory said with a wink at Zac.

"Then it's time you learned. I'm a firm believer men should be able to do for themselves. Look at Zac. He was able to make that salad himself, though I'm not sure the combination of—" She blinked at Zac then smiled. "It was a delicious salad," she said.

"Thank you, Mrs. Benson."

"Come along, young man," she said to Cory. She wheeled her chair into the kitchen with an energy Zac had never seen before. A moment later they heard her giving Cory and her husband orders.

"I don't believe it," Brianna breathed. "She said your salad was good."

"It was." He grinned. "I like those flavors together."

"Yes, but—" Brianna blinked.

Zac realized her eyes were full of tears.

"You're crying," he murmured, catching one tear on his fingertip. He slid his hand around her waist to comfort her. "Why?"

"Happy tears." She stared straight into his eyes. "I've never had a Thanksgiving like this before. Thank you."

"Me? I only made the salad," he said, loving the way she snuggled into him as if she found comfort in his arms.

"It was a great salad," she whispered as one hand brushed his jaw. "You're a great friend." Her eyes met his, huge orbs of forest green. "Thank you." Then Brianna stood on tiptoe and kissed him.

And Zac kissed her back, relishing the feel of her soft lips against his, the touch of her fingers against his neck, the curve of her waist against his hand. She fit. This was right.

A noise from the doorway disturbed them but when he looked, no one was there and the discussion from the kitchen centered on whether knives should be points up or points down in the dishwasher.

Slightly bemused, Zac eased back a fraction so he could look into the face of the woman he loved, had never stopped loving.

"Brianna?"

"Yes?" She laid her head on his chest.

"Can we do this again sometime when we're alone?"

She froze for an instant, then giggled and drew out of his arms.

"That was the wrong thing to say, wasn't it?" he asked, hating the emptiness he felt at her loss. "I seem to make a habit of saying the wrong thing."

"On the contrary, my dear friend. You always say exactly the right thing to me." And she kissed him again, though this time her peck on his cheek was much less satisfying. "Let's get out the Christmas decorations. I have a feeling this is going to be an afternoon to remember."

Brianna didn't realize, but it already was, Zac thought, following her to the family room where a live tree waited to be adorned.

But where was it going? Did Brianna really care for him or was she just being a friend, as he'd asked? Or worse, was this whole day, the kiss, the embrace, simply because she felt sorry for him?

And why did it matter so much?

Because, Zac admitted to himself, he was head over heels in love with Brianna Benson.

Again.

Still.

Brianna stared at her mother, shocked by the hearty laughter from the woman who'd always seemed so full of anger.

"You can't hang those ornaments like that," she told Zac. "It looks ridiculous."

"It does look a little goofy," Cory agreed.

"Brianna?" Zac asked, drawing her out of her introspection.

"What?" She tore her gaze from her mother to study Zac's work. "Oh, definitely goofy. Some might even say weird."

"I would." Mr. Benson shrugged. "I'd like to support you, Zac, but sideways ornaments are too much for me."

The family looked at each other and burst into laughter. At him.

Brianna realized that for first time she could remember Zac seemed unbothered by that.

"Everybody's a critic," he mumbled as he righted the ornaments. "No vision."

"That was more like a nightmare." Brianna smiled and patted his cheek as she walked by. "But you have great vision in other areas."

"They're going to start talking about the church now," Cory warned.

"What about the church?" Mrs. Benson glared at him. "Are you changing things in our beautiful old church, too?"

"I don't know." Zac was always honest.

Brianna held her breath. This had been such an awesome day. She didn't want it ruined. But then, this was Zac. He knew how to handle her mother.

"Your daughter has a couple of clients who aspire to get into the construction trade. She thinks they should help with restoration at the church and she wants your husband to teach them."

"Hugh? You never told me this." Mrs. Benson frowned at her husband.

"Because I've decided not to do it. It takes away too

much time I want to spend with you." He smiled as he covered her hand with his.

"But I won't be able to spend that much time talking to you. Brianna's got a quilt framed in my old office. I thought I'd come over and help her stitch it for a few hours a week." She looked at Brianna hesitantly. "If that would be all right?"

"Of course, Mom," Brianna said, her voice sounding wooden even to her. "If you want to help, I'd love it." However she knew her mother would criticize her efforts on the quilt she was making for Zac for Christmas.

"I think I would like to help." The older woman looked at her hands, flexed them. "Of course, there's no guarantee I can do it," she said, meeting Brianna's gaze. "If I make a mess of the stitches, I'll stop immediately. I wouldn't want to wreck your work."

"You wouldn't make a mess, Mom." For the first time in years, Brianna felt a connection with the woman who'd made her life so miserable. She knelt at her mother's side and slid her hands over her mother's weakened fingers. "A quilt is special because it's sewn with love," she whispered. "Not because of the stitches."

Her mother said nothing. She didn't have to. The harsh critical lines in her face softened. A tiny smile flickered at the corners of her mouth, then grew as she glanced around the room. Her gaze moved back to Brianna.

"Thank you," she whispered.

"Happy Thanksgiving, Mom."

As she hugged her mother, Brianna realized that her father's prayer had been answered. There was a spirit of peace and thanksgiving pervading this house.

And love.

If only Zac could be a permanent part of that. But he had other plans. He'd be leaving when he got that state job. Even if he could love her again, a future with him was impossible.

Because Brianna couldn't leave. Especially not now that she'd forged the first fragile bonds of reconciliation with her mother. Duty lay here in Hope. Duty to Cory, to her parents, to her clients. She'd run away once, but she couldn't do it a second time.

Zac would move on, but she'd given up her chance ten years ago. The realization decimated her but Brianna tried not to show anything as she drew away from her mother.

"Now, how about that pie?" she said, and hurried to the kitchen so she could dash away her tears before anyone saw them.

Chapter Thirteen

On Friday evening, Zac collapsed on his chaise longue.

"Don't you answer the door anymore?" Kent demanded a few minutes later as he towered over Zac, glaring.

"Didn't—hear—it." That was all Zac could manage as he sucked air into his starving lungs.

"Jogging." Kent's disgusted glare took in his clothes, soaked with sweat. "You're overdoing it, professor."

"Yeah."

"Why?"

The truth was too stupid to say aloud. Zac had run past Brianna's home umpteen times in hopes of seeing her, maybe getting invited in for coffee. He hadn't caught even a glimpse of her, but no way was he admitting that, so he grabbed his water bottle and drank in lieu of an answer.

"Never mind." Kent flopped down on another lounger. "I can't stay long. Jaclyn's tying up some odds and ends at the hospital. I have to pick her up in a few minutes. The reason I stopped by here is to tell you to get your sorry butt over to the church and help Brianna."

"Help her do what?" Zac raised one eyebrow.

"Cory has been regaling Brianna with her mother's tales of the church's past glory at Christmas, so for his sake, Brianna is trying to re-create it." Kent made a face. "I hid the ladders before I left and made her promise not to climb on anything, but you need to get over there or she's going to do herself an injury trying to satisfy that kid of hers."

"Where's Cory?" Zac's lungs began to lose the burning sensation.

"Working on his 'project' with his friends." Kent frowned. "What is this project, anyway?"

"I don't know," Zac admitted. "During Thanksgiving dinner he finally persuaded me to help his travel club plan a trip to Hawaii at Easter, so I don't think it's that."

"You had Thanksgiving at Brianna's?" Kent's blue eyes darkened at Zac's nod. "I see."

"You don't see anything," Zac said, rising. "It was nice. We decorated their tree. Her mother and Brianna made up. Sort of."

"And you and Brianna?" Kent said, raising one eyebrow. "Did you make up, too?"

"In a way. But it's not what you think." Sadness almost swamped him as he said it.

"Do you love her?"

The soft-voiced question halted Zac's progress inside. He stopped, turned around and sat down as he faced the truth.

"Yes," he admitted quietly. "But it isn't enough. I'm not enough."

"This again." Kent rolled his eyes.

"It's always been this," Zac told him. "Ever since she

walked away. You know my goal. I want that job in curriculum. Kent, my past with Brianna is over."

"Who's talking about the past? I'm talking about the future. A future you and Brianna could have together." Kent hissed his frustration. "What's really at the bottom of this, Zac? If you love her—"

"Yes, I love Brianna. Always have. Okay?" Zac jumped to his feet. "But so what? That doesn't make me any better suited to being her husband."

"What else do you need but love?" Kent demanded.

"This town, Hope, is your home and you think it's perfect," Zac muttered. "But it isn't perfect for me. I only came back here to take the next step on my journey."

"So you'll let your ambition ruin your relationship with Brianna again?" Kent's disgust was obvious.

"We're friends. We'll stay friends. But that's all," Zac told Kent. "Anyway what she does or doesn't feel for me isn't relevant."

"Isn't relevant?" Kent repeated.

"No, because whatever she feels, nothing can come of it." Zac watched Kent's eyes narrow and knew he had only a few minutes to make his point before his buddy would interrupt. "I've worked my entire life to get to the top, to prove that I'm not some useless brainy nerd. I've worked especially hard to prove it to the people in this town, the ones who made fun of me."

"You'll ignore what you feel for Brianna because you need revenge?" Kent demanded.

"No, but Brianna and I are on different paths now. I can't act on anything I feel because I'm not staying in Hope, Kent. Coming here was just a stepping stone onto something better. I need that state job."

"To prove you're not the poor pathetic nerd the kids in school called you?"

"Something like that." Zac stiffened at the reminder, the old scar stinging. "Brianna is not leaving Hope. She has her family, Cory has found his grandparents. She's finally working in the clinic she and her friends talked about half their life. It can't work between us."

"So you've decided, huh? Did you even pray about this?" Kent studied him then nodded. "I didn't think so. There's no room in your life for God to work, is there? Because Zac Ender already has his life all figured out, complete with barriers that no one can get through." Kent's voice hardened. "This need to prove yourself— it's a trap, Zac. And getting that state job won't satisfy you, because inside you won't have changed. You won't engage with those state administrators anymore than you did here because you're too afraid of rejection. But you can't control everything, Zac. Sometimes you just have to take a chance and trust God to work things out."

"Giving up control isn't that easy for me."

"I know." Kent nodded. "Because fear rules your life. You go out of your way to make sure nobody will reject you ever again, especially Brianna. You'll withdraw rather than extend yourself and take a chance. But the thing is, to find acceptance you have to be willing to risk rejection."

Zac recalled three occasions when he'd pled work as an excuse not to join his friends. He could have taken an hour off to join them but he hadn't, because he'd felt awkward.

"You've got your eyes focused on yourself, Zac. You talk about killing the apathy in the schools, about opening the kids' eyes, but yours are closed. You push people away, and then wonder why you're alone. I've known you most of my life and even I have to push my way into your world." Kent walked toward the gate, dragged it open then stopped to glare at him. "Fortunately for you, I happen to think you're worth the trouble."

"Thank you." Zac met his friend's blue stare with a nod.

"You're welcome. Now get over and help Brianna. I don't want her hobbling around with a cast for Christmas because you weren't man enough to get out of your comfort zone." Kent slapped on his cowboy hat. "Maybe you might even get to telling her how you really feel?"

"What good will that do?"

"Did you hear anything I said?" Kent shook his head in disgust. "You won't know till you try, will you?" He left.

Zac showered and changed in record time then drove to the church. He didn't have to. It wasn't far to walk. But he needed to talk to Brianna. When he arrived, she was kneeling in front of the manger scene at the side of the church, tenderly straightening the sheet that draped the baby doll.

She was sobbing.

"Hey!" Zac drew her to her feet and inspected her face. "What happened? Did you hurt yourself? Where?" He drew back to check.

"I'm f-fine. Oh, Zac." She shifted, pressed her face into his shoulder and began sobbing all over again.

Zac couldn't help but wrap his arms around her and try to comfort her. Finally her weeping slowed. She hiccupped once, drew away and swiped a hand across her face.

"What happened?" he asked, smoothing the damp strands away from her face.

"I'm an idiot, is what." Brianna sniffed, accepted the tissue he offered and blew her nose. "I'm so busy trying to impress my son that I slipped off a chair and single-handedly destroyed the ornaments that are supposed to go on the Christmas tree. Precious old things and I ruined them all." Her face crumpled and tears began rolling down her cheeks again. "My mother will be furious when she finds out. She donated them."

"Don't start crying again, please?" he begged. Her tears made Zac feel helpless and awkward and useless. "Besides, they weren't just old, they were mostly chipped and broken. And worse than that, they were ugly. People should thank you. I wish I'd done it. It's the kind of thing I'm really good at."

"Oh, Zac." Brianna choked back a laugh.

"You can't defend those ugly baubles," he insisted, relieved to hear that laugh. "They were awful and should have been tossed years ago."

"Well, they were sort of ugly but—"

"No buts. I'm voting we start a new tradition." Zac wanted to hold her forever. Who cared that cars were driving slowly by, their inhabitants craning their neck to see who was embracing in front of the nativity display? With his arms wrapped around Brianna Benson he was in another world.

A world that couldn't last, his brain reminded.

"A new tradition? Such as?" She blinked at him, her lashes spiky from her weeping.

"Wait here. Okay? I'll be right back." He waited for her nod, tucked one wayward strand behind her ear then turned and ran toward his car. Less than five minutes later he was back with two large boxes. "Can you help me carry these inside? And don't you dare drop them."

"I'm not a klutz," Brianna replied with an inkling of her usual spirit. "What are they?"

"Remember the day we went to the Christmas farm? I made a purchase. Turned out to be a lot bigger than I realized."

He opened the boxes and lifted out the beautiful blown glass balls he'd purchased.

"Oh." Brianna clasped her hands to her cheeks, green eyes flaring with excitement. "I love these. But don't you want to use them at home?"

"I did." Zac smiled at her rapt expression. "These are what are left. Turns out I ordered a dozen of each, instead of one. When that clerk said the price I thought they sounded awfully expensive but then Cory said you loved them so I figured to heck with the expense. If Brianna—" He stopped, aware that he'd just given himself away.

"You bought them because you thought I liked them?" Brianna's eyes grew even more round. "Really?"

Be open, Kent had charged him. *Meet the other person halfway.*

"Yes."

"Oh, Zac. I've prayed and prayed—" She put a hand over her mouth.

"You've prayed for me?" he asked, and knew from her expression that it was true. "I've prayed for you, too. For you and Cory and your parents." He slid his hand over hers. "I want you to be happy."

"I'm very happy right now," Brianna whispered, and tilted just the slightest bit forward.

Zac wasn't stupid. He knew there was no future for

them, but this was an opportunity he wasn't going to resist. He drew her into his arms and kissed her. Her lips were soft and inviting beneath his and after a second she freed her hands to wrap them around him and drew him closer. It was as if ten years had never passed.

This was right, his brain chirped as he deepened the embrace, pouring feelings he couldn't verbalize in his caress. This was what should be. But just as Zac tried to draw Brianna even closer, she pushed back, tilting her head away from him.

"What are we doing, Zac?" she whispered.

"Kissing." He grinned at her. "Didn't you like it?"

He thought she'd joke back. But her eyes darkened to a rich forest-green as she stared at him.

"I always did like kissing you," she murmured. "You make me feel like I matter. When I'm in your arms I feel protected, as if I don't have to be the strong one anymore."

"You don't," Zac told her, a rush of confidence filling him.

"For how long?" Brianna broke eye contact then eased away from him. In one fluid motion she slipped out of his arms. With a delicate touch she slid a wire hanger through the glistening glass balls then balanced on tiptoe as she hung them all over the tree. "Sooner or later you'll be leaving, Zac," she whispered.

And there it was—the stark, cold truth. There was nothing he could say to contradict her. So he worked silently alongside her, placing the ornaments on the higher branches she couldn't reach.

"Did you mean what you said?" Brianna asked sometime later.

"I always mean what I say." He fastened the last ball, then straightened. "But which time, exactly?"

"A few weeks ago you told me that back then, when we were supposed to be getting married, you would have given up your dream for me. Was that true, Zac?"

Zac took a minute to plug in the Christmas-tree lights and admire the soft shimmer of their beauty reflected in the beautiful ornaments. He needed the time to choose his words wisely because he must not hurt her.

"I probably would have, Brianna."

"But you would have regretted it." She looked deflated, as if all hope had drained out of her. "I see." She turned away but he caught her arm, urged her to look at him.

"I've learned some things about myself since then," he said.

"Such as?"

Okay. Kent told him to open up. Here it was.

"I need to be validated, Brianna," he told her. "Somewhere inside me there's a little kid demanding I show all the people who once laughed at me."

"Show them what?" Brianna's smooth forehead rumpled.

"That I'm worth their respect. That I'm not a nerd. That I've done a lot with my life." Zac waited for it, but Brianna wasn't laughing at him. With a sweet rush of feeling he realized that she never had. So he continued to tell her what was in his heart. "That's why I said it's a good thing we didn't get married. I couldn't stay in Hope. I needed to prove myself."

"But, Zac." She stopped, frowned and then waved a hand. "Look around. Who is there to show? Everyone has moved on with their lives. They're not noticing you or what you've accomplished. You're not in high school anymore."

The way she said it made him feel like a child.

"Why did you kiss me, Zac?" Brianna demanded. "Because I was here and handy? Because you were trying to comfort me?"

"Because you were sad, and I wanted to make you feel better. Because I care about you, Brianna." That was about as open as Zac could get. He looked at her but she seemed to be waiting for him to continue. "I like kissing you."

"I like kissing you, too." A soft smile creased her lips. "But is that all there is?"

"It has to be," he said softly.

"Because?"

"Because you're staying here in Hope, and I'm leaving, Brianna. Maybe not today or tomorrow, but as soon as I can." Zac squeezed her forearms then let go and took a step backward. "I wish I could offer you a future. I wish we could build on what we've learned about each other, but it wouldn't be fair to you because I won't be staying and you can't go."

"No, I can't." She wrapped her arms around herself as if seeking comfort. "Mom and I have some kind of truce started. I have to see that through. And Cory would never forgive me if I took him away from his grandparents now."

"I know." Zac reached out and brushed the curling tendril away from her eyes. "I know it's stupid, Brianna. This need I have to prove myself—I know it's childish, that nobody cares. But I care. I need to show the world—"

"What?" she whispered when he didn't continue.

That I'm worth loving.

The unspoken words shocked him. Zac stared at Brianna, realizing that the hole in his heart that had opened up the day she left still gaped.

And that when he left Hope, it was never going to heal.

"I think that if you try a few of those suggestions, you'll find it a lot easier to get along with your family this Christmas." Brianna smiled at her troubled student and escorted her to her office door. "Let me know how it turns out."

"I will. Thanks." She gathered up her coat. "I have to hurry. The Your World fair starts in an hour. Merry Christmas, Ms. Benson."

"Yes, Merry Christmas to you, Trina." Brianna sank down behind her desk only after the girl had left.

The Your World fair.

For the past three weeks she'd worked alongside Zac, preparing for today while her heart cracked and broke. Not once in all that time had he mentioned the night at the church, so neither had she. He'd escorted her home without saying anything and she'd taken her cue from his silence and kept it through every encounter.

Though his hand might brush hers, though she laughed and smiled, the approaching Christmas season left Brianna anything but happy. She missed their frank discussions, the comfort he offered whenever her mother lapsed back into her old habits. And she'd tried to explain to Cory why Zac no longer came over.

In the stillness of the night, after everyone had gone to bed, Brianna faced the certain knowledge that she loved Zac Ender with all of her heart, that she would love him until the day she died. Zac made her world sparkle and shine. Without him the day passed slowly. But Zac was leaving. And she had to stay. Her father's health had deteriorated. Her mother was not recovering from her stroke as quickly as expected. Cory had abandoned his self-destructive behavior but to uproot him now was a chance Brianna dare not take. Her place was here.

Zac's was not.

To keep facing him day after day when all she wanted was to throw herself in his arms and beg him to stay was torture. Everything reminded her of him— the apple pie she'd made last week was his favorite. The manger scene she'd set on a window ledge was one he'd given her eons ago. The green dress she wore today— it reminded her how he'd once admired a green outfit because he said it made her eyes mysterious. But that night at the church, when he'd held her so tenderly, then told her he would be leaving, that's when she'd known her love would never be returned.

"Oh, Lord, this is so hard." She squeezed her eyes against the tears. "But You are my comfort. You know how my heart hurts. You know my deepest desires and You will guide me on the best route for my life, even if it's without Zac." As she'd done for the past few months, she repeated, "Use me however You want, God. Let me be a living testament to You. Help me show Your love to others."

Thus strengthened and resting in the knowledge that God would always be there for her, she gathered her jacket and her purse and headed for the school, smiling at everyone she passed.

This would be the most difficult Christmas she'd ever spent.

* * *

"Hey, Mr. E. Pretty amazing, isn't it?" The student grinned at Zac's openmouthed gape. "We pulled out all the stops."

"You sure did." Zac had already noticed the huge banner outside announcing the Your World fair. In the foyer were directive signs leading to the auditorium but it was inside that auditorium that brought surprise.

The room was divided into booths with signs hanging over each one announcing the student's goal or dream. Charts, models, illustrations—each booth featured some practical application of their point. Students had grouped together in some cases, or gone it alone in others. The room brimmed with Christmas decorations, all handmade by the students. The total effect was amazing.

"Mr. Ender, we've kept folks waiting, hoping you'd do us the honor of saying a little something to open our Your World fair." The principal smiled at him. "Would you mind?"

"I'd be happy to." The words slipped out without thought. Then Zac caught sight of the press of people waiting outside the gym doors. He followed the principal to the small podium and took his place on it, heart in his mouth as he scanned their faces. His throat went dry. His palms began to sweat. What should he say?

He saw Brianna, standing at the rear of the group. Her eyes met his. She smiled at him and suddenly Zac felt calmer.

"Ms. Benson has been my cohort in helping create Your World," he told the principal. "I think she should be up here, too."

The principal agreed and sent a student to lead her

forward. She stood beside him, leaned closer and said, "Congratulations, Zac. But who invited all these people to our little soiree?"

"I have no idea." He looked at her and saw a flicker of sadness in her eyes, which she quickly concealed. "I'm going to try to make an off-the-cuff speech to open this thing," he murmured. "When I screw up, bail me out."

"You won't screw up. Just speak from your heart."

Zac got lost in her eyes. Why did she always have such confidence in him?

"Ladies and gentlemen, today we are going to w-witness our future, as seen by your children. You may consider their ideas mere flights of fancy. You may think their goals impossible." Zac stopped, his throat desert dry from nervousness. The room was so quiet.

Brianna stepped forward.

"We ask you to suspend those thoughts and let yourself fully experience the hopes and dreams of the young people of this community," she continued. "Examine them. Talk about them. Learn how our world looks to those who will inherit it." She laid her hand over Zac's, which held a huge pair of scissors. "So now, on behalf of the students of Hope schools—" She looked at Zac, waited.

A rush of confidence filled him. He could do this—with her.

"We hereby declare Hope's Your World fair open." He and Brianna cut the ribbon.

There was much applause then people began to stream inside.

"Thank you," Zac said to her. "I'm glad you rescued me."

"You didn't need rescuing," Brianna said. "You were speaking from your heart. People respect that."

A man stepped in front of them, identified himself as media from Las Cruces and asked many questions. When he left there was another, and another.

"How did you hear about this?" Zac finally asked.

"Press release. Want to see it?" The reporter pulled a crumpled piece of paper from his shirt pocket and handed it over. "Smart way to drum up interest," he said.

Zac smoothed the paper and studied it, conscious of Brianna leaning over one shoulder.

"Wait a minute. I recognize this." She took it from him, squinted at the artwork. "Cory did this."

"Cory? Are you sure?" But the more Zac studied the paper, the more he realized the phrasings were not those of an adult. "Your son drummed up all this interest," he said, waving a hand as locals and strangers alike filed into the auditorium. He looked at Brianna. "You're not crying, are you?" he asked.

"Tears of pride," she assured him with a teary smile.

"Well, you'd better wipe them away," he said tenderly as he dabbed at her face with his handkerchief. "You'll embarrass him."

Brianna laughed. And then her eyes locked with his and all Zac wanted to do was pull her close and hold her. Of its own volition, his hand reached out. His fingers grazed her sleeve but a voice stopped him.

"Excuse me? Are you Zachary Ender?"

"Yes," he replied.

Two men introduced themselves and gave their credentials from state education.

"We were told of this plan of yours and were intrigued. It certainly seems to have interested the kids and the town." The men explained that a letter from a student inviting them to the event had arrived at their office two days earlier. "Anyone who can generate student interest as you have certainly bears our closer inspection. Would you show us around?"

Zac wanted Brianna to come along but she excused herself. So he ushered the men inside and began telling them how Your World had started. Over the next couple of hours he caught sight of Brianna. Once she was laughing with Eve Larsen. But twice she stood in one corner, a serious expression marring her beauty as she listened to a red-faced parent.

Zac wanted to go to her, but he could not leave the state people. He could not abandon this chance to make his mark on them, to prove himself.

Brianna had been a mediator, he reminded himself. She would handle the parents with aplomb. But as the day progressed, a niggling worry kept him glancing around the room to find her.

"Is something wrong?" one of the men asked.

"Not at all." Zac abandoned his current search of the room. "Let's have lunch. The students' travel club is raising funds for a trip to Hawaii. They're selling soup and sandwiches."

Brianna would manage without him.

"Hi, Mom."

"Cory!" She hugged him then his two friends. "You guys and your secrets. You're the PR behind this event, aren't you?"

"Yeah." Cory grinned as he high-fived his buddies. "Adam's thinking about a career as a sports agent, and

Hart's into newspaper stuff so we put our heads together."

"You did a marvelous job," she told them. "I'm so proud of all three of you."

"Thanks." Cory showed her some leaflets. "We're passing these out in case anybody here wants to hire us. Then we'll be able to raise more money for the travel club."

"Get busy then," she said. "I'll buy your lunch when you're ready." They hurried away, chatting between themselves as they spread their leaflets.

Brianna spent a few moments surveying the room decorated in red, white and green—and its very engaged students. Zac had done an amazing job in the school, and she felt a surge of pride and rich satisfaction in having been part of his goal to turn around the town's young people.

That combined with the change he'd wrought in Cory had helped her face her anger at God so that she now realized He was there with her even though she didn't feel Him. She'd gained a new relationship with her father and her mother, thanks to Zac. He'd helped her cleanse the failures of the past.

But not even Zac could erase the failure she felt in her work.

Brianna had tried so hard to help kids, to ensure that they had someone there to listen to them. But it seemed all she'd done was create barriers between parents and the children whose aspirations they couldn't accept.

"I want to talk to you," Peter Larsen said, standing in front of her, his face belligerent.

"Let's get out of the way where we can talk more

freely." Brianna's heart sank as she led him to a quiet
spot behind the stage. "What's on your mind, Peter?"

"I like to be honest and up front so I'm telling this
to your face. We're circulating a petition to have the
school board remove student-counseling services from
Whispering Hope Clinic."

"Because of Your World?" she asked, trying to
stem the pain at this new evidence of her failure. "But
I thought that once you saw what the students are learning—"

"Because of you." His jaw thrust forward. "We don't
want our kids to waste their lives dreaming of something they'll never have. You've got my Eve out there,
her head in the clouds as she talks to those state people
about going to medical school. We both know she isn't
smart enough. It's not going to happen."

"But it can—"

"You think running away from this place solves everything. I don't want my kid running away, trying to
achieve something she can't get. I know all about that."
Peter clamped his lips together, as if he'd said too much.

"Is that what this is about?" Brianna murmured,
stunned by his words. "Is what's bothering you the fact
that you didn't get your dreams, and you don't want Eve
to experience the disappointment you did?"

"Yes." His anger flared. "I found nothing but pain
when I left this place. I thought I could make something of myself but all I managed was to get caught up
in drugs because then I didn't have to feel the disappointment."

"There's no guarantee Eve will go through that," she
told him, feeling his pain.

"There's no guarantee she won't. I came really close

to killing myself once," he admitted in a very soft voice. "I will not lose my baby girl."

"But that's what you're risking by not sharing her dream and helping her find a way to achieve it."

For a second Brianna thought he'd recant, but then laughter from the other room intruded and his face hardened.

"I just wanted to warn you," he said. "We're going to talk to the school board after this thing is over. We don't want you around our kids anymore."

Brianna watched him stomp away. She heard someone approaching. Quickly she moved to stand behind the stage drapes, hidden as tears of bitterness rolled down her cheeks.

"This has been an amazing display, Zac," one of the state men said. "You've taken the worst of the schools in this area and turned it around. We wanted to let you know that if you're interested, we have room for you in our office. Whenever you like."

"Thank you very much. I'd enjoy the chance to enhance curriculum."

Brianna tuned out the rest of the conversation, didn't even notice when they left. All she could think about was that Zac had achieved his goal.

And she had failed to reach hers.

Her heart was glad for him. He'd worked so hard. He deserved every success.

She loved him, but it was futile.

Zac would leave Hope. Brianna couldn't.

She finally accepted that they had no future together.

Chapter Fourteen

Zac returned to the auditorium elated that as he'd escorted the state men to their vehicle, they'd assured him he'd have a job offer on his desk in the New Year.

Jubilant that he'd finally achieved his goal, he couldn't wait to find Brianna and share the news with her. Then he realized that after he left, he wouldn't be able to share anything with her ever again. The realization knocked him for a loop.

Brianna would be out of his life forever.

Was that what he wanted?

"We have to talk to you, Zac." Peter Larsen stood in front of him, his face set in angry lines. Behind him several other parents were nodding.

Aware that the confrontation was causing a disturbance in the room, and embarrassed that they were now the center of attention, that he was being targeted this way, Zac needed to get them out of here.

"Uh, sure." Zac glanced around. "Let's go somewhere more private."

"We can talk right here. Other parents need to hear this." Pete glared at him.

Trepidation crawled up Zac's spine and took root like a hammer in his head. Everyone was staring. He was caught like a deer in the spotlights with the entire room looking on, the center of attention—the very last thing he wanted.

"I've already told Brianna that we're going to ask the school board to cancel the contract for counseling with Whispering Hope Clinic."

"What?" Zac blinked. Peter's face was white. An angry line creased his forehead. "You'd do that—after what you've seen here today?" he asked, keeping his voice low, moderated.

"This fair doesn't change anything. In fact, it makes it worse," Peter sputtered. "Now other people have latched on to the fairy tale and that's wrong. We all know nothing's going to change. Somebody has to deal with reality here in Hope. So I'll be the bad guy. We don't want Brianna filling our kids' heads with silly impossible dreams anymore. It's too hard on us parents when we can't make them come true."

"Too hard on you?" Fury banished any trace of awkwardness Zac felt at being on display. That the Larsens and other parents would do this to the caring woman who'd tried so hard to help them and their families infuriated him. Every single eye in the gym was on him, but Zac was barely conscious of the audience. He looked Peter straight in the eye.

"Have you lost your memory?" he demanded. "Can't you remember four months ago when your little girl made a desperate attempt to escape the misery of her life here in Hope because she had no goals, no dreams?"

The other man paled, but Zac couldn't stop. They'd impugned the integrity of a woman who'd gone way beyond anything in her job description to help their children. He could not sit back and allow that.

"You think dreaming about a career as a doctor is harmful to Eve because you can't make it come true? Why is it up to you? It's Eve's dream." He faced the next man. "And you, Martin? You think your son's aspiration to get into the space program is silly? And Grant? You don't want that brilliant kid of yours to go into cancer research? Why? Why would any of you want to kill such laudable goals as these?"

The group squirmed but they didn't back down.

"They're impossible goals," Grant mumbled.

"Who says they are?" Zac shook his head. "Four months ago your kids aspired to nothing. They were failing in school, destined to fail in life because nobody gave them hope and nobody told them they could have a dream and achieve it. You, their parents, had failed them and you know it. Yet not one single one of you came running to me, asking me to help you change things. You were content to let them share your apathy."

"We were not apathetic about our kids!" Martin was red-faced now. "We wanted better for them."

"Just not the better they want, is that it?" Zac shook his head. "I think you've let yourselves get so bowed down by your own unfulfilled dreams, you believed your kids didn't have what it took to change the status quo. And when they challenged that, you reacted by letting fear control you." Zac paused. If he was going to connect with these angry parents, he was going to have to be brutally honest. "The reason I believe that is because I was in the same position, believing a lie because I feared the truth."

Zac let the images of the past four months flood his

mind, the certainty that he had to leave here to be successful, the conviction that he had to escape teaching and the spotlight to make a difference.

"I was just like you, caught up in escaping my own failures, certain I could change nothing—until Brianna pushed into our lives. She's challenged us, you, your kids and me, to look beyond our safe little world and see what is around us. She defies our rigid mind-sets and dares us to be better than we are, to look beyond Hope to the world and imagine how we can affect it. To feel our fear, acknowledge it and push past it."

The room remained utterly silent. Zac knew he was the focus but it didn't matter. What mattered was making these parents see the truth.

"Yes, Brianna and I helped your kids begin to dream, Peter. We asked them to see themselves in a world where their contributions matter. And this—" he waved a hand "—this is the amazing answer your kids gave."

"But it's just a dream," Grant protested.

"What's wrong with that? Didn't space travel, the United Nations, the internet all start with a dream? The how and why of it came later." Zac let his emotions run free as he studied the other men, then moved his arm to indicate the various displays. "This is your chance for success, Peter. And yours, Martin. And Grant's. In this room lies the best chance we in Hope have to impact the world around us by equipping our kids with our whole-hearted support for whatever they dream, by not being afraid, by embracing it, by pushing them toward it."

Zac slung an arm around Peter's shoulders, the man who as a teen had berated him so often. For Zac that past was gone. The hurt was over. The need to prove himself had been replaced by the need to help the kids.

"Your businesses in Hope are important, of course, but your real legacy lies in your kids, great kids who want to change the world whether they decide to stay here in town or whether they want to move away. But their success hinges on you and me getting rid of our fear." He decided to take a risk. "Think about how different your world and mine would have been if we'd had a counselor like Brianna when we were in school, someone who told us to believe in ourselves, someone who pushed us beyond our fears to our dreams."

"But how can they do it?" Peter demanded. "It's impossible."

"That's fear talking. Fear of failure. It's what a lot of people said about going to the moon." Zac stepped away, shook his head. "And if you think like that, you're already defeated. That's why we need Brianna. She doesn't say it will be easy or fast or any of that. All she's saying is try. If it weren't for her selflessness, her vision, her foresight and most of all her courage and determination, you parents would have little to feel proud of today. But because of her, your kids' futures are wide open for whatever they aspire to. All they have to do is reach."

Zac glanced around and realized he wasn't a bit nervous. He loved Brianna, loved her more than anything. He would do whatever it took to defend her. It had never been that God couldn't use him. It had been his fear that prevented God's work. No more.

He stared at the assembly, let the silence stretch until every eye in the place was on him.

"How sad that you're rejecting the one person who's put hope back in Hope. But if that's truly the way you feel, I'm tendering my resignation. Effective immediately."

A collective gasp went up.

"No. We don't want that. You've done a great job for us, Zac." Martin shook his head. "I'm not willing to go along with you on this anymore, Peter. My kids have done a one-eighty in school. I didn't like hearing their grandiose plans because it made me feel a failure and because I was afraid they were doomed to the same. But my mess isn't theirs."

"But you don't—"

"No, I don't know how we're going to pay for my son to go to college, but he's going, Peter. He's going as an emissary of Hope into a world where he's needed." Martin's shoulders went back and his chin lifted. "I say we keep Brianna doing what she's doing. I didn't trust my kids enough to believe in them, or her. I've been walking around in fear, but that ends now."

"I agree," Grant said, his voice quieter. "My mom died of cancer. Imagine if my kid found a cure. What a legacy. I don't know how we'll manage. I have no money to send him to college. But if my boy wants to go, I'm sending him. There's got to be a way."

One by one other parents in the group murmured their assent. Somehow Peter seemed to sink back into the crowd as Kent stepped forward.

"I say we owe Zac a big round of applause. When my kid goes to this school, he's going to benefit from all the work Zac's done."

Zac cut short the clapping. "I think your thanks should be to Brianna."

Everyone cheered and called her name. Zac worried she'd run away until finally Brianna appeared from behind the corner of a stage drape. She looked stunned by the attention and accolades as she moved to the stairs. Zac walked forward and held out a hand to help her dismount.

"Three cheers for Brianna. Hip, hip, hooray!" the crowd shouted with their approval.

Zac had never been more proud.

Or more certain of what he had to do to prove himself to her and finally be free.

Brianna gulped down her tears as Cory's two friends stepped forward with a sheaf of roses. She hugged them both, then tried to think of what to say to express what was in her heart.

"Thank you. Thank you all. I know I've tried your patience." She smiled as the room erupted into laughter. "But I believe, as Zac does, in our kids. They are our future. They are so much smarter than we were. They see the world as their responsibility and they are determined to make a positive impact on it. I applaud you, students. Congratulations." She shifted her roses and clapped for them. The parents joined her.

The kids in the room laughed and bowed, their faces beaming when their parents rushed over for a hug.

Awed by the response and that her prayer to be able to help kids had been so completely answered, Brianna tried to slip away, but Zac prevented that by taking her hand. She studied his face, amazed at the transformative glow that softened the angles and edges.

"Thank you," she said and tried to lift her hand free. But Zac wouldn't let go.

"I'm not finished, Brianna. I have something else to

say," he said more loudly, drawing the attention of the room. Every eye turned on them.

Brianna shifted uncomfortably, wishing she knew why Zac had done this. It was so unlike him to draw attention to himself.

"Bear with me now, folks. Everyone knows I'm the worst public speaker this town has ever seen." He paused to let the murmur of laughter subside. "I'm also the slowest learner. For years I thought that if I could make a big enough impact, I could show everyone that I'm not the nerdy failure I thought they saw when they looked at me. Then you came back to town, Brianna, and I had to face the fact that my true failure was that I was afraid to believe in us, even though I loved you. Even though I never stopped loving you."

Brianna gasped. She glanced around the room, quivering under the interested stares. Her knees began to shake. What was Zac doing?

"I've just stood here and criticized Peter for not taking a risk on his daughter, but that's exactly what I refused to do with us. I want a future with you but I was too afraid to tell you I loved you in case you turned me down or changed your mind. Again."

A soft whiff of laughter rolled around the room.

"Zac, this—"

"This is me, Brianna. Warts and all. And I am in love with you. Still. Forever." Zac knelt on one knee. "Brianna Benson, will you marry me?"

Chapter Fifteen

Zac waited, kneeling, holding her hand.

Brianna found not a trace of embarrassment on his face.

But how could she answer? If she said yes—well, he was leaving. And she couldn't leave.

But if she said no he'd be horribly embarrassed in a town where she'd already done that to him once.

"I've never known you to be at a loss for words, Brianna." Zac's eyes held hers, strong, determined and brimming with love. For her.

And then it dawned on her. She'd learned to trust God, even when she didn't feel Him. She believed He had been guiding her to reconciliation with her mother, to help Cory change, to her own healing. This second chance at love was her test, the biggest test of all. She could accept it and believe God would work out the details, as she'd told the students so many times, or she could run away again.

Brianna wasn't running anymore.

"Yes, I will marry you, Zac. Whenever you want. I love you."

In a flash she was in his arms and he was kissing her in front of the entire assembly, to the wild applause of students and parents. He finally drew away, but refused to release her.

"I hereby declare Your World fair over," he said in a clear firm voice, a grin stretching his mouth. "But you're welcome to stay for coffee and Christmas cookies. The travel club could use your support. Merry Christmas everyone."

"Merry Christmas," the group repeated as one and then to each other.

Brianna stood by Zac's side while the townspeople filed past them, congratulating them and offering to help with the wedding, which Zac claimed would be as soon as possible.

Cory was the last in line. He shook Zac's hand and welcomed him to the family. Then he hugged his mother tightly.

"I'm sorry I messed up so badly," he said for her ears alone. "I promise I'll try harder to make you proud, even if the judge thinks I should go to detention."

"I'm already very proud," she told him, kissing his cheek. "No matter what the judge decides. We'll keep praying until your video conference with him tomorrow."

"When he hears what you've done for the fair, I'm sure he'll be impressed," Zac said. "Besides, you have to be here for the wedding. Who else would be my best man?"

Cory left them to tell his friends, his chest three inches bigger.

"If you're free for the rest of the afternoon, I think we should go ring shopping." Zac leaned nearer and brushed her cheek with his lips. The auditorium had emptied. Everyone had gone. They were all alone.

"I already have a ring." Brianna drew the chain holding her ten-year-old engagement ring from beneath her sweater. "I love this ring. I don't need another."

"This ring is okay," Zac said, slipping it free of the chain. "But it needs a few alterations because we've gone through a few changes ourselves. For the better," he added. "I promise I'll give it back to you on Christmas Eve. And I don't expect you to wear it on a chain around your neck."

She giggled and agreed, but a moment later grew serious.

"I heard those men offer you the job, Zac. What are you going to do?" A whisker of fear tickled inside but Brianna forced it away. God would work it out. She knew that.

"I'm going to decline. I want to be here to find out what happens to our first Your World graduates," he told her, fiddling with the tendril that refused to lie against her neck. "I want to be here to watch you and your mom grow closer. I want to be here to help your dad take care of our family. Mostly I want to be with you and work with you to help kids excel."

"That's what I want, too, but only if you're sure. After all, that state job was your dream."

"My dreams have changed, Brianna, and all of them include you and me together, making a difference in children's lives. Today I finally realized that if I make myself available, God can use me." He made a self-deprecating gesture. "I could never have spoken that long to all those people except that I asked God to use me. From now on I'm available to Him. And you."

He kissed her and for a few moments they basked in their joy. But Brianna had to ask.

"Why did you choose such a public forum to propose?"

"Something your mom said last night when I saw her after visiting Miss Latimer. She said, 'If you want someone to know something, Zac, you have to tell them.' I decided I'd make sure you knew I loved you. Besides, after accepting me publicly, you can't really back out, can you?"

"I'm not backing out ever," she told him. "I'm trusting God. He always knows what's best. Let's go enjoy our Christmas break, fiancé."

The Christmas Eve service at the tiny run-down church was short but filled with meaning. As Brianna sat beside Zac listening to the age-old words announcing the birth of Christ, she marveled at what God had done for her.

The judge, so impressed with Cory's work and the reports from his teachers as well as a commendation from a news agency who had received his press release, had granted an unconditional discharge. Brianna spared a moment to think of Craig.

"We'll look after him, Craig. Zac and I will love your son as long as we live."

The root of betrayal that had lain dormant for so long was gone. Brianna was finally free to embrace her future with Zac.

When the service was over, Brianna watched her father wheel her mother out of the sanctuary. They looked like newlyweds themselves, beaming with happiness as Cory danced beside them, asking a ton of questions.

"Do you have to get home right away? Can we take a moment?" Zac whispered in her ear.

"We have all the time in the world." She smiled at him, content to stand beside him, her hand nestled in his, studying the lovely Christmas tree they'd decorated together.

Finally they were alone.

"This is for you." Zac slid a ring on her finger. But it wasn't her old ring. It was a completely different one. A lovely diamond solitaire that glittered above a circle of smaller diamonds that enclosed it and kept it safe. "I love you, Brianna."

He kissed her thoroughly, and of course Brianna responded.

"It's beautiful, Zac, and I love it," she told him when she could catch her breath. "But what happened to the other diamond?"

"You'll see when I slide your wedding ring on your finger." He kissed the ring in place, then in the glow of the Christmas-tree lights lifted her face so he could look into her eyes. "I don't want to wait anymore, Brianna. Can we please get married New Year's Eve?"

"New Year's Eve? But it's so soon."

"Soon? I've waited ten years!" Zac grinned. "The whole town has offered to help us. And a client of yours, Trina, approached me today to offer her help. Seems she's planning a future as a wedding consultant and says she needs the practice."

Brianna burst out laughing. But then she looked at the man she loved, had loved, would love. The moment grew solemn. His eyes held hers, a plea in their dark depths.

"I would love to marry you on New Year's Eve, Zac."

She stood on tiptoe and kissed him. "Just tell me the time, and I'll be there."

"You're sure?" he asked, staring deeply into her eyes.

"Positive."

After one last kiss, they left the church and drove home where they announced their news to friends and family who'd gathered there.

And when they'd all departed and no one but Brianna and Zac remained, he led her outside onto the deck and pointed to the black velvet sky, glittering with stars.

"This is our world. I can't guarantee we'll be here forever, but I can guarantee that for as long as God gives us, I will always love you," Zac murmured, holding her in the circle of his arms. "Forever."

"Forever," Brianna agreed. "That should be just about long enough for us to learn to love each other enough so we can trust each other with everything. She glanced upward. "A certain elf named Cory used up many allowances hanging this mistletoe all over the place."

"Did not," a voice denied. Then a window slammed closed.

Zac's chest shook with laughter. He drew Brianna even closer.

"By all means let's not waste the boy's allowance," he murmured.

He guessed that Brianna's heartfelt response meant she totally agreed.

* * * * *

Dear Reader,

Welcome back to Hope, New Mexico. I hope you enjoyed Brianna and Zac's story. They waited a long time and waded through a lot of issues before they finally gave love a second chance. Brianna had to deal with her unmet expectations of Zac, and he had to face his fear of letting folks see the real person he is.

I love to hear from readers and will do my best to answer as quickly as possible. You can contact me at my webpage at www.loisricher.com; email me at lois-richer@yahoo.com or like me on Facebook. Or you can write me at Box 639, Nipawin, Sask., Canada S0E 1E0.

Until we meet again, I wish you overflowing joy that Jesus brought, abundant love God reserves for each of us and a peace to pass on to those around you.

Merry Christmas and Happy New Year from my house to yours!

Blessings,

Lois
Richer

SPECIAL EXCERPT FROM

Love Inspired®

Pregnant and abandoned by her Englisher *boyfriend,
Dori Bontrager returns home—but she's determined it'll
be temporary. Can Eli Hochstetler convince her that
staying by his side in their Amish community is just what
she and her baby need?*

Read on for a sneak preview of
Courting Her Prodigal Heart *by Mary Davis,
available January 2019 from Love Inspired!*

Rainbow Girl stepped into his field of vision from the kitchen area. *"Hallo."*

Eli's insides did funny things at the sight of her.

"Did you need something?"

He cleared his throat. "I came for a drink of water."

"Come on in." She pulled a glass out of the cupboard, filled it at the sink and handed it to him.

"Danki."

She gifted him with a smile. *"Bitte.* How's it going out there?"

He smiled back. "Fine." He gulped half the glass, then slowed down to sips. No sense rushing.

After a minute, she folded her arms. "Go ahead. Ask your question."

"What?"

"You obviously want to ask me something. What is it? Why do I color my hair all different colors? Why do I dress like this? Why did I leave? What is it?"

She posed all *gut* questions, but not the one he needed an answer to. A question that was no business of his to ask.

"Go ahead. Ask. I don't mind." Very un-Amish, but she'd offered. *Ne*, insisted.

He cleared his throat. "Are you going to stay?"

She stared for a moment, then looked away. Obviously not the question she'd expected, nor one she wanted to answer.

He'd made her uncomfortable. He never should have asked. What if she said *ne*? Did he want her to say *ja*? "You don't have to tell me." He didn't want to know anymore.

She pinned him with her steady brown gaze. "I don't know. I don't want to, but I'm sort of in a bind at the moment."

Maybe for the reason she'd been so sad the other day, which had made him feel sympathy for her.

He appreciated her honesty. "Then why does our bishop think you are?"

"He's hoping I do."

His heart tightened. "Why are you giving him false hope?" Why was she giving Eli false hope?

"I'm not. I've told him this is temporary. He won't listen. Maybe you could convince him to stop this foolishness—" she waved her hand toward where the building activity was going on "—before it's too late."

He chuckled. "You don't tell the bishop what to do. *He* tells you."

He really should head back outside to help the others. Instead, he filled his glass again and leaned against the counter. He studied her over the rim of his glass. Did he want Rainbow Girl to stay? She'd certainly turned things upside down around here. Turned him upside down. Instead of working in his forge—where he most enjoyed spending time—he was here, and gladly so. He preferred working with iron rather than wood, but today, carpentry strangely held more appeal.

Time to get back to work. He guzzled the rest of his water and set the glass in the sink. *"Danki."* As he turned to leave, something on the table caught his attention. The door knocker he'd made years ago for Dorcas—Rainbow Girl—ne, Dorcas, but now Rainbow Girl had it. They were the same person, but not the same. He crossed to the table and picked up his handiwork. "You kept this?"

She came up next to him. "*Ja.* I liked having a reminder of…"

"Of what?" Dare he hope him?

She stared at him. "Of…my life growing up here."

That was probably a better answer. He didn't need to be thinking of her as anything more than a lost *Englisher*.

Don't miss Courting Her Prodigal Heart *by Mary Davis, available January 2019 wherever Love Inspired® books and ebooks are sold.*

www.LoveInspired.com

Love Inspired®

Save $1.00

on the purchase of any
Love Inspired® or Love Inspired®
Suspense book.

Available wherever books are sold,
including most bookstores, supermarkets,
drugstores and discount stores.

Save $1.00

on the purchase of any Love Inspired® or
Love Inspired® Suspense book.

Coupon valid until April 30, 2019. Redeemable at participating retail outlets in the
U.S. and Canada only. Limit one coupon per customer.

Canadian Retailers: Harlequin Enterprises Limited will pay the face value of this coupon plus 10.25¢ if submitted by customer for this product only. Any other use constitutes fraud. Coupon is nonassignable. Void if taxed, prohibited or restricted by law. Consumer must pay any government taxes. Void if copied. Inmar Promotional Services ("IPS") customers submit coupons and proof of sales to Harlequin Enterprises Limited, P.O. Box 31000, Scarborough, ON M1R 0E7, Canada. Non-IPS retailer—for reimbursement submit coupons and proof of sales directly to Harlequin Enterprises Limited, Retail Marketing Department, Bay Adelaide Centre, East Tower, 22 Adelaide Street West, 40th Floor, Toronto, Ontario M5H 4E3, Canada.

52616033

U.S. Retailers: Harlequin Enterprises Limited will pay the face value of this coupon plus 8¢ if submitted by customer for this product only. Any other use constitutes fraud. Coupon is nonassignable. Void if taxed, prohibited or restricted by law. Consumer must pay any government taxes. Void if copied. For reimbursement submit coupons and proof of sales directly to Harlequin Enterprises, Ltd 482, NCH Marketing Services, P.O. Box 880001, El Paso, TX 88588-0001, U.S.A. Cash value 1/100 cents.

5 65373 00076 2 (8100)0 12391

® and ™ are trademarks owned and used by the trademark owner and/or its licensee.

© 2018 Harlequin Enterprises Limited

LICOUP44816

Love Inspired®

Inspirational Romance to Warm Your Heart and Soul

Join our social communities to connect with other readers who share your love!

Sign up for the Love Inspired newsletter at **www.LoveInspired.com** to be the first to find out about upcoming titles, special promotions and exclusive content.

CONNECT WITH US AT:

Facebook.com/groups/HarlequinConnection

 Facebook.com/LoveInspiredBooks

Twitter.com/LoveInspiredBks

LISOCIAL2018